DIFFERENT ANIMALS

MARIA —
YOU ARE A GODDESS
AND A ROCK STAR!

Love —
[signature]

7-15-2006

DIFFERENT ANIMALS

Kelley Dean Walker

iUniverse, Inc.
New York Lincoln Shanghai

Different Animals

iUniverse books may be ordered through booksellers or by contacting:

iUniverse
2021 Pine Lake Road, Suite 100
Lincoln, NE 68512
www.iuniverse.com
1-800-Authors (1-800-288-4677)

ISBN-13: 978-0-595-38156-2 (pbk)
ISBN-13: 978-0-595-82524-0 (ebk)
ISBN-10: 0-595-38156-1 (pbk)
ISBN-10: 0-595-82524-9 (ebk)

Printed in the United States of America

~ I ~

"That's right, hero. Just keep on walking this way."

The man's voice was remarkably relaxed considering the situation he was in; a situation that he had created personally only moments earlier. The woman in his grasp had finally ceased struggling and was mostly limp aside from her legs, which were still keeping her in an upright position.

"Of course, I'll have her fucking head off before you can make it over here—but yeah, feel free to keep moving, tough guy. I'm sure she won't mind."

"Now just hold on there, partner," the man behind the counter replied, using the most reasoning tone he was capable of. "I'm hearing you and I understand what you're saying...but this ain't happening, okay? Really, friend, it ain't going down like this. I'm asking you to please let her go. Please. How 'bout it?"

Jayce Daley, the part-time evening bartender of the Spitfire Steakhouse, was sounding a great deal calmer than his suddenly psychotic patron but the façade could only last for so long before his voice would start trembling. He knew it as well as he knew that he had to act fast before one of his regulars fell to the floor with a large gash in her throat. He didn't have a clue why it was happening and was starting to guess that there was no logical reason for it. There couldn't be. Just a few minutes earlier everything seemed fine.

"How 'bout I show you what she looks like on the inside?" The man mimicked Jayce's drawl perfectly as he yanked the woman around by her hair, throwing off any balance she may have had. "Would that make your night, *partner?* To see her spill all over this goddamn table? Because you'll be cleaning the floor, the walls, and the fucking *ceiling* when I'm done with her."

"Okay…*okay*," Jayce pleaded, holding out his empty hands in a sign of total submission. "What can I do?"

The man stopped moving and gripped the woman even tighter. Pulling her head back brutally, the woman's chin nearly pointed to the ceiling as the knife was laid across her throat. He stared back at the bartender with a crooked smile.

"You can watch."

*   *   *   *

It had started as normal as any other night and was still going smooth right up until closing time. Jayce Daley had worked the Spitfire's bar for over two years and hadn't noticed anything strange about the clientele that evening. There was no indication of a problem and the final parties in the room hadn't done so much as spill a glass of beer all night long.

He was just beginning to close up when a man walked in from the restaurant, which had closed up a few minutes earlier. His bill had been transferred to the bar with a total of twenty-seven dollars and he looked ready to cap it off with a drink or two before heading out into a particularly rainy night. There seemed to be nothing unusual about him when he took a seat at the bar next to two other men who had been drinking and watching ESPN for over an hour. He put his doggie-bag on the bar and ordered a beer.

The man had strolled in just as two of Jayce's regular power-drinkers were making their way to the door and, until the man's entrance, Jayce had done nothing but count downward as his regular patrons departed for the evening. Once they numbered in single digits he usually started closing up the bar and totaling up the checks. The man's sudden appearance didn't change anything. It was just one more person to shoo out the door in half an hour and the opportunity for another tip didn't bother him much either.

His presence brought the total customers to seven, which was a fairly good Wednesday night crowd considering the late hour and foul weather. The bulk of them were seated at one table and had been the loudest bunch of the night.

The four women had been drinking for over four hours and only paused for bathroom breaks. Two of them were regulars—local women from the mail processing facility—and the others Jayce hadn't seen before. They were all attractive in their own way and one of them was used to rebuffing his advances on an almost nightly basis.

It was their sheer volume that drew the first looks from the remaining men in the bar. But based on the amount of alcohol consumed, Jayce could sense them being sized up as well. He knew that each man was mentally pairing himself off with at least one of them but he couldn't tell yet how such an endeavor might go.

Working one on one was hard enough on its own. Wading through a group of four would increase the odds of companionship but would often stiffen their resistance if they weren't in the mood to be pawed at. Jayce knew it from his own experience as well as from endless hours of watching the fumblings of many a drunken man have a go at it, which was always educational if not entertaining.

As Jayce added the imported beer to the newest patron's dinner tab, he was surprised to see him take a single sip off of his drink before getting up from the barstool and making his way across the room. With the bottle in hand, he swaggered confidently toward the noisy table of women without even pausing to take a look at what he was getting himself into. There were no furtive glances or coy looks passing between any of the involved parties and he didn't waste any time before jumping headlong into it.

Jayce and the two remaining men at the bar gave each other a few surprised glances as the daring customer ventured into no man's land. For the first time in an hour they took their eyes off of the TV.

✳   ✳   ✳   ✳

"I'm sorry," Spencer said, running his fingers through his dark brown hair as he eliminated the gap between them. "I didn't catch that. What was that you just said?"

Their talking ceased abruptly. His rapid approach was the only indication that anyone had even been paying attention to them in the nearly empty room.

"I said..." the woman in her mid thirties paused with half-lidded eyes and exhaled a boozy breath across the table. "...life's too short not to live it to the fullest whenever you can. Like I was just telling Natalie over here—"

"No, before that. It was something else."

Spencer flashed her a toothy smile and grabbed the one empty chair at the table. With a quick flip, he spun the chair around into a backwards position and sat down, straddling the seat. He put two hands on the top of the back rest and set his chin down between them, peering curiously at each of the table's occupants. Four pairs of eyes stared back into the cold but entrancing blackness of his own before he turned his focus on the tipsy woman who had been doing most of the talking.

"It was right before that 'Life's too short' bullshit you were talking. You were saying something else. Remember?"

She nodded with a smile that could only be described as sloppy. Maybe she remembered and maybe she didn't. She was most likely too drunk to notice the words as they fell from her lips.

"Sure I remember. I was telling Natalie to go ahead and kill the bastard already. Just kill him and get it over with. That's what I say."

Her voice gave way to braying laughter, which Spencer didn't join her in. He simply continued to stare, grinning in a way that changed his features ever so slightly. Tiny lines and creases formed beneath his eyes, giving them warmth and a strange sense of understanding.

"She doesn't look convinced," he said. "Is that what you ladies have been arguing about? Killing some guy? Is that right—*Natalie?*"

He tilted his head to the right and shifted his attention to the girl who had been the subject of their discussion moments earlier. She blushed as she heard her own name drip from the stranger's mouth and her heart sped up by several beats per minute. It wasn't the subject matter that was making her uncomfortable—the multitude of drinks had cured her of those inhibitions. It was the man's penetrating black eyes that made her stomach go all fluttery.

Embarrassingly, a huge and totally uninvited smile covered her face and as hard as she fought to control it there was no stopping the muscular contractions that gave away any chance of playing hard to get. She couldn't help herself. The man was devilishly attractive and looked like a movie star or someone she had seen on TV or in a magazine at some time in her life. As a movie buff herself, Natalie Warner knew for sure that he had never graced the silver screen since she would have certainly remembered him, but he definitely had a quality to him that couldn't be ignored. He scooted his chair another inch in her direction.

"So, who is he, Natalie?" he asked, watching her blush yet again. If there was one thing he remembered about the real world, it was that women loved to hear their names spoken aloud. "Your husband? Boyfriend? Your boss? It's one of those—don't lie, Natalie."

"I wouldn't—I mean, I won't," she sputtered, completely captured in his dark gaze, which contrasted wildly with unnatural icy blueness of her own. "I'm sorry, but...who were you again?"

"You don't *know?*"

"Well, there's something..." Squinting her eyes at him as though it would help, she pored through her memory in search of the reason for the stranger's familiarity, praying that he wasn't an ex-boyfriend from high school or something equally humiliating. The difference in their ages—at least ten years—

quickly drove her away from that train of thought, but it was definitely something from days past that nagged at her. "Okay. I give up."

"Don't worry, it'll come to you," he assured her. "So, who are we talking about here? It's your husband, isn't it?"

"I'm not even married."

Spencer looked around the table before turning back to Natalie. "Why are you such a liar?"

The other women burst out with laughter, which drew envious looks from the bartender as well as the last two customers in the bar. Now that the man had them giggling like children, it was clear that he could pretty much take his pick. And since all four women had been self-medicated with multiple potent drinks adorned with umbrellas and pineapple wedges, he wouldn't have to drop a single dime in his quest for whatever it was he wanted. What he wanted might have seemed obvious to the casual observer.

"Separated is what I meant," she admitted, bringing her eyes back up. "Does it really show that much?"

"Doesn't show at all," he replied. "But I could smell it from across the room."

In response, the three women who were sounding more like hyenas every second laughed it up all the louder. Natalie joined in, hoping that it would have a self-deprecating kind of appeal. The attention was flattering and made her feel somewhat special. As though she had been selected. Chosen.

"So, you're still married and you want to kill your husband. Or did I not hear that right?"

"Not really, and it wasn't me—"

"It was my idea," one of the other women called out loudly, raising a hand while clutching a slushy drink in the other. "I think he's a dog and should be put down like a dog. He's a son of a bitch and needs to be destroyed."

"I'll just bet he is," Spencer replied. He scooted his chair further to his right. In turn, the woman he knew as Natalie leaned a little closer to him as well.

"It sure is getting late," she said playfully. The women she came with were forgotten a little bit more with each second that passed.

As she spoke, Natalie Warner drummed her fingers against her right cheek and batted her eyes, taking no notice of how desperate she appeared to the man who observed her from mere inches away. Though his eyes remained locked with hers and darted occasionally around her face, he was paying more attention to the other seven people in the room with him and keeping tabs on their whereabouts and what they were doing. It was pretty easy to tell what was going on if one knew what to listen for. And Spencer did.

*   *   *   *

It was just about closing time. Every squeak was noted as the bartender polished the lipstick off the last of the cocktail glasses and hung them up for the evening. The leftover bowls of pretzels and peanuts could be heard making their way to the trash can. Last to go were the ashtrays, which were only dumped and wiped down once all cigarettes had been extinguished. A moment later the TV was turned off.

Taking it as a cue, one of the last two men at the bar took a sad look at his empty glass and shoved himself off of the barstool. He tossed a twenty dollar bill on the counter then nodded to the bartender and shuffled slowly to the door. Peering back once at the noisy table that now seated five, he grunted incoherently before stumbling out the door and into the rain.

The glass and coaster were removed and the spot was wiped down quickly, though the man with the rag was barely watching what he was doing. His eyes kept straying to the table of women, only occasionally glancing to his last customer at the bar who was finishing his beer and checking out the action as well.

"That's it folks," Jayce then called out, shutting off the TV. "We're closin' it up for the evening. Time to go home."

Amid several loud groans from the table of giggling women, the man he had been watching suddenly rose from his seat and started slapping softly at his pockets. First on his pants, then up to his jacket. He reached into every pocket he had and came out empty-handed each time, looking more worried with each failed search attempt. Jayce had seen countless drunks lose their car keys but never in such a loud fashion.

"Oh, *Jesus*," the man uttered, digging through the same fabric compartments for the third or fourth time with nothing to show for it.

"What'd you lose?" one of the braying women asked as she pushed her chair away from the table.

"Yeah. What is it? What's wrong?"

It was Natalie Warner—one of Jayce's regulars, who never gave him the time of day—doing the asking this time. The man she had been nearly cheek to cheek with was now scowling and giving himself a frantic frisking of the highest order. He was checking his front pockets again and still coming up empty.

"*Damn it!*" he yelled, reaching into his jacket again then looking down at the floor around him. He ducked down, looking under the table but popped right back up. "Quick, look around. If I can't find it…" He trailed off as four pairs of eyes looked back and forth at each other. Natalie took a step back and peered at the floor around where he had been sitting. If she had to take a guess, losing a winning lottery ticket or a large roll of cash would be the only reason for such a sudden outburst.

"It's no use," the man said, throwing his hands up as he turned to Natalie. His voice went quiet as his hands dropped to his sides. "It's gone. Totally gone."

"What? What's gone?" She looked up at him and the man's scowl had vanished. It was replaced with a smirk as he reached behind his back.

"My patience," he answered in a calm voice as he pulled out the large knife and held it up for her to see. "That's what's gone, Natalie. My patience with bitches like you."

She was in his grasp before she had time to scream and was spun around with the knife at her throat when she finally did. The shriek was cut short by the blade which was harshly pressed against her windpipe.

What followed was all a blur to Jayce Daley, who was finding it hard to keep track of the words that were said and who was saying them. From what he could gather, the man with the knife was inviting him to watch a horrible murder take place.

✳   ✳   ✳   ✳

"That's what you can do, Mr. Bartender," Spencer explained. "I want you to watch this and I want you to see what it's like when a lady loses her head. How's the angle from over there? Are you getting a good shot?"

As the bartender looked on, the knife slid slowly across her throat. With her chin pointed upward, he guessed he was seeing whatever it was that was intended for him to see.

"How do you like it so far?" Spencer asked, pulling the blade away and revealing the tiny abrasion he had left on the woman who was currently urinating down both legs and into her high heels.

He looked away but kept the knife in place. The small amount of redness on her neck was almost enough to make Spencer swoon in an old, familiar way that nearly made him black out. But no blood had been spilled. All control would have been lost at that point and he couldn't say for sure what might happen if he did. It had been a while since he'd succumbed to that particular darkness.

Leaving the knife at her throat, he forced her head forward so that it locked the blade firmly between her chin and neck as he shook her around some more.

He kept a tight grip on it while her wide, streaming eyes met with those of Jayce Daley only a few yards away.

Another was watching the scene as well, though his role hadn't been dictated by the man with the knife. He sat motionless across the counter and merely observed, moving his eyes back and forth between the bartender and the woman with mascara running down her cheeks. He had a beer glass clenched in his hand but had stopped drinking from it the moment things got exciting. He turned back to the bartender to see what would happen next.

"And here comes the really bad part," Spencer said with a broad smile, stepping to the side of Natalie and balancing himself while keeping the knife stationary. He gave the bartender an unobstructed view as he twisted her neck into position and probed it for a big, fat, pulsing artery.

"I'd put on a raincoat if I was you. It's about to get wet in here."

If Spencer's eyes weren't busy poring over the woman's throat he would have seen the bartender's hands slip beneath the counter. He also missed the look on the last customer's face when Jayce pulled the gun up and leveled it off in the direction of one madman, one soon-to-be victim, and three very pale women who were glued to their chairs in horror.

Spencer found his artery and finally looked up.

It was silent for a few seconds.

"What is that—a shotgun?" Spencer asked with a disappointed tone, keeping the smile on his face as he glanced at each of the people who were within three feet of him. From where he was standing the barrel on the gun looked to have been cut down to twelve inches or less. "Just how many of us do you plan to fucking shoot?"

It was a question that Jayce hadn't pondered before reaching for the ancient and inaccurate weapon. Now that he was well beyond taking the gesture back, all he could do was aim it like a rifle—a very short one with no stock to rest against his shoulder—and play it by ear. The weapon had been a fixture under the counter since he'd started working at the Spitfire and he had only pulled it out once to break up a fight that involved a couple of pool cues and a knife. The trigger had never been pulled.

"There's only two of you in my sights, mister. If you kill her then there's only one of you and I won't hesitate if you do."

"Hmmm," Spencer wondered aloud, not showing any nervousness if there was any to be had. "I see your point. But let me ask you—what are you gonna do to keep this bitch alive? That's the big question here, isn't it? What are you gonna do now? *Right* now, I mean. You can't *stop* me from doing it. You can't do a thing about it and you know it."

"I can, mister," Jayce replied, preparing to step forward around the bar and create some room to work. "You'll see."

If he could eliminate the distance between them then it would take the other three women out of the equation. The man hadn't said anything about the others but he could easily kill the one in his grasp and then move on to another one without much trouble. And from what he had seen so far, Jayce guessed the man was up for it. He hadn't asked for any money and didn't seem interested in anything except cutting up a defenseless woman. If it was a robbery then negotiations would have begun already but the psycho in front of him didn't seem to have any kind of motive at all.

Jayce considered what few options he had and suspected that no matter what happened, he wouldn't have to take the blame for any of it if it went badly. All he could do was try. He started to move.

Before he could take the first step, Jayce Daley felt the world begin to swim around him. Like water flowing down a drain, his legs gave out and he dropped straight down in a crumpling fashion until he finally rested flat on the ground. The blood that ran into his eyes would have temporarily blinded him if he wasn't already unconscious. He was unaware of it when the shotgun was removed from his limp hands by the man who had smashed him over the head with the beer glass.

"Brilliant timing, Stan." The knife was removed from Natalie Warner's throat. He tossed the woman aside without bothering to watch where she fell. "If you waited any longer I was gonna have to cut her for real."

"Sorry," he said without looking up. His attention was directed at the firearm in his hand and his own growling stomach.

"So are we armed, or what?"

"Sort of," Stanley answered as the area underneath the bar was searched. "I don't see anymore shells back here. I don't even know if this thing's loaded or not. I'm not a gun kind of guy, you know."

"And I'm not usually a knife kind of guy," Spencer replied, relieving him of the shotgun. "How'd I look?"

"Scary like a horror movie. Did you eat all the good stuff?" Stanley reached for the doggie bag that had been left on the counter a short time earlier.

"There's plenty of everything left."

Spencer checked the shotgun and grimaced. It was double-barreled, old as dirt, and contained a single shell in its left barrel. Though it wasn't the class of weapon he had been hoping for, he was glad they didn't go through the whole thing for nothing.

"I had prawns tonight, Stan. Fucking *prawns*. Can you believe it? Sirloin and scallops too. The only thing I didn't bag was the salad."

"That's okay. Are we ready to go?"

"Eat your food, Stan. We've got cash and wheels now. I'll finish this up and then we're off."

While Stanley ate and watched, Spencer emptied the register and the tip jar then returned to the table of women that were still mute and unmoving. He guessed that for at least one of them it just might be a permanent condition.

Natalie Warner's mouth hung slack and her eyes were no longer big and round. They were glassy, half-lidded, and plastered to Spencer's handsome face. He smiled at her and dropped her into a chair.

"Do you know who I am now, Natalie?" He barely looked at her as he grabbed a purse and slung it over his shoulder. She had no response for him aside from the blank stare that followed his face around the table as he scooped up the other three purses. "You recognize me, don't you? Not at first, but I bet you do now. I *know* you do. My feelings were hurt for a minute there."

It was true, he didn't like not being recognized. He would have loved to ask her which magazine cover or TV program she'd seen him on but now simply wasn't the time for such vanities. It was time for securing transportation, traveling cash, and some form of weaponry and all three goals had been achieved. When he had everything he needed Spencer went back to Natalie's chair and knelt in front of her, putting a hand on her urine-soaked leg and shaking it lightly. He cocked his head and returned her blank gaze for over a minute. Her expression never changed.

"Well, you'll be fucked up for a while. Good luck with that."

He then moved forward and grabbed Natalie by the face, leaning in for what looked like an attempt to kiss her. It wasn't, though.

She made no move to resist as his mouth skipped over her lips and settled directly over her left eye. She didn't even flinch when he pried open the lid and buried his tongue in the opening, rolling it around on her exposed eyeball. When he was done he repeated the process with the other eye, appreciating the passive acceptance she had shown. She'd served her purpose and he was done with her.

With four purses over his shoulder and a pocketful of cash, Spencer strode back to the bar and took a quick peek at the bartender on the ground. It was just enough to be sure that he was still down without having to gaze upon the bright red stuff that leaked from the gash in his scalp. After another look around for anything they could use, he grabbed the doggie bag off the counter and headed for the door.

"Hey—" Stan protested, but couldn't get the words out fast enough.

"You can finish it on the road. Time's short."

For Spencer, it felt like a funny thing to say since their time lately had been measured in years instead of minutes, hours, and days. Time was not short—it was nothing but long. Up until a few days earlier there was no reason to look at it in any other way.

As he searched the parking lot for the perfect vehicle, he thought about his good fortune and briefly enjoyed the feeling of rain falling down around him. He had spent a good part of the last few days unprotected in similarly foul weather but it didn't bother him in the least. When Stan walked out behind him, he too paused for a few sniffs of rainy air before they would be cramped up in whichever vehicle they chose to drive west in. Neither could deny the fact that in the last few of days some kind of god had been smiling on them.

Tonight they ate steak and prawns.

Three days earlier they had been incarcerated.

~ 2 ~

After he had carefully situated the matchbook into the folded sheet of notebook paper, prisoner number H65032-48 steadied his hands and prepared to let it fly. He threaded a single match through a few of the others and bent it into an upright position. He then set it ablaze with the tip of the lit cigarette that dangled from his fingers. Before it could burn down to the rest of the pack, the small paper airplane was sent sailing past the empty cell on the left and landed close enough to its intended destination. It was snatched up quickly and the flame extinguished. The paper was unfolded and the note was read. With the message delivered, the entire sheet was quickly gobbled down by prisoner number H65032-75 in case the transmission had been observed by anyone. It was one of many precautions taken by the two neighbors to minimize any damage that could be caused by their off-the-record communications. Unlike most of the secrets passed between the cells, this one actually had a bearing on their future.

This time they weren't just comparing notes or killing time. It was an important matter and required a more confidential approach than usual. It was something to look forward to in a world where nothing much changed and the routine was painfully static. It meant freedom—a prospect that both men had given up on two years earlier.

"How'd that one taste, shitbrain?" His words echoed for several seconds before fading out.

"Like a three course meal," the elder Carroll replied, still chewing the softened paper and savoring it. The flavor of pulp he didn't really care for; it was the news that was contained in his late evening snack that made it pleasant for him. "Sleep tight, brother."

It was all they could say without arousing suspicion, though if the right people were tuned into them at the moment the small exchange would have raised a red flag or two. Fortunately for them, the only person within earshot of the speaker that monitored the two famous inmates didn't take any special notice of the few short sentences and the significance of it was sadly overlooked.

On most nights, the Carroll brothers didn't speak to one another. Since the trial, which had gone on for over a year and ended with a unanimously guilty verdict, the two thirty-four year-old men had spent more time blaming each other than they'd spent on their many appeals. Convicted of the murder of two men that they had never even seen before, they didn't bother to feel fortunate that they weren't being prosecuted for the several murders that they did happen to commit or had ordered personally. The relatively short thirty year sentence they had been given didn't make them feel any better about it.

Tonight they felt better anyway. Putting their personal conflicts aside, they would have plenty of time to sort things out in the comfort of an expensive hotel room once they were out. According to the word they had received, it wouldn't be long at all.

At precisely one a.m., as per the flaming note he had been given, the better known and slightly more photogenic brother climbed from his cot and removed the foam mattress from it. He moved to the far wall of his cell and covered himself as best he could while he waited. If the message was truly accurate, he expected the wall to come down at any minute.

*   *   *   *

Within weeks of their imprisonment, it became obvious that communication would be a problem. Woodhall Federal Penitentiary was definitely not one of the prisons on their list of mob-friendly institutions and, in fact, seemed to want to make things as inconvenient as possible for them. Even with all their connections—criminal, political, and otherwise—there would be no favoritism from their captors as they had been led to believe. If it had been a state prison things would surely have been different but the fact that they had the deaths of two DEA agents on their résumés made sure that the treatment they received would be less than cordial.

It started with the constantly shifting accommodations, which kept them on their toes and in motion much of the time. Adjusting to life in a cell was hard enough on its own. Being moved every two or three months made it even harder and had an unbalancing effect on both of them.

The surveillance was worse. Even the right to free speech had been revoked with their convictions and they were watched at all times. When they couldn't see any eyes on them it only meant they were being listened to instead. Whether the goal was to catch them implicating themselves in a completely different crime or simply to keep an inordinate amount of pressure on them, it was annoying as well as paranoia-inducing. With every word between them being analyzed, the only recourse was to commit the worst sin of all and put their words down on paper.

When they were kept in cells that bordered one another the small notes weren't a problem. Even if separated by up to three cells, the notes would be passed along by a few of the more cooperative murderers, rapists, or other career criminals that they shared the cell block with. That only lasted a few months, however. It took their jailers a very short time to figure out how much correspondence they were missing out on, so the living quarters were, yet again, rearranged accordingly.

Keeping an empty cell between them served two purposes at once. It would cut off all written communication while forcing them to speak loudly if they did choose to converse. Within weeks of the new arrangement, paper airplanes started flying and, once again, any other interested parties were left out of the information loop. It would have worked fine if the folded sheets of paper could be counted on to fly straight every time, but they seldom did. Once they flew off course and landed out of reach, the only person getting the message would inevitably be a guard.

Fortunately, the first of such navigational errors yielded little information aside from the brief statement: *Hey, asshole. Throw me some smokes.* Though it was hardly a coup for the authorities, the lesson had been learned and their communicative methods would be improved.

For a real message—one of great importance as tonight's was—the note would carry a payload consisting of a single book of matches. Once a match was lit, the airplane was tossed and one of two things would occur. Either the message was received and read before being destroyed or it sailed away in the wrong direction and burned up entirely, leaving it unreadable to anyone.

Of course, they still had to be cautious. Certain ball-point pen inks and graphite pencils left the message remarkably legible unless the ashes were scattered before a guard came along. On at least three occasions, their notes overshot the target and had to be retrieved by fellow prisoners, who generally helped out if there was something in it for them. These were not the standard wiseguys by any means and were quite a bit different than the company the Carroll brothers were accustomed to.

Probably more by design than coincidence, they found themselves flanked by some of the most despicable characters ever to have been put behind bars. Not merely bad people, but individuals that earned their notoriety through barbarous acts that the public and criminologists alike couldn't begin to make sense of. There were men they'd never heard of as well as a few that were as infamous as the brothers themselves. At least three of them had enjoyed as much newsprint as the Carroll's but their stars had slowly faded as the years flew by.

With the trial completed and sentences handed down, even the brothers were being pushed off of the front page occasionally. They were still wildly famous, but a few bombings in the Middle East or even a high profile bank robbery was enough to eclipse the imprisoned pair lately.

A massively destructive earthquake in the middle east, a headline grabbing serial killer in the northwest, a recently assassinated central American dictator— these were the latest in a series of distractions that threatened to pull attention from the brothers. Though the natural disasters were forgiven, their discontent was generally focused on the human element; especially when those humans were common murderers whose kills were performed outside of the business realm and served no purpose at all. It didn't quite seem fair that the high body-count psychos got all the really good ink—not to mention respect, admiration, and more than a few marriage proposals. It was like a sick joke.

Why many of their nastier neighbors weren't on death row was obvious. To the people who made a living identifying and capturing such animals, they were too valuable a commodity to simply execute. Likewise, the Carrolls had value too but instead of being studied for crimes they had already committed, the two were considered a work in progress. Ongoing operations were still being investigated even though they had ceased pulling the strings on the family business from the moment that they were locked up. Others were managing the empire in their absence, which was a daily source of disgruntlement for the both of them. It was time to make some changes.

*   *   *   *

Glancing once more at the clock, the time was noted and the mattress was pulled even tighter around his body. Assuming that his little brother was in a similar position two cells away, the Carroll who was older by a full two minutes covered his ears and shut his eyes against the debris that would be filling his small room in very short order. The window on their departure was closing fast.

∗   ∗   ∗   ∗

With the help of a few architectural engineers, an insider at Woodhall Penitentiary and four others for the dirty work, the plan had been in the works for over two months and finally seemed feasible enough to try. Guessing they had less than a week or two before being rotated into different cells again, they didn't want to take any chances and needed to proceed as soon as possible. The entire facility had been mapped out and analyzed over a year earlier but their locations had made it impossible to move ahead unless freeing only one brother was an option. It wasn't.

Until they were moved closer to each other or at least transferred to a cell block where they shared a common wall, there was no point in getting their hopes up. They played the waiting game for several months before their prayers were finally answered. After that, it was all a matter of timing.

Now that their cells backed up to the same concrete slab, there would only be one section of the wall to worry about instead of two points of entry in two different locations. All other scenarios required multiple explosions and drilling equipment, meaning they also required more time. And since getting the manpower into the facility would take up most of what little they could afford, it made sense to have them as close to the action as possible before it even began. That end of it had already been covered.

For the prior forty-eight hours, two laborers and four well armed escorts had been situated on the other side of the wall, only inches from either of the two cells.

Three days earlier, the six contractors had rolled through the security gate in the rear compartment of a refrigerated food service truck. From there, it was a cold two hour wait before it was dark enough to make the ten yard dash to the basement window of the former administrative offices. Once inside, a detailed map of the structure sent them through a seemingly endless maze of corridors, leaving them adjacent to the targeted building with adequate cover on both sides of them. They got right to work on the ancient brick and mortar wall that would bring them one step closer to their goal. It crumbled easily and quietly as it was picked apart by skilled hands.

Twelve hours and four walls later, the six men slept on the floor of a barless and doorless cell, which was one of many in the former solitary confinement block. The room, long ago stripped of all usable steel, was nothing more than a narrow row of naked cinderblock dividers that had been sealed for over a decade. It's main block partition had been torn down and replaced with a reinforced concrete structure, which now made up the rear wall of the current Cell Block D. The men slept comfortably knowing that cells thirty-eight and forty were right on the other side of them. At daybreak they rose and got started.

After carefully measuring and marking the areas of interest, large pieces of clay were rolled, stretched and molded against the concrete slab to form a series of U-shaped protrusions along the wall. Muriatic acid—the same variety that adjusted the pH level in swimming pools—was then slowly dripped into the clay, which acted as both a funnel and receptacle for the acid to settle into. There, it bubbled as the concrete was slowly eaten. When the fizzing action stopped, meaning that the acid had neutralized, the remains were dumped out and a millimeter or two of the affected part of the wall was silently wiped away with an abrasive cloth. Once done, the process was repeated again and again…and again. Their time had all been well budgeted and there was no reason to speed things up.

By the end of the first day they reached the steel rebar that reinforced the concrete that surrounded it, signaling that they were halfway there. At the midpoint of day two they were finished with the acid and began setting up the cutting charges of C-4 against the imbedded reinforced bars. Knowing that they only had a quarter inch of concrete left before breaking through into the cells, the utmost care was taken to avoid cracking or marring the wall in any way.

They spent the next several hours seating the detonators, testing all the equipment that would be used, and cleaning the dust from their weapons. After verifying that their watches displayed the same late hour, three of the men grabbed a backpack each and headed out. They had their own jobs to do.

*   *   *   *

At exactly 1:01 a.m., the first series of blasts came in rapid succession and were nearly impossible to pinpoint since the noise emanated from so many directions at once. Each deep thump echoed loudly through Cell Block D, though they were too distant to cause any damage to the immediate vicinity. They were merely precursors to the real thing but the effect was startling. Doing a mental count to ten, both brothers covered their heads and waited for it.

Before the last thunderous echoes had faded, the much quieter C-4 charges were detonated, cutting through the thick steel reinforcement and shattering the remaining concrete in the predesignated pattern. The cracking sound of the C-4 was a whisper compared to the first explosions and generated no smoke whatsoever. The shockwaves produced by the military-grade explosives were quite powerful, however.

In less than a second, the Carroll brothers, along with several other rudely awakened inmates, watched their small and confined prison cells become a great deal larger. The long wall that used to have a sink and toilet bolted to it was gone, leaving each inmate with his own brand new back porch. Several flashlights quickly sliced through the darkness, creating solid beams that reflected ten year's worth of dust that had been kicked up by the immense chunk of wall, which had fallen in one neat piece.

A moment later, the real noise began. The penitentiary's emergency siren, which wailed with ear shattering intensity, made the small explosions sound nothing less than disappointing.

The charges that had been placed in strategic locations around the facility were simple diversions and nothing more. Unlike the cutting charges that sliced through the wall with surgical accuracy, the others were crude, noisy bombs packed with powdered sugar, which burned quickly and created a great deal of smoke. At first glance, the entire facility probably appeared to be under some type of military assault. It was exactly what they needed.

*   *   *   *

Wiping the dust from their eyes and trying to shake the ringing from their ears, two men stepped into the newly created hallway behind their cells and faced each other. They could barely see through all the floating debris.

"Is that you, Stan?"

The man with the shell-shocked look on his face simply nodded.

"Are you coming, or what?"

"Sure...I guess," he replied, still reeling from the blast that left his head spinning.

First it would be the guards then the dogs they would have to worry about. The smoke helped for a short time but dissipated before they were in the clear. Shots—some near them, some not—could be heard clearly as they took advantage of the mayhem that fell over every cell block on the sprawling acreage of the maximum security prison.

From there, it was over three fences and into a long stretch of sloping, rocky land that went on for several miles. The surprising lack of trees in the surrounding area left very few places to hide when the helicopters flew over but it was still quite dark outside, which helped more than a secret hideout would have.

Amazingly, the dogs they'd expected to sniff them out never even showed up.

After more than six hours of walking in a zigzagging line, they slept on the ground in the first decent place they could find and laid low until darkness fell again. It wasn't their last day of sleeping under a drizzling sky while being hunted like prey and the process was repeated until they ran into their first paved road, which was almost seventeen hours later. They spent another half of a day walking parallel to the narrow strip but kept their distance from it.

Their first bite of food in years that didn't taste like prison came in the form of two hotdogs purchased from a twenty-four hour gas station over forty miles from where they'd started. They cost ninety-nine cents, which was almost as much change as they had found by the gas pumps before entering the store. They couldn't afford to purchase a paper but read one anyway before placing it back in the rack.

According to the Salt Lake Tribune, the infamous Carroll brothers—Martin and Jensen Junior—never even made it out of Utah. Both had died a fiery death along with six heavily armed accomplices outside of Logan only an hour after their daring escape attempt. The authorities were still tracking down a few stragglers but the situation was slowly getting back under control at Woodhall Penitentiary.

There was no mention of Stanley Lewis Hewitt or Spencer James Stoning, who disappeared at the same time. No stories were dedicated to them at all. There wasn't a paragraph or even a single sentence that gave any indication that two of the nation's most notorious multiple murderers weren't locked down anymore. Not a word.

~ 3 ~

"Jesus Christ—the *both* of them?" Doctor Beverly McGrath uttered, taking a deep breath as she finally understood the reason she had been summoned. The thirty-six year-old psychologist was a only year into her own private practice and working the public sector was a memory that she'd hoped to keep her distance from. "Two escapes in three days? How many hours has it been?"

Of the three men in the room, none of them seemed to be in any hurry to answer her question. Based on what she knew about both prisoners, it surprised her to see the facility in such a quiet state. She had received the phone call four hours earlier and was on a plane an hour after hanging up. Based on the urgency of the call, she expected to hear sirens still blasting when she was dropped off in the parking lot. Instead, it just seemed like any other day at Woodhall Pen. After several years of avoiding the place, she couldn't fathom why they had flown her all the way back to Utah.

"Go ahead and tell Dr. McGrath what she wants to know."

The voice was well known to her and hadn't changed in the years since she'd last heard it. As a writer, psychiatrist, and professional expert witness, Dr. Perry Burgess had already assumed what both of their roles would be. He had arrived only fifteen minutes ahead of her but it was enough to get a decent grasp of the situation.

Beverly looked around the room and waited for an explanation. Dr. Burgess let out a small chuckle and stepped forward.

"What they're all really eager to tell you, doctor, is that our favorite inmates have been walking the earth freely for over three days. Both of them. They're out there."

"Out where?" she asked in disbelief, receiving no form of reply. "Jesus, they made it off the grounds? How far off?"

No one was talking yet.

"Ryan?" she said, looking to the uniformed guard with a hopeful but worried smile. Their familiarity with one another was apparent, though greetings and the formality of shaking hands were ignored for the moment.

"Just the path they took," he answered. "They hitched a ride out of their cells with Marty and J.J. but that's as far as they went together."

"Marty and J.J.?"

"Martin and Jensen," he rephrased, seemingly uncomfortable with the sudden attention. He was a shift supervisor after all, not a public speaker. "The Carrolls, ma'am. It was their deal from the start. They went right out the front gate in one of the delivery rigs with heavy fire support all around them. Three guards wounded—none seriously. There was a chopper waiting for them quite a ways north of here but they never reached it. The Logan County Sheriff's boys took the truck out about five miles shy of where they were probably headed. All eight of 'em got torched pretty good."

"And Stanley?"

"He and Stoning went in the opposite direction. They were probably climbing over the first south fence when the Carrolls were making their exit out the front. They could've made it over fences two and three in a few of minutes without us seeing a thing. We were blind for nearly half an hour, you see."

"This place has ten miles of wire surrounding it—" Beverly started to argue but found herself cut off.

"No juice, ma'am," he said, lowering his eyes. "It's the same reason we were blind. The electrical systems are redundant in case of any emergencies so that we never lose power completely. It's mainly set up to keep the fences alive but they blew the main grid, two backup lines, and a generator all at the same time. Even our communications were down for a few minutes. They knew what they were doing, ma'am."

"The Carrolls, you mean."

"That's correct, ma'am," he replied. "They and whoever was working with them."

"Tell her what the dogs found." Burgess already knew but looked anxious to hear it again anyway.

"Well, ma'am…," Williams paused, looking uncomfortably at the others around him. "The way I heard it, they picked up the scent pretty quick and took off running. It was nearly morning by now, you see, and there was still a lot going on. They had ten guys trying to get the lights back on and everyone else dealing with convicts from Blocks A, B, and C in the dark."

A new voice chimed in. "Just tell her, Williams."

It was the first time Matthew Chase had spoken since they had gathered. From a business standpoint, the entire facility was his responsibility and he reported to a board of directors instead of any kind of penal authority. The prison was designed for incarceration but was run for profit like any other industry. He loosened his tie and listened to the guard go over it again. If it wasn't such a serious matter he probably would have been laughing.

"Well, ma'am. Like I said, it looks like the two of them went over on the south side."

"And after that?" she asked.

"We're not sure. Every one of the dogs got fried when they hit fence number one. I…uh…guess they got the power back on." He was silent for a moment after that.

Burgess folded his arms and looked up to the ceiling as did the others who couldn't find a better place to let their eyes settle. Most of it wasn't his concern but he felt embarrassed for all of them regardless. Williams was the only one who didn't look like he needed to feel sorry about anything.

"By the time I was called in—I'm still on days, you know—they'd brought in some new dogs. We got them working the perimeter of the first fence but it was raining pretty good by then. They caught the scent for a while and followed it about half a mile to the east. The rain came harder and it was gone for good after that. Helicopters didn't see a thing, which shouldn't surprise anybody. There's too much ground to cover once your past the perimeter."

"And this happened three *days* ago?" she asked, though the answers had already been given. She had heard about the Carroll's escape attempt like everyone else in the free world and bristled at the fact that it was already old news when the real news hadn't even been reported yet. "I guess it's safe to say they're not on the grounds then."

"That's correct, ma'am."

"*Okay.*" She slapped a notepad on the table and took out a pen, turning her eyes on Matthew Chase, who she had dealt with in a limited capacity before. He looked extremely tired and his tie was all the way off now. "First, I want to know when the Associated Press will have this. Their faces should have been on the cover of every paper on the planet the moment this happened."

"It's done, Beverly," Chase replied. "It'll be in print as soon as the presses roll and on TV even before that. It's going public as we speak. The photos are really recent and they won't be able to move ten feet without someone giving us a call."

"Okay...who's *us*?" She gave Perry Burgess a glance but all he could do was shrug his shoulders. Apparently, this was where they were when she walked in.

"Dr. Burgess?" Chase beckoned, gesturing toward a chair at the table. He then looked up at the guard. "That'll be all for now, Williams."

With a look of relief, he nodded and was turning for the door when it suddenly came flying open in front of him. If he had been walking through it at the time, he guessed he would have been knocked flat by the man in the dark suit who moved swiftly into the near empty conference room. He toted a large briefcase and wasted no time taking a position at the end of the table. He was already pulling items from the case when he looked up to Williams, who was venturing toward the door.

"Where do you think you're going?"

"Back to my shift?" he answered, though it sounded more like a question. "I'm working the yard until—"

"You'll need to stay."

"He's right," Beverly agreed, offering the man a smile that wasn't returned. "You're still D Block, Ryan?"

"That's correct, ma'am. Up until a few days ago."

"Then you probably know more than all of us put together."

She then turned her attention to the man in the dark suit. Having spent a great deal of time interviewing all types of law enforcement officials, she didn't have to ask what agency he worked for. FBI was written all over his face as well as his choice of clothing. If the man left a vehicle in the parking lot, Beverly McGrath knew she'd be able to pick it out within fifteen seconds.

"Special Agent Hildebrandt," he said dryly, extending a hand to her. "I'm heading up this end of the task force and I'll be your contact from this point forward. I alone will handle all communication in regards to this matter and you'll speak to no one else about it. That includes everyone from your colleagues to the press and all the way up to the governor. Are we understood?"

"You sat on this from day-one, didn't you?"

"Of course we did. Are we understood, Dr. McGrath?"

Before she could respond, Agent Hildebrandt turned his stare on Burgess, who hadn't said much and didn't even have a pen in his hand. So far, he was merely a spectator.

"Me—I'm fine," he said, looking uninterested if not outright bored. "I don't need anything and I'll keep my mouth shut. Sign me up."

"Dr. McGrath? Last chance."

"Okay," she finally answered. "I'd be happy to share my thoughts with you. How do you want to start?"

"We already have," Hildebrandt replied, taking out his own notepad.

~ 4 ~

"Stanley Hewitt fits the role of the classic serial killer in several ways with only a few exceptions, Agent Hildebrandt."

She had shifted into the same voice she used when speaking to large groups. It was obvious that Beverly McGrath had spent a great abundance of time educating the scholarly as well as the morbidly curious on the intricacies of Stanley Lewis Hewitt.

"In every book on the subject, including my own, you'll find that he fits the profile in terms of race, age, and the big three childhood indicators of bedwetting, fire starting, and torture of animals. His maternal issues are right off the chart in terms of abuse and his upbringing is as bad a horror story as you'll ever hear. His environment was a prime foundation for deviant behavior of all kinds."

She had to take a deep breath. It had been years since anyone had requested a lecture from her and she was already nervous enough.

"As a serial murderer, however, you'll find he lacks the narcissistic and possessive personality traits that are commonly associated with his contemporaries. His IQ is below average—another inconsistency when it comes to the common profile—but his operating mode has signs of calculation that he shouldn't be capable of."

"And what would that be?" Hildebrandt asked as he pulled two books from his briefcase and laid them on the table. He put down his notepad and took a highlighter from his jacket pocket. "His MO, doctor. Give me a page number."

"The MO is riddled throughout the book, but Chapter eighteen has the real depth on it," Beverly told him, watching the agent flip through the book that she had penned herself more than twelve years earlier. "The first several chapters deal with chronology and physical evidence, so you'll want to check those out too if you haven't already. A lot of my information was gleaned from the Bureau's own files and I'm sure they're much more extensive than what I've put together."

She waited as the FBI agent thumbed through the best-selling manuscript that essentially made her life what it was. Without it, Beverly suspected she might be working in Social Services or writing articles for a local newspaper back in Santa Barbara. Once Hildebrandt found his page and looked ready to listen, she continued.

"Stanley Hewitt uses a knife as his weapon of choice—or lack of choice, from a psychological standpoint—and bleeds his victims slowly from multiple locations. He doesn't stab his victims and never penetrates the skin past a few millimeters. He's a cutter, agent. Slow and with purpose. He drains them."

The agent appeared shocked with disgust for a moment. "You mean they're alive the whole time? Right up until they're heart stops?"

"That's correct. It can take minutes or it can take hours. If one of the cuts is bleeding too slow, he won't hesitate to open up another. They don't always have to be over arteries, either. Some of them were used to keep the victim awake and alert for as long as possible."

"Did he ever say anything to them?" Hildebrandt asked, seemingly riveted to his seat.

"Nothing that we know of. There was only one survivor and if he was as consistent with her as he was with the rest, he didn't say a word. He gave them no reason or indication why he was doing what he was doing to them."

"Well, that sounds absolutely horrible," he said with an overly squeamish look. "Didn't anyone fight back or at least make a run for it?"

Beverly started to answer, but hesitated as her eyes narrowed slightly. It didn't feel right for reasons that were plain to her but she had his full attention and proceeded anyway. "No, agent. Nobody ran anywhere. They were rendered unconscious through strangulation or blunt force to the back of the head to gain initial control over the victim. Once unconscious, they were completely immobilized before he got started. And once he got started, Stanley Hewitt didn't stop until he was finished with them."

"And how exactly did he immobilize them?"

Williams and Chase shot each other a squinty-eyed glance. Only one of them had read Beverly McGrath's chronicle on the crimes, capture, and trial of Stanley Lewis Hewitt, but they both knew what he did with his victims before killing them. It was the kind of thing that stuck in one's head upon hearing it, even if they only heard the story once. Everyone knew what he did; everyone except for the FBI agent, it seemed. It wasn't very confidence inspiring.

She paused, sharing the same disconcerted look with Perry Burgess. She hoped they were thinking the same thing and decided to clear the matter up.

"Can I see some ID, Agent Hildebrandt? Because if you don't know the answer then I think I'd rather speak to someone else in your agency."

While Williams appeared amused with her audacity, Matthew Chase grimaced and reached up to loosen the tie that was no longer there. Since he couldn't strip down to his t-shirt, he settled for wiping the sweat off of his forehead and massaging the spot between his eyes. Burgess simply stared at the agent with as much suspicion as his younger female counterpart.

Unflustered by the request and ignoring her demeaning tone, Agent Dwight Hildebrandt calmly removed a wallet-sized object, unfolded it, and pushed it across the table. His face was very businesslike and matched perfectly the picture on his ID. It appeared to back up what he claimed to be.

"You'll speak to *me*, Doctor McGrath." He leaned toward her and snatched the ID back. "If this would have happened a couple of years ago you'd probably be here with Agent Schultz instead and I'm sure you'd answer any questions he had for you without hesitation."

"I've interviewed him a few times," she said, conjuring up an image of the man who had played the FBI's main role in Stanley Hewitt's manhunt a decade and a half prior. "He's a good agent—a good man. How is he doing?"

"He's dead, doctor. He had a stroke late last year. I occupy his position now and I'm pretty well up to date. He knew you—I don't. And just because you wrote one of the fifty books out there on Stanley Hewitt, it doesn't necessarily make you the ultimate authority on him. I've got a lot of bases to cover on this one."

"I've spent over a hundred hours with him face to face and—"

"And that's the only reason you're here." He picked up her book again and grinned as he flipped through the pages. His face, mannerisms, and even his eyes looked a great deal different than they had only a minute earlier. "I've read your book, Dr. McGrath. It's...cute. You really seem to know our boy Hewitt on a completely different level. You've got a whole chapter in here about your time together and how pleasant he was with you."

"It's only because he was," she said, dispensing with his name and title as she moved into a more defensive mode. She had been scammed but guessed she still had time to recover.

"Well, I'm happy for you but it's time to forget about all that, okay? Williams, this goes for you too." He looked briefly at the prison guard then back to Beverly. "A man on the loose is not the same as a man in an interview room or in a cell. You think you know him—both of you. You don't."

"Have *you* spoken with him?" Beverly asked.

"Only through you, doctor, except I wasn't present to be manipulated by him." The statement could have been made in a sarcastic or superior way but was completely void of such sentiment. He continued in an even tone, tapping his fingers on the dog-eared manuscript that looked like it had been read a thousand times. "I've got all your notes and all the hard data with none of the emotion to clutter it up. Each of your appointments was set up by Agent Schultz and monitored by him in case you don't remember. You may have written the book, Doctor McGrath, but *we* supplied the ink and the pages. I think it's important for you to recognize that."

"Why?"

"Because of that attitude of yours. Because you don't know half of what you think you do. Really. Try to remember we have a three day head start on you. Even more, remember what he did with his victims before he killed them. Because I know what he does, doctor. Of *course* I know. I want you to think about that and keep it in your head for as long as we're working on this."

"Agent Hildebrandt, I am well aware of the capabilities of—"

"No you're not. And we're not writing a true-crime book here. What I need from you, doctor, is the intangible aspects of your interviews with Stanley Hewitt and how they could possibly tie in with Spencer Stoning. The kind of things I can't get from reading your transcripts or listening to the tapes—which I've already done, by the way. I need to see him from a more human side, assuming he has one."

"He does," Beverly replied. "He's more human than you might imagine."

This time all three other men looked away and would have rather been locked in one of the prison's cells than have to remain in the room with the two of them. Judging by what they had heard already, the woman was approaching the situation from the most wrong of all possible angles; that, or she was merely trying to antagonize the agent into a shouting match.

"That's good, Dr. McGrath," he said with a slight smile. "That's exactly the kind of crap I'm looking for. It sickens me, but it'll do the trick." He looked done with her for the moment and turned to Dr. Burgess.

Beverly knew that it was a mistake but felt the need to open her mouth again anyway. She was fine with letting him have the last word or two, but it was his choice of those last words that bothered her.

"I understand your disdain for him, agent, but you've got to admit he *is* human, first and foremost. His psychosis is based on a human response as a result of extreme mental trauma and unthinkable abuse he received as a child. Unimaginable acts, agent. These are things he told to me and no one else. I was the only one he confided in. Did you know that?"

Hildebrandt didn't nod or shake his head, but merely shrugged his shoulders in a noncommittal gesture. He remained silent for a few seconds and seemed to consider his words carefully rather than just blurting them out. His response was given in a slow, soft, and controlled manner, pausing for maximum effect when it seemed appropriate.

"Did *you* know that Spencer Stoning and Stanley Hewitt nearly killed two people at a restaurant two nights ago in Black Pine, Idaho? Did you know *that*, doctor?"

He blinked his eyes slowly as a pair of deep lines appeared on Beverly's forehead just above her eyebrows.

"Well...no...I..."

"Did you know that they're traveling by car now and can drive just about anywhere in the world they want to go?"

She remained mute this time and started gnawing on her lower lip. It hadn't started trembling yet but she kept it locked down with her teeth just in case. She was probably only a minute or so from crumbling but it didn't stop him from continuing on his present course.

"Did you know that five hours ago, a woman was found in a Vancouver, Washington apartment with about sixty-five gashes on her twenty-three year-old corpse? Can you guess how she had been...*immobilized?*"

"It couldn't be—"

"Keep telling yourself that, doctor. Convince me of it and you might even get published again. Just make sure you leave my name out of it. Now, Dr. Burgess..."

The psychiatrist hoped his flinch wasn't perceptible when the man finally got around to him. He wasn't happy about it but couldn't help but admire the way that Agent Hildebrandt worked. The best-selling author of *Understanding The Sickness* was almost in tears and he hadn't even raised his voice to her.

"...I've read your book too."

~ 5 ~

Good luck, Dr. Burgess, Ryan Williams thought as he eased himself another inch from the conference table. *If you knew what I knew, you would've stayed home.*

Since calling in sick wasn't an option for the forty-six year-old corrections employee, maintaining a low profile was the best protection he could currently afford. Flying under the radar had been nearly impossible for the last few days and it was causing a serious upheaval in the monotony of prison life that he had come to enjoy. Even though he wasn't an inmate, the idea of breaking out of the place did have a certain appeal at the moment.

The Carrolls had obviously been in the same frame of mind.

They never did get with the program and they couldn't adjust—that was their main problem. From day-one, they never thought it was real. They didn't understand it and thought they could make it go away if they wished hard enough. Their frivolous appeals were just a cruel tease.

Guys who were going to be sent back out soon were not locked down in Williams' sector and he wouldn't want them there if they were. Williams liked the lifers and the lifers liked him. The Carrolls never belonged since they never expected to stay. Exceptions had been made for them and that was what botched the whole deal.

Routine was the magic ingredient. Keeping it simple and keeping it the same was the golden rule when it came to bringing order to men who had never known anything but inconsistency. It was easy to maintain and it worked miracles in subduing those persistent thoughts of ever living a life outside of a cage again. They would have gotten used to it eventually but the Carrolls never had the opportunity to try it out. Routine was never an option and Matthew Chase had made sure of it.

If the Carrolls rehabilitation was ever an issue, it had been tossed out for the same reason that the east end of D Block's wall had fallen as easy as the first little pig's house that was made of straw. It was the money, plain and simple.

Matthew Chase wanted to go Supermax. It was the goal and it showed in every bit of his decision making since the first of many facilities in the country dispensed with their bars in favor of fully sealed, single occupant cells. One per customer. No more riots and no more inmates knifing each other in the yard. There would be no more messy rapes and no more violence between ethnic groups, who fought each other tooth and nail over territorial issues of all things. It would all be a distant memory if the numbers were crunched in the right way and the budget could be met.

Supermax was the future; Ryan Williams knew it as well as Chase did. It did away with much of the security from a personal standpoint, but as long as a human being was still required to peek in through the glass a few times a day and another got paid to cook and slide food through a slit in a ridiculously heavy door, he had no problem with it. The efficiency of such a system couldn't be overlooked and employee safety would be at an all-time high, though he had his doubts that protecting the men who held the keys was high on Chase's priority list.

He distinctly remembered the day that Chase had returned from his tour in Terre Haute, Indiana where all the celebrities were locked down. It was the Alcatraz of modern incarceration and was worthy of housing anyone from Al Capone to Timothy McVeigh to Adolf Hitler. Those guys weren't around anymore but at least one of them had enjoyed a brief stay at ground-zero of the federal penal system before taking one in the vein. Chase had practically drooled while he detailed the facility's organization and prisoner isolation techniques. He had even mentioned a few of the inmates that he'd peered in on and what they were doing when got his first good look at them.

Like a thirteen year-old girl who'd got an autograph from the teen sensation of the moment, Matthew Chase had described looking through a metal blind at the Unabomber. He had been stretched out on a cot reading a book, though the way Chase had spoken while relaying the valuable information left Williams expecting something more sinister, malevolent, or at least a little more exciting than a man in a bed. If Ted Kaczynski had been doing a jigsaw puzzle, he guessed that Chase might have gone and shit himself.

He was like that, though. Easily excitable and impressed with notoriety, regardless of the reason. Quite often Chase walked D Block like he was another guard instead of the Chief Financial Officer of ACT, Inc., one of the newest players in corrections privatization. He loved his murderers and rapists. They were money in the bank and were guaranteed to keep paying dividends as long as they were locked away in Chase's own personal vault. The longer they stayed, the better the bottom line was.

Lifers were the cash cow but it was men like the Carroll brothers that made him feel on top of the world. They were a living and breathing advertisement for Woodhall that couldn't have been put together better by a team of ad execs from Madison Avenue. Williams could always tell when Chase was walking the block, even before he saw him. The sound of his shoes echoing through the halls was unmistakable. Nobody on D Block—or the whole prison for that matter—walked like he did, as though traipsing through a shopping mall in which every store belonged to him.

For a brief moment in time, he owned the Carrolls and wore it like a feather in his cap. Before them it was Spencer James Stoning and before that it was Stanley Lewis Hewitt. He loved them like a boy loves his baseball card collection. Now they were gone and all he was left with were plain old, vanilla-flavored felons. The Carrolls were gone for good but Williams was hopeful that the others would be back in short order.

While Matthew Chase massaged his forehead and Beverly McGrath massaged her bruised ego, Williams focused his attention on Spencer Stoning's former doctor and tried to avoid the agent's eye completely. They hadn't spent the last three days sharing space with him like Williams had been forced to do and only now were they getting to know what he was about. Williams already knew and was sick to death of him.

~ 6 ~

Perry Burgess sat quietly while the agent thumbed through his own sordid masterpiece that had debuted a good seven notches lower than Dr. McGrath's on the *New York Times Bestseller List*. He remained still and knew that it was through more than luck alone that Hildebrandt had played his little game on the psychologist instead of himself. The agent was right. She dove right in without testing the water first. He wouldn't make the same mistake.

"It's not quite the same story with Spencer Stoning, is it?" Hildebrandt noted as he set the paperback book down.

"Different animals entirely," Burgess acknowledged, knowing that he was correct, but ready to agree with the man even if he was just a little off base. He shifted into his own special seminar voice and gave them all a simple rundown. "Stoning is a spree killer and doesn't resemble Hewitt in any way. He had no police record and no history of any kind of violence before he went off in Janesville, Wisconsin ten years ago. While Hewitt did his thing over the course of a month, Stoning's spree was a one-time deal, most likely due to his rapid capture. In little over an hour, he killed twenty-nine people in two states. He was arrested without incident at the second murder site in Rockford, Illinois. He tried to plead temporary insanity…"

"The blackout defense," Hildebrandt inserted with a cynical nod.

"That's right, and the jury didn't buy a word of it. They hardly ever do when I'm testifying for the prosecution. He got seven consecutive life sentences out of it then had the nerve to request *me* as his psychiatrist. He's smart—not nearly as smart as he thinks he is—but he's a strange one for sure. What else would you like to know?"

He was pleased with himself and it showed. He had given all the basic data without much interruption and didn't receive as much as a sideways glance from the man in charge. He hadn't sold as many books as Beverly McGrath but his mind rested easy knowing that he wouldn't get humiliated like she did.

"I said I've already *read* your book, Dr. Burgess. Everything you just told me is right here on the jacket."

There was no apparent snideness in the remark but it stung nonetheless. Having spent more than a thousand hours in the witness box in front of judges and juries, Burgess knew better than to show his displeasure with the statement. Snappy retorts would be saved for a more appropriate time if they were needed at all. It was quiet for almost a minute as the agent went back and forth between two piles of paperwork and the doctors themselves.

"Different animals," Hildebrandt uttered quietly as if to himself, echoing the line that Burgess had used. He nodded to no one in particular and finally spoke to the group as a whole.

"I've got a million reasons here that these guys wouldn't pair up for more than a day or two. We know they've stuck it out together at least that long and we also know that they worked as a team for money, a car, and a firearm. Why did they leave in the same vehicle?"

"Well, they probably felt a need to—"

"Out of five cars in the lot," Hildebrandt continued, ignoring Beverly McGrath completely. "They have keys for all of them but they leave together. Why?"

Nobody bothered to answer him this time. No one even twitched a muscle as the agent's passive intensity took over the room.

"Did they split up later? In Idaho? Washington? Were they together in Vancouver? Are they still together? Are they still on the move or have they found a place to lay low for a while?"

He paused briefly as his concentration appeared to go a level deeper. His eyes moved down to the table and seemed to stare straight through it. His trance-like state lasted less than thirty seconds before he looked up and nodded to himself again. The scattered paperwork was quickly gathered up and thrown back into his briefcase.

"Why are they together, where are they going, and at what point can we expect them to split up if they haven't yet?" The tone of his voice made it seem as though he was wrapping things up. It was confirmed when he removed two cards from his front pocket and slid them across the table. "That's it. That's what I need. You can reach me at any of those numbers if you feel it's necessary. I'll be around here somewhere if it's something that can't wait. Mr. Williams will answer any questions you have and give you a tour of what's left of their cells if you care to check them out. They've already been picked through by a dozen of our men but feel free to take a look around. We'll meet back here again in...." He looked down at his watch. "...an hour and ten minutes. If you come up with anything important before then, have Mr. Williams track me down or call my cell number."

He snapped his briefcase shut and rose from his seat. He was halfway to the door when he paused and turned back to table. The agent nodded once to Williams and Chase then quickly ran his eyes over the two doctors.

"Nice to meet you," he said with his best FBI smile and walked out through the door as quickly as when he'd arrived.

~ 7 ~

"Well, thanks for all the warning, Matthew," Beverly said in a growling voice as she tossed her notebook across the table. It skipped once on the flat mahogany surface before flying into Chase's face like a flapping, rabid bat. He knocked it away easily, not bothering to look upset or surprised.

"No shit, Matt," Burgess agreed. "This is a chance to give us some credibility and you throw this guy at us. I didn't even get to the good stuff. If I would have known—"

"I looked like a know-it-all prima donna and a complete idiot all at the same time." Beverly was breathing heavily and shaking her head while she tried to remember everything that she'd said and figure out how bad it must have looked. "Why did they call us if they were just going to kick the crap out of us? I thought they *wanted* us here."

"They did...they do," Chase replied. "More importantly, I do. It's just Hildebrandt's way of doing things. You should've seen poor Ryan a couple of days ago."

"It was no problem, sir," Williams replied. "He just lets you know real quick how he wants it to go."

Beverly was still raging, however. "What a *prick*."

"I'm surprised we didn't all have to synchronize our watches," Burgess added. "What's with this 'one hour and ten minutes' shit? Who keeps time like that? I can't just sit here and have the guy expect me to brainstorm for him on his FBI schedule. It doesn't work like that. Where did he go and what's going on in the other offices?"

"Lots," Chase said, looking as though he was only going to let them complain for a short while longer. He didn't let on, but Hildebrandt had steamrolled over him in much the same fashion that the doctors had just experienced. His response was on par with theirs but being a man who reported to basically nobody, he had no one to complain to.

"Conference rooms one and two are packed with feds—administrative staff and whatnot. They'll probably move along once they have an idea of where these guys are headed, but until then, they stay on site. It shouldn't be more than another day or two before they relocate. Yesterday they had a team of engineers checking out D Block to find out why the wall fell so easily."

"What'd they say?" Burgess asked.

"Along with the professionalism of the blasting job, which everyone agrees was executed perfectly, they said the same thing that I've been telling everybody for years. This place is old and it wasn't in great shape when we purchased it from the state way back when. Taking it over meant private investment for upgrades and new facilities. D Block was on the list but we've been waiting seven years just to get the old admin buildings torn down. It'll be a priority from here on out."

Beverly rose from her seat and picked the notepad up from the ground. There was no apology for the reason it found its way there. "So, what are we supposed to be doing right now? Do we just kick ideas around and see what sounds the best? I haven't even had time to think about this. What did they tell you when they called, Perry?"

"Consulting job—just like you, I guess. I thought it probably had something to do with the Carroll's escape since I've spent a lot of time here and know the layout. I'm not on any cases right now and I haven't written a book in a while. I figured 'What the hell?' I sure wasn't expecting *this*."

"Me neither. Who decided to call us?"

"That'd be me," Chase said. "They wanted some doctors who were familiar with the way Hewitt and Stoning's heads worked and I threw your names out. They aren't looking for miracles and it's not like you're the only people working on this. The Bureau has a thousand of their own shrinks and profilers already doing the same thing, but you two were the last ones from the private sector to get your hands on them. A lot of people have read your books and it'll show that we're going the extra mile on this thing. I thought it couldn't hurt."

"And Ryan?" Burgess asked.

"He's here for you. Nobody knows more about the goings on of the block better than he does and you already know each other from before. I know it's been ten or fifteen years, but maybe he can help you out with some of that *intangible* shit that Hildebrandt was huffing about. It's just a shot, guys. If nothing else, I've got to at least look proactive. If it turns out that Hewitt killed that woman in Washington—and I'll eat a fucking bug if he didn't—it opens Woodhall and ACT up to legal action that I don't even want to think about."

"You're going to have to get me some more information on that, Matt," Beverly said, still insistent but sounding more open to the idea than before. "If we can get Hildebrandt to throw us some information it would be a good place to start."

"What kind of info are you thinking?"

"Some details on this Washington murder for starters. It's way too coincidental and I don't like the sound of it. I'll want exact time of death and a work-up of all her injuries. A name wouldn't hurt either. Photos would be even better. Get me a few clear ones of the scene and I'll be able to tell you if Stanley did it or not. Can we get that without being yelled at?"

"He didn't yell, Beverly," Burgess noted, still feeling that he was ahead of her on points.

"Shut up, Perry. He kicked your ass too."

"Let's relax for a minute, people," Chase said, scrambling up from his chair before the catfight could begin in earnest. "I'm going to see about getting you the help you need. You can use any of the equipment we've got—phones, fax, computers, printers—and I'll find out about some stuff from the fed's side of things. Hildebrandt agreed that you should be here so it wouldn't make any sense for him to cripple you by not sharing. And do me a couple of favors. Don't argue with each other if you can help it and certainly don't talk down to me in front of him. It looks bad. I know we all share a past together but Hildebrandt was right about your attitudes so far. I need you to turn it down a notch."

"Hey, I'm not arguing with anybody," Burgess protested as Chase moved past him and headed for the door.

"It's all in that smug tone of yours," Beverly started but didn't get any further.

Chase turned on both of them with a stern look. "Do you want to be part of this or not? Because if you think that it's *you* doing the favor here, let me just tell you that you're wrong. This is my place of business, okay? I've got about a million things to do and, like I said, there are plenty of people already doing the job I've asked you to help out with. If you play your cards right, everybody benefits."

"Jesus, Matt," Burgess said. "What makes you think we need this so bad?"

"I didn't say you needed it. I just thought that maybe we could help each other out on this one."

"What do you mean?" Beverly asked.

"What I mean is…" Chase replied, searching for adequate words. "…I guess I'm just pointing out that it's been a while for the both of you. I won't lie to you; *Understanding The Sickness* and *Man Of Rage* were top-notch when they were hot and no one will ever be able to take that away from you. But you're out of print now. You're out of circulation and have been for years."

"Does it really look that bad from where you're standing?"

"I don't know, Beverly. Does counseling a bunch whiny people do it for you? I don't think that's what you're about." He then turned to Burgess. "When was your last book signing? When was the last time you destroyed somebody's insanity defense on the stand and really stuck it to them? I know it's been rough lately, Perry. Tell me it hasn't."

Nobody told him anything. Instead, they watched in silence as Matthew Chase gave them a final sympathetic look and opened the door. He stepped from the room and pulled the door shut behind him without another word.

Suspecting that he was still on the other side of the door with his ear pressed up to it, they waited for over a minute before speaking again. Even then, Burgess kept the volume down when he finally spoke up. The amount of truth in Chase's statement was made apparent by the look on his face as he turned to the only man he might possibly outrank.

"Three whole days ago? They've got to be pretty hard up to call us, don't they, Ryan?"

"That's a correct assumption, Dr. Burgess."

In a refreshing turn, the guard seemed to lack every bit of the brutal sympathy that Matthew Chase had offered them and was going to skip the condescension as well. Unlike the doctors, who were only just starting to figure out the depth of their locations in the investigative food-chain, he understood his position perfectly and was happy just to be asked the question in the first place.

"Does this mean we were last on the list?" Beverly asked.

"Pretty close, ma'am. You'd be surprised by how many people didn't make the cut at all, so I wouldn't worry too much about it. You're here now and you'll be in the middle of it real soon. If you can come up with something brilliant, I think it'd put a few of these suits in their place; especially that Hildebrandt character. I'd like to see that."

They both nodded politely, though neither was absolutely certain of what the D Block guard's last couple of sentences were about. They had both tuned out the moment he mentioned that there were others who were even further in the back of the line than themselves. In a rare moment of unity between the pair, they glanced at each other and tried to figure out who would ask the question. It was Burgess who got the honors.

"So, uh…" His opening was less than stellar as he stumbled his way through the awkward and unnecessary query. "…who *didn't* make the cut?"

If Williams was disappointed by the self serving and face saving effort, he didn't make it obvious. The fact was, he wasn't sure what to make of either of them at the moment. Before today he had always thought about both of them the way they were before fame had enveloped them. There was no reason to think about it in such terms but Williams was pretty sure he liked them better back then.

"Well, I can think of at least one guy who didn't get a call."

~ 8 ~

With the target clearly in sight, it was only a matter of a short walk from the front desk to the periodicals section to move in for the kill. The rear doors of the facility were alarmed and the only other route out of building was the main entrance, which wouldn't do him any good now. His prey wasn't much of a runner anyway.

The short, balding man in his early fifties sat cross-legged with a newspaper folded neatly across his lap and gave no indication that he had been spotted. As he heard the footsteps brush quietly along the carpet he only gave a brief glance up before returning to his article. He let out a sigh as his eyes moved faster over the newsprint in an effort to absorb as much as he could before the inevitable occurred.

"Oh, *Henry*," Floyd Madison said with a small smile, quietly singing the man's name as he approached.

He spoke softly not just because they were in a public library, but simply because it was his way of doing things. The tall, muscular black man had learned over the years that when he spoke in his natural voice, which fit his persona to a tee, people tended to get a little intimidated. Sometimes that was a good thing and he used it accordingly. Times like now required more subtlety if he wanted it to go smoothly and without incident. He suspected this one would only require a minimum amount of effort.

"Just a second," Henry Torres replied in the same hushed tone without looking up as he pored over his paper. "I'm just about done here."

"Take your time." Floyd sat in the seat next to him, the handcuffs in his rear pocket jangling with metallic finality as he dropped down into the chair.

Out of courtesy more than anything else, he only took one quick peek at the story being read, not wanting to hang over poor Henry's shoulder and make his last few free hours any more uncomfortable than they already were. Though they were currently in San Francisco, it was an article from the Colorado State Journal and the subject was none other than Henry himself.

"How bad are they making you look this time?" Floyd asked.

"Like the fucking weasel I am, but it could be worse. They left my wife and the kids out of it, thank God."

"Which ones?"

"Iowa...I mean Idaho," Henry said, correcting himself quickly. He had wives and children in both states—other places too—but, strangely enough, polygamy wasn't listed in any of the charges that had been brought against him. "They've got all the previous convictions in here and everything. Old jobs, old names—my phony certifications and diplomas. It's pretty thorough but they could've been less kind, I suppose."

The man seemed to have a pretty good grasp of his situation and was dealing with it in a remarkably levelheaded manner. This was their third meeting and the computer-hacking embezzler was still a model of consistency.

"How much are you getting for me this time?" It was the same question he always asked and he always wore the same million dollar smile while asking it.

"Ten grand on delivery," Floyd answered. "It'll pay my rent and keep my fridge filled up for half a year, so don't even start with me."

"Oooh, food and rent for six whole *months*. Is that the beach house in Malibu or the Bel-Air estate?"

"It's the one without the bars," Floyd quipped back humorlessly as he reached into his pocket for the handcuffs. Henry's rapid-fire apology followed quickly.

"You know I'm just kidding with that shit, don't you, Floyd? No cuffs, man. *Please*, no cuffs. I'd rather have you pierce my ball-sack and lead me around on a chain than put those fucking things on me." Henry held his hands out for him anyway. "Really, Floyd—let's not do this. I didn't mean to make fun of you and your future life of welfare checks."

Henry Torres was cuffed and led out of the library before he had time to get any wittier and found himself in the passenger seat of Floyd's car even quicker. It was the kind of standard nondescript, white Ford Ltd. that screamed anonymity and Henry would have been embarrassed to be seen in it. He didn't like being dragged around but knew he had brought it all on himself by not keeping his mouth shut when it was critical that he did. Whether by some genetic defect or simply a personality flaw, he could only remain silent for short periods before his lips started moving. When they moved, they said all the wrong things.

He admired the plain interior as Floyd pulled out the paperwork on him. Even as he looked down at his own wanted poster, the curse still plagued him.

"Nice car, Floyd...but you should have gone with a Bronco instead. With me being a fugitive and all, we could do a pretty mean O.J. impersonation together. I'll get in the back and act suicidal. Can I borrow your gun for a minute?"

Floyd ignored him and shuffled through the mountain of charges that Henry was wanted for. It wasn't that the bright, middle-aged man had done anything truly horrendous to demand such attention; it was just the amazingly huge amount of white-collar felonies he'd committed that made him stand out.

"Okay—*you* can be O.J." Henry said, holding out his bound hands as if Floyd was done playing around and would uncuff him immediately. His arms got tired after a minute or two and his hands went back into his lap. "You wanna be one of those slick dream-team lawyers and get my sentences reduced?"

Floyd started the engine.

"Wait, wait, wait. Just wait a second." Henry's hands were up again. "When I crack jokes about your penniless, low rent, minimum-wage-earning ass—I didn't mean *any* of that—all I'm doing is pointing out just how valuable you really are. Don't you know that?"

Floyd gunned the engine several times. He released the emergency brake.

"Come on, listen to me. Of all the guys that chase me across the country for money that they can't earn by using their brains, you're my favorite. You're the best, I swear. And you're the only one that *ever* caught me more than twice. That's got to count for something, right? We have a history, man."

"Someone snagged you *twice?*" Floyd asked, acknowledging the man for the first time in several minutes. The engine slowed back down to a steady idle. "Who was it?"

"Devereaux. The bastard got me in Spokane and then again in Reno."

"Back to back?"

"No, *years* apart," Henry replied, sounding hurt. "I wouldn't let that guy do a catch and release on me twice in the same year. I've got principles, you know."

"What were you worth then?"

"Six thousand to him...okay, seven." It probably meant eight.

"And what'd you give that old man to let you go?" He wasn't sure if Henry Torres thought he was actually going to jail this time, but it was best to stress him out a little before the negotiations began. "Because I'm not easy like Devereaux."

"Of course you're not."

"So, what'd you give him?"

"Double," Henry answered. It didn't even sound like a lie. "Both times."

"Well, I'll want triple," Floyd said, raising an eyebrow as he searched for a reaction. "Yeah, triple sounds fair to me. How's that sound to you?"

"Sounds great, you fucking degenerate." Henry held his hands out confidently this time. In no time at all, he was unchained and the million dollar smile returned to his face. The ordeal hadn't changed his pleasant demeanor in the slightest. "Is a check okay?"

"Aren't they always?"

They weren't just kidding around with each other. He never had a problem accepting checks from Henry Torres and he knew they would never bounce no matter whose name was printed on them. Spreading money around and hiding it in the middle of the electronic world he exploited was Henry's specialty. It was also the main reason he had evaded capture for as long as he had. If it was anyone else besides Henry, Floyd would have insisted on cash or, more likely, would have just carted them off to jail to get his payday from the bondsman. It was what he did for a living after all.

The amount was written in, a squiggly signature flew from the pen, and Floyd took the check without hesitation. He would even pay taxes on it.

"Until next time," Henry said, exiting the vehicle as though he was merely stepping from a very expensive cab ride.

"Yeah, see ya, Henry."

Floyd waved and watched the little man wander back into the library to finish his reading. Though he would never say anything to the effect, he genuinely liked Henry Torres and admired the man's outlook on things, not to mention his balls for going right back into a building that he just been dragged from in cuffs. Floyd guessed it must have been a pretty damn important article he'd been reading.

As soon as the library's front door closed behind him and Henry was out of sight, Floyd drove out of the lot and immediately pulled over at the nearest curb. He got out and returned to the parking lot, looking for Henry's car. He found it easily. The plates and color were different but there was no mistaking the only vehicle that Henry Torres ever drove in. It was a Cadillac the size of a three bedroom house.

For the third time in as many years, the once-famous bounty hunter swapped out the global positioning tracking device on Henry's car. At the same time, he yanked the wires on a second and more advanced GPS model that had probably been planted by a skip-tracer named Tom Devereaux. As long as the man didn't get a new car anytime soon, Floyd could count on another thirty thousand dollars or so whenever he needed it. All he had to do was catch up with him again.

Back in the old days he didn't have to cheat so much to get the job done. He also didn't make a habit of letting them go when they gave him more money than the bail bondsmen were offering—not as often as Devereaux, anyway. Back in the old days he was treated like a rock star.

Returning to his car, Floyd pulled away from the curb and headed for the Interstate. He couldn't wait to get back down to LA to take care of more than three months worth of unpaid bills on an office that had seen very little business lately. The short day and a half he'd spent in San Francisco catching up with Henry Torres had been way too cold for him anyway.

~ 9 ~

"No kidding?" Burgess mused, looking for Beverly's reaction to the new information. "You'd think they'd ring him up for PR reasons if for nothing else. Is he dead or something?"

"Your guess is as good as mine," she replied. "And as far as the Bureau not contacting him, I can see them wavering on something like that. He made them look bad and they don't like that kind of thing. Law enforcement hates a solo artist."

"Is it because he didn't give them any credit?"

"He didn't need to," she told him, starting to write notes again. "Floyd Madison bagged Stanley Hewitt on his own with no assistance whatsoever. Every federal, state, and local agency had twenty-four hour dragnets out for him and Madison brings him in all by himself. He got victim number ten to the hospital before she bled to death and walked Stanley right into a Santa Barbara police station in handcuffs. Walked him right through the main entrance and brought him to the desk sergeant. Everyone went crazy. My God, what a scene that was."

Although she hadn't actually been there to witness the first few minutes, the image she had constructed in her mind was full of all kinds of details both big and small. Only a few blocks away from the scene at the time and still just a student herself, twenty-one year-old Beverly McGrath had descended on the police station as eagerly as the many journalists and TV reporters who got the word at the same time. In less than an hour, the numbers had swelled into the hundreds and included everyone from national networks to students from the university.

The word spread around town quickly that there was a tenth victim. She was alive and she was one of their own.

Though it was early Spring, the atmosphere had been more like that of New Years Eve. Stanley Lewis Hewitt, the west coast murderer who had killed nine women and had only been identified by name a week earlier, was in custody. It was a reason to celebrate and many people had done just that.

"And thus begins the illustrious career of Doctor Beverly McGrath," Burgess offered with a broad smile, hoping it didn't come out sounding snotty. It wasn't intended that way and he genuinely enjoyed watching her eyes light up as she spoke about it.

"Almost, Perry. It wasn't until number ten started talking that I got involved and that was out of sheer luck. She was the key."

"Right place, right time," Burgess said, shooting a look over to Williams, who was quiet and still listening intently. "You see how it works, Ryan? Ten years of school plus a medical degree for me and it took even longer than that before anyone besides my mother knew who I was."

"He's right," Beverly agreed, drawing a small grin from Williams.

"That was a pretty good start for you *and* Floyd Madison," Burgess added. "What do you think ever happened to the man?"

"Who knows?"

The last time she had heard a word about Floyd Madison was over nine years earlier. He was on Good Morning America and it was his final TV appearance that she knew of. Before then it had been tabloid TV, afternoon talk shows, interviews on the evening news, and even a couple dates with Leno and Letterman. For a year or so the viewing audience couldn't get enough of him. The clips were always short and entertaining and he had a sound-bite for every occasion.

It didn't last very long, however.

If he could have kept up the pace, bringing in a fresh serial killer once a year and generating a happy ending for every high profile missing persons case he accepted, he could have made a brilliant career of it. Things didn't tend to work out like that, though, and both she and Burgess were familiar with the phenomenon. Since being reminded of her own personal failings wasn't what she need at the moment, shifting back to the subject at hand seemed appropriate if not required.

"Frankly, I'm more curious about what happened to Stanley. If he's out there doing a repeat it would really surprise me. This isn't like Ted Bundy getting loose and trying to kill a dorm-room full of girls because of pent up hostility. Stanley works on a whole different mechanism."

"Hildebrandt sounded pretty sure of himself." Burgess then shifted his attention to his favorite prison guard. "I don't want to be a bother, Ryan—"

"I'm here to please, doctor." He was already getting up from his seat. "Time of death, injuries, a name, and some pictures—I got it. I'll see if I can crack a few skulls and get some of the suits on your team."

He was thrilled to finally have something to do that didn't involve speaking. For a little while he was concerned that his part of it was going to be nothing but more of the same interviews like he'd had with Agent Hildebrandt and many others like him. Three days worth had been quite enough. Getting coffee for people or even mopping up the restrooms would have been preferable to another dreadful Q & A session. Both doctors thanked him before he stepped from the room and that in itself was more than enough to keep him momentarily happy.

As soon as the door closed, Burgess leaned closer to her with a semi-serious look. He dropped his voice even lower than when Matthew Chase had departed.

"We might want to take a minute and focus on what Hildebrandt wanted from us. It sounds easy enough and I could really use this right now. He wants to know if they're still together. If we give them an answer and it turns out to be the right one…we're gold, Beverly. Back in business for real."

"And if we're wrong?"

"Then they can hardly hold it against us."

"So, *are* they still together?" she asked of herself and Burgess at the same time. Giving the question her complete attention for the first time since it had been brought up, she realized that she didn't have a clue. She had an instinctive feeling but wasn't sure if it qualified. "I'd have to say no myself and I don't see them sticking close together for any length of time unless it was absolutely necessary. Of course, I also didn't think that Stanley would ever leave these grounds, so what the hell do I know?"

"I think you know plenty…about Hewitt," he replied. "And I know Spencer Stoning backward and forward. These guys don't mix; that's my opinion. We're dealing with some weird circumstances here, but I can't picture them driving clear to Washington and committing a murder together. Can you?"

"I don't think Stanley did it at all."

"Okay, Bev," he said, holding a hand up before she went any further. "First of all, stop calling him 'Stanley'. He's 'Hewitt' or 'Stanley Hewitt'. 'Stanley Lewis Hewitt' would be the norm if you were in front of a crowd or putting his name in print, but you've got to stop calling him by his first name for God's sake. That's why Hildebrandt jumped all over you."

"Why'd he piss on you then?"

"Because you irritated him before he got to me. Secondly—stop saying he didn't do it. I know we're all innocent until proven guilty but Hewitt's been proven guilty once already. Maybe Ryan will be back here in a minute with photos that don't match Hewitt's MO, but until I see them I'm going to assume the worst."

"And what do you think 'the worst' would be?"

"I'm not qualified to get that specific," he replied. "But I'll trust your judgment on this and agree with anything you want to tell them as long as it doesn't involve defending the guy. Think about it from that agent's perspective and just give him what he wants. He knows you can make a few educated guesses. So do I."

"Thanks for all the confidence, Perry, but how specific do you think I can be?"

"Very," he answered, wanting badly to give her the answer himself. "You know the history better than anyone. Hell, you made a best-seller out of it. Taking everything the agent told us into account, I want you to ask yourself, Beverly—seriously ask yourself—what's his next move? If you'd never met Hewitt and only knew what you'd read about him, where would he be going next? Where?"

She considered the question and tried to step further from herself and take a look from the outside. From an evidentiary viewpoint it didn't look too good for Stanley. If she didn't know him on a personal level she'd have to say it looked pretty damn bad; not to mention the fact that it could be even worse than it already appeared. Taking it all into consideration, she imagined the worst possible scenario she could think of and threw it right out there.

"I guess he'd be on his way to Altamont, Oregon." It was the answer Burgess had expected. It made perfect sense in a very bad way. "So, where would that put him right now?"

"Anywhere in between there and Vancouver. So, where's Stoning, Perry? You know him backward and forward, right? Tell me where he is."

Perry Burgess wasn't even embarrassed by the fact that he had nothing. Spencer James Stoning was a man with no return address. The majority of people he had ever known were cut apart by bullets in a killing spree that rivaled anything of its kind. Before that happened he had never so much as kicked a dog. No rap sheet and no arrests. There was no history to run home to and he could disappear in any number of ways.

"I don't know, Beverly. He's alone, though—I can tell you that much. To say that they're somewhere to the west of us is the best I can do."

"But they've separated by now," she stated and asked at the same time, making sure they were on the same page. If they were going to present their ideas to a man who could make or break any possible future for either of them, their findings would need to be in complete agreement with one another.

"They've split up. Absolutely."

"You're sure?"

"Positive," he replied, feeling confident that he was indeed correct.

~ 10 ~

"Hey, Spence," Stanley asked timidly, tapping lightly on the door even though Spencer had given him all the time he needed while he occupied the room. Though there were still a few hours of daylight left, getting some solid sleep was the main thing on his mind. "How much longer is it going to be, man?"

He heard a loud sigh on the other side of the door. Stanley would have felt bad but it had been over an hour now. Spencer's response reverberated in the small, tiled room.

"Leave me alone, Stan. I'm taking the best shit of my life in here. Go watch TV or something."

Knowing what the man was experiencing, Stanley wandered back to the main room and climbed back onto what felt like the most comfortable bed he had ever laid on. It was almost *too* comfortable for his liking. It wasn't quite as relaxing as crapping without an audience for the first time in a decade and a half, but it felt better than he expected. Such a small thing and yet it had slipped away over the years without much notice.

Stanley had spent better than forty-five minutes on the toilet himself. The act only took the usual few minutes, but it was letting the seat warm under his ass and taking his time even though he was finished that made it something out of the ordinary. He took five minutes alone just playing with the toilet paper, which was a great deal softer than the sandpaper they gave him in Woodhall. It was pure white instead of recycled beige and appeared to made of at least two layers of something that resembled tissue paper.

In his excitement, Stanley Hewitt had nearly wiped his ass into oblivion. He guessed that Spencer was doing the same.

So far, Oakridge was a bit more dull than Vancouver had been. In Washington the heat hadn't been turned up very high yet and laying low in public was still a safe bet. Now it wasn't and the temperature was rising steadily. Spencer had told him that it would only get worse and he believed him without question, as usual. He had always been right about everything for as long as they had known each other and it was only one of the reasons Stanley worshipped him.

"Anything yet?" Spencer asked as he finally emerged from the bathroom. The TV was on but the volume was turned all the way down and neither of their faces were currently being displayed.

"Not since I've been watching. I can only stare at that thing for so long before it gives me a headache. I used to watch TV for a days at a time when I was a kid and I don't remember it hurting so bad."

"Then stop looking at it, Stan," he replied with a sideways glance. It seemed the simplest solutions were the hardest for the guy to grasp sometimes. "That clock next to you is also a radio. Put it on AM and roll that dial around. And turn it up, will you? I was taking a dump in there and it kind of ruins my serenity knowing you're listening to me."

"I didn't hear anything."

"I hope not, man," he chuckled with a faint glint in his eye. "Because it was a real steamer, I'll tell ya. Burned my ass and everything. Did you ever take a shit that made your fucking ears ring?"

He could have gone on for several more minutes regarding the particular merits of his bowel movement but it wasn't required. Stanley had already fallen over sideways and was howling into the pillow next to him. He hit the bed with his fist hard enough to make the springs squeak as his body spasmed uncontrollably, making it hard to keep air in his lungs. From Spencer's end, it was a tiny moment of triumph.

There was another laugh in the room as well but Spencer ignored it for the moment since he didn't feel like being the bad guy right now. It was a pleasant sound and wasn't intended as a form of ridicule or mockery. The small voice was only doing the natural thing when presented with bathroom humor and he loved the contrast of the two distinctly different voices giggling together.

Then the kid's father had to go and open his mouth and ruin the whole thing. It was necessary that he did so, but Spencer wished he had waited for a more opportune moment.

"Shush, Kevin," the man hissed, still gazing at the floor as he been doing for the last several hours.

The laughter vanished suddenly and the atmosphere that hung over the room made it seem as though it had never existed there at all. Everything shifted from levity to deadly serious in less than a second. Everyone in the room had seen the transformation once already and it hadn't worked out too well for them the first time. The father in the trio of unfortunate travelers still wore a welt over his right eye from their initial encounter.

"Are you *talking* again, George?" Spencer asked.

The man put his arms up to fend off the blow he knew was coming but it never connected. He heard the sharp crack of skin on skin but didn't feel a thing because the backside of Spencer's hand had met with his wife's left cheek instead of his own. Instinctively, she pulled her head back quickly and did more damage to herself banging into the wall she was leaning against than Spencer would have done with his empty hand. With a thud that dented the drywall behind her, she now had two injuries to moan over.

"*Oh, God no,*" her husband wailed as he lowered his hands to a position covering his face, which was nothing more than an uncontrollable mask of fear by now. The abuse had been pretty steady throughout the day and the pressure was still building as the evening approached.

Their seven year-old son pulled his legs up closer to his chest and buried his head in between his knees. Spencer knew that the kid probably already felt horrible about what happened because of a single laugh, but the fact was it didn't matter what the reason was; they just needed the man to say another word so their evening could proceed on schedule. He could have been speaking to any of them and it wouldn't have made a difference. It was only a matter of time.

"You shouldn't talk to him like that, George," Stanley said, grabbing the man by what little hair he had. In a flash, he was forced against the same wall that his wife had just bounced off of. "Give me some scissors, Spence. I'm gonna make George start taking me serious."

"Which pair?" He stepped away from them and moved next to the bed furthest from the door. "The long ones or the little stubby guys?"

"Huh?"

Spencer looked down into one of the drawers in the nightstand. "I'm sorry, Stan, but I've got to know what you have in mind if you want me to pick one for you. If there's one important thing that my old buddy Kenny Keyes used to say, it's that you need to use the right job for whatever tool you're going to do. He was a fuckwit and was always mixing his shit up like that, but I usually knew what he meant anyway. Are you gonna take off a finger, Stan?"

"I—"

"You'll want the short ones if that's the plan. You'll have more leverage and the web of your thumb won't get all bruised when you get to the bone. If the grip's too thin, you won't get past the tendon."

He watched the man's head begin to sway back and forth in a mix of fear and disbelief. Spencer guessed he was screaming the word "*No*" in his head while Stanley hovered over him.

"Now, these pointy barber-shop jobs, on the other hand—I think you already know they're only good for skin and other kinds of stabbing, jabbing, and flesh-poking. Silly looking things. You gonna do any poking, Stan?"

By now, Stanley knew better than to answer since it made the most sense to let the specialist handle the situation in his own special way. Spencer was on a roll and looked ready to close the deal.

"Because if you are, these are the ticket. I especially like this little deal hanging off the end." He pointed but didn't reach into the drawer yet. "I've always wanted to ask the guy who designed these why he left that little extra finger gadget on there. It's not a loop but your finger rests against when you're cutting. That half moon piece of shit just sticks out all the time. Am I the only one who's ever wondered about that? Why not just make it a full loop like the other two?"

Stanley's eyes shifted quickly to Spencer before they rolled upwards toward the ceiling. He didn't want to admit that he had always been mystified by the strange differences there were between regular shears and the clippers that his barber used to cut his hair with when he was a kid. Of course, he didn't feel a need to respond since he was halfway convinced that Spencer had pulled the idea right out of his head.

"And why are they so damned long? Real thin and way too skinny at the tip to cut anything more than a few wisps of hair at a time. You can't do much else with them, can you?"

He went quiet briefly before reaching into the drawer and moving his hand around. Dramatic pauses were always good for effect and often said more than a book full of words ever could. He let the clock tick away as silence took over the room and a moment of calm returned. It wasn't until their breathing had almost gone back to normal that he started right back up again.

"Which brings us back to that poking I was just referring to. What do you suppose your wife's threshold for pain is, George? Does she have any cataracts that need removing?"

Spencer peered at the cowering man to see if he would look up. According to his drivers license, the man's name was Paul Lang but they had both been calling him George ever since they had knocked on his hotel room door and forced their way in seven hours earlier. Spencer liked using people's names when he addressed them and if he didn't have that particular piece of information just yet he would make one up on the spot and run with it. Stanley followed suit and they continued using the name even after the license told them different. On top of everything else that was occurring, Spencer correctly surmised that the effect would be most disorienting to the man and his family. It was working out quite well so far.

"Wait…does she still have her tonsils? I'm talking to you, George. Look up here at me and stop being rude."

He still hadn't opened his eyes and his defensive posture had been going strong, off and on, for several hours. They both knew from various experiences that living in constant fear of imminent bodily harm was taxing on the mind as well as the body and could only be handled for so long before one or the other gave out. Sometimes they both caved in at once and that was the goal for the moment.

If they wanted to get any solid rest tonight, the Lang family would need to be broken down and kept in as much disorder as possible before bed time. The kid wouldn't be much of a problem and the wife had just been shoved an inch or two across the line of normal fear and into the realm of terror. She could still bounce back from it relatively easily over time, but she wouldn't be screaming or escaping from the room tonight, meaning that more than half of their goal had been met.

Taking a step back from him, Stanley looked down at the man they had been calling George and guessed that Spencer might have talked him even further over the line than his wife had ventured. His shaking form had wandered away from average fear too quickly and the terror was probably waist deep by now. Backing it off a bit would be required if they didn't want poor George to slip any lower and drown in it. There would be no bouncing back from it at that point.

"What about the boy, George? Does he have any parts that need trimming? Any dirt under his fingernails that Stan here can dig out for you? He's real talented, you know. He'll go right down to the bone if he needs to."

It was using the proper tools that made it work and Stanley knew that Spencer was dead-on right, as usual. He was full of tricks like that. Aside from a quiet tap on the head from the shotgun and a slap across the face, no one had been physically harmed. With that little bit of groundwork already laid out, it was only a matter of a few well-placed, mentally torturous moments that guaranteed absolute submission from them during the dark hours. It would be hell on their delicate little minds and might take years to get over completely, but it would keep their bodies healthy throughout the night if they were lucky.

"*Come on, George,*" Spencer whined angrily. "You're going to look up here at me or I'll have to snip your wife's pretty little eyelids off. Because I'll tell you, George, somebody—*somebody*—is going to give me some *fucking* attention and they're going to give it to me right this *instant.*"

Profanity also had its place in the process; especially when there were children present. Since no parent would want their child exposed to such foul language, stripping that control from them was just another part of the program. Spencer felt confident that no one would attempt to censor him. If it was the husband by himself, a completely different game would have been played and more physical contact would have been necessary. Luckily for him—or unlucky, depending on the point of view—his wife and son were the perfect tools for the job; or jobs for the tool if you ever listened to a fuckwit named Kenny Keyes talk. When it came to leverage, Spencer knew that there was no better asset than loved ones if you really wanted to snap somebody in half.

"Let me ask you, George," Spencer went on, rapidly shifting both his tone and facial expression from angry and frightening to pleasant and curious. "Is your wife still…you know…*fertile?* I know it's a personal question, but I guess what I'm really asking is if she still has her ovaries. It's not for me, George. I don't even know what I'd do with them personally, but Stan here actually collects things like that; like they were coins or stamps or something. Isn't that just about the worst thing you've ever heard, George? Isn't it?"

Stanley watched in awe as Spencer took George right up to the edge of insanity with nothing more than a few scary suggestions and an open drawer that probably contained a Gideon Bible at the most. And as far as the ovary thing went, he didn't have a clue what that was about.

When he had asked for the pair of scissors a minute earlier, it was just a bluff; an excuse to take a shot at being as horrifying as his partner—if Spencer didn't mind being referred to as such. He hadn't expected Spencer to carry it any further but he did and he did it with an amazing amount of flair. It was so good that Stanley could picture both pairs of scissors in the drawer and he could see them with uncanny detail. The barber's snippers were shiny, long, and complete with the extra half-loop that the middle finger would rest against. The shorter ones hadn't been described but he saw them anyway. They were bulky with extra thick ends and could cut through cardboard all day without ever getting dull. They would slice a leather belt in two without a minimal amount of pressure and would go right through those tendons that Spencer had been talking about.

After a few seconds of giving it a little more thought—maybe too much—he began to question if there were really scissors in the drawer or not. He didn't remember seeing them but, then again, he didn't specifically remember *not* seeing them. He decided not to be surprised if Spencer pulled a pair out and handed them to him.

It wouldn't come to that, though. Scissors or just a bible; it didn't matter what was in the drawer. Paul Lang had finally reached his limit of anxiety.

His hands dropped to the floor and his head hung down, rolling slowly from side to side. Every few seconds his eyes would widen for an instant then the lids would creep back down to a half closed state. His breathing had slowed down a great deal and came at long intervals in giant lungfuls. His mouth was currently too dry for a good string of drool to get going, but it probably wouldn't be very long before he started soaking the carpet.

Stanley remembered seeing a girl devolve under Spencer's spell in much the same way in a restaurant a couple of nights earlier. It was a completely different scenario with the girl herself being threatened, but the results were equally admirable. While George probably couldn't focus his eyes even if he had a rational thought left in his head, the girl at the restaurant had been different and couldn't stop looking into Spencer's face.

Stanley found himself with the same problem from time to time. He didn't know what it was, but the famous mass murderer he'd escaped with had something going on that couldn't be put into words.

They observed the trio quietly for over a minute before Spencer suddenly slammed the nightstand drawer as hard as he could. The boy flinched the most while his mother only uttered a short squeal that was barely audible. She was slumped against the wall with one hand covering her face up to the eyes, which were still clenched shut. She was sobbing in a gasping and muffled way but was finally beginning to wind down. Her free arm was wrapped tightly around the child that sat between herself and her husband.

Paul Lang had no response whatsoever to the sudden sound that had killed the silence. For all intents and purposes he wasn't even there. He was mentally blank, momentarily deaf, and was pretty sure his name was George.

"Wrecked another one, didn't I?" Spencer said excitedly, staring down at his latest accomplishment. "Who's the bad guy, Stan? Who's the fucking bad guy?"

"You are, Spence. You're the bad guy."

"Your acknowledgement is appreciated." He crossed the room and checked the door. It was already locked but he engaged the deadbolt and chain as well. "Give me a hand here."

Together, they each took a side of the heavy table that sat in the corner of the room under a hideously ugly lamp that hung from the ceiling. With a little effort they moved it directly in front of the door and left it there. It wouldn't really keep anyone out but would work beautifully keeping everyone in, assuming they had the guts to give escape a chance. Neither man suspected they were up to it and if they did they wouldn't be able to move the table without making enough noise to get themselves killed.

Tonight Spencer and Stanley wouldn't even sleep in shifts. They wouldn't hide any blunt or sharp objects that might be used against them in their slumber and they wouldn't leave a single light on to keep an eye on things. There was no need to.

"What time are we heading out tomorrow?" Stanley asked as he climbed into the bed.

"As early as possible," Spencer answered, hopping onto the bed closest to the radio. Turning the volume up slightly, he shifted across the bed and leaned closer to Stanley, keeping his voice semi quiet. It was supposed to sound like a whisper but was much louder than that.

"Altamont's about a hundred and fifty miles from here and I want it to still be dark when we roll in. I'm thinking we leave about four, which is a full twelve hours from now. That's tons of sleep for the both of us and at least one good meal in between. How's that sound?"

"Sounds fine," Stanley replied with a yawn that lasted about ten seconds.

It had been a long day and sleep would come easily. Constantly thinking about the near future and recent past was tiring work but was necessary if they wanted to stay ahead of the authorities and walk the earth for another day. Finding transportation they could hang onto for more than a few hours was hard enough without worrying about food and accommodations.

In Vancouver they had driven through two fast food restaurants with nothing more than sunglasses to obscure themselves and had no trouble at all. They would be headline news shortly and it would never be that easy again; especially where they were headed.

"They'll be expecting us, won't they?" Stanley asked in his own loud whispery voice as he reached in between their beds and dimmed the lamp.

"Some, I guess. It wouldn't take a brain surgeon to figure it out. I've got it covered, though, so don't start worrying just yet. Getting through to Redding will be ten times worse if by some miracle we make it out of Altamont."

Spencer rose from the bed and clicked off the bathroom light before giving the room a last look. The door was barred and their three roommates were as inanimate as the floor they sat on. It was all they needed for a decent night of sleep with one exception. He stepped toward the three figures and stared down at the one in the middle.

"Do you have to go to the bathroom, little guy?"

"No, I already went."

"Not *you*, Stan," he said stiffly, turning his head to see Stanley already curled up with a pillow. Even in front of a child and two nearly catatonic adults that he didn't know from a hole in the ground, Spencer managed to feel embarrassed anyway.

~ II ~

"What do you think now?" Burgess asked as they pored over a series of grisly images supplied by Ryan Williams, who had returned a few minutes earlier. "Hildebrandt will be back in exactly thirty-six minutes by my watch and he's going to want an opinion. What does it look like?"

Beverly held one close-up shot to her face until her nose was almost touching the glossy print. After a minute of staring at the various cuts that covered the woman's entire body, she set the photo down and rifled through a file with some preliminary forensic findings. The results were consistent with one another and it wasn't at all what she had hoped for.

"I've seen a lot of pictures that look just like these."

"You're not really surprised, are you?" The only thing that surprised Burgess was that she did seem shocked. She shouldn't have been and if she was, she certainly shouldn't have shown it. "What other realistic possibilities were there?"

"I was pulling for some other old-fashioned Washington State serial killer myself. They're a dime a dozen out there. I swear, I think every single one of them either moves to the place or at least passes through. Think about it. The Beltway snipers, Ted Bundy, Kenneth Bianchi—"

"Bianchi...he was one of those Hillside Stranglers, right?"

"Yeah, he came all the way up from LA to kill in Washington. And just for fun, let's throw in the Green River Killer, the .22 Caliber Killer, the Want Ad Killer, the I-5 Killer, the Roadside Butcher, the—"

"Hey, why does he get to be the 'Butcher'? Why don't they just call him the Roadside Killer like everyone else?"

"I don't know, Perry, but that's exactly the kind of thing that I'm talking about. What *about* the Roadside Butcher? He's been busy in the region lately. Last time I read about it, he was going at a pace of about one every month and a half. He was due and it was in Washington. I'm sure someone's already considered it."

"Maybe," Burgess allowed. "But like the agent said, it was *Vancouver*, Washington, and that makes it a little more significant. It was where Hewitt got started. Victim number one. You know it, I know it, and Hildebrandt sure knew it when he threw it in your face the way he did."

She could only nod since he spoke the truth.

"And that Roadside Butcher shit?" he continued. "It's like Jack the Ripper and the Zodiac Killer all over again. It's what do you do when you've got a mutilated corpse and nobody to blame for it. You make it up. You give it a scary name and throw it on the front page. You consolidate. That's what you do and they've been doing it for years. When they finally caught the Green River guy they tried to tack every unsolved homicide from Oregon to B.C. on him. Maybe they were his and maybe they weren't. Who really knows? Remember Henry Lee Lucas from way back when? Ottis Toole?"

"Who doesn't?"

Even Ryan Williams nodded in recognition of the names of the two self proclaimed, allegedly prolific serial killers. With more than three-hundred supposed murders under their belts, the duo appeared to be kings at the top of the psychotic heap. It wasn't so simple, however, when looked at from an investigator's viewpoint where actual proof of a crime was required. Perry Burgess didn't buy it.

"They've made movies about them and they *still* haven't confirmed most of the murders they confessed to. A lot of open cases got closed because of those two and they still don't know how much of it was outright lies. I'm guessing almost all of it."

"You're probably right," Beverly agreed. "But nobody's going to pay money for a book about what a person *didn't* do and the people he *didn't* kill. Nobody would write it and no publisher would print it. Neither of us can afford to tank on the bestseller list again."

Burgess winced slightly at the comment but kept his eyes from narrowing. Hearing her admit that her writing career was in a shambles was fine. Taking note of his own recent failures, however, was not.

As much as Stanley Lewis Hewitt and Spencer James Stoning were a mismatched pair, Burgess knew that he and Beverly McGrath were different animals as well. While her second book may have "tanked" in the retail market, Burgess would never have used such a word to describe his personal lack of sales. He preferred to think that he was on a slightly higher level than the *True Detective* crowd they often shared shelf space with and was catering to a much more exclusive and educated reading audience. Of all the lies that he told himself daily, the legend of the discriminating reader was his favorite.

"Now, if we really wanted to screw our careers, we could write a book about the Roadside Butcher together," he offered. "You and me—I can picture it. We'd fill it with quotes and facts and all kinds of ingenious horseshit and narrow our suspects down to the usual young, solitary, white male that everyone loves to hate. A year after publication they find out that the murders were committed by ten different people with no connection whatsoever and we'd win the Asshole of the Year award."

"My agent would be thrilled," Beverly added sarcastically.

"Mine too—if she's even speaking to me anymore. The Butcher and the Zodiac Killer are just somebody's excuse for poor police work and I can't be involved in one of those. I think Hewitt's our man and we should start from there."

"So, it's *we* now?"

"Yes, it is," he answered plainly. "If Stoning decided to blow away a few rooms full of people again, I'm pretty sure you'd be on my coat tails in a heartbeat. I can't help it if your patient is the one who wants to relive his past. Hildebrandt wants an answer from the two of us anyway and that alone should be enough to join us at the hip for a little while."

"Stanley was never my patient. He was just an interview and that was it."

Beverly knew it looked as though she was trying to suddenly distance herself from the killer whose first name she couldn't seem to stop using, but it obviously wasn't playing to the room very well. While Ryan Williams avoided eye contact with her for the moment, Burgess gave her a direct look that was almost cruelly sympathetic. At first she had pushed too hard in one direction. Now she had pushed too hard in both.

"Okay, so it was a few weeks of interviews. We talked and we got comfortable with each other. It was necessary if I wanted to get the full scope of him and as far as the psych end of it goes, I'm the only person he ever opened up to."

Even as she spoke, Beverly realized the ignorance of her statement considering the people she presently shared the room with. While Perry Burgess could write her words off as merely pompous, Williams could most likely prove them to be inaccurate if he cared to. It was true that Stanley Hewitt hadn't spoken about his crimes on the record before Beverly McGrath appeared, but anything that happened after those crazy few weeks she couldn't comment on with any real credibility. The only one who probably could was Ryan Williams himself.

"I know you've already been asked this a hundred times in the last couple of days," she said, turning to Williams, who was queuing up his answer before she asked the question. "But what was his mood like for the last month or two? Were there any drastic changes or anything else I need to be aware of?"

"Same here, Ryan," Burgess chimed in, hoping for a clue about Spencer Stoning's current mental state. "Anything odd that sticks out in your mind."

"And any communication that went on between them would help out a lot too. Whatever you think might help."

"Plus anything either of them said to you or any of the other guards."

"...or to anyone else in D Block."

"And don't forget correspondence, Ryan. Letters, cards...any kind of mail."

Williams' eyes bounced back and forth between the two of them as they piled more requests and questions on top of one another as he had expected them to do. It was no different than how the federal agents had worked him over except he would only have to tell the story to the doctors once if he was lucky. And like he had already told them, they were very far down on the list and he didn't foresee anyone standing in line behind them to ask the same questions yet again. At least he hoped not.

When they finally stopped talking over each other, it got quiet as they waited for the guard to respond. He slowly rose from his chair and pulled out a chain with at least twenty keys on it.

"We've got about half an hour before Hildebrandt gets back. You should come with me. If he finds out you haven't asked to look at their cells by then, he's gonna feel worse about you than he already does. I'll tell you the rest along the way."

~ 12 ~

It was 4:38 p.m. exactly when the car made its first wild lurch out of the far left lane and moved to the right, nearly smashing into the smaller car that he hadn't even seen. From the eighty-five miles an hour he was going a minute earlier, his speed dropped down to fifty-five in one second and down to twenty even faster. Another second later he was on the shoulder of the busy I-5 and at a dead stop surrounded by the smoke from his own tires.

Floyd Madison didn't wave or apologize to the many commuters he had almost killed and didn't give any thought to his own mortality. He chose instead to roll up his windows to block out any traffic noise and turn up his radio to make sure he heard what he thought he had just heard. The voice on the radio was still rambling about one thing or another, neglecting to repeat the exact words that had grabbed his attention. The story sounded like three day old news at first and he had barely been paying attention to it. He had already heard enough about the Carroll brother's short lived escape from prison and couldn't imagine why they were beating a dead horse.

It was while he dwelled on the sad redundancy of what KCBS radio considered to be headline news that the announcer said something that jarred Floyd Madison right out of the fast lane. It was a name.

"Say that again," Floyd growled, giving his radio a fiercely dirty look. He knew what he heard and suspected that his speakers weren't just lying to him. "Go ahead and say it. Say what you just said."

The news anchor was reading with a voice that stood out from the usual monotone, teleprompter-inspired traffic reports and had a sense of urgency backing it up. Still halfway convinced that the man was simply rehashing the same Carroll's story from a new and different angle, Floyd pulled out a cigarette while he waited and wasn't sure how he was supposed to feel about it yet. The shaking of his hands while he lit up his smoke didn't answer the question in any way.

"…*on the heels of Martin and Jensen Carroll, who were killed early Friday morning during a firefight with state troopers and local…*"

He took a heavy drag and tried to separate the old news from what he hadn't heard yet. Frequent bursts of static jumbled the words occasionally and left him wondering if he had heard anything at all.

"…*weather conditions hampered all efforts…*"

This part was new. He had read in the paper that the Carrolls were wasted during a rainstorm but it didn't seem to impede the marksmanship of whichever local boys were credited with shooting up their truck until it burst into flames. From what he had heard and read about it, all efforts had paid off grandly and weren't hampered by anything, much less weather conditions.

"…*proceeded on foot…*"

The doubts Floyd had about what he thought he had heard were fading even more. Nobody had gone anywhere on foot unless policing up a bunch of smoking corpses qualified as legwork. It was beginning to sound as though the focus was shifting away from the two brothers that Floyd had already been sick of before they were even imprisoned in the first place. The two spoiled rotten, pretty-boy gangsters had never interested him in the least.

"…*from a gas station security camera in Tremonton, Utah. Fourteen hours later local authorities were summoned…*"

He knew the Carrolls never even made it close to Tremonton. This he was sure of. They were killed somewhere near Logan, only a few miles from where they started along with the men who busted them out. CNN had been very clear on the point that no one who wasn't wearing a badge of some sort had walked away from it.

"…*Black Pine, Idaho, where multiple witnesses positively identified the assailants…*"

Assailants? Idaho? He still wasn't completely sure what it meant but he was definitely interested by the sound of it. Whoever they were, they weren't the Carrolls and they weren't in Utah anymore.

"…*as convicted murderers Spencer James Stoning and Stanley Lewis…*"

"…*Hewitt,*" Floyd finished as he involuntarily gnashed down on the cigarette that was lodged between his teeth. He was almost through the filter when he yanked the ruined butt from his mouth and stuffed it in the ashtray. After a full minute of taking slow, deep breaths and listening to his radio, he steadied his hands and lit another one. The news was horrifying, yet strangely encouraging.

"*Stanley Fucking Hewitt*," he uttered again, trying to remember the last time he had heard the name spoken aloud by anyone. Since he couldn't think of a specific time or occasion in the last several years, he guessed that his own name had been used even less frequently. "This ain't right at all. What the hell have you been doing, Stanley?"

As though responding directly to his question, the voice on the radio proceeded to tell Floyd Madison exactly what the hell Stanley had been doing. And he had been doing it in Vancouver, Washington apparently.

For some—most, in fact—the news would have been bad, if not utterly tragic. Floyd tried his damnedest, but couldn't manage to see it in such black and white terms. Though he knew enough to feel badly for the unfortunate victim and the family that was surely in mourning, putting a positive spin on the current situation wasn't beyond him. Desperation had quickly filled in all the gaps that a long lost sensitivity had left vacant.

"Man, that's fucked up," he said with no expression as the radio voice finished its Cliff Notes version of the latest grisly news item and moved onto the next story.

Grabbing the rearview mirror, he angled it downward so he could look into the only face available to him and search for the thing that was missing. While his own eyes stared back at him, Floyd put the car back in drive but kept his foot on the brake, trying to come up with a reason to feel badly about the unexpected information he had just heard. So far, he had nothing and it nagged at him. The only consolation was that he was very aware of the deficiency, meaning that all wasn't lost yet.

Before making the acquaintance of Stanley Hewitt, Floyd had often found himself shocked by many of humanity's repulsive and aberrant offerings. He remembered being disappointed at times and even sickened by acts that went miles beyond explanation no matter how long or how hard one tried to make sense of them. But those days were gone thanks to Hewitt and the sideshow of freaks that had followed in his wake.

There had been others prior to the infamous serial killer, but bringing in men who had neglected to pay their child support and shoplifters who failed to make their court dates never landed his photo on page-one. In fact, nobody had even bothered to waste a single drop of ink on him before fate stepped in and handed him the score of a lifetime.

Single-handedly pulling in the west coast's latest source of terror had been fantastic for business but would only be the beginning of Floyd's faith-shattering quest for greatness. There had been much to learn in a very short amount of time.

Following Hewitt's arrest and the fanfare that accompanied it, Floyd Madison had become the full time, highly paid, one-man industry that he had always dreamed of being. It didn't last for long—a couple of years at the most—but the shock of his chosen profession had worn off much faster than he would have ever thought possible; faster than was healthy for him he eventually came to believe.

He couldn't pinpoint the day he graduated from throwing up to simply shrugging his shoulders when presented with the unimaginable, but becoming desensitized to it was part of the process. It was a bad part but he knew that it was exactly that kind of thing that made him who he was.

He recalled a phrase that his mother used to say about the things that did not kill us were the things that made us stronger. In Floyd's experience, however, it was the things that killed others while he continued to live that had a much greater impact. And to complete the package, it got him paid, too.

Eventually, he lifted his foot from the brake and reentered traffic as dangerously as when he had pulled out of it. He wanted to wait until at least a tiny glimmer of disconnected sadness or empathy set in but it wasn't happening and he simply didn't have the time to grow a new soul.

He wove recklessly through the cars ahead and raced for the nearest off-ramp to make a call, ignoring the cell phone that was a permanent resident in his coat pocket. It was strictly for show and hadn't been activated for over a year due to lack of funds.

His secretary had been the first to go. The desk and other office furniture followed quickly after her and it wasn't much longer before his answering service and voice mail was replaced with a small plastic box purchased from a K-Mart for twelve dollars and ninety-nine cents, plus tax. As he thought about the cheap answering machine that rested on the floor of his nearly empty office space, Floyd tried to guess if his one remaining phone line had been cut off yet.

"I hate to say it, Stanley, but I think you just made my day."

It was the God's honest truth and he really did hate to say it. Considering the fact that he already had a thirty thousand dollar check in his pocket, it was a fairly heavy statement.

~ 13 ~

"Is this all of it or has anything been removed?" Beverly asked as she surveyed what was left of Stanley Hewitt's prison cell. Aside from the gray dust covering everything, it looked as if he was accustomed to keeping things as simple as possible and other than a cardboard box, he appeared to have no possessions whatsoever.

"It should all be here," Williams replied. "Some stuff's been moved around a little but they mostly just photographed the heck out of it and left everything where it was. There's really not much to it, as you can see."

Aside from a cot that was chained to the wall and the box beneath it, there wasn't much to look at. Beverly turned her attention to the rear wall that was no longer standing and carefully peered through the opening. The odor of ancient dankness mixed with fresh, caustic chemicals assaulted her sense of smell but she did her best not to even wrinkle her nose at it, feeling the two pairs of eyes that were on her.

She stepped up onto the concrete structure that now laid flat and could see the light pour in from the other eight cells that were now exposed. Avoiding the sink and toilet that seemed to stare up at her from their new positions on the ground, she ventured as far as she dared go without a flashlight. To Beverly it felt like stepping through a time machine and into a completely different world.

"How old did Matthew say this end of the block was?"

"Well, where I'm standing it's about thirty years old," he yelled back. "But the part you're walking in was built before World War Two. It was all solitary confinement until about thirteen years back when they shut her down. That was when D Block went solo. The block was just an annex off of the building back then. If you asked Chase, he'd tell you it was all scheduled to be upgraded ten years ago but he needed more funds."

"And what would you tell us if we asked the same question?" Burgess inquired as he walked the hallway and probed each of the damaged rooms, noting their contents.

"I'd say the funds were there but they got spent on other things. Lawyers, lobbyists, public relations—I'm guessing anybody with a hand out got a piece of Chase's action."

"And what did he get in return?"

"Expansion into Arizona, Colorado, two more in Oklahoma, and three in Texas. He gets five of them as is and he's taking bids for contracts on the two facilities that ACT gets to build from scratch. They'll be bigger, harder, and won't look a damn thing like this." He turned his eyes back on Stanley Hewitt's cell. "How are you doing back there, doctor?"

Instead of answering, Beverly stepped back through the opening and brushed the dust off of her sleeves before taking another look at the walls that were still upright. They were absolutely bare and free of any of the scribblings that often covered the walls of the average convict's cell.

She moved to the cot and reached underneath it. The cardboard box she pulled out appeared to be full of old newspapers and nothing more. "Not much too go through, is there?"

"No, not much," he echoed. "I was here when the first batch of investigators started picking through it and this is exactly how it looked then. There isn't anyplace to hide anything in here. Believe me, they checked it all out. They even checked the drains and x-rayed the mattress. It's just what's in the box."

Carefully, Beverly began removing the papers one by one and started stacking them next to her on the floor. When there was room to get her hands inside, she pulled out several at a time, making sure to keep them in the same order and position as they were in the box.

"Don't bother flipping through them," Williams cautioned, more worried about the time than anything else. "There's nothing in between the pages. No papers or notes and he didn't write anything in any of the them. The only thing with extra markings in it is sandwiched in there somewhere. You'll know it when you see it."

"Where?" she asked, carefully lifting out the remaining contents. There was only one item that wasn't a daily paper and it jumped right out at her. She scooped the book up quickly, looking at the front and back covers before flipping it open to the front page.

"What is it, Bev?" Burgess asked.

"It's a copy of *Understanding The Sickness*," she replied, taking what appeared to be an eerie kind of pride in what she was looking at. "It's autographed. I sent it to him when the book was released. I forgot all about that."

"The older stuff is on the bottom," Williams offered. "We only let him keep so many newspapers before he has to throw a bunch away, so anything he wanted to keep for any reason is probably underneath the new stuff."

"Why's that?"

"I guess he found something interesting in them."

"No, I mean why did he have to throw any away?" she asked. "I thought reading material didn't qualify as contraband."

"It doesn't. But one time we had this piece of shit convict named Juarez down in B who used to save up his papers. A real pack rat, you know? Now, laying flat in a stack, newspapers don't take up a lot of room. But if you take one or two sections at a time and wad them up into a ball, they get real big and you can fill a whole cell up with them."

"So?"

"So, that's what Juarez did. One night he wads up about three months worth of papers until he was up to his knees in them. His cellmate didn't say anything about it until Juarez said goodbye to him and lit a match. You ever see forty pounds of newsprint go up all at once in a twelve by nine room?"

She hadn't, but could picture it a little too vividly. With a grimace on her face, Beverly shook her head and started flipping through the seemingly endless pile of pristinely kept newspapers, finding it hard to focus on any one page. They were all from the Salt Lake Tribune and spanned a period of at least thirteen years, though they could have passed for being a few days old.

"All I need is the dates. We can go through the Tribune's archives when we've got some more time if someone gets us a list. Can we get that, Ryan?"

"Shouldn't be a problem, doctor."

"Excellent. Anything interesting next door, Perry?"

Burgess gave her a squinty-eyed grin before stepping back from the bars and looking down the hallway in both directions. The next look was directed towards Williams and was followed by an embarrassed smile.

"I give up, Ryan." The psychiatrist's powers of deduction were pretty rusty when it came to the felon he'd stopped thinking about the moment his sales had gone cold. "Which cell is it? I've got two guesses and I really don't feel like being wrong twice."

"Four doors down. It's the one that stands out."

There was only one that fit the description and it wasn't one of his first two choices. The Spencer Stoning he had chronicled, testified against, then counseled for two years wasn't close to being a quiet type of man, but the state of his latest habitat was a bit louder than Burgess had anticipated. It was a confusing and surrealistic display that nearly hurt to look at.

Though it differed in no structural way from any other cell in the block, the intricate designs, text, and drawings that blended in together gave it both a sense of open space and tight confinement at the same time. At first glance—and if one didn't realize they were in a penal institution—it might have looked like the back of a van decorated by an autistic child; a *brilliant* autistic child tripping on acid while suffering from a simultaneous attack of claustrophobia and agoraphobia. Upon closer inspection it also could have looked like the small room that it was except for the huge windows that were drawn on each of the walls.

Depending on the angle, the "outside" changed drastically and it became clear where the occupant spent most of his time and what his primary point of view was. Only once Burgess squatted down next to the bunk and aligned himself to where Spencer Stoning would be propped up in bed did the pictures begin to make sense. From the center of the room each pseudo-window had its own shape and symmetry and seemed to have no correlation between one another. None were perfectly square and there wasn't a ninety degree angle to be seen in the whole room.

But from the cot they looked real enough to climb out of.

In between the windows the walls were covered with what looked like random swirls of colored shapes that bled into each other almost imperceptibly, making it almost impossible to tell where one color ended and the next began. A closer look revealed that the shades themselves were connected by tiny letters, then words, then whole sentences tied together with no punctuation, no grammar, and not bound by any rules of the English language. Some of it didn't appear to be English at all.

As his eyes squinted down to try to distinguish at least one readable phrase among the seemingly thousands that were available to him, Burgess found his attention pulled away to another location and then to the next as though it would make sense if he just kept reading.

But reading wasn't what he was doing and it took him longer than he was happy with to realize it. He didn't know exactly what he was doing but he knew he didn't like it.

"Creepy, huh?" Williams asked, killing the silence. "The FBI's guys went over the whole thing with a high resolution camera if you want a peek at it and they're willing to share it with you. It's a wall to wall freak show in here, that's for sure. Did you see the weird part?"

"The weird part?" Burgess echoed with an incredulous look as his eyes rolled from the wall to the ceiling and back down again, not seeing a single thing that could be described as even close to normal. "Oh, sure. How could I miss it?"

"What is it, Ryan?" Beverly said, walking up behind him and getting her first look at Spencer's world. She didn't gasp, but blinked several times in a manner so comical that it would have made her laugh if she had seen herself do it. "*Jesus. And this gets weirder?*"

"Check it out," Williams said, motioning toward the large blank space to the rear.

Like Stanley's cell, there was a sink and toilet smiling up at them but there was quite a bit more. Even through the dust that had settled everywhere, they could see that the rear wall had been painted just like the others.

"Another window?" Burgess asked.

"Nope," Williams answered confidently, having already had the chance to view it at length. Lying on its back, the image lost much of its meaning. Upright, it had fit in perfectly with everything else in the room and now had a significance that couldn't be ignored. "It's a door."

~ 14 ~

"Oh my God," Beverly uttered in amazement, shifting her eyes around the various shapes until Spencer's door came into focus. "Is it supposed to be open or closed?"

Williams watched the doctor's minds try to bend their way around Spencer's cell in the same way that the federal agents had done. He preferred the wide-eyed awe of his current company to the sterile and unimpressed faces that the agents had worn.

"Well, it sure looks open now, doesn't it? Stoning started on the walls a few years ago. It's mostly felt tip."

"Felt tip?"

"Yeah, he started the whole thing with a Magic Marker one day and kept at it. It was just real thick lines here and there and didn't look like anything at first. The crazier stuff came later when he switched to smaller pens. He'd ask for another one whenever they ran out and I guess nobody saw a problem with it. They let him have one a day—no sharp ones or anything he could get high off of, of course—and he'd go to work on it. I kept waiting for the day that Chase would send a guy from maintenance over with a can of paint and cover it up, but it never happened."

"Why not?" Burgess asked. "Isn't it against the rules?"

"In general population, sure. But that's just crude nudie pics, profanity, or group stuff. You know, Aryan Brotherhood and all that crap. Mostly slogans and symbols and the kind of stuff that guys mark their territory with. In general population the inmate gets written up and the wall gets painted over."

"Why the exception for Stoning?"

"Why not?" Williams asked in reply. "There aren't any wars going on in the block. It's strictly psychos and high profiles up here and each guy has his own cell. Hell, these guys don't see but one hour of sunshine a day and they're alone when they do it. They don't even shower together. Everyone up here is a special case in one way or another and we have the least amount of trouble in the whole facility. If drawing pictures on the wall keeps an inmate from throwing his turds through the bars then I can see how they'd let him get away with something like that. Chase seemed to be intrigued by it anyway and that's the only reason we're looking at it now."

"How long did it take?" Burgess asked, pulling out a pen and his notebook as his eyes pored over the walls. "Or was it something he was still working on?"

"He'd take a few whacks at it whenever he was in a mood. But most of it what you're looking at was done a couple years ago. It was pretty neat looking and I didn't mind walking past it twenty times a day, so I really didn't have any feelings about it. Then about a month ago he throws the door in."

"A *month* ago?" Beverly wasn't doubting him but simply required confirmation of what the guard had just said.

"That's right."

"*One* month ago?" Burgess asked, sharing the same stunned expression as his female counterpart.

"About a month, give or take a few days. It wasn't too long after they tossed J.J. to him that he started working on the rear wall. Two weeks later he's got a new door to stare at and two weeks after that, he's gone. Now, listen—"

Williams stopped talking long enough to chuckle as Beverly brought a hand to her forehead while Burgess stared at the floor, looking like he had been kicked in the stomach. Instinctively, Williams tried to cover the smile on his face but put his hand down when he remembered that he didn't need to. Laughing at the feds would have been a costly mistake but laughing at the two doctors wasn't out of bounds in any way. He liked the both of them and could sense their excitement.

"We need locations, Ryan," Beverly spat out as she took a few steps away from the cell and took up a position in the middle of the hallway. "Okay, who was where when the escape happened?"

Williams strolled down the hall to the first cell that was missing a rear wall and pointed a finger at it. He spoke slowly, making sure they writing it all down.

"D-35—Bill Hersch. He's doing life for a triple homicide and has been bouncing around up here for about six years. He didn't even make it into the yard before a couple nightshift guys scooped him up. He's down in C now."

He moved to the next cell and pointed with his finger again.

"D-36—Gerald Knaziak. Serial rapist doing life. He made it to the fence line but that was it. When they caught up with him he was still standing there trying to gather enough balls to touch the fence and see if it would shock him. He never did, which is funny because the power was down the whole time. I hate that guy."

He only paused briefly in front of the next one before moving on.

"Stanley was here in D-37 and his next door neighbor was Martin Carroll here in thirty-eight. They didn't get along so well. D-39 was—"

"In what way did they not get along?"

"Let me finish," Williams said, holding up a hand for a pause in the questions while he moved down the row. "D-39 was empty—just a little buffer space between the brothers. It was the DEA's idea and they were still probing the Carrolls for their own reasons right up until they busted out. When they were moved up here to D, they were next to each other in thirty-nine and forty for a few weeks before getting split up."

"So, that puts Jensen Carroll in D-40," Burgess noted, writing it down.

"That's correct; right next to Stoning in forty-one. D-42 was occupied by a kidnapping snitch named Tony Potts and he didn't even try to leave when the wall came down. Either he knew he wouldn't make it or he couldn't find anyone to tag along with, which wouldn't surprise me. Potts was scared to death of Stoning and nobody likes a snitch anyway."

With that, Williams paused for a breath and looked down at his watch as he prepared for the barrage of inquiries that he knew was coming. He was almost happy to see that they had to get moving in a few minutes.

"So, you say Martin Carroll and Stanley Hewitt didn't get along?" Burgess asked.

"That's right. Martin started right in on him when he and Jensen got the transfer to D. It was the first block in all of Woodhall where there was someone as infamous as the Carrolls and I guess he didn't like it."

"How bad did it get?" Beverly asked.

"Not that bad at all. Kid stuff, actually. If you don't like a guy on D Block, the most you can really do is yell at him."

"So they'd get into shouting matches?" Burgess asked, going over the layout of the floor again and trying to picture what one could do to annoy another individual in the vicinity.

"Not those two. They were a pair of quiet ones, which is why it was so scary when they'd start going at it. It was mostly just threats and insults but I can tell you Martin Carroll was *not* used to it. I don't think that guy had been threatened in his whole life and you can bet that Hewitt didn't give a damn one way or the other."

"Can you think of any specific threat?"

"Well, sure," Williams answered, checking his watch. "I remember Hewitt once told him he was gonna have someone crap in his laundry. I don't really ever see that happening but it got Marty pissed something awful. He wouldn't change his clothes for a week. Another time Hewitt had Marty convinced that he'd stuck his toothbrush up his ass. It would be pretty damn hard for him to get a guy's toothbrush out of his cell but it drove Marty nuts anyway. They were both real paranoid like that."

"In what way?" Beverly asked.

"Well, with Martin Carroll, it didn't have to be a big deal for him to start getting all bent out of shape. Mostly he thought that people were trying to kill him from the outside—probably a valid concern—but he'd lose sleep over just about anything. Did you know he had a wife? I'm sure you can imagine how hard that would be. Guys can be real cruel about things like that in here."

"And what was Stanley so paranoid about?"

"Only one thing, really," Williams replied. "Theft. It was the same thing every time. He was just sure that someone was stealing from him—like he's got a bunch of priceless items laying around. He'd say it all the time. I never saw anything go missing but every now and then he'd act like a kid whose bike got ripped off or something. It had been getting pretty bad lately."

"What about Jensen Carroll and Stoning?" Burgess asked, finally getting his question in. It wasn't that Hewitt was less important; it just seemed to make more sense to focus on the guy with the door painted on his wall.

"I'd say they got on pretty good for the most part. They didn't argue too much, but then again, when it came to getting on his bad side, there weren't a lot of takers. Saying that you're gonna kill a guy in here is the norm and Stoning never did any of that. He'd just say something off the wall; maybe something about your mother or a family pet or your fifth grade teacher—*real* off the wall stuff—and he'd get you thinking in ways your mind doesn't want to go. He's got a real strange way with words."

"I recall," Burgess said thoughtfully, knowing first-hand what the guard was referring to and he was glad to hear that Spencer's interesting behavior hadn't been manufactured for his benefit alone. "It took me over two weeks of sessions with him just to get used to it."

"Yeah? Well, it took Hewitt even longer. I'll tell you, if there was a way for two guys to get at each other up here, they would have figured it out. They smoothed it out eventually but I don't think they even spoke to each other for the first couple months."

"You mean when Stoning first arrived at Woodhall?" Burgess asked.

"No," Williams replied as he checked his watch again then stepped to the left of Spencer's cell and pointed his finger at Jensen Carroll's former abode next door. He couldn't wait to see their reaction to this one. "I'm talking about when Hewitt was moved here to D-40. It couldn't have been more than five or six years ago."

Instead of gasps or more of the stunned looks that he was expecting, Williams was given two of the nastiest glares he had seen in a while. Burgess glanced back and forth between the two cells and then back to the guard.

"This keeps getting funnier, Ryan. What you're telling us is that Stoning and Hewitt were kept in adjacent cells? Right *here*? Right *next* to each other?"

"That's correct, doctor."

"For how long?" Beverly asked.

"Right up until the Carrolls transferred over from C Block. Yeah, six years sounds about right. We've got to get going now. You guys have about five minutes to figure out what you're gonna tell them."

*   *   *   *

While the two waited nervously in the conference room with no solid idea of what they might say to the authorities, Dwight Hildebrandt's stringent hour and ten minute time period expired without much notice. His tardiness was appreciated but put another awkward spin on a situation that already anything but accommodating. Every single minute of extra time was spent dragging as much useful information from Ryan Williams as they possibly could before the agent would arrive and, very likely, shoot each one of their theories into tiny little pieces. Based on what they had experienced so far, there was no reason to expect anything different.

When the door finally did fly open twenty minutes later, it was Matthew Chase instead of the bland Agent Hildebrandt stepping through it. With three sentences it was made abundantly clear that for them to develop any expectations at all would be pointless.

"Hildebrandt is gone." He pulled an envelope from his jacket pocket. His tie was back on and his hair was now combed neatly. "They're tearing down the shop here and moving everything to Redding, California. Most of Hildebrandt's staff is either already there or on their way."

~ 15 ~

Fine by me, Williams thought as he breathed a sigh of relief. *Go away and stay away, you bastards, because I'm really tired of talking to you. I don't mean you, Doctor McGrath—I think you're the only one here besides me who really even sees the big picture—but the rest of you are invited to leave as early as yesterday. Maybe you should go with them, Mr. Chase. Oh...and don't come back any time soon.*

He couldn't tell yet whether Beverly or Dr. Burgess would be asked along on Agent Hildebrandt's hunting party and he guessed it didn't matter one way or another to anyone involved. The groundwork had already been laid and regardless of how it all played out, one or both of the doctors would have some kind of story to tell. Either of them could bang out a sequel to their previous work with a minimal amount of effort. Just about anything would do as long as Woodhall Penitentiary, ACT, Inc., and Matthew Chase were painted as the swords of justice instead of a group of greedy, lazy bouncers who neglected their duties and let the wrong guys into the party.

It wouldn't even have to be about Hewitt and Stoning at this point. With enough of a marketing push, Williams knew that the blame for this one could be shifted entirely to the Carrolls and leave Woodhall Penitentiary in the clear if they did everything exactly right. Even if Stanley and Spencer decided to go postal from coast to coast, some well-written documentation from a best-selling author or two would go a long way towards keeping the attention on the escape itself, giving Woodhall some breathing room when it came to lawsuits and the like.

It had been a bang-up job after all with an amount of precision that was almost inconceivable. Seeing as how even the feds couldn't deny how brilliant the whole thing was, Williams suspected it wouldn't take too much more to keep the words *gross negligence* off of any legal papers that happened to cross Chase's desk. Perhaps they would simply call it an unforeseeable act of God and leave it at that.

The real shame was that the doctors would be leaving with so much left unsaid. It would just be the same essential information that the everyone else had been denied by him but Williams had fully intended to share it with Beverly McGrath before they ran out of time together. The way it looked now, he guessed it was probably already too late to make much of a difference anyway.

~ 16 ~

Chase gazed down at them with a knowing grin, making no move to conceal his approval in regards to the latest development. Half relieved and half reluctant, they waited to hear the rest of it and try to guess what level of involvement they would have, if any at all.

"*And?*" the doctors uttered simultaneously.

"Oh…here you go," he finally replied, tossing the envelope on the table between them. "Your flight leaves at six a.m. sharp and you'll land at Redding Municipal about an hour and a half later."

"Redding?" Beverly asked in a desperate voice. "They've *got* to know about Altamont. If the FBI's trying to plot the next location and Stanley's going with some sort of repeat scenario then why are they skipping number two?"

"Don't worry about it. They've already got a team on site in Altamont that should give them all the information they need. It'll make the rest of the job a lot easier and they'll know for sure what we're all dealing with."

"What kind of team are we talking about?"

"Forensics," Chase replied. "Hildebrandt has the best guys in the business on the ground in Oregon right now ready to sift through the leftovers of whatever happens next. By the time Hewitt gets into California they might have an idea of what's going through his head."

"I see where you're going with this," Burgess said. "But it's not a very active approach, is it, Matt? If they weren't able to find anything in Vancouver that tells them where Hewitt's headed when he gets to Altamont, then what in the hell is a body in Oregon going to tell them about where he'll end up in Redding? *Alta-mont* is the place to stop this guy."

"I'm sure you're right," Chase agreed, still hanging on to his suddenly sunny disposition. "You should mention that to Hildebrandt when you land."

Beverly had a suggestion of her own. It wasn't offered with a smile.

"Or maybe *you* should do it right now. Last time I checked, Altamont held about eighteen thousand people. The population in Redding is closer to ninety thousand. Add it up and tell me where the best odds are at."

"Sorry, doctor, but I have to stand with the feds on this one for all the obvious political reasons. If someone's going to jump into this with both feet, ruffle some feathers, and take a shit on the FBI's theories and practices, it sure isn't going to be me. It has to be you if we want a believable point of view from an outside source. It *needs* to be you."

"But if they're right about this then we've only got until tomorrow night before we're looking at another body. It sounds a lot like they're just waiting for it to happen."

"That *does* seem to be the plan, doesn't it?" Chase agreed, wisely dispensing with his beaming face for the moment. He locked eyes with Beverly and gave her the most serious expression he was capable of. "But if someone could finish this thing up before it even reaches California, I think a lot of people might take notice of something like that. All kinds of people, Beverly. I'm not saying it's likely or even possible at this point." He paused to take a deep breath as he shifted his eyes between the two of them. "But it would be huge and I think you know what I mean."

"Yeah, we got it, Matt," Burgess replied with a scowl that made Chase's serious expression seem child-like. It wasn't the insinuation of trading lives for notoriety that left him feeling somewhat whorish—those ideas already had a permanent home in Burgess's mind and he seldom had trouble forgiving himself—it was the persistent feeling that Chase was offering up the situation as though it was nothing more than a corporate kickback instead of a heartfelt request for assistance that nagged at him. "We hear what you're saying."

"We sure do," Beverly agreed, echoing Burgess's sentiment in the tone of her of voice.

"All right then." Chase clapped his hands together once as the smile returned to his face. "I think we're in business."

With a confident bounce in his step, Chase walked them from the conference room and escorted the pair personally to the main entrance where he vigorously shook hands with each of them before retreating at a quick pace. To the psychiatrist and psychologist who had been dragged across multiple states for the short two hour visit, it seemed he could hardly get them through the door fast enough.

*　　　*　　　*　　　*

Matthew Chase's walled palace was practically FBI free now and the rest of them would be gone shortly, leaving him with the run of prison again. Along with the guards and inmates, his own routine had been taking a beating for the last few days and now it would return to some kind of normalcy—at least for a while. In an undetermined amount of time, he was sure his world would be flipped on its head again but the reasons for it would be nothing but good.

He had lost four of his star attractions in one night—two of them forever— and the whole country would shortly be aware of it. They would be back, though, and as long as Woodhall could avoid being held liable for their unauthorized field trip, every lemon that had been handed to him would be squeezed into the biggest glass of lemonade anyone had ever laid eyes on.

If he played his cards right, his two missing bad boys—everyone from the old D Block, in fact—would be back home soon and spending their days in the comfort of the latest and greatest Supermax facility, compliments of ACT, Inc. All he had to do now was find a reason for the federal government to cough up a big fat subsidy for it.

Fortunately, that end of it was serendipitously being handled by two convicts who were loose and currently terrifying a large portion of the tax-paying population.

*　　　*　　　*　　　*

"Like you were never here, huh?" Williams offered with a light smile as they watched Chase disappear back into the concrete city that was Woodhall.

"Something like that," Burgess sarcastically agreed. "Is any of this for real, Ryan, or are we just part of the show?"

"I guess that all depends on how everything turns out," Williams answered, motioning for the tower guard to open the gate. At the same time, he removed a printed sheet of paper from his pocket and handed it to Beverly. "Stanley's newspapers, Doctor McGrath. All the dates are there."

"Thanks, Ryan—for everything. I'd like to pencil you in for a sit-down when we reach some kind of conclusion with this."

"Maybe when the time's right, doctors. I'm guessing there'll be plenty to say and plenty of time to say it when everyone comes home. Good luck out there in California and don't let those feds walk all over you."

As he finished speaking, the gate returned to its closed position with a squeal followed by a loud crash of metal. Williams appeared pleased by the jarring sound and gave the gate a good hard shake before being absolutely convinced of its ability to keep the bad guys inside. Only after verifying its locked status did he wave once to the doctors and start heading back indoors. He didn't get far.

"Wait—*Ryan!*" Beverly yelled and ran quickly to the closed gate. Williams stopped where he was and turned around. He was over ten yards away and made no move to come any closer. *"Are they still together?"*

Williams shoved both hands into his pockets and stared back at her through the bars she was grasping on to. From where he was standing, she looked like a confused prisoner stuck on the outside wanting very badly to get in. With a small chuckle, he turned away from her and continued walking, only looking back for an instant. He nodded his head once as he stepped through the door then vanished from sight.

~ 17 ~

"Okay...*okay*," Floyd Madison mumbled as he dug into his pocket, wishing that the clerk would keep his voice down. He didn't know anybody in the lobby of the hotel but it was still humiliating for him regardless. "I'll just pay cash for the room if that's all right."

If it wasn't all right, Floyd was ready to drop his voice an octave and turn the volume up to eleven. Even though he was dressed in one of his few remaining expensive suits, he could sense a vibe from the thirty-something desk clerk that felt strangely like superiority. He was used to it to some extent but seldom did it come from the type of guy who worked the evening desk at the third cheapest motel on Riverside Boulevard for something close to minimum wage.

The man had eyeballed him from the moment he walked into the lobby and had let out a quiet but obnoxious sigh when he was approached for a room. It wasn't until Floyd's credit card was rejected that he sighed again, leaving him with just one more before he would go over Floyd's three-sigh limit and find out what it would feel like to breathe through a collapsed lung.

"Cash will be just fine," he replied with a flat tone and a plastic smile as he started punching numbers into his computer. "And how long do plan to stay with us here in Sacramento?"

"Why, do I have a time limit?"

The clerk snorted out one short, nervous laugh at the comment without bothering to look up from his terminal. "No, sir. I was just curious if you were going to stay more than one night. We'll need you to pay in advance if that's the case."

"No, it's just for tonight."

Actually, it would be even less if he could help it. Floyd could have returned to the dive he had stayed at in San Francisco but chose instead to go further north and get a little closer to where he needed to be. At the moment, he wasn't sure where that was and Sacramento felt like a decent place to figure it out. It had already been an excruciatingly long day and he knew that he would vacate the premises as soon as a decent destination came to mind.

"What's the total?"

"That'll be forty-seven fifty," the clerk told him, punching a few more keys as Floyd pulled a fifty from his wallet. "And there's a twelve percent room tax…plus key and phone deposits."

Floyd remained silent, holding the fifty dollar bill in his hand. He had already asked the question once and didn't feel like asking again. Almost a full minute of staring went on before he finally did.

"You waiting for me to do the math, or what, chief?"

"Oh, sorry," the clerk stammered. "That'll be fifty-eight twenty. I'm also going to need a picture ID."

With his wallet already out, Floyd removed another ten dollar bill and pulled out his license at the same time. Dropping both on the counter, he cracked his neck and said a quick prayer that his drivers license hadn't expired. Being on top of things hadn't been his strong suit lately. As the money had dwindled away to nothing, it became much easier to let things slide unnoticed rather than come face to face with each setback and still not be able to do anything about it. As a result, most of his disappointments were now considered simple accidents instead of outright failures.

The clerk took a long look at both the ID and Floyd himself before finishing the transaction and handing the license and some change back. When the receipt was finished printing, Floyd was handed a pen.

"Sign here."

Though the words came out less cordial than he usually put up with, Floyd scribbled his signature anyway and slid the form back across the desk. They barely made eye contact when the room key was handed over.

"Thanks," Floyd said out of pure reflex, wishing he hadn't wasted his breath.

"Yeah."

It was all the response he received.

Yeah? Floyd repeated silently in his head, feeling his anger slowly give way to depressed exhaustion. Turning his back to the desk, he started for the elevator and decided not to get too worked up about it. If the guy wanted to throw attitude at every black man who walked through the door then that was his business.

Floyd guessed that eventually he'd be rude to the wrong person and find out the hard way that a little courtesy went a long way, even if he had to fake it. When he stepped into the elevator and turned around to press the button for his floor, he wasn't surprised to see the clerk still eyeing him.

✳   ✳   ✳   ✳

Yeah? Gary Mooney thought painfully as he watched the elevator door close. The last few minutes had been nothing but a blur to him and he was still trying control his respiration so he didn't appear to be the heavy breathing, fidgety idiot that he felt like. *Yeah? Did I really say that? Tell me I didn't do or say anything stupid in front of Floyd freakin' Madison. I can't believe I just had his drivers license right in my fucking hand!*

The last time he had even thought of the man was when he was twenty years old and still suffering through college, which he eventually dropped out of. He had been watching the *Arsenio Hall Show*—a huge late night TV program in its peak years—and Madison had a three minute spot in the chair next to the host. It was short and sweet but the large, imposing man exuded a selfless confidence that set him apart from the various actors, comedians, sports stars, and musicians that often graced the stage.

Before seeing the show, Gary Mooney had heard very little about Floyd Madison; just enough to figure that the guy was some kind of crusader or part-time super hero with a deathwish who'd brought in a big league bad guy named Stanley something. He turned out to be quite a bit more, leaving an impression that stuck around for a while. When the three minute bit was finished and for at least a week afterward, Gary wanted to be the man that he'd seen on his TV.

The hum of the elevator told him that Madison had cleared the lobby and was on his way to his room. As he returned to his desk duties and tried to wipe the silly smile from his face, Gary wondered whatever happened to him. Not Floyd Madison—aside from some odd problem with his credit card, he looked to be in fine shape and was still enshrouded in the powerful aura that Gary remembered so vividly. It was Arsenio Hall that he was concerned about.

Now, there's a guy who just plain disappeared.

~ 18 ~

The room was tiny with only one bed in the middle and a small fridge containing food that Floyd wouldn't be able to afford until he cashed the check in his pocket. A Coke, a miniscule bottle of Jim Beam, or even a bag of Macadamia Nuts was currently out of his price range unless he was in the mood to chow down and split without paying.

Discovering that he was in that mood, Floyd grabbed up two expensive shots of Vodka and poured their contents into a plastic cup. In his very large hand, the empty bottles looked like syringes that were missing their needles as he tossed them in the trash. The disappointing amount of booze was whisked down his throat in a flash and the slight sting of alcohol in his mouth was quickly blunted by the cigarette smoke that followed it.

In the past four years, Floyd had whittled his habit down to five butts a day. Starting from when he awoke in San Francisco only fourteen hours earlier, he had filled his lungs with over half a pack, most of them being devoured during the jaunt from San Francisco to Sacramento. He would need to buy more before too long.

While he took an inventory of his tobacco situation, Floyd picked up the phone—the only real reason to waste money on a hotel room aside from a TV and a shower, he thought—and dialed his number back home. At the first sign of a click, he set the phone down on the table and counted to ten before picking it back up. If there was one thing he hated, it was the sound of his own voice on the answering machine.

Back in the day—"the day" being anything longer than nine years ago but more recent than fifteen—his out-of-office message was a full blown production that had been recorded in a Hollywood recording studio. It cost over fifteen hundred dollars for the twenty second message, along with the other five submenus that you got after pressing the appropriate button, and it was as flashy as the rest of Floyd's operation.

When the number was called now, any perspective clients were treated to Floyd Madison minus the flash. His voice echoed slightly in a room that sounded as empty as it was and had a distorted quality to it that reeked of terminal cheapness.

Guessing that his own voice was done humiliating him, Floyd placed the phone to his ear and listened for the tone. When the short beep was finished— too short to hold out any hope—he punched in his five digit code and retrieved his messages. All one of them.

The bad news was that no one had bothered to shoot a call in his direction regarding Stanley Hewitt's return to public life. Not even the press had called to get his reaction to the latest events.

The good news, as the message had confirmed, was that he could now get instant credit protection on his Citibank Visa card...*and more!* apparently. If the message wasn't from the same company whose credit card had just been rejected at the fifty buck-a-night hotel he was currently staying in, he might have been more enthused with the offer.

With the useless phone call out of the way, television became the next priority.

He found it sad that his only outlet for any information was the same mass media that everyone else had access to, but he would take what he could get at this point and pray that more sources would open up before too long. Depending on how things were going up north, he supposed he could put in a personal appearance or two and get a few of the old police contacts talking since their information would be the freshest.

Where to actually *go* up north was the big question. He turned on the TV and only flipped around for a few seconds before finding that what he was looking for was on practically every station on the dial. They had pictures and everything.

So far it was mostly shots of squad cars. Black and white, solid blue, solid white, and quite a few black sedans flashed across the screen as multiple scenes in several locations were covered simultaneously.

Woodhall Penitentiary in Utah and the parking lot of some restaurant in a place called Black Pine were delivery points for much of the live coverage, though there appeared to be little or nothing going on at either location. These sites were only relevant in terms of activities that had already come to pass, but Floyd knew as well as his journalistic counterparts did that the viewing public loved nothing more than returning to the scene of the crime.

Uninterested in the past, Floyd flipped to the next channel and then the next, searching for a glimpse of the present. He only had to wait a minute for it to show up. He recognized the face instantly.

There you are, he thought silently as he sat straight up and moved closer to the TV set. *I see you, Stanley.*

It had been fourteen or fifteen years and the guy hadn't changed a bit that Floyd could tell. His hair was shorter and neater, but age didn't seem to have torn into him the way it had affected most of the people that he was acquainted with. He suspected it had something to do with staying indoors and out of the sun, which Stanley Hewitt had plenty of opportunity to do.

At the same time, he wondered briefly if maybe they were just showing an old picture of Hewitt and he was mentally tacking on a few years of his own without realizing it. It wasn't unheard of and Floyd knew some of the tricks a person's mind could play on them when it came to memory and assessing age.

With seldom seen relatives the differences were always a shock. A few years would go by and those aunts, uncles, and grandparents he remembered from his youth would have changed to the point of looking like completely different people. They would act, dress, and wear their hair in varying fashions to keep up with the times but depending on the amount of time that passed between visits, those differences could be huge, if not frightening.

Childhood friends—the ones he never saw again after grade school—were doomed to live in a permanent state of prepubescence when viewed through Floyd's memory. He couldn't help the way their faces had been burned into his brain with no capacity to adjust for the time that had passed. It wasn't to say that they never aged at all in Floyd's head; they just never grew up completely regardless of the years that had flown by.

High school and college friends were much the same, remaining static and locked within the confines of their yearbook photos unless he ran into them again for some reason, which did happen occasionally; especially after he became famous. At that point, and only then, would the mental portrait update itself and replace the faded memory with something real. He didn't know why exactly but it certainly wasn't due to a lack of imagination. Knowing what he knew and seeing what he had seen, Floyd could imagine just about anything. He could imagine himself right into a bad case of the jitters if he really cared to. He didn't right now, but couldn't keep his mind from wandering to some of those old faces that still haunted him.

Many of those old faces still looked like children and the images would never—*could* never—be updated. No growing up and no growing old. They would remain as still-photos, unchanging in Floyd's mental scrapbook until the pages fell out.

As Stanley's photo faded from the screen and was replaced by another man in an orange jump suit, Floyd shifted his eyes from the television and searched for the mute button. He had seen him and he had marked him as a target. It was enough for now. Since there was no point in dwelling on the man until the next move had been mapped out, he dwelled on those old faces instead; for motivation if nothing else.

Some of them went good. Some of them went bad.

Prior to his capture of Stanley Lewis Hewitt—the sole catalyst for Floyd's short-lived fame—his biggest accomplishment in life had been the apprehension of a man named Kirk Faust who'd had a warrant out for assault.

Through luck more than anything else, when Floyd made his regular Monday trip to the courthouse downtown to see who was wanted for what and for how much, he recognized a man in one of the posters. He hadn't known where Faust was staying but he definitely knew where he drank. He had seen him at the same location dozens of times and had no idea that he was on the run.

Alcohol was the reason Kirk Faust had lost his job and it was the reason he beat his wife. It was the reason he punched an officer while being arrested and played a good part in why he never showed up for trial. But it wasn't until Kirk woke up in jail that he realized he had a drinking problem.

If the police officers weren't lying to him, he had walked into the precinct on his own two feet. They said he was absolutely shit-faced, had his arm around a big black guy, and was demanding to see the maitre d'. They also said the black guy was laughing his ass off.

Floyd wished they could all be that easy, but using finesse only went so far.

Six weeks later Stanley Hewitt would be in custody and Floyd Madison would be known far and wide. It should have made life easier but things would only get harder from that point forward.

When he was contacted by Richard Nylander—a broken wreck of a man who had been living in a perpetual state of worry—his fifteen year-old daughter Janine had already been missing for over a month.

Coming down from the highest point of his life, Floyd found himself surprisingly haunted by the idea that a child could simply vanish—so haunted, in fact, that he was unable to deal with it in such simplistic monetary terms. He would get over the malady in short order but Floyd Madison's first legitimate case would end up costing the Nylander family absolutely nothing.

~ 19 ~

Janine Nylander was fifteen years old and a straight-A student according to the thin stack of paperwork that had been given to Floyd by her father. The manila file folder contained a copy of a birth certificate, medical history, fingerprints, a brief bio, and enough photos to keep Floyd up all night. It wasn't the quantity of pictures that stole the sleep from him; it was the quality of the young woman who was in them, though referring to her as a young *woman* might have been pushing it. If asked, Floyd would have said they were pictures of a child. She wasn't even old enough to drive yet.

If he had seen only one or two of her pictures, he could have passed off her innocent look as merely a trick of good photography. But the fifty or so that he did have all showed the same consistent image; a beautiful young girl who wore sickeningly cute clothing and whose face glowed brightly without the benefit of cosmetics. From what he could gather, she seemed to be fond of pony-tailed hair, homemade jewelry, and sweaters with little bears on them. The very fact that she was missing made him furious.

He knew she wasn't missing, though, and that was the part that got to him.

Homeless people who lost their minds and wandered the street were "missing". So were all the other social dropouts and mentally defective MIAs. Even a guy who slips into a river and gets washed away could be qualified as "missing", but Janine Nylander wasn't any of those. There was no doubt that she was missed by her parents and other family and friends, but Floyd felt strongly that somebody out there wasn't missing her at all. In fact, he suspected that somebody was probably very close to her right now if she was still among the salvageable.

Floyd didn't tell the Nylander family that finding what was left of her abused corpse was probably the most realistic possibility that they could hope for. It was an awful thing to consider but as bad as that option sounded, there was always a good chance that she would simply be gone forever with no clue at all what happened to her. Deciding which option was worse was just one of many things he didn't care to discuss with them; not until it was necessary.

Maybe she had been raped and murdered—that was one of them.

Tortured *then* raped and murdered—another winner.

Being tortured and raped daily; still alive and still a few long brutal weeks from being murdered—no, her parents wouldn't want to hear that either.

Every possibility was a different nightmare with its own special elements of horror, but seeing as how it was his first real case, Floyd was ready to settle for just about anything as long as she still had a pulse.

The police detectives he spoke with the following day were open and honest in ways that they had probably avoided with Mr. and Mrs. Nylander, giving facts and assumptions that were none too pleasant to think about. While praying for the typical runaway scenario, they also noted that she didn't fit the profile and took it as a bad sign. It fit just enough for the authorities to delay declaring her as a missing person for forty-eight hours but now they were doing everything within their power to locate her or anyone she might have had contact with.

After digging into the details of police procedure, which was a totally new experience for him, Floyd discovered that "everything within their power" added up to a huge truckload of very fucking little.

There was a file in a cabinet somewhere with her name on it and Xeroxed photos of her on display in various state and federal institutions around Los Angeles County. There was no media coverage whatsoever and it would take over a year just to get her face on a milk carton if it came down to that. Of all the people interviewed in connection to Janine Nylander's disappearance, there were several that stood out to the detective in charge but none that would warrant a valid investigation.

Naturally, the Nylander parents were the first to be scrutinized and they passed with flying colors. Neighbors, friends, and any local registered sex offenders were next on the list, though it gave them very little to go on. Most of them didn't even look worried when the cops showed up on their doorsteps.

The main problem was all the talking that was going on. Everyone was doing it and everyone was answering every question in all the right ways. Almost anyone who might have been considered a suspect could quickly be ruled out by their eagerness to be forthcoming if nothing else. All alibis were rock solid and there wasn't a single lead to be followed up on. Not even from the only person they interviewed who'd been a pain in the ass.

✳   ✳   ✳   ✳

"*Pain in the ass?* What do you mean?"

"Just like it sounds," Detective Adams replied quickly before having to remind himself of who he was dealing with. "Short answers…irritated real easy, that's all. The kid's only sixteen and that's the way they act in confrontational situations. Even the smart ones are fucking retarded at that age. You'll need to get used to it."

The detective didn't seem put out in the least while he gave a basic clinic on adolescent behavior to the rookie private investigator. From Adams' position in the driver's seat, the sharp looking celebrity next to him was so green that calling him an amateur would have been flattering. He was still on the clock but the information he was passing along to Floyd Madison fell well outside of his job description.

"I'm only telling you this so I don't have to save your ass a week from now. He's already been interviewed twice and unless you want some kind of harassment suit to be thrown at you, you'll need to take your time with this."

"Maybe I will," Floyd said, shifting around uncomfortably in the coat and tie, which both felt very foreign hanging off of his body. "But I'm not buying some old guy from the end of her street who's lived there for twenty years flipping out and grabbing her and her parents seem solid enough to be ruled out. She sure ain't the type to get into a car with a stranger and she doesn't seem like the kind of girl that would sneak out of her house at night. This girl's different, man."

"Different from what?" Adams asked in reply. "I'll tell you a little secret that just might make your job a little easier in the future, Mr. Madison. It's *always* some guy from up the street, if not right next door. They *all* get into cars with strangers and they *all* sneak out at night. That sweet young girl in the photos you've been gawking at isn't special, okay? She'll be smoking and drinking and swearing like everyone else in her class—maybe even get herself knocked up before she turns eighteen…if she's still alive. She's probably not, you know."

"Probably not," Floyd agreed dryly, staring out the window.

"And get used to that too. From what I've heard about you—that Stanley Hewitt shit was fucking beautiful, by the way—I gather you've got some pretty thick skin under that flashy suit your wearing. You'll need it if you want to make it in the people-finding business. You'll also need a little patience."

"Sorry, I'm fresh out," Floyd replied with a smile that only lingered for a moment.

He had been working on different faces and expressions in the mirror since his many televised interviews and knew that the smile didn't always work for him. The fake smile he eventually came up with was a real charmer and looked great on TV. He'd get more than a few miles out of that toothy grin. The tough look he used was pretty good and his serious expressions looked genuinely severe. A few days earlier he tried out a harsh face that was so scary it freaked the hell out of him when he saw it in the mirror. It was the one he planned on using today and it didn't mix well with the goofy smile that appeared from time to time.

"Most of these end real shitty, Mr. Madison. Once it gets to be a few weeks or a month into it, all the parents can really do is pray for some kind of closure, which they hardly ever get. If you're prepared for it, it's not nearly as bad. Trust me."

"I do, detective," he stated seriously. "And I appreciate you taking the time with me on this. But I think you guys might be a little off base this time. I know you've got a lot of experience with these deals and I understand what you're saying, but didn't you ever have a gut feeling about something?"

"Sure, when I was young and full of crap. You'll grow out of it. We all do. And if it turns out we're wrong about this little shit, make sure you don't apologize. It makes it look like we're just guessing, which is pretty much what we're doing with this one. I'd handle it myself, but this whole thing got started through the official channels so the kid and his parents have already seen my face."

"I hear you, detective. How much further?"

"He's just around the corner. Are you sure about this? You won't be able to say that you weren't warned."

"Don't worry about me." Floyd opened the door and stepped from the car. "I won't be saying shit."

"It'll be the end of you if you don't do it right," Adams warned one final time, grinning through his opened window. The warning was real and so was the smile on his face. He knew that this Madison character was a different sort, but to take a chance on such an obvious career-ending offense was going above and beyond the call of duty. "Fuck it up and they'll own your ass after this. And I'll swear to God that I was never here."

"I don't even see you now, detective. What's the number?"

"Hang a left up there and walk about fifty yards. He's thirty-one fifty-nine on the right. His parents will probably be home and they're gonna be all over you just like they were with me. Act nice and don't piss them off if you can help it.

Just get to him and rattle his cage a bit. But try to remember you're dealing with a minor."

"Don't worry. I'll be real sweet."

Floyd turned away from the car and started his three minute walk to the Madrid residence. He understood the detective's reasons for remaining out of sight and off the record, but he didn't see what the harm would have been to at least drop him off a little closer to the kid's house. He guessed that Detective Adams probably knew a thing or two about lawsuits and wasn't just making up all that stuff about being prosecuted for what he was about to do. If it wasn't absolutely true, Floyd knew he wouldn't have been shuffling down the residential street in search of four numbers.

3159.

He found it easily and paused before approaching the large house that belonged to some people who were obviously very well off. He hoped he still looked sharp since straightening his tie and smoothing out his jacket were things he hadn't learned about yet.

He walked casually up the driveway and cleared his throat as he neared the front door. Before knocking, he tried out his harsh face one last time. It felt perfect.

He knocked and after a few seconds the door came open for him. The silence that followed was expected, though Floyd wasn't quite used to their reactions yet and had to wait for the initial shock to wear off.

The fifty year-old man who answered the door had nothing to say. If he did, it wasn't coming out. All he seemed capable of was a long, slow stare at the black giant who had nearly shattered his door with one large fist when he'd rapped on it. There was nervous recognition in those eyes and it made Floyd happy.

"Do you know who I am or do I need to tell you?" he asked in deep, *deep* voice, breaking the silence right when it looked like the man was about to start speaking.

The question had cut James Madrid off and left him floundering for something to say. His eyes blinked in disbelief at first and his face wore an expression of bewilderment. It wasn't long before it gave way to sad horror as it finally dawned on him why the man was at his door. The answer to the question was immediately obvious but Floyd was going to make him say it anyway. He wouldn't let him say much, though.

"You're the one who—"

"Yeah, that's me. If you know that, then you know what I do and you know why I'm here. Where's he at? I want to speak to him right now."

"Listen," the man said, taking a step further back from the door, trying to replace his surprised look with something that would pass for impatience. "I'm his father and I'm going to tell you the same thing I told—"

"I didn't ask to speak to his daddy, did I?"

Floyd straightened up a bit, forcing his chest out and tilting his chin upward slightly. The simple, subtle movements seemed to add about a foot and a half to a body that was already scary enough. The gun in his shoulder holster was showing now too, which added to the effect. In response, James Madrid took another two steps back from the doorway and gave Floyd a look of anger mixed with uncertainty. He wasn't moving, though, and he crossed his arms in a silent gesture of defiance.

The gesture, his arms, and the look on his face all dropped in the same instant when Floyd Madison stepped across the threshold and into the man's house. The biggest rule of all the rules had just been broken.

"Wait...you can't just walk into my—"

"Do I look like a cop to you or something?" Floyd asked in a stern but calm tone, advancing slowly toward the retreating man while casually checking out the living arrangements. "That's the *police* department you're thinking of, Mr. Madrid. It's the *police* who need warrants and all that shit to gain access to your home and your property and your family. Not my style at all, man. Too many regulations and guidelines to follow. Me—I'm just an intruder. How do you like it?"

"What?"

"Me being in your house, Mr. Madrid. How do you like it?"

He stopped a few feet short of the living room and looked at a framed picture that hung on the wall. They were a handsome family of four with a daughter that looked to be nine or ten.

"It's okay, Mr. Madrid, you don't have to answer if you don't want. It's not a good feeling—we both know it—so let's get this done as quick as possible. Tell me where he is?"

"He's not here." His tone had changed sharply. Instead of just plain fear, it was now blended in with a protectiveness that gave Floyd a little hope. "And I'll be calling the police if you're not out of my house in ten seconds. I don't care who you are or what you've done. I know what my rights are."

Floyd knew those rights too but he'd gone way too far to back down now. The only alternative was to keep pushing forward with all he had. When the push came, it was harder than he'd thought himself capable of.

"Lies are bad for your kids, Mr. Madrid." He wasn't even totally sure what he meant by the sentence, but he knew he didn't like the sound of it—even coming from his own mouth. "And it'll only get worse from here on out. They don't send in heavy hitters like me without good reason, so maybe you should just let me speak with him for a few minutes before everything gets as ugly as you've imagined it. Call him down or I'll let him know I'm here in my own way. You decide."

James Madrid seemed to stressfully consider the options put to him, which told Floyd essentially everything he needed to know. If he was right, the man knew nothing about any of it and was simply terrified of what might occur if his son was coaxed into speaking freely.

He also looked like he had been expecting something of that nature eventually and was tired of waiting for it to happen. It wasn't long before he relented.

"*Scott!*" he yelled, seemingly tortured as he tilted his head to the ceiling. "*Come on down here for a minute.*"

Together, they heard a set of footsteps quickly make their way down the hallway and then to the top of the staircase. They were the awkward, heavy steps of a boy in his mid-teens who hasn't yet adjusted to his rapidly changing body. The sixteen year-old high school student was halfway down the stairs when he saw the both of them looking up at him. It caused him to slow his pace a little but his legs kept moving.

"What's up? Who's yelling?"

"That'd be your father," Floyd answered, watching the youth's eyes move all over him as he made his way to the bottom. There was also a lot more of the recognition that Floyd loved so much.

"One more time, Scott," James Madrid said to him, sounding apologetic as he pulled his son toward him. "Don't worry. Just tell him what you know and he'll be on his way."

Taking a position on his father's left side, Scott Madrid became smaller and smaller as Floyd took his time measuring the kid up. For the first thirty seconds or so, words weren't necessary. He simply stared at the young man until he looked ready to speak. When he was finally ready, Floyd wasn't going to let him. It was an old trick that his mother used to use on him when he was in trouble.

"I've already told—"

"Just *stop*," Floyd said impatiently. "I already know exactly what you've told and who told it to, so don't bore the fuck out of me. And if you *really* knew how much I *really* know—well, you wouldn't be standing this close to me, so there's no point in going over it."

The teenager hardly flinched as he waited for the standard questions to be presented to him yet again. He felt confident, knowing it was obviously desperation time for whomever had pointed the large figure in his direction. He took a deep breath and relaxed, happy that he had spent all the time he did preparing for it.

"I want you to tell me about your sister, Scott."

To this, the boy could only scrunch up his face and shoot an odd look between his father and the man he had seen on TV not too long ago. It wasn't the question he was expecting and differed quite a bit from the kind that the other two detectives had grilled him with. For the last couple of weeks he had been sure that the whole thing with Janine was winding down and would eventually go away completely. They were grasping at straws now.

"Theresa?" he asked with a small chuckle, feeling fortunate that the little one wasn't around for this particular scene. "What do you want to know about her?"

"I want to know where she's at, Scott."

"She's at dance class with my mom. Why?"

"How sure are you about that? On a scale of one to ten. How sure?"

While the kid merely looked confused, his father's discomfort rose rapidly to the next level. "What in the hell kind of questions are these?"

"They're not the regular kind, Mr. Madrid. How old is your sister, Scott?"

"She's ten."

"Dance lessons?" he asked again.

"Yeah, that's right."

"And you're sure she's there?"

"Where *else* would she be?" Scott Madrid asked, tiring of the strange inquiry. The other detectives had asked a series of questions that were meant to trip him up and give himself away in any number of ways. This was a great deal harder.

"*Where else would she be?*" Floyd repeated back to him and waited. "That's a good question you're asking. *Great* question, in fact. *Where else would she be?* I like it."

He only let the Madrid's take one breath before continuing.

"Can you think of anyone else who might be asking a question like that right now? Someone else with a little girl, maybe. I want you to picture this, okay? They're sitting there at home knowing that she's not in any of the places she's *supposed* to be and it doesn't make any sense at all. It leaves only one question, Scott. Just one. You know what it is and there are a lot of places somebody could be. Girls, man…they disappear all the time. It's an awful thing, huh?"

The younger Madrid was thrilled with Floyd's little speech because it meant that the guy was going to attempt to tug on his heartstrings to find out the answers. For some, it might have had the desired effect. For this particular teenage boy it wouldn't work at all.

The elder Madrid, on the other hand, felt saddened by what the girl's parents must have certainly been going through and sympathized with them deeply. Imagining himself in their shoes was a very horrible, yet easy thing to do. His sympathy only lasted for a few seconds.

"What are you *saying*?" he screeched. "You think you're gonna do something to my daughter, you son of a bitch?"

"Not at all, sir. That wasn't my intention in any way and I resent the implication." He hoped he had said it right. In all of Floyd's thirty-one years, he had never said or even imagined that he would ever utter the words *I resent the implication*. Coming out of his mouth, though, he thought it sounded rather spiffy.

"The last thing in the world I would want to do is see something happen your daughter or *any* girl for that matter. It's common enough already, as you're well aware of."

Both of them got equally heavy doses of Floyd's glare and the boy began to shift around nervously. It was the first sign of any real progress.

"But there's two sides to every story, Mr. Madrid and one way or another, your heart's gonna break because of this. Honestly, sir, that's the part I feel worst about right now."

"*What—?*" The elder Madrid was ready to beg for clarification, but Floyd was already a mile ahead of him.

"I'm saying that it's not always girls who are vanishing." Feeling eerily like the bad guy in the Nylander drama, Floyd looked directly into the man's eyes then shifted them slowly to his son. Since neither was used to being threatened directly, it took them a moment to realize what was being said. Actually, it was slightly less than a moment.

"Boys are turning into smoke all the time too, Mr. Madrid. Check out the statistics if you don't believe me."

*   *   *   *

And that was pretty much the end of it. Aside from a few details and arrangements, Floyd's first case was over.

The next word that had come out of Scott Madrid's mouth was the name of a city only two and a half hours away from Van Nuys. It was followed by an address and even a zip code to go with it. The girl had received a D in Trigonometry and had been hiding at a friend's house in Escondido for almost five weeks.

Even the smart ones are fucking retarded at that age, Floyd remembered Detective Adams saying.

When the boy had burst into tears and tried his hardest to explain, Floyd put a comforting hand on his shoulder and nodded knowingly, as though the information was old news and had been the whole time. Keeping his excitement bottled expertly inside, Floyd listened quietly and thanked God that his gut instinct had been wrong. He'd thought she was dead for sure.

The only thing he had really known for sure and accurately predicted was the part about the boy's father. As they all sat down and talked it through, Floyd could feel the man's heart breaking as he'd said it would. It was a terrible thing to see but much of that pain was alleviated when James Madrid was informed that no one need ever hear about it. And unless the kid wanted to face the police, the Nylanders, and everyone else over the information he had withheld…no one ever would hear about it.

When she was missing, Janine Nylander wasn't important enough to rate five seconds of air time on a local cable TV station. When Floyd Madison brought her home, the buzz that was generated could have lit up a city.

~ 20 ~

"So he takes an empty suitcase, hops in his car, and heads down to Escondido—it's a place just north of San Diego. He waits for her to come out of the house then walks right up to her all slow and smooth like. He says 'Your parents miss you and would like for you to come home now'. She breaks down sobbing and he takes her back to her family. Cue up the weeping right there, Perry. I mean, the guy is like a walking, talking, movie of the week."

Burgess had been laughing while she told most of it and now the muscles in his midsection were threatening to tear themselves apart completely. They were almost through their first bottle of Merlot when Beverly started the story but were now working on their second. Burgess poured each of them another glass as he tried to get himself under control. As crazy as his day had been, he had to admit that he was enjoying himself.

"But how did he *do* it, Bev?" he asked in a mildly frustrated tone. "How does a person do what he does without being a goddamn psychic? I don't get that end of it. I mean, straight research I can deal with, and you don't do too bad yourself. But locating a person in another city or state who doesn't want to be found sounds pretty far out there."

While Beverly smiled and sipped her wine, Burgess spoke with his hands, as though putting together an invisible jigsaw puzzle that was floating in front of him. It was clear that the pieces weren't fitting together any more for him than they did for her. Of course, it didn't mean she had to let him know that they were equally ignorant on the subject.

"It's all about talent and experience, Perry. Same as us—but different."

"Is it? In what way?"

The question wasn't put to her in an inquisitive manner and his tone would have been more appropriate had he said *And just what the hell are you talking about now, woman?*

"Well, think about what you do. There isn't any school you could go to that would teach the kind of things that you've learned when it comes to testifying on the stand and saying what the jury wants to hear. There aren't any classes or seminars on how to read people the way that you do, Perry. It's just an ability that you've recognized in yourself and you use it to your advantage. Everyone's got one but not everyone is aware of it. There's got to be a lot of wasted talent out there."

"And what would your great ability be?"

She answered the question without any hesitation whatsoever. "Getting people to shoot their mouths off about anything in the world, no matter how personal or painful it might be. It just might be the only talent I've got but I use it in every way that I can."

"Oh, I'll bet you've got plenty of talents," Burgess added with what he thought was a pretty slick smile. The woman across from him was smiling even wider and he took it as a good sign.

"You're cute, Perry." She then wrinkled her nose and laughed with a tiny snort. "But there isn't enough wine in the whole state of Utah, okay?"

"Enough *wine?*" he repeated with a confused look. He hoped it looked confused, anyway, because there was no misinterpreting the statement. Another one of Burgess's talents was taking rejection slightly better than an eight year-old child. "I'm sure I don't know what you're talking about. The point that I was in the process of making was completely and totally in regards to your remarkable, uncanny ability to—"

"*Ohhh...*you mean my remarkable *blah-blah?* And my uncanny *blah-blah-blah?*" With her eyebrows raised in a smug fashion, she held in as much cruel laughter as she could. To Burgess, her smile looked even better than before. "You're very sweet, Doctor Burgess."

"And you're *not.* So, how did he do it, Bev? Tell me. How did he find her?"

"Part bloodhound, I guess. Not a very scientific assessment, I know, but if everyone could do it then everyone *would* be doing it. Do you remember what it was like when Stanley was finally identified and his picture was all over the place?"

"Sure, it was right before Madison caught him."

"Actually, it was a whole *week* before Madison caught him. With the half-million dollar reward they were offering and his face on every newspaper in the region, every citizen, police officer, bounty hunter, and wannabe private eye was looking for him. It worked like a charm when they were trying to catch the Night Stalker."

"Richard Ramirez? That was a good one."

Burgess distinctly remembered the day that the Night Stalker was finally captured. Though every law enforcement agency in California had been tracing his steps from Orange County to San Francisco and beyond, it was a group of angry citizens who got the credit for subduing him. They also got the honor of beating him senseless—considered to be a genuine perk by many in the Latino neighborhood who punched and kicked him until he had cried.

"And Ramirez's picture was only out there for one *day*," she continued. "For a whole week nobody had a clue where Stanley was or where he was headed next but Madison scooped him up as easily as he'd found the Nylander girl. I don't know how he does it, Perry, but I trust it and I'm impressed by it."

He could tell by the look in her eyes that she wasn't just rambling. In *Understanding The Sickness*, Beverly McGrath had spent a single chapter on Floyd Madison's role in the apprehension of Stanley Hewitt, but it was easy to see that the subject could have filled up quite a bit more. His own book had dwelled on Spencer James Stoning's arresting officers for less than three paragraphs.

"Do you think Hildebrandt and his outfit have any of that kind of magic in them?"

Responding to the query, Beverly began to look seriously irritated for the first time since they had sat down for dinner. "Well, if they don't, they sure should have plenty of resources to make up for it. Maybe I'm thinking on the wrong scale here, but wouldn't it make sense to just surround the whole city? I'm talking about putting up a roadblock at every freeway off-ramp, street, and dirt road into the place. How hard could it be?"

"If deterrence was the goal I don't think it would be much harder than what you just said. But it's not about that. These guys—state police *or* the FBI—they aren't going to be satisfied by simply preventing a murder that nobody's even sure is going to happen. This whole thing is about capture and recovery and until something happens in Altamont nobody is going to lift a finger to stop it. There's way too much speculation involved."

"What's your point then?" she asked.

"I think you just heard it. Everyone's waiting. That's the point. Aside from a few minor measures, Hildebrandt isn't going to risk moving his operation to

Altamont and then move it again in two days because his field agents weren't able to stop one small murder in one tiny little city in Oregon."

Burgess paused long enough to fill his glass again. As he poured, a thoughtful look crossed his face and he shook his head in frustration.

"And the crazy thing is, the more I try to criticize Hildebrandt for thinking that way, the more sense it makes to me. I know the guy's no crusader but I can see how he can't afford to put all his eggs in one basket. What if the murder in Vancouver was a fluke? What if Hewitt only went to southern Washington because he felt comfortable there or he knows somebody there and this murder just...*happened?* What if it was a spur of the moment thing and doesn't figure into his past killings at all? It's not too likely and I know it sounds horrible to say, but Hildebrandt, regardless of his resources, can't throw everything he's got at one small target."

"Why not?" she asked, growing more annoyed with each word he used to defend the FBI agent. "It's a place to start."

"Because...well...I guess it's because Hewitt's just a fly-speck on the map to him. Hildebrandt wants them to be together, Beverly. He's *praying* for it and that's got to be why we were called in the first place. If he can be absolutely sure about it...yeah, if he can be one-hundred percent on this, then he's just waiting for another murder to happen. I guess I'd be too."

"Oh, *Jesus*, Perry—"

"No, just wait a second," he continued, hoping his point could be made without making him look too heartless. "From where Hildebrandt is sitting, he's dealing with two—pardon the expression—evils. I know it sounds nuts to say, but out of all the options what would be the lesser of those two evils? One murder every three days or a houseful all at once? How about a library...or a school full of children? A church packed with people on a Sunday morning? It's got to be the reason he wanted us working together."

"So, you think he's preoccupied with *Spencer Stoning?* Is that realistic? He was a one-shot deal—you said so yourself. You even wrote that he—"

"Do you believe *everything* you read, Beverly?" he replied incredulously, wishing he had a copy of *Man Of Rage* on hand to browse through. It was so far in his past that he had trouble remembering much of what he had committed to paper. "I wrote that book about a man who was looking at seven consecutive life terms and was never going to see daylight again. I have no *idea* what's going through his head right now. It was hard enough to figure out all those years ago when I sat face to face with him."

Most of what he said was completely true. The only thing he wouldn't have been able to pass on a polygraph test was the part about figuring Spencer Stoning out. As hard as he said it was, the fact remained that he never even came close to understanding what would motivate a man to kill twenty-nine people in one afternoon; not this particular man, anyway. *Rage* had sounded like a safe bet—a good bet even, considering that a person would have to be at least a little angry to mow down the kind of numbers that Stoning had.

Man Of Rage. He had a totally different title in mind but the publisher over-rode the request. It sold well anyway and he had to admit that the word *Rage* looked great in print too.

"I can't stop thinking about that cell of his," he continued with an exaggerated shudder. "And I'll bet Hildebrandt can't get past it either. He's been working on this for a few days and he's got to be seeing that painted door in his sleep by now."

Beverly finished off her wine and pushed her plate away. "Okay…I've lost my appetite. If you're right about this then Hildebrandt already thinks he has an answer to the question he asked us. He wouldn't be waiting for it to happen if he didn't; at least I hope not. He thinks they're together and he's betting that some-one will die tomorrow."

"That sounds about right."

"And if it doesn't happen, Hildebrandt will be crushed because he thinks it'll mean that something worse is on the way."

"Worse, yeah," Burgess agreed with a disappointed nod. "And as far as what *worse* means and just *how much* worse, well, I've already written that book."

*   *   *   *

With mildly upset stomachs, they split the check and returned to their hotel across the street from the restaurant. After spending less than an hour determin-ing their next course of action, Burgess made his way to his own room and flopped onto the bed.

When he drifted off, the only thoughts running through his head were fanta-sies involving a scantily clad psychologist performing acts on him that would be considered highly unprofessional to a peer review board. When he was jarred from his sleep only a few hours later, it took him a minute to realize that he'd been dreaming. It hadn't been a scary dream and wasn't nightmarish in any way that he could remember. He wasn't sweating or trembling, but was simply agi-tated and confused beyond reason.

The clock on the nightstand read 3:56 am. As he vainly tried returning to a state of slumber he realized that Agent Dwight Hildebrandt wasn't the only one seeing Spencer's door in his sleep.

~ 21 ~

At 3:58 am the near blackness of room twenty-eight at the Oakridge Motor Lodge was disturbed for the first time since the sun had gone down ten hours earlier. Instead of police flashlights or broad beams thrown by helicopters from above, it was the soft glow of the television set that slowly filled the room and allowed Spencer's eyes to adjust. Before turning it on he had sat silently for almost an hour staring at the red digital numbers of the alarm clock, thinking and waiting patiently while the minutes ticked away. He deactivated the alarm only minutes before it would go off and found quickly that the television was much more fun to watch than the time. As quiet as he could manage, Spencer roused Stanley from his sleep and told him that he was on TV.

There would be no continental breakfast for them. With both their destination and daylight only two hours away, relocation was essential if they wanted to stay on schedule. Both men shaved, brushed their teeth, combed their hair, and put on the nicest pairs of clothes that Paul Lang had brought along on his family's vacation. The jacket and tie fit Spencer's smaller frame fairly well but Stanley was left with a button down shirt and a sweater vest that he thought made him look like his old science teacher from the junior high school he'd occasionally attended. The pants and underwear were left on the floor in the hotel room while pullovers, T-shirts, and socks went into the suitcase they kept for themselves.

The change in clothing had nothing to do with trying to disguise their appearances; that would need to wait until later. Even as they took a long look in the mirror, it occurred to Spencer that they didn't look any different from their prison photos aside from pricier outfits. It didn't matter to him at all. He simply thought that if they had to get captured or killed on this particular leg of their trip they might as well be dressed sharp while it happened. He wasn't as optimistic about Stanley—he looked like little more than a psychotic crammed into cotton—but sometimes it was the thought that counted.

The Lang family was quiet as the two men walked out of the room without so much as a glance in their direction. They remained silent for a quite a while after the door had closed.

∗   ∗   ∗   ∗

"What do you think Ry's doing right now?"

"You mean besides sleeping?" Spencer asked in reply, keeping his eyes on the lookout for any headlights in the rear view mirror. So far, there were no red and blue lights flashing behind them.

"You know what I mean. What do you think he's doing now that the block's shut down? They wouldn't fire him or anything, would they?"

"I doubt it, Stan, but if you're so curious you can ask about it when we get back to Woodhall. It shouldn't be more than a few hours if they take us straight there."

"Do you think they really *would?*" Stanley asked, not hiding his enthusiasm with the idea very well.

"Sorry, no chance, Stan," Spencer replied, sighing and yawning at the same time. He had known the man next to him for about ten years and was still unable to use sarcasm around him without having to explain what he meant each time. It was a daily battle. "They wouldn't take us back there for a good long while if they decided to at all. We'll be bound for Terre Haute or some other place when they catch our asses."

"What'd you say it for then?"

"*Jesus,* Stan, I'm just pointing out that we're driving right down the middle of route fucking ninety-seven and we'll probably be arrested any minute now." He twisted his head and took another look behind them, as though the rear view mirror might not be as accurate as a real pair of eyes. "To be honest, I can't believe it hasn't happened yet. When it does, though, I don't think you should get your hopes up about seeing Ryan or any of those guys again. Shit, you can probably kiss my ass goodbye too."

He didn't really want to bring it up right then but Spencer didn't see any reason for it to be a surprise when it happened. From the corner of his eye, he could see Stanley painfully considering the information. It was always easy to tell when he was thinking about something. The effort involved was apparent on his face as it took on a far-away quality.

"What if they just send *you* to Terre Haute?" Stanley asked as his worried expression grew more fearful. "Where's that gonna leave me when—?"

"Shut up, Stan. You're totally supermax, okay? There's no way in a million years they're going to put you in some shitty little bomb shelter like Atwater or Souza. Not you, man—no way. It's supermax for sure. You'll see."

It was an old argument that had been going on as long as their friendship. It wasn't just because of all the talk at Woodhall about upgrades and new buildings, either. In fact, neither of them would have felt the same about it if Woodhall simply upgraded and it would have seemed more like getting a tiny pay raise instead of the full promotion to supermax treatment. It would have cheapened the whole thing.

"Do you think he's mad at us?"

"*Ryan?* Who the fuck cares? Don't get me wrong, man—I liked Ry as much as any of the other assholes in D. It's just that he plays for the good guys and I don't think you should waste too much time worrying about him."

"He wasn't such a good guy," Stanley argued.

"I didn't say that he was. I said he *played* for them. There's a difference."

"But he—"

"*What? What, Stan?* We can talk about him all day and it won't make him suddenly appear in the goddamn car with us. I know it's been fifteen years, man, but are you really so fucking institutionalized that you actually miss the guy who watched us for ten hours a day?"

"Well—"

"Yeah, me too," Spencer admitted, mimicking Stanley's far-away look for an instant. "It's weird, isn't it? Ryan, J.J., Potts—fucking Potts, man. I couldn't go a day without making that little shit cry. I'll bet you don't miss Marty too much, huh?"

"Screw that guy."

"I'm sure he returns the sentiment," he replied with a toothy smile. After a silent moment, his smile widened then turned into a laugh.

"What's so funny?"

"I was just thinking about that prick and I was..." For a few seconds, Spencer couldn't speak at all. If he couldn't squeeze it out before the laughter shut him down completely he was afraid it would never come out. "Sorry, man, I was wondering—do you suppose he ever got the taste out of his mouth?"

"*Oh, maaaan,*" Stanley moaned but started laughing as well. He shook his head wildly from side to side and made some pretty authentic gagging noises. For almost a minute they howled together, kicking their legs out and slapping at the dashboard. "You *see*, man? You *see*? Ryan *was* the coolest."

"You're right there, Stan. I guess I can't argue with that." Spencer was down to controllable giggles by the time he asked the required follow-up question. He was pretty sure he had asked it before—positive, in fact—but he just had to ask again anyway. "Going in or coming out? Which one was worse again?"

"Coming out," Stanley answered, involuntarily moving a hand to the seat of his pants. "What is it about a toothbrush that tears up your asshole so much?"

"Bristles, Stan," Spencer replied as he started going off again.

He never actually saw the act—something he was glad he missed out on—but he remembered Ryan Williams' reaction to it quite well. After handing over Martin Carroll's toothbrush to Stanley, the guard watched for a moment then suddenly slapped two hands over his eyes and violently spun himself away from the scene, coming mighty close to vomiting and laughing simultaneously. He was an all right guy once you got to know him.

"I'd definitely say it's the bristles."

*   *   *   *

At about the same time the two men crossed safely into Altamont, Oregon, the youngest member of the Lang family was dialing 911 from the Oakridge Motor Lodge. His mother, Doreen, technically could have made the call and had even started to reach for the phone before taking a curious peek into the drawer in the nightstand.

Instead of calling anyone, she had spent most of the last hour on her knees doing a combination of crying, praying, and trembling uncontrollably. His father was on his knees as well but wasn't doing anything that could have been considered remotely productive. The boy waited as long as he could but decided he was going to have to make the call himself if he intended to eat any time soon; a problem that his parents didn't seem very concerned about at the moment.

When the first of the sheriff's deputies arrived, they were treated to two wild stories from the only Lang's who still had the power of speech. They concentrated on the one who wasn't busy speaking in tongues.

The seven year-old, who could have been a poster-child for resiliency, explained the ordeal in incredible detail. Starting with the first knock on their door nearly twenty-four hours earlier, he walked the two deputies through the events as they had happened and didn't stop until he described the men's departure. He had names for them as well, which sent one of the two officers rushing back to his vehicle to send out an urgent message on the police radio.

A few minutes later, Kevin Lang joined the officer in the car and was allowed to sit in the front seat. He got to flip on the spinning lights, made the siren wail, talked into the radio, and, under the condition of absolute secrecy, was permitted to eject a shell from a real live twelve-gauge pump shotgun. He thought it was neat. Over time, it was the only thing he would really remember with any clarity.

The thing Doreen Lang remembered the most was the miracle that had saved them all. Instead of raising the dead or turning water into wine, she discovered that the Lord had transformed two pairs of razor sharp scissors into a thick, black Gideon bible.

The Lang's had never been a religious family. From now on, they would be.

~ 22 ~

While Beverly McGrath looked over the list of cars that the rental agency had to offer, she checked her watch for at least the fifth time since they'd landed. The flight was shorter than she thought it would be, though it certainly felt later than eight o'clock in the morning. She had already spent more than half an hour waiting for one of the rental desks to open and every extra minute wasted was like a thorn being driven deeper into her side.

Perry Burgess hung back, feeling no particular need to be involved in the transportation negotiations as he went over the rental agency's nearly useless map of northern California. Beverly was making arrangements for the return of the vehicle when he finally stepped in. He didn't want to have to go through the same thing nine more times if it came down to that.

"It says here you've got an office in Chico. Can we drop it off there instead?"

He received a polite nod as the young woman pored over her computer screen. "Yes, sir. We have two locations within a mile of the airport."

"What about Yuba City?" he asked, embarrassed with his inability to make sense of the tiny map. Getting a real one would be the next move and he knew he'd find one before they walked out of the terminal.

"We have one office in Yuba, sir," she replied, smiling pleasantly.

"Sacramento?"

They had six there.

"And what about Pleasanton?"

"Pleasanton?" Beverly asked, hoping he was just being extra organized and not trying to predict the future. "You're getting awfully far south, Perry."

"I know it," he replied, still waiting for an answer from the woman behind the counter. "Salinas, Santa Maria, and Santa Barbara. What about those?"

They had a branch in the first two locations and two others in Santa Barbara. If nothing else, it meant that transportation was covered for a while. It would also give them freedom to move about independently and would be one less thing for them to worry about.

"Can we leave this open-ended?" he asked.

She answered in the positive, explaining that all it would take was a driver's license and a major credit card. He accepted the offer and gave Beverly his first genuine smile of the day. She returned it, though only for a moment.

"I'll let you take care of this while I go find us a decent map. Can I get you anything?"

She didn't answer him. Instead, she took out her credit card and signed for what could potentially become a purchase in the one to two thousand dollar range over the course of the next couple of weeks. It could also be as little as a three hundred over a couple of days if everything worked out right. She was pulling for the cheaper scenario but had a feeling that they'd be spending more than a few hundred on gas alone.

When the transaction was completed and she had keys in her hand, Beverly took a seat about twenty feet away near a bank of phones and searched for a data line for her laptop computer. In less than a minute she was linked up and viewing her daily work schedule, fuming about the multiple cancellations that filled the screen. Unless they got some good news very quickly, she knew there would be plenty more.

While trying to put together an itinerary for their day, her eyes were drawn to a slow moving Perry Burgess who had returned to the last spot he had seen her and was now looking around. He had a folded map under his arm and a styrofoam cup in each hand. Not knowing he was being observed, his face lost much of its false confidence and his mouth hung slightly open as he craned his head from left to right, finally settling on the person who had rented them a car. For a moment, he appeared ready to ask her a question but couldn't quite get the words out.

When Beverly locked eyes with the young woman at the rental desk, they were wearing similar smirks. Beverly didn't call out to the lost man and the rental clerk didn't point him to were she was sitting, both obviously fine with letting him figure it out for himself.

Not only was she paying for the car they would be traveling in, but Beverly suspected she would also be doing the navigating and most of the driving as well.

By the time he found her, he looked worn out, the latté he'd purchased for her was cold, and she knew that she'd probably be pumping the gas too.

The Pontiac Grand Prix assigned to them was found easily in a parking lot that was nearly empty. After cold coffee and a few Tic-Tacs, they drove to the address where they were told Agent Hildebrandt would be waiting for them.

*   *   *   *

He wasn't there and he wasn't waiting. As it turned out, he wasn't even in California anymore. Special Agent Dwight Hildebrandt had fled to the city of Altamont only one hour earlier with a pared-down version of his crisis team in tow. The question—the one single question that was the sole reason for the doctors' involvement in the matter—had already been answered by a deputy from the Lane County Sheriff's Department in a place called Oakridge, Oregon.

The agent who relayed the information to their stunned faces didn't tell them about the Oakridge Motor Lodge and he didn't mention that Stanley Lewis Hewitt and Spencer James Stoning had been identified and were assumed to be traveling south together. He didn't tell them about the Lang family or much of anything really.

He thanked them, though, and smiled broadly while he did it. He thanked them, shook their hands, and politely explained that their services would no longer be required. Then, just as politely, they were asked to leave the premises.

~ 23 ~

If it was Portland, Eugene, or Salem, the public might not have noticed the additional police presence that was suddenly placed in their midst. In Altamont, however, practically every one of it's eighteen thousand five hundred ninety-one residents was aware that something very odd was happening around them.

It wasn't as if the National Guard had descended on their small town but may as well have been, considering the way the federal agents stood out against the serene, tree-lined backdrop of Klamath County. In addition to the new faces in the dark sedans, it also didn't go unnoticed that every police officer within a fifty mile radius seemed to be on duty today and were confined to a relatively small area. If there was supposed to be a convention in town, nobody had heard about it.

Starting at about ten a.m., the first set of cruisers had taken positions in various locations around the outskirts of the ten square mile plot of land that was Altamont. By eleven, another group moved into residential areas where the population was at its most dense, concentrating on the neighborhoods near schools, shopping centers, and public parks. Though the coverage was still somewhat sparse, nobody who drove a car through any part of the town would be able miss the abundance of law enforcement vehicles that had invaded their small corner of the earth. By noon, it had gotten around why they were there.

The word didn't come from anyone wearing a badge of any kind and was, instead, relayed in a second-hand manner by the first news vans to arrive on scene. The network affiliates as well as a local crew came from two different directions and showed up at about the same time. The news team who came in from the south had been shadowing Dwight Hildebrandt's every move since his first day at Woodhall Penitentiary and were his public soundboard whenever the man felt the need to speak, which was rarely.

The local group from the north came down from Eugene and had already driven forty-five miles to the Oakridge Motor Lodge before speeding another hundred and forty miles to their current location. As far as they were concerned, it was their story.

It wasn't an anonymous tip or even a solid lead that sent the reporters and journalists scurrying to the small city in south Oregon—it was simply common sense. It was highly speculative as well, but anyone with a camera and tape to roll was ready to take advantage of that speculation. With so many officers and various federal agents in such a visible position, there would be a story in it whether the guest of honor showed up or not.

If anyone in Altamont hadn't known where Stanley Lewis Hewitt's second murder took place fifteen years earlier, they would certainly know now. It was spelled out in black and white in every newspaper and was now being broadcast directly from in front of their homes, churches, and schools. If not for one horribly unoriginal murder in Vancouver, Washington three days earlier, the sleepy little town would still be sleeping. Now they were wide awake and thoroughly annoyed with all the attention. For those who had been residents of the city fifteen years ago, the situation looked remarkably familiar.

The general consensus was that if there was a chance that the murderer who brought cameras to their community the first time was planning to make an appearance, he certainly wouldn't be doing it now. With his face splashed across every TV screen and newspaper, not to mention the siege-like atmosphere that had taken over the city, it was very unlikely that he would be able to make his way in without being recaptured—if that was even his intention to begin with. Most doubted the idea but it was obvious that a few were hoping for it, which was the annoying part.

Aside from the overly curious, most of the citizenry stayed indoors and watched the scene from the comfort of their living rooms. On two stations the carnival of law enforcement was nonstop with only a few commercial breaks while every other channel had updates that ran each half-hour. It was overwhelming from a local point of view where anything remotely newsworthy was a rare event. It was the place that they lived and now they were a live TV show in at least three states.

Staring into their television sets, the residents of Altamont saw nothing but strangers walking their streets. The strangers wore varying outfits that came with badges of many different shapes and sizes. If they weren't wearing a uniform of some shade of blue, brown, green, or black then they were clothed in suits that were supposed to make them appear very businesslike.

At the moment, there were only two kinds of business that fell outside of the uniformed man's realm: speaking into a camera and not speaking at all. The ones that spoke wore loud clothing that screamed *Look at me!* while the quiet ones wore darker colors that said *I was never here.*

There were so many strangers that the man-on-the-street interviews ran out of townsfolk to fire questions at, leaving only other strangers to fill the void. They had no personal connection to the town or anyone in it but were more than willing to give their take on the days events—events that had yet to occur, though it had no ill effects on the festivities. Some of the perspective interviewees were less glib than others and a few even shunned the camera's eye.

If one was an avid true-crime reader they might have caught a brief glimpse of one or two authors who had made their mark in the genre, though both had declined to comment on what was currently happening in Altamont. The respective authors of *Understanding The Sickness* and *Man Of Rage* bolted out of sight and were quickly replaced by someone more anxious to look bad on TV. There was no shortage of them.

An hour or so later, the same television viewers could have seen another man turn down an interview in a manner that was hard to read from a TV screen. The large and sharply dressed black man looked quite ready to spew forth a fifteen minute diatribe on the subject before the woman with the microphone kindly asked him for his name and occupation. When she did, the man simply smiled— an odd, tired kind of smile—and shook his head before turning away from her without another word. Within seconds, she found another target to harass and moved along with her cameraman following close behind.

While there was no real story to report on yet, the various news crew did a splendid job of creating one wherever they could find it. At least two shoving matches broke out over the intrusive and aggressive nature of the many reporter's queries and by the time the sun went down a lone cameraman had gotten himself mugged and beaten. In a town that had no crime to speak of until the media showed up, a bruised up man whining about the theft of his camera was the best anyone could come up with on this particular day.

By ten o'clock in the evening, which was bedtime for much of the local population and dinner or drink time for the news crews, things were winding down on the street. Rain was beginning to fall, forcing most of the non-natives into the shelter of restaurants or hotels. Many of them favored their own news vans, instead, hoping that some clever editing would make an entire day's worth of taping look like something resembling the news. So far, it didn't.

At about eleven-thirty the city shut down as though under curfew. The last of the news crews that weren't planning to spend the night in Altamont had departed and the rest moved into their hotel rooms for the evening. There was still plenty of business for the bars and twenty-four hour coffee shops but the streets were finally empty of pedestrians. The rain that had been falling for hours forced the last of the residents home and sent most others back to wherever they came from. Any police cruisers that weren't scheduled to be camping out on a corner all night had been recalled to their respective departments an hour earlier.

By two a.m., the only audible sounds were the patter of raindrops and the buzzing of streetlights. Aside from the chatter of local wildlife and the occasional barking dog, much of the city rested peacefully throughout the night.

Even though Special Agent Dwight Hildebrandt was wide awake at 3:16 a.m., still staring at his hotel room ceiling as he had been doing for the past two hours, he was unaware of the murder that was taking place a only few hundred yards from where he was laying. Beverly McGrath and Perry Burgess were awfully close to the scene as well, staying in adjoining rooms at a slightly cheaper motel just down the street from him. Floyd Madison, who had recently cashed a thirty thousand dollar check, was checked into an expensive bed and breakfast but he didn't sleep at all.

Regardless of whatever rest they got that evening, the citizens of Altamont were oblivious to the event that they had been waiting all day for.

They couldn't hear the desperate screams that were trapped behind three layers of duct tape or the tapping of the Craftsman hammer that caused them. They missed the reflective gleam of the knife and the whisking sound of the sharp blade as it sliced repeatedly through the air—among other things—and the frequent, muffled, pleading moans were way too weak to travel much further than the bedroom that they originated from. Along with the slow, wet, dripping noise that lasted for over two hours, all other sounds were lost to the pouring rain and wouldn't be noted by a single soul. It was a quiet affair.

*   *   *   *

Lindsay Stauffer, a twenty-one year-old waitress who sculpted and made pottery in her spare time, wasn't found until 1:00 p.m. the following afternoon. Much like a series of murders that had taken place over fifteen years earlier, as well as another that was only days old, she was still upright when the first officer encountered her. After three hours of taking photos, lifting fingerprints, and scouring the room down to the most minute of details, the FBI's forensic team finally started removing the carpenter's nails that had been pounded through each one of her bare toes. Aside from the duct tape across her mouth and the nails that held her feet in place, she hadn't been bound in any way.

She was propped up in the north-east corner of the room with her knees in a locked position. She had a bluish complexion and multiple gashes in all the important places. They estimated the time of death at around 5:30 a.m. and found over four pints of blood coagulating in her carpet. After more than ten hours of being stuck against her wall like a humiliated and horribly anemic mannequin, they pulled the final nail from the small toe on her left foot and let Lindsay Stauffer slide to the floor.

The nails were placed in a plastic bag and taken to the lab. So was Lindsay.

Like any other shocked community, the residents of Altamont turned out in large numbers for her funeral, which was a full six days after her death. By the time she was lowered into the ground, Margaret Hobin of Redding, California and Shelly Eagan, a student at Chico State, had already joined her. Gwendolyn Rossi of Yuba City would follow three days after that.

~ 24 ~

"Sacramento?" Spencer wondered aloud as he took in the view of the latest city on their journey. It was three in the afternoon and he hadn't seen a busier city since they had driven through Portland an eternity ago. "I'd ask you what the hell you were thinking but that wouldn't do any good, would it?"

"Probably not," Stanley admitted, taking his own obstructed glances at their new locale. "Just another place that I ended up at, I guess."

"Whatever. Just make sure you don't tell anyone that if they ask you. Say it had a special purpose. I'm not sure what the word *Sacramento* means but I'll bet it's Spanish for something religious. Something to do with the word *sacrament* is what I'm thinking."

"So?"

"So, you should always play the religious angle whenever you can, Stan. It freaks people out. There's nothing like it."

"Why didn't *you* do it then?" Stanley asked, feeling surprisingly quick for a change. It wasn't very often that he noticed any verbal slippage from his partner. "You could have said you wasted all those people for St. Peter or the Virgin Mary, or something."

"Nice try, Stan, but a man with twenty-nine kills gets to skip all the religious innuendo and go straight to God status. I didn't have to say a word or even allude to any of that supernatural or theological shit. Some things just speak for themselves. What can I say?"

"I don't know, Spence…" Stanley replied in a hesitating voice. He shifted around nervously. "…but you sure say it a lot."

For a few seconds, it seemed like the conversation had ended but both knew that it hadn't. Moments of silence were commonplace between the two and usually it was just a brief pause to let Stanley catch up to something that Spencer had said. Other times, like now, it was a chance to let something else distract them before a serious argument could begin. There was a lot to look at and they still had a ton of work to do but this one had been coming for at least a week.

"Go ahead and start whining," Spencer said without a single change in his facial expression. His tone was still dangerous but his handsome, smiling face remained steady and calm. "Just don't get too loud on me, Stan. I'll leave you right here with your little fourteen victim hit parade and I won't look back."

"It's always gotta be the numbers with you. Your big *two-nine*. Why do you throw it in my face like that?"

"I'm not throwing anything anywhere. You're the star on this road-trip and I'm the sidekick, okay? Seriously. I'm fucking Tonto over here, man. I'm just a convict. I'm nothing to nobody right now and I can prove it to you. You know what I heard on the news this morning?"

"What?"

"*Spencer Stoning*. That's what I heard." Spencer watched Stanley wince a tiny bit and suspected that he might have heard it too. It was only one news anchor probably just trying to save a little time but the faux pas wasn't missed. Not for a second. "That's who I am at this particular moment. *Spencer Stoning*. Two words; four syllables. I may as well be a fucking shoplifter."

"They've done the same thing to me before."

"So, we're *lying* to each other now? When did you hear it? When has anyone on the news called you 'Stanley Hewitt' in the last week? How about in the last fifteen *years*?"

"I don't know."

"Well, then you don't know what it feels like, so quit acting like I'm stealing something from you. When they call me 'Spencer Stoning' they may as well be cutting one of my limbs off instead of just whacking out one third of my identity, which is exactly what they're doing, by the way. Now, I didn't kill John Kennedy but if I did I would insist that people call me Lee *Harvey* Oswald. Say 'John Gacy' to someone and they won't know what the fuck you're talking about. Say 'John *Wayne* Gacy' and they immediately picture that fat bastard in his clown outfit with a big, pointy, faggoty fucking smile painted on. You've got to have three names, Stan. It's *so* important. I can't stress it enough."

"What about—?"

"If you mention Bundy or Manson I swear to God I'm going to slap you."

He would have too. Spencer knew it was probably one or the other that Stanley was about to refer to since he didn't follow up on his reply. Ted Bundy, Charles Manson, and maybe a few others were rare exceptions to the rule. The good ones almost always had three names. If a prospective killer didn't have a multi-worded name that rolled off the tongue easily and frightened people at the same time, Spencer didn't see the point in trying.

"Stan, do we really need to have this conversation right now?"

The argument was an old one but a lack of access to each other had always kept their mutual antagonism on a verbal level. At one time or another, he suspected they would tangle physically for purely therapeutic reasons. He also knew that he'd lose badly, which was fine with him since he knew that therapy came in many forms.

"If we *have* to do this, Stan, let's find an area a little less public so you can get it off your chest once and for all. We can punch it out or just have a slap-fight if you're not up to having your face bleed a whole lot. *Or* we can skip the whole thing and just go into an alley and measure our dicks if you really want to."

"Spence—"

"But if you want to go by size then I **suggest** we whip out a list of dead folks instead of our peckers. Honestly, man, **you** may have a big one in there—don't tell me if you do, *please*—but my twenty-nine will always beat your fourteen as long as we're talking sheer volume. I'm **sorry** and I apologize for it but there's no way around it."

"*Jeez*, Spence—"

"And there you are, taking it all **wrong** like you always do. It's apples and oranges, Stan. Numbers versus style. There's no point of reference and as far as I know, nobody's created a scale to judge what's right and proper when it comes to smoking God's children. You really need to keep that inferiority complex in check. You're supermax all the way. Quit worrying."

"So, you're saying we're equal?"

"Of course we are," Spencer replied, putting a reassuring hand on his shoulder and giving him a light shake. "We're just equal in different ways. Relax and try to enjoy it while it lasts."

Stanley nodded and seemed satisfied for the moment. They returned to their current job of scanning the streets for anything that stood out. It was only quiet for a minute or two.

"What did you mean with that *'smoking God's children'* thing? That's a hell of a weird thing to say, man."

"I'm glad you noticed. Like I said; always play the religious angle. It doesn't have to mean anything for it to make people squirm." With his point well made, Spencer moved on to more serious business. "Have you seen any potentials yet?"

"It's hard to say. I can't see too much from behind here. My arms are getting tired and everybody's starting to look the same to me."

"Well, grab a seat behind me and act busy. I'll keep looking." Spencer noticed that sweat was beginning to build up on Stanley's forehead and realized that they'd been hanging out in the same spot for almost half an hour without a break.

"And you're not going crazy, man, the reason all these people look familiar is because they're the same damn people we've been looking at since we left Oregon. The fed dressed like a tourist, the fed dressed like a mailman, the fed who just hangs around for days on end—yeah, they're all here. Go ahead and sit down for a few minutes. Draw me a nice little picture or something."

Stanley nodded appreciatively and pulled the baseball cap lower on his face as he lifted the large and heavy television camera off of his shoulder. When held correctly, the bulky and awkward box covered the right side of his face completely while the viewfinder made even a momentary glimpse from the front virtually impossible. From the left side, the man in the glasses and baseball hat looked a lot like the same person they'd stolen the camera from in the first place. It had been just over a week but Altamont felt like years ago.

Setting the camera down next to him, Stanley sat down on the rear bench seat of the stolen van they were currently borrowing and left the door wide open. There was no reason to turn off the large camera since he could never get the thing to work anyway. He kept his hat low and pulled out a pen as he opened up the spiral notebook that Spencer had bought for him.

With his head down and his face practically buried in the notebook, he did as requested and drew a nice little picture. It wasn't nearly as neat as the stuff that he'd seen Spencer draw but it was quirky in its own way.

Before getting back to business, Spencer took a long look at his partner to gauge his recognizability. From where he was standing, the figure sitting in the van just a few dozen yards from the Capitol Building didn't look like a raving psycho at all and bore little resemblance to the Stanley Hewitt that had been displayed on TV. Spencer felt pretty good about his own radically altered appearance as well.

The messy brown hair that the networks had been showing was now shorter, fashionable, and as blond as it could get without looking transparent. On top of that, his deep black eyes were now a bright and brilliant blue, which brought out the star quality that he knew had always been there. In fact, he thought the colored contact lenses looked even better on him than they'd looked on Natalie Warner back at the Spitfire Steakhouse in Black Pine, Idaho over a week earlier. It probably wasn't something she would ever forget and he remembered her fondly for it.

Above all, he thought it was sweet the way she didn't struggle with him or even flinch as he'd sucked the two small pieces of shiny blue plastic right off of her eyeballs. She was marriage material for sure.

Only after he was convinced that Stanley wouldn't give himself away did Spencer turn back to the street, which was crowded with people from all walks of life. Like he had told Stanley, there wasn't anything terribly new about anyone he saw and they didn't see anything new about him either. He and Stanley had been making intermittent appearances around them since Redding and hadn't received so much as a sideways glance. They never got in the middle of anything and had always stayed pretty far away from the action. This one was a little more risky considering the press conference that was about to take place, but that was what made it so much fun.

"It looks like our favorite fed finally decided to show up," Spencer said from the corner of his mouth, causing Stanley to stop scribbling for a moment. "If we make it another hundred miles south I swear I'm going to interview that guy."

Looking down at the microphone in his hand, Spencer was very tempted. Of course he wouldn't do anything stupid like that and jeopardize their mission, but the idea had a lot of appeal. Special Agent Hildebrandt had been on TV almost nightly since the college student from Chico was murdered and he hadn't mentioned Spencer's name once. Not many others had either. He was officially off the radar and if he wanted to stay in the game, he knew something would need to be done on his behalf in the not too distant future. It wasn't quite time yet.

"Or maybe I'll go over there and interview your girlfriend instead. She and that prissy little shrink of mine have been tenacious as hell, haven't they?"

~ 25 ~

Like clockwork, Floyd thought as he watched Beverly McGrath slide from the driver's seat and step out onto the street just a hundred yards or so from the state capitol. He had pulled into Sacramento ahead of her by no more than an hour and knew almost exactly where he would find her. With his tracking skills as limited as they were, he felt fortunate to have figured out her pattern so quickly. He guessed that her traveling companion had his own place in the scheme of things but he hadn't paid too much attention to him since they left Oregon.

And he's always in the passenger seat. Every damn time.

Today, just like every day for the last week, Floyd didn't look like a man with almost thirty-thousand dollars in the glove compartment of his car. He wasn't dressed sharply and he didn't look very good at all, in fact. The clothes were from a thrift store up north and were purchased solely on how average they appeared. He'd stopped shaving as well and already had a decent amount of stubble going.

He was nobody and he wore it well. It was the kind of look required to maintain relative invisibility while tailing someone that knew your face.

He still smelled nice, though, and that in itself could have presented a problem if Floyd was planning on being scrutinized up close. Since he wasn't, he didn't see any reason to go stinking up the place. A seasoned pro like his ex-employer Tom Devereaux would have seen right through the ruse but good old Tom wasn't around right now—at least he hoped not. No, Tom was probably still driving around in San Francisco trying to hunt down a polygamistic embezzler named Henry Torres and wondering what happened to the tracking device he'd planted on the man's Cadillac.

As Floyd watched the regular cast of characters begin to arrive, he made sure to take a few over-the-shoulder glances behind him before getting too comfortable. It would have made perfect sense for Devereaux, or any other lowlife private investigator for that matter, to do the same thing that Floyd was already busy doing and he certainly didn't need any company. Keeping an eye out for vultures, leeches, and other assorted lurkers was a priority.

Ironically, it was Devereaux himself who had shared all the good secrets about the parasitic nature of their chosen profession. And in educating the young Floyd Madison, good old Tom was unknowingly making one of biggest and most expensive mistakes of his life.

Exploitation of information, Tom had told him, *is the key to any investigator's livelihood.*

He'd always laughed a little when he spit the line out and said the word "investigator" in a tone that implied he had slightly less than zero respect for men who shared their line of work—himself included. He was right, though, and Floyd had been listening. Floyd had always been a good listener, even back when his sole source of income came from roughing up the inebriated and escorting them to the ground.

Floyd was all of twenty-six when Tom Devereaux saw him toss his first drunk from The Fifth Street Lounge. The victim was over three hundred pounds, stood around six-six, and had consumed an amount of alcohol that probably would have killed him if he weighed twenty pounds less. He wasn't a regular and would have been cut off much earlier if the bartender had known just how unruly he was about to become. When he was finally cut off, the man responded by throwing a shot glass through the ten foot wide mirror over the bar and proceeded to go after anyone within arm's reach.

In a barroom as crowded as Fifth Street was that night, the spectacle soon turned into a savage, running-of-the-bulls type episode with many patrons being harmed merely by trying to get the hell out of the guy's way. Not a soul had dared to make a move toward the man until Floyd stepped up to perform the ugly part of his job.

He usually spent much more time checking IDs and schmoozing tipsy women than rolling drunks out the door but he didn't get his job at the Fifth simply for being big. He'd wrestled on the playground, wrestled in high school, and would have wrestled in college had he chosen to attend. On this particular night, he viciously wrestled a three hundred pound drunk out of a bar and onto the sidewalk, where he left the freshly unconscious man to fend for himself among the street people of LA. Devereaux liked what he saw and within a few days he'd hired himself a brand new skip-tracer.

For a while Floyd wasn't sure what his job title meant.

Tom Devereaux owned and operated an agency that catered mainly to the bail bonds industry and skip-tracing seemed to be the general theme. Floyd knew that his job was to bring in the men who were ripping off the bondsmen by skipping their court dates, but he never did any tracing that he was aware of. He was always told by his employer exactly where to go and was told whom he was to return with.

Generally, he was instructed to take them straight to the police station for processing or back to the bondsmen who had guaranteed their bail. Other times—much of the time, in fact—he was told to bring them back to Tom instead. These were the guys who got to walk if they had the cash to change Tom's mind about handing them over.

To Tom Devereaux, there was nothing like the look on a felon's face when he thought he'd been arrested only to realize that he'd been kidnapped instead. Their ransom was always suspiciously close to whatever their warrant was worth and they almost always paid. The ones that didn't pay found themselves quickly back in jail with a brand new set of rules regarding any future bail arrangements. In short, they were never offered the chance to skip out again.

If you don't know the answer, chances are that somebody else does, Tom was also fond of saying.

Floyd was still listening and by now he was watching exactly how the game was played as well. And it *was* a game to Devereaux, which was why it didn't work out nearly as well for him as it could have. The lessons were short and few but they were an education that Floyd couldn't have received at any school.

It was all about information and information came cheap if the donor of that information didn't know they were supplying it. For the first few months under Tom's wing, Floyd exploited everything that was handed to him. It was there to use and it was accurate, which was all that was required. With a name, a face, and a location, the only other thing Floyd needed was a reason and Tom always had a good one.

It wasn't until a particularly expensive fugitive skipped out that Floyd was given his first shot at what Tom would have laughingly called "investigating".

The target was all mapped out and Floyd was given every detail he needed to keep close tabs on a person named Dane Vario. The job was simple: track every move made by the man. Day or night, Floyd's one and only task was to see where he spent his time. There would be no physical harassment and no bringing the man in. There was to be no interaction at all, in fact. It was a simple chore that left him wondering why anyone would bother with such an operation.

A few days later, he found out exactly why when Devereaux swooped in and picked up a first-class fugitive worth eighteen thousand dollars to anyone who delivered him to the authorities. The real target wasn't Dane Vario as it turned out but a man named Ivan Galana, who was wanted on a manslaughter charge. Dane Vario was simply a very good bounty hunter with even better information and he had been slowly catching up with Ivan over the course of a month. When he finally nailed down the man's location, Floyd was still shadowing him and passed the news on before Vario could make his big move. Every scrap of information gathered by Vario was made irrelevant by three days worth of surveillance and his rather large payday vanished straight into the pocket of Floyd's boss.

If you don't know the answer, chances are that somebody else does. Dane Vario sure did and he wasn't the only one who knew a thing or two. There was plenty of information to exploit and The Devereaux Agency took advantage of every bit of it.

While Floyd kept a close eye on his two latest targets, he couldn't shake the feeling that Devereaux was out there somewhere, shadowing his moves and taking notes. If not him, then maybe some new flunky that he had trained specifically to ride Floyd's ass and steal away any chance of a revival for Madison Investigations. It would have been fair after all. Even Floyd couldn't deny that.

As he abandoned his position and cautiously moved closer to Doctors Burgess and McGrath to try to see which room numbers they would occupy, he wondered for at least the fifteenth time if he was on the right track or not.

His first instinct had been to follow the caravan of feds from city to city and step in front of a camera or two along the way, creating a decent little buzz for himself whether he was able to be productive or not. The idea had merit but his focus shifted immediately when he had first caught sight of Beverly McGrath in the tiny city of Altamont. Not only was she very well educated in the ways of one Stanley Lewis Hewitt, but she would certainly remember the man who had caught him—unlike the hellish bitch of a reporter who'd had the gall to ask him his name on live TV back in Oregon. In a world where good ink was getting harder to come by, the doctor looked like an angel from heaven.

In the end, he decided to hang back and not worry about whose ass he chose to follow. The FBI or the woman who wrote the book on Hewitt; it didn't really matter. They were practically inseparable even if the feds weren't onto her yet, though they probably were. It took Floyd all of three days to realize that Beverly McGrath and her companion had been mirroring the FBI's moves in exactly the same way that he would have done himself. It was the same way he did it in the old days and wasn't much different from how he was tailing her right now.

It was also pretty close to the way he had followed Tom Devereaux to Santa Barbara fifteen years ago and caught himself a serial killer named Stanley Lewis Hewitt. A lot of time had passed since then but Floyd had a strong feeling that his old boss might still be sore about it.

~ 26 ~

"Don't worry about me, Perry. Just take up whatever room you feel you might need."

It came out as sarcastic as she'd intended and Beverly was nearing the end of her patience, which had been waning more and more with each passing day. She seethed as she watched Burgess stake his claim to all the available table space in the small hotel room without bothering to ask her permission first. Beverly figured she was owed at least that much respect since, like almost everything else on their trek thus far, she was paying for it. In all the miles they had driven together, this was the first time they were forced to share a room.

"Why the hell do you need it so bad?" he asked, not really caring how nasty he sounded. His own nerves were terribly frayed and he had stopped making an effort to please her somewhere between Chico and Yuba City. "I've got about a million eight-by-ten photos to go over and all your shit's on the laptop. Who do you think needs more space?"

"Use one of the beds, Perry."

"Why don't *you* use one of the beds?"

"Because I need an electrical outlet and a phone line for the modem," she replied in a heated tone, nodding toward examples of both which protruded from the wall next to the desk.

Instead of harping back at her, he turned away from the cluttered desk and stomped over to one of the two queen-sized beds which took up most of the room. He picked up her laptop computer and plugged the power cord into the socket next to the nightstand. Without looking the least bit put out, he then disconnected the nightstand phone and plugged the empty hole with her modem cable. He fluffed up both pillows and set them upright against the headboard before leaning back into them with an exaggerated sigh of deep comfort. The computer was then turned on and rested easily on his legs as it booted up.

"Oh, damn. This sure is a bitch."

Four or five days ago it might have made them laugh. Two or three and it might have forced a small smile onto their faces. Today it didn't and it wasn't meant to.

Burgess immediately climbed out of the bed with a sneer and returned to the table—*his* table—without a word. While Beverly finished unpacking behind her own wall of silence, Burgess sat down in a chair that felt like it was made of broken glass and started spreading the latest batch of photos around on the sparse, laminated tabletop.

Feeling no need to watch him huff and puff, Beverly threw open each of the three suitcases they were now traveling with and dug around for some bathroom supplies. The two suitcases they had each brought to Utah originally were now packed with a mixture of wrinkled clothes, half-filled notebooks, and just about any item that could be stolen from the cheap hotels that had become a fixture in their lives.

She hadn't showered in two days and had neglected many of the other more involved duties for over a week. After a minute of sorting through the mess, she rounded up some Q-Tips, tweezers, facial cleanser, and most importantly, a razor. It wasn't hers but she took it into the bathroom with her anyway.

It might have seemed a bit childish, but she got a little satisfaction from knowing that the next time that Burgess shaved the stubble from his face he would be using the same razor that she had dragged across her spiky legs, armpits, and maybe a couple other places too. With a wicked sort of satisfaction, Beverly took the longest, hottest shower of her life and thought about how it would feel to strangle Perry Burgess with her modem cable or put one of those big, fluffy pillows over his face while he slept. She wondered how much of a fight he would put up and how long it would take for him to stop kicking—if he kicked at all. There were some serious doubts in her head about the man's survival skills.

The sick visions of Burgess's demise amused her for a short time but her main thoughts were about cutting out and going home. It wasn't the first time she'd considered the possibility but the road was beginning to chew her up in more ways than she could count and the climate between Burgess and herself was growing harsher with each mile.

When they had arrived in Chico after leaving Redding, it was the second time in a few days that she placed a call to her administrative assistant with orders to reschedule her counseling appointments. Many of them had been cancelled more than once already and that was something she simply did not do to her clientele. It was a rule and breaking that rule was bad for any kind of business; especially when something as fragile as sanity was on the line. It was only getting worse, though, since the latest call to her office wasn't just to cancel more appointments but also included instructions not to schedule any more until further notice.

She was less than four hundred miles from her home and office in Santa Barbara and at their current pace, she knew that they would make their way there in about a week. Perhaps she would go no further at that point. Perhaps she wouldn't need to.

Fifteen years ago, the Stanley Lewis Hewitt saga had ended in her home town and the event made her existence what it was. She wondered if it would end there again, but wondered even more what was next if it didn't. There wouldn't be hindsight to fall back on anymore and Stanley would be creating new history instead of repeating his old one. It would be like starting from scratch but already deep in the hole. The idea of it gave her hand a quick bout of the shakes and she had to wait a moment before reapplying the razor to her skin.

How long before he starts cutting his way through LA, Orange County, or Riverside? Where to after that? San Diego? South to Mexico? East to Vegas? Phoenix? And what if he doesn't go anywhere after Santa Barbara? Who say he has to? Why not settle in for while?

She had those plus plenty more scary thoughts while scraping the last wide band of growth from her lower thigh, just a couple of inches higher than her shortest skirt would fall. She stopped there but suspected that if she was traveling with just about anyone besides Perry Burgess she would have shaved all the way up. The road was a lonely place but it sure wasn't *that* lonely.

The last thought got her laughing quietly as the water poured over her and rinsed all the tiny severed hairs off of her body. Just watching them go down the drain seemed to have a mild revitalizing effect all by itself. Her legs were so smooth that they felt brand new to her and after another minute under a stream of the hottest water she could stand, the rest of her didn't feel so bad either.

She shut off the shower and basked in the steam, being careful not to cut herself while she ground the head of the disposable razor against the faucet. It was a bit on the childish side but she hadn't had breakfast yet and was still feeling mildly sadistic.

*   *   *   *

"You were right about the shower," Burgess confessed as he stepped out of the still steamy bathroom to let the air clear. "I *do* feel about a hundred times better. Almost human, even."

"And you're looking better too," she replied, flashing a surprising smile in his direction. It was an out-of-character expression he hadn't seen for days.

Instead of continuing to stare at him and grinning like a dope, Beverly quickly pointed her face back down to her computer screen. She was still giggling on the inside but kept it at bay while Burgess stood there in his cheap terry-cloth robe and bled for her. He had eight tiny squares of toilet paper pasted to his face and at least five oozing cuts that hadn't received medical attention yet.

"How much longer?"

"Ten minutes or so. They're still setting up. Who's it going to be—Hildebrandt or the governor?"

"Probably neither," he replied, trying to rub the pain off of his face as he returned to the bathroom. Leaving the door open, he wiped down the mirror and reached for his aftershave. "That Hildebrandt looks like a robot when he talks into the microphone so it wouldn't surprise me to see a new federal mouth-piece pretty soon. The man's not built for public relations. Now, the governor on the other hand...*God damnit! Shit, fuck, shit...shit...shit...*"

Beverly didn't bother to ask what was wrong. She could smell the aftershave as clearly as Burgess could feel it burning into his raw, wounded skin. It completed her morning and gave her a brighter, more positive outlook on the day ahead.

"*Ooh-ahh-ooh...son of a...*" he muttered, clenching his fists together and bouncing from foot to foot as though it would help quell the stinging sensation. By the time his dance of pain was finished, Burgess was covered with enough sweat to justify another shower. "That does it—I'm switching to an electric. What the hell was I just saying?"

"The governor."

"What about him? I forgot where I was going with that."

"You were about to say that the governor isn't going to lay it on the line just so the feds can feel loved. If he talks about the additional measures to hunt down Stanley, he's admitting that they don't have any kind of handle on the situation—which they don't. If he says anything positive or indicates that they're making progress then he'll look incompetent when the next murder happens right here in the capitol."

"It's a no-win situation."

"Which is why he won't be speaking," she replied. "He won't chance it and I don't blame him."

"Who's it going to be then?"

"Your guess is as good as—" Beverly stopped speaking abruptly and turned up the volume on the television. She yawned and closed up her laptop. "Well, here comes Mister Personality now."

It was as dull as any of his other efforts in front of a camera and Special Agent Hildebrandt's basic announcements only lasted for the usual few minutes. There was nothing new about his facial mannerisms—there were none—and his body language was still consistently rigid. The question and answer portion, which was the only reason he had an audience at all, lasted a bit longer and clocked in at just under fifteen minutes. The questions were long, the answers were short, and it only varied slightly from his many previous outings. There was very little information and even less excitement.

~ 27 ~

"*Chapter Twenty-Seven: Dwight Hildebrandt Doesn't Know Dick.* How's that sound?" Beverly turned off the TV and tossed the remote aside.

"It sounds accurate. I was thinking something like *Slaughter In Sacramento*, but yours has such nuance. How's that chapter looking, anyway?"

"Same as the others," she answered, scrolling backward through the rough manuscript that was really nothing but a jumbled mass of names, dates, and cities. Aside from those few facts, each of the sections after chapters one and two were so similar that there wasn't much to write without sounding repetitive. Fortunately, it was the brutal kind of repetition that made the story interesting and guaranteed readership. "But let's not get too hung up on chapters just yet. It's nothing but pieces and parts so far and the editors will probably rearrange the whole damn thing anyway."

"I think I remember how it works, Bev. I was just asking how the Yuba City narrative was going. That's all."

"Same as the others," she said again. "I'm going to have to throw in about a thousand quotes from the local police just so the reader knows they've moved on to another chapter in totally different city. There's only so much I can do with the individual murders but I'll manage with whatever personal stuff we find out after some more interviews and we'll fill in the blanks later on. How's your project working out?"

"Scary enough for a chapter of its own." The desk was completely covered with the glossy photos that had been mailed to him. "I've got maybe two-thirds of this crap transposed and it gets creepier every time I look at it. What was that Ryan said about Stoning's cell—it's a *wall-to-wall freak show?*"

"Good line."

"It is, isn't it?" he replied, grabbing a pencil and writing the quote down. "And he wasn't lying, either. I've been over these pictures a thousand times and it's like something new jumps out at you every time you look at them. I've got words here that make sense on their own but mean nothing when you try to string them into the sentences they're supposed to be part of. Backward, diagonal, upside-down—I've tried the usual stuff but it's not getting any clearer. Then I've got whole sentences and phrases that just float out there on their own with no rhyme or reason. There're quite a few names in here too."

"Anyone I know?"

"Probably just the ones that everyone else would recognize," he replied, shuffling through his notes. "He's actually got Gandhi in here. Buddha's in there twice with a Bundy crammed in between them. How weird is that? He's got a few Jesus references among other bible figures. Job, Cain and Abel, Noah, Abraham, Joshua; a bunch like that. On the other end we're looking at Baal, Astaroth, and a few other assorted demons. He writes about the nephilim—bad angels, I guess—but steers clear of the word 'Satan'. Probably too ordinary for him."

"Is your name in there?" She could tell immediately from the look on his face that it wasn't.

"No, thank God, but it wouldn't have surprised me if it showed up. He's got plenty of average Joe's in here. No family stuff but the whole cell block was pretty well represented. The Carroll's names are in here—Jensen a little more than Martin—and Hewitt got at least a square foot all to himself. Out of his twenty-nine victims, only one of them made it onto a wall. The name 'Kenny Keyes' appears three times and that doesn't surprise me either."

"Who's Kenny Keyes?"

"He was Stoning's best friend," Burgess answered with a well-hidden scowl, only now knowing for sure that the woman he had been traveling with for over a week had never even read his book. In *Man Of Rage*, Kenneth Keyes had rated almost half a chapter and would have stood out for obvious reasons if she had bothered to read it.

"They worked together at Kerslake Machinery in Rockford. Kerslake had two facilities; a new production line in Illinois and their sales and administrative offices just across the border in Janesville, Wisconsin. And the people who called in sick that day were the only survivors from the whole damn company. I interviewed all three of them and they each said that he and Keyes were pretty tight."

"Do you think they really were?"

"It's debatable. Stoning blew him away during the second round of killings, so it's hard to say. There sure isn't anything written on his walls that'd tell me. I'm not even sure if the stuff that makes sense is his own work or somebody else's. I'll need to run a few searches on them and try to figure out how original they are, but I'd be willing to bet that half of them are song lyrics or poems or something like that."

In truth, he wouldn't have been willing to bet on anything when it came to the drawings on Spencer's walls. They almost hurt to think about. Along with the windows and single door that were painted with the same remarkable skill, the whole arrangement made his head spin for its lack of logic. If the photos had been around during the time of Stoning's trial, Burgess guessed he could have gotten off using the insanity defense that had ultimately failed him.

"Was Matthew able to send anything else, or was that all?"

"These were the last of them. And it's a miracle if you ask me. Now that the feds don't need us, I can't see any real reason for Chase to keep helping us out with this stuff."

"I can," Beverly replied, looking up at him. "Chapter One for starters. I don't know what this book will look like when we're done with it, but I can tell you for sure what Chapter One will deal with."

"The escape?"

"No question," Beverly said with a nod. "Chase wants to be totally absolved of it and he wants it in writing. I don't know how much this book will help him out but it's the least we can do with everything he's provided us with. We could fill up four whole chapters with nothing but stuff pilfered from the first two books and still sell a million copies, but it *has* to start with the escape."

"Why?"

"Are you kidding? We've got two good-looking criminal brothers locked down at Woodhall maximum security who are media darlings and more popular than the president. They bust out military-style, getting themselves and their crew killed in an ultra-violent explosive shootout with local boys while our killers are busy sneaking out the back. I don't even see Stanley and Stoning making a real appearance in the first chapter except for the last few sentences, but it all starts with the escape."

"Who says?" Burgess asked, a devious smirk moving across his lips. "That's just what everyone will expect. Why not start it off at the restaurant? You know—that place in Idaho. The first place they struck after busting out."

"The steakhouse in Black Pine? You think?"

"Yeah, it's brilliant. Start at the restaurant with their first non-fatal horror-show and segue straight into the Carroll's prison break. Let the thing build up a little then we go into the background on Stoning and Hewitt."

"Or Hewitt and Stoning."

"Whatever," Burgess conceded, not ready to get too concerned about who went first until the presses were set to roll. "We move from the restaurant to the escape to our meeting with Hildebrandt. Depending on how he treats us when he finds out we've been tagging along, we can make him look like a genius or a total idiot—author's discretion. We throw out some history on the prison and maybe a few of the notable felons locked up there—"

"And that's another chapter, right there. We can write up the penitentiary, the Carrolls, the other inmates in D Block, and cover Chase's ass all at the same time. That's *if* we can get some credible demolition guys to back up what he says on the record, I mean."

"Exactly. And now we're into chapters two, three, maybe four, and we still haven't touched on Stoning and Hewitt. It'll all be good stuff, but the reader has just paid between seven and thirty dollars for a book—"

"*Thirty?*" Beverly jumped in, unable to help herself. "You're thinking *hardcover?*"

"That'll depend on how this mess turns out. We're five murders in, which I think will guarantee us a decent paperback run as it is. We'll talk hardcover next week. But back to what I was saying—the reader has just spent his hard-earned money on a book about our two antagonists and he's four chapters in before they're even mentioned. That won't work and the reader will be unsatisfied. But if we start with a bang in Idaho then feed them the rest in small doses, we're already a quarter of the way done before we even start to cannibalize pieces of *Man Of Rage* and *Understanding The Sickness* for the background. You know how much time and work that will save?"

"It won't be like we're stealing it from somebody either," Beverly agreed. "It's our own work and we'll only be plagiarizing ourselves. We could have this thing halfway done before we get to the Vancouver murder."

"And it doesn't even get any harder at that point," Burgess added. "Since the murders are happening in the same order as before, we present the old murder alongside the new one and do a little comparing and contrasting. Each one is brand new chapter. That's five so far on top of anything that new happens from here on. It could mean a whole lot of new chapters and a great big fiery finish when they're captured or killed. This is huge, Beverly. It won't be a very tough sell to any publisher out there. They'll be bidding on this before the rough draft is finished."

He was practically drooling over his stack of photos as Beverly set her pen down and sat up straighter on the bed. She had been leery from the start about co-authoring with Perry Burgess but his points were getting better even though his end of their psychotic duo hadn't been doing too much aside from horrifying families and the like. Stoning couldn't remain complacent forever, though, and that was the main reason she had agreed to share space on a book jacket with the psychiatrist. It wasn't so much a partnership as it was an insurance policy.

"It *is* huge, Perry, but it's got potential to be even bigger and I know you've already considered it." She watched his eyes light up as she read his mind. It wasn't hard to do. "So, how long before he goes off? Do you have a clue?"

"It could be any time now. If they're still together, Spencer Stoning isn't just along for the ride. He loves attention and Hewitt's getting almost all of it right now. He won't like that."

"And what happens when he loses it?" Beverly asked, trying to imagine what it would take for anyone to eclipse Stanley's trail of victims. "Unless he plans on driving all the way back to Illinois, I don't see a way to prepare for this."

"You're not supposed to. That's what spree killers are all about. They usually suicide or get sniped by the SWAT team before they get the chance to answer too many questions, so they're more of an enigma than their serial killing brethren."

"How did it happen in Rockford?"

"Actually, it was Janesville first," Burgess corrected. "There were two concerted efforts in two locations and that makes him a bit of a peculiarity."

"In what way?"

"I wrote a whole book on this, Bev," he replied, his sneer returning briefly. "Maybe you should go grab yourself a copy."

"Maybe you should go grab yourself," Beverly fired back expertly. It wiped the nasty look from his face and replaced it with something that would have passed for a smile. "If you finish up with those pictures and give us a clue what level of psychosis we're dealing with, I'll see what I can get on the rest of these newspapers that Stanley thought were important enough to hoard in his cell."

Though she had only located and downloaded six of the eighteen archived periodicals from the list Ryan Williams had supplied, there was already a notable pattern that could have simply been a coincidence. It wouldn't be as eye-catching as Spencer Stoning's walls but there would be a little more material for the book if they ran short on the page count for some reason. She hoped sincerely that nobody at Woodhall had done anything to D Block since they'd left the place.

She had a feeling that the key to the whole thing lay somewhere on a wall in cell D-41.

"I've got at least another four hours on these," she said as she closed up her laptop and slid off of the bed. "How much time are you looking at?"

"A few hours to get it on paper and possibly the rest of my life trying to figure out what it all means."

"Getting it on paper is good enough for now. Let's grab some breakfast and get a few pages on the local scene so we don't have to bother with any of it tomorrow. I want to be finished up with all the evidence from their cells before it gets too late. I think I'll sleep better when it's done."

~ 28 ~

And she's driving again, Floyd noted, staying a good twenty yards back as usual, though he wasn't actually afraid of losing them. He always knew where to pick them up again if that was the case. He was also pretty sure he knew who would be driving.

So far, he wasn't very impressed with Dr. Perry Burgess and it wasn't just because the man didn't seem to know how to enter a vehicle from the left side. It had started back in Altamont when he got his first close look at him. It was all in his face. There was something about it that gave the impression that he was above much of what was going on around him or was privy to some special information that nobody else knew about. Floyd tried to avoid looking directly at him if he could help it.

By the time he had purchased a copy of *Man Of Rage,* which was three days later, he couldn't look at the picture on the back cover without getting angry. There was just something about his face that cried out for an educational beating.

The book made it worse. Since picking it up, Floyd had skimmed through it three times and was disappointed with just about every conclusion the man had come up with. If not for all the chapters devoted to the trial—a trial highlighted by the testimony of Burgess himself—Floyd couldn't see how he could have filled up a whole book on the subject if not for the gruesome stuff. It was awfully thin. The details were sufficiently morbid, though, and were purported to have come straight from Stoning's mouth during a series of lengthy psychiatric sessions.

Since even the craziest of crazy people had certain rights, Floyd had to assume that Stoning gave special permission to have his sessions published, and if all that he said was absolutely true then Floyd was worried about more than just Burgess's crappy writing style. Floyd only had to look as far as the newspaper on the seat next to him to know that Stanley Hewitt was potentially the undercard to Spencer Stoning's main event and he assumed it was the only reason that Burgess was along for the ride.

As a rule, Floyd read the paper not to learn what he didn't know, but to learn what others thought they knew. He rarely believed it and never trusted a word that was deemed newsworthy enough to print. The only thing he could count on without much skepticism was the obituary page. It was the same page he turned to at each stop on his trip and he was keeping score in every city.

According to the papers he had read, there wasn't a town in the United States where somebody wasn't dying. They died everyday from a thousand different things and there would be more of them dying the very next day.

In the city of Altamont, a city of only nineteen thousand, one other person had died along with Lindsay Stauffer on her special day. He was a man of eighty-six who'd had a cardiac arrest and passed away four hours before her. In Redding, roughly five times the population of Altamont, six others had died on the same day as Margaret Hobin; one car accident with two fatalities and four of natural causes. The stats in Chico and Yuba City were comparable to the others and only varied based on the size of each city.

The conclusion, sick as it was to the man doing the concluding, was that people died every day and Stanley Hewitt was barely making a dent. The more he thought about Spencer Stoning, the more he could see where the numbers came into play and he had to admit that Stoning's body count was impressive in the worst kind of way. He found it odd that no one had seen fit to mention it out loud yet.

His thoughts were briefly interrupted as the car out in front of him made a quick turn and disappeared for a moment. They were probably just going out for some breakfast but he didn't want to miss it if their wanderings took them somewhere that didn't include a meal. It was a fifty-fifty shot since all they seemed to do was eat, sleep, and make nuisances out of themselves.

As with the other cities they had visited, Floyd expected them to end up at a few predesignated locations within the first two days.

The first destination was always a local police department. There, he assumed they would be requesting a sit-down or conducting interviews with the officers who were around when Hewitt ran through their town the first time. Judging from what he had read of both of their books, vague and foggy recollections from the people who had been on scene were essential to the process. From where Floyd was standing, that was the easy part.

The next place they would go had to do with the victims themselves and Floyd didn't approve, regardless of what their motives were. These trips led to the mothers, fathers, siblings, and other relations of Hewitt's initial victims with no other purpose than to dredge up a few horrible moments of their past and to get their reaction to it. They were no longer doctors of any kind at that point and became the journalistic vultures that made death into a spectacle and made trage-dies even more tragic. The only up-side was that Floyd's own scavenging seemed tame in comparison.

Within fifteen seconds he had caught up to the car again and watched as it pull into the parking lot of a coffee shop. He dropped speed and maneuvered his way around the street one more time before pulling in and backing into a parking space. By the time Floyd killed his engine, they were already inside.

If he thought it would be any different than their last twenty conversations, he would have ventured in and sat nearby. He didn't think so. Not this time. It had been tense between them lately and he guessed they probably wouldn't even speak to each other. Instead, he would stay where he was at and, for the fourth time, read through a book by a man that he didn't even like. It might have all been horseshit but there was just something about a guy who could do what Spencer Stoning had done that made Floyd keep remembering that this was for real.

Burgess wasn't the real target anyway and he could be safely ignored. It was the woman who interested him for a variety of reasons; some selfish, some not. If they ever split up, there wasn't any question about who would be followed and who would be allowed to fuck off. It was an instinct Floyd was willing to follow at least as far as Santa Barbara if they needed to go down that far.

He put the small, paperback copy of *Man Of Rage* up in front of him, leaving just enough exposure to be able to keep an eye on the doctor's car while he read. He had already breezed through the first several chapters and was getting to the day of Spencer's rampage, which was his favorite part; something he couldn't jus-tify in the least. It was just a poorly written snuff book but was awfully hard to look away from at times.

Within a minute he was lost in it again. He didn't even mind being led along by Perry Burgess's horrible narrative as Spencer Stoning made his way to work on "that fateful day".

That fateful day? The cliché was so bad that it pained him to look at the phrase. He had seen it for the fourth time now and it would get worse before it got better.

"I may not be any kind of writer, Dr. Burgess," Floyd said aloud, hoping nobody would wander by and hear him talking to himself. "But I could fart a better book than this."

*   *   *   *

It took almost a full page for Spencer Stoning to wake up then eat his breakfast and find his way out the front door of his apartment. By the end of that page the reader would know what type of cereal he liked, what size shoe he wore, what side he parted his hair on, and whether he shaved every day or just every other day.

The car he drove came next and took up several paragraphs by itself. Typical of everything else in the book, Stoning's '67 Camaro was described in enough detail to be a pamphlet written by the folks at Chevrolet.

"Not a hot rod but just for getting around in," Stoning would explain in an excerpt, since he didn't want to be viewed as *"One of those tiny-peckered, muscle-car-driving morons. It's just wheels, man"*. Though Burgess had filled up much of the book with his own conjecture and opinions, it seemed that almost all the good lines belonged to the bad guy.

The weather took up half a page even though the phrase *"It was a sunny day in Rockford,"* would have sufficed. The next three paragraphs detailed Stoning's route to work, which included the actual street names plus all of the lefts and rights that he took to get there. These were the kind of irrelevant items that peppered the entire book and drove Floyd crazy.

A page later Stoning had finally completed the arduous three mile journey from his home to his job at Kerslake Machinery, where he parked in his usual space. Floyd guessed it probably took Stoning less time to cover the distance between the two places than it took him to read about it when the book came out.

From there, Stoning walked in through the main entrance, where he encountered Isabelle Robles—the receptionist and soon-to-be victim number eleven—then greeted her as he usually did.

It was noted on about every other page that anything that took place inside either of the two Kerslake facilities on *that fateful day* was relayed to the author by Stoning himself as opposed to eye-witness accounts. This too was another example of redundant irrelevance since it had been made clear right up front that there were no survivors at either location. To Floyd it was clear that any time Burgess had the chance to mention his intimate conversations with the killer, he definitely made sure to mention it. The man couldn't get enough of himself.

It took another paragraph just for Stoning to pour himself a cup of coffee (Yuban with cream and six sugars) then say hello to a few of his doomed coworkers before he clocked in. Five minutes later he was at work in front of a lathe, doing the same thing he had done at Kerslake Machinery for the last two years; shaping metal rods that went into products that he would never get to see. Whatever the alleged products were, they were never mentioned again; something Floyd found upsetting since he was genuinely curious about them now.

According to *Man Of Rage*, Stoning spent almost two hours in the machine shop before things went bad. That was how it was described. *"Things went bad".* Floyd wasn't sure if the understatement belonged to the author or to Stoning, but things certainly did go bad. Not so much at first, but everything had to start somewhere.

"You're on fire, Spence."

That was the quote that set everything in motion and it was the last sentence on the page. It was just a little build-up to get the ball rolling and it was enough to let Floyd know that the gratuitous parts were about to ensue. Apparently the author knew it too since he killed the chapter at that point and started a fresh one on the next page even though he didn't need to. It was probably just for dramatic effect.

~ 29 ~

"You're on fire, Spence." The words were attributed to a drill-press operator named Kenneth Keyes, who worked in the station directly behind Stoning's lathe. If one believed what they read, he was also Stoning's best friend.

"So, I turned around and that's when I noticed that my gearbox was burning," Stoning was quoted as saying. The next one was the same quote that appeared in bold letters above the book's description on the back cover and gave the reader a clue of what to expect from the man they were reading about.

"I tried to remedy the situation but ended up killing everybody instead. Isn't it funny how things happen sometimes?"

It was probably the main reason the book sold so well.

Though he still thought it was a dreadful exploitation piece, Floyd was impressed with the way certain words and phrases were presented. The last two sentences he read seemed to fly off the page at him. Maybe it was just an odd font or the way the words were italicized but most likely it was the sentence itself that made it so attractive. There was so very much that was so very wrong with it.

What followed next was supposed to be Perry Burgess's attempt to present the facts through the words of the killer, but Floyd wasn't buying it as such. Comparing it to Beverly McGrath's chronicle on Stanley Hewitt, Floyd thought Burgess's book looked like a novelized version of a tabloid interview. Regardless, it was still compelling on the most basic of levels.

"I flipped open the gearbox on the lathe to get a look at what was going on and sparks and flames started shooting out of it. If I'd had more time to think about it I probably would have done the smart thing." Floyd suspected that Stoning's words

were delivered in a friendly and very casual manner based on what he had read so far. One of the points that Burgess had reiterated in several chapters was how chatty Stoning could get when the subject excited him. *"But all I could think to do was to start slapping at it with a shop rag. I've got a fire caused by a bunch of high-torque gears grinding together and I'm trying to put it out with a cloth. I can't really explain that one."*

Floyd thought he could hear Stoning's self deprecating laughter even though it wasn't noted in the text.

"Now the rag's on fire too and it gets sucked straight into the gearbox. And it was loud, man—that screechy kind of loud that you can feel in your spine. I didn't like that sound at all. By now, everyone else in the shop is powering down their machines and trying to see what's going on. That should have clued me in right there what I was doing wrong but it just didn't occur to me. I was pretty embarrassed by then, so I reached right in there and tried to pull the rag out. If the gears were working like they were supposed to be working then I'd have lost my hand. Instead, I lost about six layers of skin across my knuckles and my sleeve caught fire. That was when I started seeing red."

Floyd could feel the mood change. Whether it was Stoning's words or Burgess's style that did it, the mission had been accomplished. He could picture the scene and knew from experience that quick and sudden pain was as good a reason as any for an angry outburst. Floyd had been injured quite a few times himself and was well aware of what kind of emotions came to the surface when the pain reached its maximum. In his opinion, it was a nasty feeling but could usually be quelled by a swift bout of swearing instead of the need to commit mass-murder.

"About two seconds later everything gets quiet. No more sparks. No more flames. Just a whole shitload of smoke and a bunch of guys laughing at me. I didn't like it."

"Spencer, if you had a brain, you'd be fucking dangerous." The quote was the second one that belonged to Kenneth Keyes. The book said that the drill-press operator had cut the power to Stoning's lathe before it could start throwing metal around the room. *"Forgot about the kill-switch, didn't you? Way to go, moron."*

"That's the next thing I hear. Fucking Kenny, ragging on me about the kill-switch. That's what he has to say to me while I'm standing there with wringing ears, a scraped up hand, and smoke pouring off of me. The fucking kill-switch. It probably started right about there."

There was a break as Burgess explained to the reader exactly what a kill-switch was. He could have called it an "emergency power switch" or simply an "off button" but he never did and Floyd didn't need to ask why. It was all about the drama and the word "kill-switch" had a nice ring to it. Floyd had taken metal-shop in high school and knew what he was trying to allude to, though he'd never heard it referred to in such a way. It was the biggest lesson in safety next to that whole lecture about keeping your goggles on at all times and was a frightfully easy concept.

Two buttons; one green—one red. One meant "on", the other meant "off". It wasn't something you needed a degree in physics to figure out.

"Every piece of heavy machinery in the world has that big red button, but it's no good unless you remember to press that thing from time to time. Kenny remembered but I didn't…and he was a goddamn idiot. No shit. Don't get me wrong, Kenny was my buddy and all. It's just that he was too stupid for words most of the time. And I'm not just being an asshole when I tell you that he shouldn't have been talking to me the way he was. There was no need for it. I was already scared and hurt and cranky as hell so I guess that was when I started getting really upset. I stayed cool externally, though. Don't think I didn't."

Floyd didn't want to rewrite the book or anything, but he was pretty sure that Stoning didn't stay too cool.

"I can usually play it off so that no one can tell when I'm feeling moody—it's a talent of mine, you know. I was actually doing okay for a little bit there and after a while I even forgot about the pain in my hand. That's how fast it happens, man. One second the monster's there and the next it's gone. I was glad too, because in no time at all the guys were done laughing at me. A minute later, the smoke had cleared, the machines started running again and they had a tech checking out my lathe, which is really good news because without that lathe spinning, I'm out of a job. Everything cooled out so fast I should have known something was up."

Floyd had already read the chapter, so he knew what was up. He read it again anyway.

"The foreman—a guy named Jack—he talks to the technician and tells me that I may as well clean myself up. He says 'You're outta here, Stoning' and in half a second I'm starting to see red again. Now, when I say that, I don't mean I'm just getting angry. I mean I start seeing things with a weird rosy tint—like I'm looking at everything through a sheet of red cellophane. And that's how it was when I was looking at Jack. He was just this dark shape surrounded by a big, red aura and I know I'm about to black out at any second."

Burgess interrupted to remind the reader of the blackouts Stoning had experienced since his early teens. He'd mentioned it at least once much earlier in the book but the author apparently thought a few of the less brainy folks needed to hear it twice. The blackouts generally followed moments of intense stress or anger and lasted anywhere from five to thirty minutes. As expected and rather conveniently, Stoning could never account for any of the time that passed while in the condition.

Floyd rolled his eyes as he read about the patented blackout excuse again. He wasn't sure if he was supposed to be disappointed with Stoning or upset with the author for such lameness but it was one of the main reasons he thought the book lacked any credibility. This was more than just an *"on that fateful day"* type of cliché. It was the classic defense for horribly guilty people and it actually worked some of the time. Floyd didn't believe in blackouts as an excuse for murder and he believed in Stoning's blackouts even less. From what he had read and heard about the man, Floyd wasn't even sure if he was truly crazy or just a fantastic liar who tried to get off with an insanity verdict.

"It didn't happen, though. Not then. I could feel myself slipping but I wasn't ready to pop. I was just about there when Jack tells me I'm going to the old plant in Janesville to pick up a new motor and whatever else the tech needs. I thought the guy had just fired me but all he wanted me to do was drive up to the main office and pick up some new parts for my lathe. I was glad he told me because I was about to throw a fit."

"Don't worry, you'll get around to it," Floyd said quietly as he peered over the book for a quick look at the doctor's rental car, which was still present.

"So, I relaxed a little and went back to my station. Casey was there—he's the technician who was fixing my lathe—and he gives me a parts list to take to the old shop in Janesville. Now, he's already angry about the lathe being all temperamental but he keeps his mouth shut in front of me because I'm pretty fucking temperamental myself, in case you hadn't heard. Maybe he'd start bitching once I was out the door but he kept a tight lid on it in my presence, which I appreciated. Just about anybody in the place could have told you that it wasn't a good time to be fucking with me, seeing as how my morning had been going. That fuckwit Kenny couldn't help it, though, and it wasn't too much later that it started going down."

There were no more quotes attributed to Kenneth Keyes. Instead, whatever abuse Stoning's best friend had hurled at him was now rerouted through Stoning's mouth, leaving a whole lot of room for embellishment if he had chosen to rearrange a few of the details. Floyd guessed he probably did.

"I can't remember all the words exactly but I remember the look on his face while he said them. It was like we were having a laugh or something and that's probably what made it so bad. He just couldn't understand that my cool had all been used up. Maybe we'd been friends too long—that's what I think. I don't mean that I thought it was time to stop hanging with the guy, I just mean that he might've thought he had special privileges when it came to riding my nuts. If we were in private—maybe in a bar or out in his backyard shooting at cans—I don't think it would have bothered me

so much. And to be really honest with you, I'm not sure exactly what it was that made things go black. Next thing I know, Casey and Jack are pulling me off of Kenny and dragging me across the shop floor. By the time they separated us, I could feel some real badness coming up from way deep inside me and I knew it wasn't gonna be backing off too quickly. All I needed was some time to put out the fire. You know...just a little time to hit my kill-switch."

There was that word again. It was growing on him by now and made him wonder why it hadn't appeared in the title of the book. *Man Of Rage* didn't really do anything for him.

"I didn't get it, though...not even for a second, man. They didn't give me any time to cool down at all before Jack's calling me in to his office. He's telling me I can still go to Janesville if I want but only to pick up my last paycheck. I waited for the punch line but it never came. I'm sitting there in his office and I'm thinking 'Is all this happening because my lathe caught fire?' Everything seemed to escalate from that point on and I'm still not sure what was really important and what was just pure escalation. Jack didn't give a shit, though, I can tell you that much. He just kind of smiled at me with that stupid fucking face of his while I was gathering my stuff. I can still see it in my mind even though I don't remember seeing him again after that. They tell me that I did, though."

Floyd set the book down for a moment and lit up a cigarette. He was up to a pack a day again and the habit returned to him like an old friend. He checked his watch and estimated another thirty minutes before the doctors would be finished with their meal. By the time he had exhaled his first lungful of smoke, his nose was back in the book.

"They tell me that I saw all of them again...for a little while at least. The whole thing is just a blur so I guess I have to believe what they tell me."

Stoning's dialog abruptly gave way to Burgess's narration and wouldn't return until the end of the chapter. In most parts of the book, the author's voice on the page was a sorrowful thing to read and was distracting to say the least. During this chapter, however, the action filtered right through the empty words and made the scene tolerable. It was much faster than anything before or after the current chapter and read something like a *Reader's Digest* condensed police report. It was pretty good.

The next thing Floyd knew, Stoning was in his Camaro and heading back to his apartment. There was no mention of which exit he walked out of or how many steps it took for him to reach his car door. There weren't any notations indicating how much gas was in the tank or what kind of mileage he got either.

For whatever reason, it appeared that Dr. Perry Burgess had momentarily and blessedly run out of blank space to fill up.

Only three lines down from where he was a second ago, Floyd found Stoning in his bedroom, packing several unregistered firearms into a duffel bag. Two lines later he was on the interstate and crossing into Wisconsin. The thirty-four mile drive was barely noted.

He arrived at Kerslake Machinery headquarters at 10:35 a.m. and shoved two fifteen-round clips into matching nine-millimeter handguns. When he strolled in through the front door of the small building, he had four more clips in his pockets and was now toting over ninety rounds of ammunition.

Fifty-four year-old Rose Chen was working the phones on that day—it had ceased being *that fateful day* for at least ten paragraphs—and she quickly became victim number one. They knew it was quick because of the way she was gripping her pen. It was held in a light grasp and it's tip was still touching paper regardless of the hole that had been blown through the divot between her top lip and her nose. She was still sitting at her desk when they found her. Though the description of her wound was brief, Floyd could see it all too clearly.

From there, he could picture Stoning moving swiftly to the office on his right and dispatching an overly curious George Bent, who was the president of the small but rapidly expanding company. He was found in his doorway with much of his left eyeball blasted through his head, indicating to the investigators that he had probably poked his head out the door to see what in the hell that loud bang was.

Two doors down was the single room that served as the Accounting department and the occupants became victims three, four, and five. Two were still in chairs and the other was on the floor in the middle of the room when they were found.

Through a trail of bloody footprints, it was determined that he backtracked past George Bent and Rose Chen on his way to Purchasing. Jim Piscietti, the company's buyer, was found face-down halfway between his office and the reception desk. The footprint on his back led investigators to believe that he was dropped in just enough time for Stoning to step over him and get a clear shot at the company's lead project manager.

Wes Norheim was number seven and had fallen only five feet from his favorite purchasing agent. Each had a hole in his head and one of them had received a vicious throat wound as well.

Artery, vein, or trachea? Floyd asked of the book again, thinking it an odd time to start getting cheap with the information since it was already filled with a ton of garbage he didn't care about at all. At the same time, he could forgive it since things were finally moving along at a brisk pace.

It was determined that Stoning had to go through two sets of doors to reach the last three of the Janesville victims, all of whom were in Sales and located adjacent to the old machine shop. Since most of the hardware had already been moved to the new facility in Rockford, there was really no need for the sales and administrative offices to be sound-proofed anymore. They were though and the same thick walls that had kept the machine shop's racket from disturbing the rest of the employees worked just as well dampening the sounds of multiple gunshots. The authorities claimed it as the reason that none of the three salesman were able to get a call out of the building before they were killed.

There was no such excuse for the first seven victims and their silence was chalked up to the rapidness of their demise. Based mainly on bullet holes and location of the bodies, the consensus was that they had all been killed in a span of about eighteen seconds. It left barely enough time for Stoning to make eye contact with each of them if he had bothered to do so.

Before the smoke had even cleared, the book placed Stoning behind the wheel of his Camaro again and had him driving the thirty-four miles back to Rockford, where he would continue his rampage. It was a peculiarity that stood out to Perry Burgess and had been noted to the jurors during the trial as well, destroying any chance for Spencer James Stoning to live outside of a cage again.

The blackouts and the insanity defense; they simply couldn't stand up in court, given the circumstances. The extended time period involved and the mileage that had been covered didn't completely rule out insanity since there was plenty to argue in favor of it, but the cold-bloodedness of the killings gave it a personal touch that was guaranteed to keep Stoning out of the psychiatric ward. There was way too much time involved for it to be considered a spur-of-the-moment rage-killing and the blackout scenario was effectively hammered to pieces.

Crazy by itself would have landed him in a padded cell. Crazy and mean-spirited got him the same basic cell; just less padding, fewer drugs, and much uglier nurses.

As he lit another cigarette and continued to read, Floyd found Stoning back in Rockford. He was parked in his usual space, reloading his nine-millimeter clips and removing the other weapons from his duffel bag. Though Janesville had required relatively little firepower, a shotgun and an AR-15 assault rifle accompanied the shooter into his current place of business and nearly every round of the various sized ammunition was used up before he was finished. The book got a little long again but Floyd didn't mind so much at this point.

In Burgess's *Man Of Rage*, every killing in Rockford was accounted for and dwelled upon more than the Janesville killings. There were nineteen victims this time and Stoning had known each and every one of them on some kind of personal level. It took longer to read because of all the extra details and it got repetitive very quickly but Floyd managed his way through it again without much trouble.

Burgess covered all nineteen murders over eight pages, which Floyd had found morbidly interesting the first couple of times around. It was still interesting, though he thought the author could have saved a lot of time and ink by simply writing: *Victim #12 (see victim #11)*…and so on, instead of spending paragraph after paragraph going over entry points, exit wounds, and blood patterns. It was all pretty much the same after the first few but Floyd supposed those sick little details were the ones that got people to throw down their money for the book.

The only victim that really stood out from the others was the last one. Burgess probably could have filled up another page or two on the death of Stoning's best friend but chose to stick to a few simple facts for the moment. Kenneth Keyes had been shot repeatedly and was the only one to take a bullet from a distance of less than a foot. It was the most personal killing by far and had left the man with seven holes in his chest on top of the single gunshot to the side of his head that had been fired close enough to burn his hair around the entry wound. It also appeared that he had been battered somewhat prior to his death.

Damn, Stoning, Floyd thought as he took a long drag and flicked away the ashes. *I'm glad I don't have any friends like you.*

The last few paragraphs dealt with Stoning's capture, which was quite the anticlimax to an otherwise frightening chapter.

Unlike the situation in Janesville, two people had the time and the presence of mind to dial 911 before being killed. One was an administrative assistant—a poor woman who had the rotten luck of being murdered on tape—and the other was an unknown male who would never have the opportunity to be identified. When the police arrived, Stoning had already disarmed himself and was sitting on the steps in front of his former workplace. He gave up without any struggle whatsoever.

"I was just sitting there and kind of waiting to wake up, you know? I had about twenty cops inching up on me with their guns out and I couldn't stop wondering; did all this happen because my lathe caught fire? I guess it's possible, but it was probably just a case of really bad timing. Isn't it funny how things happen sometimes?"

That was how the chapter ended and Floyd closed up the book with no intention of reading any further. He knew that the one chapter would be reread a few more times but he wasn't going to spend any more brain power trudging through the rest of Burgess's self-serving waste of paper. He already had to watch the guy eat three times a day.

Floyd waited only fifteen more minutes before they returned to the car. Much like *Man Of Rage*, their actions were predictable and repetitive. They would spend a few hours bottom-feeding at the precinct before harassing a local couple and reminding them that their daughter had been murdered fifteen years ago. They would eat again and go back to their hotel room to add a chapter onto their new book. With each stop they made, he would find it easier not to care for them very much.

And she's driving again.

~ 30 ~

"Believe it or not, I think we've almost got too much stuff to work with here." Beverly flipped through her fourth notebook that was now completely full. It had been a big day for information, but then again, they all had lately. "It's already pretty good, but just wait until we trim it down and cut out the dull parts."

"You mean like being called an *opportunistic bitch?*" Burgess offered, not quite smiling as he said it. The woman who had referred to Beverly in such a way only a few hours earlier hadn't been smiling either.

"They can't go smooth all the time, Perry. How would you like to go back to all of Stoning's victim's families and ask them how they feel about his being loose? I can't help it if they have resentment towards me about what I've written. It's not my job to worry about that."

"Your job as a writer or that other one?" he asked in reply. "You know—the one where you counsel fragile people with various emotional difficulties and make them feel better about themselves. Or is that a part-time thing for you?"

"Different job, different client."

"Just another unsatisfied customer, huh?" he asked, immediately wishing he could tuck the sarcastic barb back into his ass where it had come from. The day had gone fairly smooth, though she had made him wince quite a few times with some of her questions.

"No, Perry," she replied calmly. "Each one of them is integral to the theme we've got going and every chapter needs their reaction if we want to stay consistent. Whether it's a good response or bad response it'll be a *real* response and that's what we need to give to the reader." She paused, glancing up at him and catching him looking back. It was hardly a look of admiration. "So, you think I'm the dragon-lady now? Is that what your problem is?"

"I wouldn't go that far, but still—"

"Well, it's going to get worse, so you may as well start adjusting. I've got an idea that I've been kicking around and I think it's a good one if we can make it work. I only hesitate to share it with you because you're acting like a pussy all of a sudden."

"Oh, am I? We're already cluttered up with more information than we can possibly use, but I'd just love to hear this bold, new idea of yours. And I should also let you know that every time you use the word *pussy*, all I can think about is your vagina, so—"

"We need murder scenes," she said, cutting him off before her face could redden fully. "I'm not talking about photos and forensic reports, I'm talking about being there. On site and up close. No more empty quotes from medical personnel, just straight narrative right from our point of view. Think of what it would add."

"Now, that is *definitely* not our job. First of all, it means going to Hildebrandt and begging for access—and that isn't going to happen. We're not asking and he wouldn't let us anyway. Just because he hasn't chased us away yet doesn't mean he's going to invite us inside the investigation. Secondly, we're not even investigating these crimes. We're documenting them and preparing them for public consumption. That's it. Let's try not to get confused about what we're doing here. We've already got plenty on the murder scenes."

He turned away from her, hoping he had put his foot down hard enough. It was only a half-hearted attempt to dissuade her and he knew he could have pushed much harder than he did.

With her eyes burning into the back of his head, Burgess kept his own directed into his notebook and tried to put on a look of deep concentration. The page he was currently staring at held the newly completed text that he had painstakingly disseminated from Spencer Stoning's cell walls, but he wouldn't have been able to fully focus on it right now to save his life. On top of Hewitt, Stoning, Agent Hildebrandt, and everything else he had to deal with, there was now a pretty vivid image of Beverly's vagina floating around in his head. Even as she eye-balled him, he was already thinking of ways to get her to say the word *pussy* one more time.

"Why pick now to get squeamish, Perry? You've seen bodies before."

"And you haven't," he replied, happy with the route she was trying to take. "If you think that I'm worried about myself then you're sadly mistaken. Try to remember that I'm a psychiatrist and not a psychologist like yourself—no offense. I've been an M.D. more years than Hewitt's spent in prison and I've had more blood on my hands than he'll ever be able to spill. I know you've seen some photos, but it just isn't the same."

"I know it isn't." Beverly didn't even bother to look perturbed. She was well aware of her lack of qualifications when it came to real live dead people. There had been plenty of natural deaths at the hospital where she interned in Santa Barbara but the old folks with sheets over them didn't really count. "But I'm the only one who's spent any quality time with the corpse that got away and that's saying a lot. I've seen the mess he makes. Sure, I know it isn't exactly the same thing but the only difference between number ten and all of the others was a pint of blood at the most. I think I'm prepared for it. If not, I'll learn the hard way and throw up like everyone else does the first time. It has to happen eventually."

"But you're comparing Gail Rainier, a living, breathing person that spoke to you, to a dead person who's cold and stiff. I doubt if you even saw an open wound."

"I saw her feet, Perry." She was seeing them right now in her head as she spoke. "I saw her toes all swollen up with a dark little dot where the nails went through. I was there when her bandages were changed and I saw how many stitches it took to keep her together. I couldn't count them but I saw them when the cuts were cleaned. Do dead people scream when you sanitize their wounds, Perry?"

His silence indicated that they generally did not.

"Well, she did—and she screamed loud. She screamed like it was happening all over again and she did it every time they touched her."

"And what were you doing while this was happening?" he asked, picturing a beautiful, young Beverly McGrath taking notes and gleefully putting exclamation points after each painful shriek.

"I was holding her down so she wouldn't tear out the stitches. I'd never seen fear like that in someone's face before. It was the kind of fear that made me feel like there was something in the room that *I* was supposed to be afraid of too and I haven't seen anything like it since. They started sedating her after the first few times and that made it easier."

"Made what easier? Cleaning her injuries or holding her down?"

"A whole lot of both, but mostly it's what got her talking to me."

Very subtly, she winced at the admission that had just come from her mouth and she tried to hide it quickly. It was a simple slip of the tongue and might have gone unnoticed if she hadn't winced again when she realized that wincing the first time was a mistake. She nearly winced a third time while thinking about the second one but decided to give it up before things got even worse.

"I didn't just say that, okay?"

It was silent for a moment and was now Burgess's turn to stare her down. It wasn't a judgmental glare, but one of mere professional interest—the journalistic profession; not the other one.

"Drugs?" he asked with an oddly disappointed tone. "Barbara Walters wasn't able to get Gail Rainier into an interview chair but you stroll into her hospital room and ask her questions while she's *stoned?* I don't know whether to be disgusted or impressed."

"Be impressed, Perry. Just be impressed."

"What was it—Demerol?"

"Dilauded," Beverly conceded, knowing that if the girl had been on something as mellow as Demerol there probably wouldn't have been a book at all. If she'd happened to write it anyway, Gail Rainier wouldn't have had many quotes in it, if any. "They started with Diazepam to relax her since they didn't want to have to restrain the poor girl, which would've only made the cuts on her wrists and forearms even worse. It kept her quiet throughout most of the day but didn't help a bit when they had to change her dressings."

"So they give her heavy duty pain meds just to relax her? You should know that they're not administered that way, Beverly."

"What's not painful about having your skin cut open in twenty different places? Naturally, the first concern with cuts in those locations is blood loss and arterial damage, but how often do you think about how much it actually hurts? I sure didn't. Not until I got my first look at her. She looked like a botched autopsy."

"And that's when some genius pumps her up with the most powerful stuff in the pharmacy?"

"No, they went the Percodan route first," Beverly answered with a sigh. "She was a little more comfortable but it didn't cure her mute streak when it came to talking about Stanley."

Burgess's face wrinkled up into an indignant sneer again. "Tell me you never called him *Stanley* in front of her. Please."

"Don't worry, I hadn't even seen him yet. The Dilauded was temporary and was only used to get her through the second week or so. It stopped the screaming and kept them from having to strap her down. Once the wounds healed, she'd be headed straight to Psych anyway, at which point she could scream all she wanted to, so it really worked out. Regardless of what I got out of her, she's still a well balanced human being the last time I checked and I think the doctors made all the right choices. Husband, kids, great job—I hear she's doing really good now."

"And you're not doing too badly yourself, doctor," Burgess said with a smirk. It wasn't necessarily a nice one. "All thanks to a little physician-prescribed truth serum. Dilauded—that did the trick, huh?"

"I couldn't get her to shut up on the stuff."

~ 31 ~

Beverly McGrath had just clocked out from her job at Santa Barbara Cottage Hospital when the word came that Stanley Lewis Hewitt had been arrested. The wildly excited girl, a junior named Amy Esparza that Beverly shared two classes with at UCSB, was nearly crying as she passed along the news to a quickly growing crowd in the hospital cafeteria.

There was nothing on the TV or radio to confirm her hyperventilation-ridden announcement and there were plenty of skeptics not ready to believe anything that television hadn't told them first. It seemed that something so important would have been very big news and most of the people present doubted that the information would be handed to them before the network gods got their hands on it. Then they heard about Gail Rainier and the place pretty much stopped.

Within minutes it was rumored hospital-wide that a twenty-two year-old senior from the university was in the ER and was currently being topped off with as much O-negative that her body could handle before it had the chance to spill back out of her. According to the out-of-breath storyteller, there were plenty of places for the blood to escape from and they were having a hell of a time keeping it all in. She said she was at the Admitting desk when the girl was brought in and claimed to have seen her injuries at their brutal and unclean worst.

She also said that Gail Rainier wasn't rolled into the hospital on a stretcher by EMTs. She'd been carried in by a man who's hands were already more than full.

Amy Esparza's crowd had swelled to more than fifteen staffers along with a surgeon and two administrators when the first of several uniformed police officers arrived. By the time they made their way to the jittery woman doing all the talking, the very thing she was talking about flashed onto each of the three television screens that were suspended from the ceiling in the cafeteria.

Only a person familiar with the area would have been able to tell that the image was a live shot from the police station only a few blocks away since it was too dark to get a very clear picture of what was going on. It was obvious that the single camera doing the filming was also the only thing lighting the scene and hadn't had much time to prepare for what was occurring. The sound was poor, shadows were being cast with every movement, and the person holding the camera was almost as shaky as the woman who was currently relaying the story to everyone in the room.

"That's him! That's him!" she yelled, pointing to the nearest television screen as her voice crumbled and the tears started flowing freely. There were now over twenty people in the room qualified to slap the hysterical woman but nobody did. *"He's the one who was carrying her. He's the…"* Her voice gave way to a series of gasps in the room as the lighting crew at the police station finally got it together.

In a bright flash that suddenly illuminated the front steps of their local Santa Barbara police station, the viewing audience was treated to a large black man in a gray leather coat who was turning away from the camera and shielding his eyes from the light. The blood that covered much of his clothing was spattered in different patterns from his neckline all the way down to his shoes. It was fresh enough that it hadn't turned the dark brown of old blood yet and some was still smeared on his face like war paint. A crimson stained cigarette dangled from his lips and he could be seen taking a tremendous drag while adjusting to the brightness. Strangely, he seemed very unconcerned with what was going on around him.

He was still squinting when he turned to face the camera as a second bank of lights were powered up behind him and turned the area into near daylight. He exhaled at exactly the same instant, magically transforming a simple shot of a man on some steps into the vision of a gigantic, battle-scarred African warrior that breathed smoke and fire. It may have been nothing more than a trick of the light but anybody who saw it found themselves with a serious case of chills straight up their spine. There were over twenty of them in the cafeteria experiencing it simultaneously.

As the lights were adjusted properly and the smoke blew away from his face, the man was quickly flanked by two older gentlemen on either side of him. Both were vying for his attention and asking unheard questions at a rapid-fire pace. Neither was in a uniform but it was clear that the police station was their place of business. The camera panned left and right, taking in the chaos of the scene while several people ran around yelling orders, taking photos, laying cables across the ground, and setting up microphones. It was about as live as live could get.

While this was happening on-screen, a trembling Amy Esparza found her voice again. It was hard to tell whether she was addressing the arriving police officers or her fellow staffers, but she had no shortage of avid listeners. It all came out in a half ranting and half mumbling kind of way, but everyone seemed to get the basic idea.

Just ten minutes earlier, a man—*the* man on *their* TV right now—had rushed through the sliding emergency doors fast enough and hard enough to knock one of them off of its track. He had a bleeding and ghostly pale girl over his left shoulder and was dragging a blood-covered man behind him in handcuffs. Wordlessly, he'd set the woman down and immediately bolted back through the door he had just broken.

The man being pulled along was passive and appeared ready to collapse at any second. He also looked suspiciously like the man in all those pictures that had covered everyone's TV screens for the last week.

She shuddered as the words *Stanley Lewis* came out of her mouth but fainted before she could say his last name out loud. Nobody caught her. The men on the television were beginning to speak and Amy Esparza would lay motionless on the floor until they were finished. Beverly McGrath might have taken the time to pay attention to her but she was already long gone by then.

She missed the first couple of minutes but had run fast enough to beat much of the press to the police station. With a deep red face and a heart rate she could feel pulsing in her ears, she arrived in time to hear the name *Floyd Madison* spoken aloud into a microphone for the very first time. While her counterparts watched it unfold from the hospital cafeteria, Beverly took it all in from a distance of less than ten yards. She couldn't take her eyes off of the bloody man who looked eight feet tall from where she was standing. He wouldn't speak for a while but when he finally did, he looked even taller.

The first person to take the microphone was a captain at the precinct and he gave a brief round-up of what the department thought they had their hands on. The speculation was that their relatively small jail now held a man believed to be Stanley Lewis Hewitt, though they were still seeking confirmation before stating it as an absolute fact. It was clear that they were confident but were taking a defensive posture to avoid what could quickly become a very embarrassing incident if they turned out to be wrong. Many of the scene's main players, including

Floyd Madison, came and went from the makeshift stage several times to converse with one another while more and more people poured into the area.

It wasn't until Hewitt was positively identified that the Chief of Police replaced the captain at the podium and made the announcement. By the time he did, the police station was surrounded by a crowd of over a hundred and it was still growing. The cheers that erupted from both reporters and spectators alike were filled with jubilation and relief and would be replayed on various news stations nationwide for the next twenty-four hours. On that particular evening and for a few days afterward, there would be little news to report that didn't include the name Stanley Lewis Hewitt.

Police Chief Robert Charbonneau kept the din of the crowd to a minimum while he doled out the few details he had on Hewitt's arrest, giving a nod to the still silent Floyd Madison. Since accepting Hewitt into custody was the department's sole involvement in the matter, the information was restricted to events that occurred only after Madison and Hewitt had walked through the police station's doors together. Anything that happened before then would be answered shortly but not by Chief Charbonneau. He simply didn't have the answers yet; not even about Gail Rainier's condition.

Likewise, the next person to step up didn't have much either aside from older news that everyone was already aware of. The man was a special agent with the FBI and had been assigned to the case since the third murder in Redding. His name was Alvin Schultz and over the next couple of years would play a direct role in the advancement of Beverly McGrath's career as a writer. She didn't know it yet, but within a few months of her graduation from UC Santa Barbara he would introduce her to Woodhall Penitentiary, a businessman named Matthew Chase who ran the place, and one locked down serial killer who would turn her into an overnight success.

In *Understanding The Sickness*, Agent Alvin Schultz would get a chapter of his own, though it was little more than a forum for him to vent his frustrations with the bureaucratic inadequacy of his federal employer. It didn't make or break him and he would die of a stroke fourteen years later with very little fanfare. In the public eye, the main thing that Agent Schultz would be remembered for was stepping aside for Floyd Madison on the crowded steps of a Santa Barbara police station.

He didn't introduce the man and didn't shake his hand. He just stepped aside.

A brief silence enveloped the throng of reporters as Floyd Madison moved in front of a steadily growing tangle of microphones. He slowly scanned the crowd from left to right, making eye-contact with anyone willing to stare back at him.

There were quite a few who did but his eyes lingered a little longer over the young woman in a candy striper's uniform whose intensity was the closest to matching his own. He would remember that face and she would forever remember his.

For over twenty seconds there were no words. When it became clear that the immense figure had no statement of any kind to make, approximately thirty reporters fired off a fusillade of questions at him all at once. It seemed to be what he had been waiting for and the first hint of grin appeared on his face. It was just a little smile but even that tiny gesture had a deep and stoic strength to it. His form disappeared in a hail of flashbulbs while the journalists shouted each other down and jockeyed for position.

How did you find him? Was there a struggle? Were you injured? Who's blood is that? Where are you from? Is she still alive?

For almost a minute the questions poured in. Still staring out into the crowd, he waited for one that appealed to him. He didn't have to wait long.

What do you do for a living? It was as good as any but seemed like the place he wanted to start. He answered this one without hesitation.

"I do what I can."

The PA speakers struggled with the sudden amount of bass flowing through them and everyone present felt those five words vibrating through their chests. His voice was deeper than anything anyone had expected, thrilling the reporters to no end. He had uttered only one sentence and was already a story unto himself.

This was no badge-carrying, uniform-wearing, feel-good kind of hero. This was Goliath straight out of the Old Testament and he was representing the good guys this time.

For almost an hour, Floyd Madison fielded questions, answering with a cold confidence and drawing laughs as well as horrified gasps seemingly at will. He never interrupted anyone while they were speaking, never got flustered by the sheer volume of simultaneous queries, and only spoke when spoken to. The man would soon be known for his gift of gab as much as anything else but he didn't try to show off on his first night of stardom. He didn't need to and didn't know how to yet. It would all come to him in time.

Only two months later he would be celebrated again for bringing home a missing fifteen year-old girl named Janine Nylander but for the day of Hewitt's arrest, his repertoire consisted of responses to direct questions only. His status as a savior was already written in stone. There was no reason to go overboard.

Beverly McGrath, who was already taking notes, didn't speak to him that night but would get answers, opinions, and plenty more wisdom from him during the following eighteen months. Eventually, she would spend countless hours with many of the same characters who were scattered around the police station that evening, but her first order of business was a simple task; much simpler than corralling an FBI agent or a suddenly famous bounty hunter in the midst of real, professional reporters with many year's worth of credentials.

Her task was to get an 'A' in Journalism for the Spring quarter and Beverly knew she had the means to earn it. She didn't have access to Floyd Madison or Special Agent Alvin Schultz just yet, but she certainly had access to a brand new patient named Gail Rainier.

Beverly was only an intern—an unpaid intern, earning a few college credits for her Psych degree by emptying bedpans and delivering meals—but it put her in a much closer proximity to the victim than any genuine reporter could ever hope to achieve. The territory would be familiar and she would return to work with a renewed sense of purpose.

Day-one was a bust. It was only a failure because Ms. Rainier was still in the ICU and didn't have the courtesy to remain conscious for more than a minute at a time. The good news was that no one else was getting to her either. It was enough to keep her hopeful.

Day-two netted some progress, though the girl was still physically and mentally unreachable. She was in and out of consciousness throughout most of the day and Beverly was able to approach her room without much notice. Actually entering the room was a problem that she hadn't overcome yet, but that issue would work itself out once she was transferred out of the ICU.

Day-three was what made it all happen and was through an equal combination of luck and tenacity. Gail Rainier's painful thrashings played a good part in it as well, but the good fortune belonged to Beverly for hovering around the girl's room at the best of all possible times.

It was an early shift and the patient was partially awake and alert for the first time since she'd been brought in. The physician in charge that day made the mistake of sending in only one nurse to check Gail's wounds for signs of infection and the mistake was heard clearly from one end of the floor to the other. There were plenty of other doctors and nurses nearby, but when the screaming started and the flailing began, the nurse's urgent call for help was responded to by the person nearest to them. Naturally, it was the person who had made sure to be near her for days.

With the moment finally upon her, Beverly didn't hesitate and soon found herself pinning a terrified woman to her hospital bed while the RN struggled with her bandages. The examination ended abruptly and all their effort went into restraining the patient without inflicting any further damage. By the time help arrived, Gail Rainier had stopped screaming and was reduced to mere sobbing and fear-induced paralysis.

The doctor who administered the sedative found his patient grasping tightly to the young intern who had been holding her down moments earlier and she didn't look ready to let go any time soon. She didn't fight the hypodermic needle and was unresponsive to all stimuli, with the exception of the soothing words being whispered into her ear by the girl who was cradling her in her arms while trying to keep the gaps in her wrists and forearms from widening further. They hung on to each other until a relatively light shot of Demerol sent Gail deep into the land where things stopped hurting and mattered much less. She was examined and got fresh bandages while she slept.

The doctor didn't ask Beverly why she was in the patient's room and didn't ask what she had been saying to her when he walked in. All he asked was for her to be present the next time they tried to change her bandages. He insisted, in fact. The patient had been calmed, the doctor had been impressed, and Beverly McGrath had been connected. There was no need to be sneaky after that and the rest was simple.

*   *   *   *

The patient recovered slowly over the following weeks, though she wouldn't knowingly speak of her ordeal with Stanley Hewitt to anyone. All requests for interviews were rebuffed and she refused to even acknowledge the incident, much less speak openly about it. While every accomplished journalist in the business was ready to kill for a chance to find out the details of what Stanley Lewis Hewitt did behind closed doors, somebody else was finding out a little bit more every night, compliments of an IV tube and the chemicals that dripped through it.

She would remember Beverly McGrath as a friend of sorts—a friend who only seemed to appear through a hazy fog of pharmaceutical bliss—but it was better than being alone when the darkness came.

By the time she was released, Gail Rainier was given a clean bill of health and through a great deal of unhealthy repression would be able to block out much of that had happened to her. In six months time she would graduate only a semester late and in another six months would finally be able to sit alone in a room by herself. Gradually, life became normal again.

About a year or so after that she would read a brand new book called *Understanding The Sickness* and for the first time would remember what it was like to be nailed to a floor. It set her back a little.

~ 32 ~

"Now...exactly who's sickness is it that I'm supposed to be understanding when I read this book?" Burgess asked, browsing the cover of a fresh looking copy. He guessed she didn't go anywhere without one. "Hewitt's or yours?"

"Keep being clever, Perry. I think the sickness you're talking about right now doesn't have a thing to do with Stanley or Spencer Stoning. You and I are both afflicted with it, so you can take your self-righteousness and stick it up your ass."

They turned their backs on each other at the same moment and returned to their own pursuits rather than let a night's worth of work turn into a verbal slug-fest. Her newspaper articles were much more coherent than the rantings of Spencer James Stoning that Burgess was dealing with but they were probably just as baffling. Since she had just shut him down pretty hard, there was a tendency not to ask him for any kind of assistance. It was a team effort, though, and she decided to ask anyway.

"And when you're done sticking it up your ass...could you tell me what I'm supposed to know about the Roadside Butcher and explain to me why I'm reading about him?"

Burgess put his notebook down and faced her; mostly to see if she was kidding or not. "You just lost me in about ten different ways. Why are you reading about the Butcher?"

"I'm not—well, I *am*, but I'm talking about Stanley. These are his papers. They're what he kept in his cell back in Woodhall."

"And that's what he was reading about?"

"I can't be sure," she replied. "He didn't keep little snippets or articles. He kept the whole paper. They were all were in good as new condition like they were part of a collection. I've got eighteen of them from the archives here and twelve of them mention the Roadside Butcher in at least one article. What's that about?"

"He's probably a fan." There was no sarcasm in the statement.

"It wouldn't surprise me, but it's weirder than just a few articles. He cut up his victims. Did you know that?"

"Who—the Butcher?" Burgess asked in reply, trying to keep his face straight. "Is that why they call him that? Give me a second and I might be able to explain the significance of the word *roadside* to you next."

"Shut up and get serious for a minute. The papers with the Butcher articles are all recent. There are twelve from the last six months and they include five murders from the Seattle area. Five of the papers broke each story and seven more were strictly follow-up pieces to those same stories. The other six issues on the list are older—about fifteen years older."

"Right around when Hewitt went inside," Burgess mused.

"Way too early for the Butcher, right?"

"Fifteen years too early," he agreed.

She scrolled back and forth from the oldest paper on the list to the newest and converted it into one long flowing document. After marking each of the articles that interested her, she deleted the rest of the text and was left with eighteen stories on less than five pages. It was much easier to look at as she skimmed several of the articles and noted the differences between them. What was stranger still were the similarities between them. Even the ones that were fifteen years apart.

"The older papers have murders too," she noted. "Not first-run type material, but just the leftovers. Follow-up pieces."

"So?"

"So, look at the MO."

She handed him the five sheets of paper. Seemingly unimpressed with what he was reading, he skimmed briefly over each page then handed them back.

"It's not exactly something we need to go see the Oracle about, Beverly. Yes, parts of the MO are roughly the same: female victims, multiple slashings, and the bodies dumped—wait for it—by the side of a road. It's no different from the Green River Killer or the Hillside Stranglers or any of the others who didn't have a better place to dump their leftovers. What does it all mean? It means Hewitt has a thing for unimaginative cutters. I don't find anything odd about it."

"You don't find anything odd about—?"

"From Hewitt's standpoint," he clarified, quickly. "To the average person—a normal person with normal tastes—it would definitely seem weird. For a guy like Hewitt though, it would make perfect sense for him to take an interest in a killer like this. *Any* killer. If you were one, wouldn't you be curious about what the others were doing? It's a pretty exclusive club."

"Why just these two then? Explain that. Why save articles on these two Washington killers with similar MOs with such long a gap in between? There have been plenty more to choose from over the last fifteen years."

"I've got two answers for you and then I'm going to sleep." He yawned widely to illustrate his point. "One—and this is just a guess—I'm thinking Hewitt likes something very specific about this type of crime. Like his murders, these weren't hatchet-jobs and the victims weren't just hacked up. None of these were the work of some idiot running around with a machete and cutting people's heads off. They were slow and methodical. Anybody could kill someone with a knife if they really needed to, but I don't think there are too many people capable of the examples we're talking about. It'd be hard to cut a person like that. Maybe he admires these guys for what they do or how they do it…or maybe he's just envious."

She wasn't upset by his response and even seemed to think about it a little. "And the second answer?"

"It's pretty simplistic. You'll be disappointed with me."

"Nothing new about that," she said. "But share it with me anyway."

"I think—just another guess—that he probably *is* interested in other serial murderers and lots of other things, for that matter. If he read something in the newspaper and he thought was remotely notable he'd probably save it. He keeps his little mementos for a few months and then guess what happens."

"Okay, what happens?"

"Ryan Williams or some other guard at Woodhall tosses his cell and tells him he's got too much shit laying around. They start thinking about an old inmate named Suarez who lit his newspapers on fire."

"Actually, I think it was *Juarez*," she inserted, agreeing with his point but keeping the playing field level by correcting him at the same time.

"Whatever. He probably throws them away, Bev—that's all I'm saying. The old ones are keepers for whatever reason and the latest batch that he hasn't gotten around to throwing away yet would be on the top and would naturally have the most recent news in them. Haven't we got enough to work with already without having to resort these kinds of page fillers?"

"I didn't say I was going to write about it," she protested. "I was just looking for an opinion. Maybe I should have asked someone else."

~ 33 ~

"No, they're good, man," Spencer argued, feeling ridiculous that he had to sell it so hard. The notebook he'd bought for Stanley was filling up slowly and he was finally asked to take a look at what appeared to be a disjointed and disorienting coloring book. He knew it would happen eventually but he hadn't been looking forward to it. "*Really* good. How come I've never seen you draw anything before?"

"No one's ever asked me to do it," Stanley replied, avoiding eye contact and staring down at his shoes. "I know they're not as neat as yours, but—"

"Stop saying that, Stan. It's pathetic."

Spencer took another look at each of the pages that were covered with some of the worst shit he had ever seen, struggling to keep the pleasant expression on his face. He guessed that if Stanley tried to draw a dog or a house, the images would be somewhere around the third or fourth grade level—which really would have been fine. In this case, however, he had tried to emulate Spencer's own style of weirdness and it came out as badly as could be expected.

"Are you trying to get me to tell you that they're ugly?" he asked. "Because I'll do that if you really want me to. And if you're fishing around for some suggestions then you should just come out and ask. I can do that if you want but then they'll be more like me and less like you, which really defeats the purpose of being artistic in the first place. Is that what you want?"

"I just want you to show me how to do it."

Spencer sighed heavily and scooted across the stolen minivan's bench seat and moved closer so they could view Stanley's artwork together. The theft of Spencer's technique was blatant but was only slightly irksome to him. If it was something bigger or of great importance he guessed he would have been as livid as Stanley got whenever someone stole from him. He picked up the pen and pointed to the first image that grabbed his attention.

"This thing—what's it supposed to be?"

"It's a palm tree."

"Okay, then," Spencer said with another sigh, putting the pen to paper. "Are you sure you want me fucking with this? It's already good."

"Come on, man."

There was no getting around it. He wasn't sure if Stanley would truly get it or not but he didn't see any reason to leave him in the dark when it came to inducing shivers through creativity. He suspected none of it would stick in his brain anyway.

"Okay—first you need to darken all the borders. It's got to be bold. Every one of these lines needs to be heavier so the person who looks at it knows you were serious as fuck when you drew it. Understand?"

He received a nod. Stanley didn't take his eyes off of Spencer's hands while he worked.

"Now, all this blank space here in the leaves—these *are* leaves right?"

"Yeah…or palms, I guess."

"Well, that space is empty right now and it needs to be full. It needs to be busier so it catches the eye…but only for a second. You see, you're gonna have another thing over here on the…uh…"

"It's the sun."

"Right—the sun," Spencer agreed, already shifting his pen to the not quite round object. He started darkening the borders as he spoke. "We're gonna put some stuff in here that's gonna pull their eyes away from the palm tree…" He shifted back to the leaves of the palm tree and started writing. "…then right back to it." The word *death* now filled up the newly darkened outline of Stanley's palm leaf. It was barely noticeable. "After a second, they find the next one and a little idea starts wiggling around in their head." He went to work on Stanley's imperfect sun and within a few seconds the sun was nearly black. "Maybe they'll see it…" The few miniscule white spaces left in the dark disk formed the word *pain*. "…and maybe they won't." He turned his attention to something that looked like a bird. "They can still ignore it if they don't look too hard at this." The bird had quickly morphed into a cloud, giving more depth to the whole picture. "But then they're screwed because they've already seen it." It was a puffy white thing that now covered almost a quarter of the page and contained strange curved lines and textures. He didn't adorn the cloud with any words or images. "They'll read whatever they want in this one even though there isn't anything there. You'll see what I mean in a minute." His hand flew across the page as he put the finishing touches—many of them—on the lined sheet of notebook paper. "They'll want to make some sense out of it..." Random words, phrases and even a few numbers were scattered about the scenery. "...and when they find out they can't, it eats them all up; especially those FBI profiler types who think they can read your mind by feeling the lumps in your shit. Do you get it?"

"I think so," Stanley replied, still looking uncertain. He pointed to a spot on the page. "But what are these things down here in—?"

"No, you don't get it yet," Spencer explained, trying to keep his patience reined in tightly. "Look here where we started. *Death*. *Death* hidden in the palms of this tree right here. Next we've got the black sun of *pain*. *Pain* in the sun and *death* up in the tree. Wicked, huh? Now, over here we've got our cloud. What do you see?"

"I see lots of stuff. What does it mean?"

"That's the question, Stan. What does it mean to you?" Spencer thought he was almost there. "Do you need any *help*?"

"Okay—I see the word *help* right there. And there's *peace*. And *love*. I can see it now. And a few numbers maybe. A two and a six."

"That's good. Add them up. What do you get?"

"Eight," Stanley answered with what Spencer thought was surprising speed.

"That's right. Now, take everything else you see there and add *that* up too. The words, the numbers, the tree, the sun—everything—add it all up. Then look back at the cloud. What do you see?"

Stanley did as instructed and took his time scrutinizing the details of what had become of his happy little beach scene. After a minute, he started to shake his head in frustration. It was all there and every bit of it was fighting for his attention, pulling him in many directions at once. He looked back to the cloud and still saw nothing. He could have lied and made something up but he didn't.

"I don't see anything in the cloud. Whatever it is, I'm not seeing it. All I see is *peace, love, death, pain, help*, and a two and a six that add up to the number eight. What does it mean?"

"The cloud should tell you. Hell, I already told you when I drew the fucking thing. What's in the cloud, Stan?"

"Well..." he stammered, going over his options one more time. He knew what each of the words meant and he could count a lot higher than eight, so he didn't see why it had to be so damn difficult. He wanted it to be there so bad. "…I guess it could be a—"

"You *lose*, Stan," Spencer said suddenly, waving him off and hoping that some kind of point had been made. "You were right the first time and you should have stuck with your gut feeling. I pushed you, so it's not really your fault, but it's not always necessary to read between the lines or search for the answer to the riddle. Sometimes words are just words and numbers are just numbers…and sometimes it's just a fucking cloud. Get it?"

Stanley's face went from confused to pleasantly stunned. He didn't get it very often but he certainly got this one.

"So, it's really nothing? It doesn't mean anything?"

"Well, it's not *nothing*," Spencer replied. "It's still a nice little picture with plenty to look at, but it *is* just a big flurry of brain crap. It's scary and pretty and bold and stuff but it sure doesn't add up to shit when it comes to creeping into *my* fucking head. It's fun and games—not much more too it than that."

"All that stuff on your walls back at Woodhall?"

"Tom-foolery," Spencer answered dryly. "A bigger workspace means your eyes are bouncing back and forth between two things six feet apart instead of only six inches. It'll scare you, give you a headache, and get you dizzy as hell too, I swear."

"The windows?"

"Something pretty to look at, Stan. Fun and games."

"Even the door?"

"No, you got me on that one," Spencer told him. "I did it mostly to be a smart-ass but it'll make everything more interesting later on, you'll see. Maybe it was ego, but I couldn't stand the idea of letting people actually think that the Carrolls set *us* loose. I couldn't help it."

It was already past nine p.m. and they hadn't found a place to sleep yet thanks to the early press conference on top of the regular preparation that kept them busy most days. As before, finding shelter would be the next order of business since the minivan would only be safe for another few hours. They would ditch it as soon as possible; probably before it would even be reported stolen if their luck was still with them.

From there, they would remain on foot and exist for two days within the same half-mile perimeter; a perimeter they shared with hundreds of people who wanted them to die. Once situated, they would scour the streets for a face that had some meaning; someone with potential.

For two days it would be a game of looking and waiting. Waiting and looking. Looking for the pattern they knew was there but was hiding somewhere among the clouds that surrounded them.

For now, they would settle for a night of sleep wherever they could find it. It could be a hotel room, an apartment, or even a house in a residential neighborhood. It was all the same to Spencer as long as there was someone at home to let them in and they didn't mind being called George for an extended period of time.

~ 34 ~

For the past two weeks, the third day in any one city meant that the big moment had arrived and things were about to come to a head. The FBI knew it and thanks to the media machine that churned out every nasty detail they could get their hands on, the average citizen knew it too. They were the target audience after all and this was a roller coaster ride that they didn't have to stand in line for. In a very low kind of way, it was just another form of entertainment at its greatest extreme. The required build-up had been completed, the opening acts were done performing, and the day-three finale was set to begin.

For the agents involved it meant coordinating with the city's police force and keeping a profile so high that even the garden variety felons skipped town and went on vacation for a few days. Aside from a single murder that everyone knew was coming, the crime rate in Sacramento dropped over ninety percent for the three day period.

For Floyd Madison, the third day meant an endless night of cruising the streets in his car, eyeballing every face that he passed and keeping an ear tuned in to his police radio scanner. It was the same futile routine he'd started way back in Redding and it hadn't helped in the least. On a more positive note, however, it meant that if and when the shit hit the fan, he would be able to get to the scene in a matter of minutes and upstage any latecomers to the show. He already knew that luck didn't just happen to most folks; it required at least a tiny bit of persistence. He had nothing better to do anyway.

For Doctors Beverly McGrath and Perry Burgess, the last evening meant that it was time to start packing for the next stop. They already had the car gassed up and hotel reservations in a place called Pleasanton. The third days were quieter, almost somber times and things between them generally rolled a little smoother on that third day. It also didn't hurt that their collaborative effort was practically writing itself by now.

To all interested parties, the end of the third day had been a foregone conclusion since the murder in Altamont. It was right about 9:40 pm when time ran out in the city of Sacramento.

✳   ✳   ✳   ✳

Danielle Morgan, a twenty-seven year-old single mother of two, made orphans out of her twin boys in less time than it took to conceive them. She would be the victim that stood out from the rest. Her wounds were much deeper and in a greater abundance than the others; only two of the indicators that Ms. Morgan was more of a fighter than the women that had fallen before her.

Unlike the murders in Vancouver, Altamont, Redding, Chico, and Yuba City, Sacramento's Danielle Morgan wasn't still standing when her body was located. She was found in her hallway only a few feet from her children's room and had all the signature markings of a standard Hewitt outing with a few exceptions. Those exceptions would generate bigger headlines on the following day than any of the other victims.

This one wasn't bled slowly and, in fact, wouldn't die from blood loss at all. She was stabbed deeply and repeatedly in the back until her heart stopped from the sheer damage to it. Though the scenario differed mildly because of some extenuating circumstances, there was no doubt about whose MO was at work before things shifted gears and deviated from their usual course.

The forensic team counted seventeen stab wounds that had occurred while she'd crawled along on her belly, struggling to cover the twenty feet that separated her from her children. Aside from the brutal stabbing, it was obvious to see why she had been crawling.

When the first officer found her, the three layers of duct tape were still covering her mouth, her eyes were still wide open, and six of her ten toes were still nailed to the floor in her bedroom. Some of them had torn free, leaving large splits in the four toes that remained attached to her feet while the others were wrenched off at the bone and had stayed behind. The six tiny digits were found tacked to the floor in the corner of the room with carpenter's nails protruding from them.

For whatever reason—fear, survival, or maternal instinct—she simply refused to play the game as it had been advertised and made the decision to move, regardless of whether her toes came with her or not. It didn't make any difference in the end but spoke volumes for the woman's constitution.

In the rough draft of Beverly and Burgess's as of yet untitled work of non-fiction, Danielle Morgan would get chapter nine all to herself. It was agreed that she'd earned it.

The two children were found in their own room unharmed but, much to the doctor's chagrin, were entirely too young to be interviewed. It was a genuine pity since a decent description of what they heard on the other side of their bedroom door that evening might have extended the chapter another couple of pages and given the reader an idea of the kind of sounds a person made while being nailed, slashed, mutilated, and stabbed to death. The children had no such input to offer.

No, the twin three year-olds had probably slept through the ordeal and were essentially useless to the process of documenting their mother's slaying. Journalistically speaking, it was quite the tragedy.

~ 35 ~

This one was making his stomach turn and, amazingly, it wasn't such a bad feeling. It was a nauseous sensation that Floyd hadn't felt in a few years and he momentarily enjoyed it before the novelty had a chance to wear off. Even at its worst, he didn't throw up—he never did anymore. Instead, he set the newspaper on the passenger seat, climbed out of his car, and crossed the street, ignoring the yellow tape that surrounded the house like a shiny bright bow on a really bad present. It was seven-thirty a.m.

Taking out a pad of paper, he confirmed the address he had written down, though the yellow tape already told him he was at the right place. The four numbers were right next to the name *Danielle Morgan*, which was directly below five other names and addresses and, as before, there was no mystical clue climbing off the page to tell him what to do next. There was nothing similar about the data and nothing dissimilar enough to be noteworthy; just a few names and numbers that had absolutely nothing in common with each other no matter how long he looked at them. There was no pattern at all. He'd known it even before pulling up to the house but figured that it couldn't hurt to do a little sleuthing.

He walked across the driveway and stepped up to the front door of the small house, where he paused for a moment and peered down at his notes. He wasn't really reading, however, and his eyes weren't even focused on the small page. He was simply waiting. Patiently, he started counting silently in his head.

When his mental clock reached ninety seconds he turned around quickly and dashed back to the sidewalk across from his car. Like a child learning to safely cross a street for the first time, he looked left, right, then left again. There was nothing to see. He repeated the move quickly enough to put a kink in his neck then looked back to the house, then back to the car. He scanned the houses all around him and even looked up into the trees that lined the street. Nothing.

Tom Devereaux wasn't behind him and he wasn't anywhere down the block on either side of the street. Nobody was there and nothing had changed since he had pulled up, which temporarily cleansed away the paranoia that had been nagging at him. The only sign of life came from the house that he had parked in front of.

From between the curtains that were slightly parted, an old woman gaped at him with unhidden curiosity. It wasn't unexpected. She'd probably seen a lot of people come and go from her former neighbor's house over the last day and a half and didn't look very concerned with his presence.

After a minute of staring, he raised a large hand and slowly waved to her. She took the time to wave back before disappearing, letting the curtains drop back into a closed position. Aside from the few people he'd had brief monetary discourses with—waiters, waitresses, and motel clerks, mostly—it was as social as he'd been in two weeks. Maybe longer. He returned to the doorway and entered the house without hesitating this time.

By the time he had picked the lock, cut through the crime scene seal, and stepped in through the door, he had committed at least two felonies that he was aware of. There might have been a few more but he shrugged them off as easily as the first set of infractions.

Don't worry, he told himself sarcastically as he scanned the living room and kitchen for other points of entry. *They're just federal charges. I'll only do three or four years if my lawyer's a slick bastard.*

One of the first things he noticed was that the house had been cleverly remodeled by the FBI in some areas, though there was little in the way of fingerprinting dust to be seen. He could also smell a variety of chemicals, indicating that the old-school methods had been tossed aside in favor of high-tech laser devices, photography, and probably a bunch of other advances that he hadn't had the time to read about yet.

He noted two large windows in the living room and one in the tiny kitchen just over the sink. None of them had screens or any kind of locking mechanisms that would deter a person carrying anything more sophisticated than a screwdriver. The large sliding glass door that led to the backyard was in the same unsecured state. He suspected it would be the same in all the rooms and stopped thinking about break-in scenarios at that point since an intruder could have stealthily entered from just about anywhere.

And some of us intruders come in right through the front door. Jesus, Ms. Morgan, didn't you even watch the news? Didn't you know what was out there?

Of course she did. Everybody did. Like everyone else though, she just didn't think it could happen to her. If Hewitt had wanted to come in through one of the many windows, she could have saved her own life with a two dollar purchase at any hardware store. A six foot wooden dowel was fifty cents the last time he checked and they were incredibly easy to cut in halves, thirds, or quarters to lay in a window track, making it utterly impossible to open without breaking some glass and making an ungodly amount of noise. As he browsed through the rest of the house and counted up the windows, Floyd shook his head sadly and readjusted his figure down to a buck fifty. For the price of six quarters she could have lived or, at the very least, heard him breaking in and prepared herself for death a little better.

When he reached her bedroom, a bout of the sweats replaced his queasiness. It wasn't the dried blood that covered the walls that got to him or even the fact that this was the place that she only *started* to die in; it was the little movie that ran in his head when he pictured her rebelling against what was certainly a no-win situation. His mind's eye showed him the whole deal from start to finish with nothing omitted.

He could see her bleeding from gashes on her wrists, forearms, inner elbow joints, thighs, the backs of her knees, and finally her ankles, right in the sensitive area adjacent to the Achilles tendon. Of course, the tendons and various ligaments themselves were never severed completely since it would be like cutting the strings on a marionette. Without strings, the puppet wouldn't be able to stand and for reasons that he didn't care to think about, Hewitt's sickness required it.

A book he had read by the very woman he was tailing claimed to offer some type of understanding of that sickness. Of course, it didn't really—not by a long shot even though Floyd managed to feel bad for Hewitt at various points throughout. Sure, he'd had some tough times in his younger years but so did a lot of people and those people didn't solve their internal nightmares with a hammer and nails.

Although her book was a pretty smooth read and had more technical background than Dr. Perry Burgess's book—not to mention a hero that Floyd thought was the greatest in all of literature—it struggled to answer an unanswerable question by asking the reader to actually understand it. As if Stanley Lewis Hewitt was worthy of understanding. Somehow, he doubted that Danielle Morgan would care to understand it.

Floyd could picture her feet stuck to the floor in the most painful way imaginable and cringed at the thought of what that first moment of defiance must have felt like. With blood flowing from every appendage, he guessed she might have known that she had very little to lose aside from another pint or two of fluids. But still, the pain had to have been several increments past the maximum that a body found tolerable.

He wondered if her toes had torn apart and popped out of their moorings one at a time or if it happened all at once in some adrenaline filled moment of desperation. There were several ways it could have gone, though it would be hard to pick a preference.

He prayed that it had been quick. He hoped it was a swift and final grasp for life that ended only a few seconds later in her hallway under a hail of uncharacteristically merciful plunges of steel through her heart by a man who hadn't yet bothered much with the concept of mercy. It seemed a strange thing to hope for but one that far outweighed the alternative; an alternative that might have included a couple of children. It wasn't part of Hewitt's MO but, then again, neither was stabbing someone to death in such a crude fashion.

To many people—lay persons outside of the *"missing and presumed dead"* industry—there might not appear to be much of a difference between hacking, slicing, and good old-fashioned, between-the-ribs organ puncturing; but the differences were huge and said as much about the criminals as it did their crimes. Floyd knew the difference and had seen it up close. The victims and the criminals alike—up close. Men and women of all ages—so close he could smell them before locating what was left of them.

Children—*too* close. Way too fucking close.

*   *   *   *

Taking on jobs that involved kids sounded ideal at first; even noble to a certain extent. In theory, they were an angle that really couldn't miss when it came to the publicity side of things. They were worth more to the clients, which were almost always parents of the missing, and would garner much more attention than the average adult because of the vulnerability factors involved. Another bonus was that there were tons of them missing out there.

Sure, there were plenty of folks in the upper age brackets that dropped out of sight on a daily basis but, by virtue of their adulthood, were legally entitled to fade away into the land of the vanished if they so desired. Many did it for a multitude of reasons, but there were plenty of others that were dragged kicking and screaming into it, having made no plans of their own that involved "turning into smoke" as Floyd once liked to say. He didn't say it so much anymore.

While Stanley Hewitt made him a name, and Janine Nylander made him the recognized and celebrated Protector of the Realm, a six year-old boy named Brian Lee knocked him down a few pegs. He had been missing for less than a week when Floyd got the call. The lucky guess and the gut feeling—Hewitt and Nylander, respectively—had now been replaced by a genuine case of a missing child.

Things would be different from that point forward.

He was paid a hefty advance this time and didn't make his first investigative phone call until the check had cleared. It wasn't that the inexperienced man-hunter's ego had inflated to a ridiculous level, rather it was the sheer volume of messages on his new voicemail system and paper flowing from his fax machine that forced him to be selective about which jobs to take on. Now was the crucial time to decide in which direction he wanted to go.

When he tallied his first two day's worth of offers, along with many beggings and pleadings from those not endowed with fat bags of cash, he chose to go the route that was more TV friendly. Plus, kid-finding was still a nobler pursuit he had reminded himself. There was no doubt in his mind that his life could have turned out much different had he gone in another direction.

If he had chosen the skip-tracing and bounty-hunting scene, where the assignments were open to all takers with no pressure or commitment to produce the bad guys, he could have failed without anyone ever knowing about it. Bounty hunters weren't offered cash in advance and they didn't make any promises to deliver. Nobody really cared about the missing party, plus the client—a jilted bondsman or state or federal agency—wasn't too particular about what condition his fugitive was returned in. In hindsight, it was the safer bet.

A bounty hunter could have fifty jobs going at one time, placing priority on those which paid more or the ones that had the hottest leads, not to mention the targets of opportunity that might drop into their lap. It wasn't the same when it came to locating people's loved ones.

On top of the advance, which was a retainer much like a lawyer would require, there would need to be money for expenses—a concept that Floyd quickly found himself comfortable with. Accepting money implied a certain amount of effort on the part of the payee, making it much more difficult to create the huge case load he imagined himself having while still being effective as an investigator. It wasn't long before he wished he hadn't decided to specialize—or that he'd specialized in something a little tamer; perhaps finding lost dogs or taking surreptitious photos of cheating husbands and wives. A lot of people made a living doing such things but, then again, they didn't get to see pictures of themselves in *Time* magazine either. For the man in his late twenties, still young and still a wild trouble-seeker, the choice had been ridiculously easy back then.

It got more difficult when it took over a month for Floyd to find Brian Lee scattered around in his own backyard, but he justified it by the fact that the police with their dogs and other vast resources hadn't found him either. Apparently, the gardener who had sodomized and strangled the child knew a thing or two about covering up his messes and had become quite proficient at masking the odor of one type of decay with another. By the time his trial was over, he had been convicted in a federal court for four similar murders in three other states.

Those weren't mine, Floyd remembered thinking defensively as he'd read about the other murders at the trial's conclusion. It wasn't to say that six year-old Brian Lee's death was his responsibility—it most certainly wasn't, and they later learned he was dead even before anyone knew he was missing—but it was still Floyd's case. There was no blame, but still there was guilt for it. He took their money, gave them hope, and had given precious little in return.

He couldn't even offer retribution for the crime, which was something he was sure he would have done if the murderer had been available to him. In a not so odd way he even felt obligated. It wouldn't quite be a refund but would show that he cared in ways that couldn't be put into words. Whether it be by gun, a piece of piano wire, or a simple but thorough pummeling with a Louisville Slugger, he felt it was a debt owed to the boy, his parents, and to himself as well.

This one, however, he would never get close enough to. In fact, the imprisoned man would do himself in several years later in a bizarre act of self immolation, using newspapers of all things. It happened right there in his prison cell, though Floyd was sure that if the man was ever paroled for any reason he would have burned anyway. Maybe he wouldn't have gone up like a human torch but one way or another, figuratively or literally, he would have burned.

There were some that were avenged and even more that weren't. It was a give-and-take arrangement that often required more giving on his part than taking. They weren't all bad, though, and there were quite a few successes along the way.

These were the ones that shot across the airwaves and onto TV screens while the failures were downplayed, if they were even mentioned at all. And, realistically, there was no reason to mention them. He didn't snatch the children to begin with. That honor belonged to others.

It belonged to strangers much of the time, acquaintances most of the time, neighbors more often than he was comfortable with, and direct family members enough of the time to make him want to puke. It wasn't anything he would ever discuss on the talk show circuit and some of it was too outlandish to be believed anyway. Explaining that many of his cases didn't need to be investigated any further than the family's own home or neighborhood probably wasn't something that people wanted to hear.

During the Janine Nylander ordeal, Detective Adams had warned him about the reality of his profession but his words had seemed too cynical at the time. They didn't now. Just once, Floyd wished he could go on the record and tell it like it really was.

The pair of young siblings killing the newborn that drew too much of their parents attention: *Happens at least once a year, Montel. Jealousy is a scary thing. They tossed that one in an orange grove like a piece of bad fruit. Go figure.*

The little girl who vanished right out of her own upstairs bedroom on a school night: *Daddy's regular Wednesday night session got a little out of hand, Sally. He played too rough and broke his favorite toy, that's all. Tried to make that one look like a kidnapping—they always do when they pull the rope too tight and fuck their kids to death. If his wife's parents hadn't hired me, they'd still be hanging on to their sad little hopes for her recovery…and that wouldn't be fair, would it?*

The twelve year-old softball star who never came home from practice: *Found her in the weeds a mile away and two weeks too late. I heard she had a great throwing arm but all I got to see was plants growing around what was left of her. I went after her coach on a gut feeling. Rode him pretty hard for a few weeks before I found out I was wrong. Didn't even apologize to the fucker. I usually don't.*

The wife of a local snack-bar manager who hadn't seen her husband in over a month. He hadn't packed any clothes, his credit card hadn't been used, and his car was still in the driveway: *He wasn't a kid but I did that one for free, Maury. Felt obligated, I guess. The guy's wife didn't have any money and, to be honest with you, I already knew where his body was. You see, I put him there myself…well, Detective Adams may have helped a little. He was always good with that inadmissible evidence kind of stuff and hated being handicapped by the judicial system. I figured the woman never needed to know that her husband had raped and murdered a twelve year-old girl since we wouldn't have been able to prove it in court anyway. It would have made her feel foolish and I was already feeling foolish enough for the both of us—you know, for wasting all that time on the softball coach instead of the guy selling the candy.*

It's a sick world, friend, and that sickness is contagious. It'll warp your mind if you're not careful—just take a look at me. But that's all between us, Geraldo. You're not taping this, are you?

He could imagine the host's response to such inspired banter if he'd ever had the guts to say it out loud. It would have made for some great afternoon TV.

✳   ✳   ✳   ✳

Walking out of the tainted bedroom and stepping carefully around what was left of the floor in the hallway, Floyd moved back into the living room and took a seat in what looked like the most comfortable chair in the house. He removed his gun from the shoulder holster and took the clip out before setting both on the coffee table in front of him. He didn't want there to be any misunderstandings if and when his party arrived. He doubted there would be but he planned ahead for a quick escape anyway, just in case things didn't work out.

Remembering the work he did with Detective Adams back in the day, he knew that his latest gamble had the potential to provide an overwhelming amount of information if a little cooperation could be had. If not, he'd probably be arrested on the spot. Either way worked for him.

~ 36 ~

"Can you tell me what's happening now?" he asked the old woman as he held the knife over the subject. There was no immediate reply so he couldn't be sure if she'd heard him or not. *"Mrs. Forbush?* Can you tell me what's *happening?"* He annunciated the words loudly and slowly the way an American might speak to a foreigner, as if shouting would somehow help. It worked though and he got her attention this time. In a few quick movements of the sharpened blade, six incisions were made and he was immediately proud of the results.

Spencer hadn't made a sandwich in over ten years but he thought the three PB & J's on the plates in front of him looked pretty damned good. And they were now cut into fours like his mother used to do when he was a kid. He poured milk into three glasses and wandered back into the dark living room, carefully balancing everything with two hands.

"He's still in that poor girl's house from what I can see," she answered in the sweet old-lady voice that all grandmothers and great aunts seem to acquire at a certain age. She let the curtains close again and turned back to Spencer with a look of concern. "Is that a bad thing?"

"Not at all, Mrs. Forbush," he replied, watching Stanley squirm in his chair. He knew it wasn't just the ill-fitting dark suit and nearly black sunglasses that were making him uncomfortable. "The man's an important part of this investigation, so I wouldn't worry about him."

He set one of the plates and a glass of milk down next to her then handed the other to Stanley. In between bites of food, the interview continued, which had begun much earlier in the darkness of the pre-dawn hours when she'd discovered the two men in black going through her kitchen. She was confused but didn't look as scared as she could have. Spencer surmised that she was either very trusting or very senile.

The suits helped out quite a bit and their wardrobe was now an eclectic mix of business and casual that could be discarded after each use if they didn't need them anymore. For the current leg of their road-trip Spencer decided to go federal, seizing on the opportunity it would give them to move about a little more freely. The ruse wouldn't allow them to walk into FBI headquarters by any means but it certainly made driving less nerve-wracking. They had a few guys named George to thank for the ensemble.

"Now, the first set of men who came through here—the ones you were telling us about—you wouldn't remember their names, would you? I'll want to follow up with them and compare notes to make sure we haven't missed anything important."

The fragile looking woman who was probably in her early eighties from Spencer's estimation, rose from her chair and ventured slowly to a table that was cluttered with knick-knacks and scattered paperwork. She ran her hands over the table as though searching by touch alone and came up with two small business cards.

"An Agent Peck…" she said, putting on the glasses that swung from her neck and squinting her eyes. "…and…it looks like Barnes. It was just the two gentlemen."

"And you never spoke to an Agent Hildebrandt, Mrs. Forbush?"

"I'm pretty sure, Agent Payne."

Agent Payne; the name was the first thing to come to mind and had popped right out of his mouth when she'd first stumbled across them. In his head, the word was spelled a little differently than what Mrs. Forbush was probably thinking. He liked her face, though, and felt no need to do his regular terror routine on the old woman.

Stanley, on the other hand, appeared less happy with the arrangement and had been wearing a frown of worry since their arrival. It only got worse when the white car had pulled up in front.

"Peck and Barnes," Spencer wondered aloud, turning his eyes to Stanley. "They must have come down from the Northwest Division, right?" He didn't get an answer or even a nod at first. It was an opportunity to put two more names with the many faces they saw everyday but it didn't look like he was even paying attention. "Excuse me, Agent Orange. I'm asking you a question over here."

Or perhaps it was the silly, off-the-cuff name that Spencer had given him that was getting him down. The name was only temporary, though he should have known that his companion wouldn't see as much humor in it—or even understand that he was being referred to as a toxic substance that caused cancer. Then again, if he'd waited for Stanley to come up with a name of his own he suspected they might still be standing in the lady's kitchen trying to introduce themselves.

"Uh...yeah, sure, Peck and Barnes," Stanley finally replied. "Tall guys—hair cut real short. A couple of stiff-walkers, if you know what I mean. One in a dark blue suit, the other one in brown. Is that them?"

"Yes, tall and very upright with very short hair," she answered with a nod. "They sound like the fellows I spoke with. But—and pardon me for saying—I think it would be awfully hard to tell who a gentleman is by the color of his suit. They might have changed clothes since yesterday."

"Not these guys, Mrs. Forbush," Spencer replied. "Federal agents like us need to wear the same exact thing every single day of our lives. I can't really explain it but sometimes making a decision like what to put on in the morning is just too much to handle. We're not nearly as smart as people think."

Mrs. Forbush thought they were a great deal more friendly than the two agents that had shown up a day earlier, but they were definitely a strange pair. It was strange the way she had found them in her kitchen and strange the way they left through her back door and jumped over into the neighbor's yard as an exit. If Mrs. Forbush's eyes were a little better, her memory was sharper, and her mind worked a bit faster she might have found them stranger still. She might have even been frightened.

*   *   *   *

"You said there would be a stakeout. There wasn't any stakeout."

"Sure there was," Spencer replied, stomping on the gas as they headed south. "What do you think *we* were doing?"

Stanley's face went slack for a minute before he turned back to Spencer. "Maybe you'd better tell me what we were doing."

"It's a fundamental rule of investigation, Stan. Scene of the crime. Guys like us always go back to it, don't we?"

"Not once," Stanley answered honestly, wondering what in the hell anyone would do that for if they didn't have to. "What about you?"

"Me neither—like I'm a habitual fucking criminal or something. I was just thinking that these feds wouldn't want to blow off such a basic concept and I figured they'd send a couple of their lackeys to case the place."

"*Lackeys?* You mean those little guys who ride on—?"

"No, those are *jockeys*, Stan—totally different thing." The misunderstanding seemed perfectly reasonable. "A lackey is someone who's like a delivery boy or a foot soldier. A grunt. Like the two losers who visited that lady yesterday instead of the special agent coming in person. They're someone who's in on the deal but not all that important. Get it?"

"Like most of the people looking for us, you mean?"

"Exactly...well, almost. We've got to give *some* credit to the one guy who bothered to show up." Spencer was about to refer to the man as Stanley's nemesis but held back since he didn't feel a need to explain the meaning of that particular word right now.

"You're talking about Madison."

"Yeah, that's who I'm talking about." They had to be many miles away from him by now but Spencer could sense Stanley squirming again anyway. "Relax, man. He isn't here right now...unless he's in the back seat. You checked the back seat, didn't you?"

Stanley's head only turned halfway around before he caught himself. He faced Spencer instead. "That ain't funny."

"Maybe not from where you're sitting." Spencer chuckled quietly while Stanley did his best to give him the silent treatment. Only once his face was completely turned away and staring out the window did Spencer take a quick look into the back seat to make sure that Floyd Madison really wasn't there. He wasn't.

"But seriously, Stan, I think it's kind of important to keep an eye on what these guys are doing and how they plan to proceed if we want to hang onto our edge. I was halfway expecting to find a couple of them in that old lady's house when we went in. It's the perfect spot to watch things from."

"And what if they *were* there, man? What if they were staking it out like you said and we just walked in on them?"

"Then we'd be wearing brown and blue suits now. That taller dude looked about your size, didn't he? We'd have genuine FBI badges to flash and we'd be better armed now too. They were probably packing a couple of nine-millimeters and maybe some smaller revolvers down by their ankles for backup. Now that I think about it, I wish they *had* been there."

"*Damn*, Spence."

Stanley was holding their sole firearm in his hands and wasn't feeling quite as untouchable as the man driving the car. Regardless of the several homes they had invaded over the last two weeks and the multitude of clothing they taken and food they had eaten, they were still limited to the single sawed-off shotgun they had stolen back at the restaurant in Idaho. Or was it Utah? Or Washington? *Oregon?* Stanley couldn't remember. What he did remember was that the shotgun still only contained one shell and they weren't even sure if it would fire or not.

Stanley didn't know much about police or FBI procedure and knew even less about tactics in a gun battle. He knew about General Custer, though. He'd learned about him in grade school and from the cowboy movies on TV. The man died because he was in the wrong place at the wrong time and because he was overconfident and outgunned.

"Don't worry so much, Stan. If anything nasty starts going down you can just turn around, plug your ears, and wait for it to end. I'll take care of it. No problem."

Stanley didn't know anything about *delusions of grandeur* either but he used to live in a cell next to Martin Carroll. Martin Carroll had a brother named Jensen and they both thought they were untouchable too; not unlike that Custer character he had learned about. All three of them seemed to have problems with...

"Quit having deep thoughts, Stan. It smells like a fart in here when you do that."

Though Stanley didn't apologize, he did as he was told. It hurt for him to think so much anyway.

"It's okay," Spencer assured him. "I know it's hard having to lay low and sneak around all the time but it'll be worth it. I'll make things right before we're finished. I promise."

Stanley didn't look soothed or convinced of anything. As if grasping for something more reassuring than Spencer's words, he reached over and put his seatbelt on. He pulled the thick strap tightly around himself.

"They're gonna shoot us on sight, Spence."

"That's right—on *sight*. Repeat that to yourself ten times and try to remember how much we've been seen by anyone who actually matters. Meanwhile, we've seen all of them. Even the ones who're supposed to be super fucking secret agents."

He chuckled a little while saying it and Stanley joined in with him. It wasn't really all that funny but there was something about the way some of the agents acted that cried out to be laughed at.

"How about that dipshit with the camera and the fruity-ass shirts and the black socks who just happens to be at every location just a few minutes before the feds show up?"

"Yeah, Black-Sox is funny with those short little pants of his."

"No shit. You know, I'll miss that guy if he's not in Pleasanton when we get there." He would be, though. Spencer was sure of it. "And Taxi-Fed—let's not forget about him and his stupid yellow cab that seems to have the same phone number painted on it no matter what city he's in. Couldn't they even change the area code? If I thought that shit actually fooled people then I'd be even more optimistic than I already am."

"He should get a meter. It doesn't look like a taxi without the meter."

"I'll make sure to tell him that when I see him," Spencer replied, happy to see Stanley smiling and taking a stab at being thoughtful. "And while I'm doing that, should I tell Hang-around Guy to lose that bippity-boppity bouncy fucking walk he's got going on?"

Hang-around Guy was in a league all his own when it came to being low pro-file and had supplied both of them with many a serious gut-spasm. When he wasn't strutting his way down a sidewalk, he was standing in one place and just sort of…hanging around. His specialty appeared to be moving from one location to another then staying there for a short time while he eyed every person who happened by. Much like Black-Sox and the other federal shape-shifters, his outfit would change occasionally but there were some things that he just couldn't shake. One day he showed up on the street with a full head of dreadlocks under-neath a big, gaudy, pimp-looking hat. Aside from all the laughter, they didn't get much done that day.

"Man, it wouldn't matter if he was in a tuxedo or a bathrobe. He sticks out like one of those twenty-seven year-old high school narcs who used to ask me if I knew a good place to score some weed. Hang-around Guy—what a peckerhead."

"He doesn't really glide so smooth, does he, Spence?"

"No, no he doesn't. But at least he doesn't move like Agent Sloth." Depend-ing on the amount of time spent watching, the names might change with any new and annoying mannerisms that the subject acquired. It didn't matter since they always knew who they were referring to. "He must have a ton of time to kill because that fucker moves like he's walking through a sandbox."

"It's like he's in slow motion."

"Like his fucking feet were weighted down with lead."

"Or nailed to the floor," Stanley added, giggling to himself.

Spencer laughed as well but could tell immediately that Stanley had no idea of what he'd just said. It didn't compute at all. The sentence that fell from his lips had slipped right by his brain somehow and appeared to be a completely natural thought to him. Not feeling like pointing it out—or dwelling on it himself, for that matter—Spencer changed the subject quickly.

"Anyway, I'm just saying it should be easier from now on. We already know who the feds are since we've seen them every day for two weeks and the state people won't change because we'll be sticking to California from here on out. That leaves us with city and county cops to worry about—like I'm totally fucking terrified—plus whatever citizens feel like sticking their necks out."

"You're talking about Madison again."

"That's right," Spencer replied. "But I wouldn't worry about him if I was you."

"Why not, man? He got pretty close to us this morning."

"Well, for one thing, the poor guy's probably being arrested by those two agents that visited Mrs. Forbush...if those lame-asses are even still around. He knows it, though, so I'm not too sure what's up with that. Like any of us, he's got his own agenda but I haven't been close enough to him to ask about it yet."

"Okay, that's one thing. What's the other?"

"I can take the guy—that's what." It was as confident as Spencer had always sounded and left little doubt in Stanley's mind that it was a fact. "He likes the dramatic stuff and the theatrics of it all—like me, but kind of different. I don't know exactly how yet, but I think his heart's in a different place than all the other folks around here who want to kill us. It's a good guy, bad guy thing, Stan. You wouldn't understand."

"But *I'm* a bad—"

The screeching of tires cut him off in mid-sentence and his head was violently thrust forward. Stanley was glad he had out his seatbelt on since the car went from sixty-five to zero in about two seconds. When they came to a complete stop and the smoke began to clear, Spencer was calmly staring at him.

"I'm sorry, Supermax. *Who's* the bad guy?"

"Well..."

"Who's the fucking bad guy, Stan?"

"You are, Spence." There was really only one valid response and even Stanley knew the answer to this one. "You're the bad guy."

~ 37 ~

"No, *you* go in." He actually nudged her a little and Beverly almost went sprawl-ing into the covered entryway, which was just on the other side of the yellow tape. They'd been standing in the same spot for five minutes. "Your scene, your perpetrator, your problem. I didn't even want to be here."

"So you said." Beverly stomped past him and lifted the yellow tape before slip-ping under it. She stepped closer to the door and put two feet on the welcome mat before turning around to see Burgess looking as unimpressed as ever.

There was no mystical glow or dark foreboding from her view of the world now that she was on the other side. The boundary had been breached and, amaz-ingly, nothing seemed to have changed at all. After all the build-up and warnings, the scene of a horrible murder that had left two children parentless was bordered by nothing more than thin bands of yellow plastic. It was a slight disappoint-ment.

"Are you coming, Perry?"

For at least the tenth time in the last few minutes, he shook his head at her. "This is as far as I go."

"Don't be like that. It's the only angle we haven't covered yet."

"Yeah? Well, we've got so many angles this thing's starting to look round to me." He peered back at their rented car and longed to get back behind the wheel of it—or behind the glove compartment anyway. With Beverly walking out front he guessed it wouldn't be long before they found themselves in the kind of trou-ble they couldn't just talk their way out of. "Please, just knock on the door and apologize to the nice FBI agents so we can get moving. We're down to a little more than forty-eight hours before Pleasanton happens and we haven't even checked into our hotel rooms yet. We should just go."

"We've got plenty of time."

"Time to get situated, sure, but how's the next chapter going to look when we don't have any interviews from the old Pleasanton murder?"

"Plenty of time, Perry," she repeated in a distracted tone as she probed the tape on the doors. Her fingers slid smoothly between the space that separated them. "How long do you think it's been since they sealed this place up?"

"Since the initial discovery and evidence collection, I'd guess. About twenty-four hours or so."

"Then where in the hell is everybody? This place should be crawling. They can't possibly be finished here."

"They're stretched mighty thin, Bev. With five cities behind us, this one, plus another coming up in a couple of days—where would you put your resources if you had any?"

"Right here."

"Just because it's the most recent out of the six?"

"No," she replied, pulling her hand away from the door and gesturing toward the street behind him. It was the same white car he had seen when they pulled up to the house. "Because this seal's already been broken and somebody's probably here right now."

"You can't know that for sure." Burgess looked at the vehicle and tried to figure out where he might have seen it before. Looking at it from the side, he was drawing a blank. If he'd stood in front of the hood with his back to it and viewed the car through a mirror it might have looked a great deal more familiar.

"And the door's unlocked too."

"How can you be so sure about...?" he tried to ask, but didn't get to finish. It was too late to ask anything.

"See?" she said, as the knob twisted in her hand. Sure enough, the door was unlocked. As if to illustrate the point, she gave it a light push and the door swung inward. A moment later she was several feet into the house.

Perry's shoulders, which had been tense enough to make his back ache, dropped into a position of surrender as he let out a sigh that felt thirty seconds long. He followed her through the door and quietly closed it behind him, never losing the stony expression that now graced his face. When he turned back around, he was momentarily blinded by a sudden flash of her camera. A small blue dot now resided in his field of vision and would last for almost ten minutes.

"I'll print this for you when we're all set up in Pleasanton. And when you see it, trust me, you won't ever want to make *that* face again."

He was still wearing the scowl anyway and if she wanted to take another picture right there and then he wouldn't have been able to stop her. He couldn't see shit.

"I can't see shit."

"Quit whining. We'll be out of here in a minute."

She stepped further into the murdered woman's house and swung the camera to her left, focusing the lens as she moved. It was deadly silent and it appeared that nobody was home. While Burgess remained within feet of the door—now officially an exit as opposed to an entrance in his mind—Beverly began snapping shots of the framed photos that hung on the wall. They were pictures of Danielle Morgan in her livelier days. There were pictures of her kids as well.

Slipping into the roll of photographer made the job more tolerable but there was a feeling of too much reality in the room to keep things at their proper level of professionalism. It wasn't until she made her way along the wall and into the next room that much of her detachment faded, as though it had been submerged in a strong solution of bleach.

Moving into the kitchen, she took several photos, including a picture of some soggy cereal floating in a bowl half filled with milk that hadn't completely soured yet. The dishes soaking in the sink were covered with bits of food that still looked somewhat edible. The two small matching cups with straws poking out of them were still wet with juice on their insides and didn't yet have the sticky effect that evaporation would cause in a short while. The tall plastic trash bin was full and uncovered but hadn't had the time to develop any type of strong odor yet. The food in the refrigerator, the scraps on the countertop, and the mustard smeared on the table were in the same state everywhere she looked. Like the murder itself, the scene was horribly fresh.

Relieved to be moving on, Beverly aimed her camera at the wall again as she followed the framed portraits like a trail of bread crumbs, snapping away as she went, barely looking at what she was photographing. After completing the circuit through the entryway, kitchen, and dining room, she headed back toward the door where Burgess was waiting for her. He read the sorrowful look on her face without much trouble.

"And that was the easy part. You want some company for this next bit?"

Afraid that her voice might crack, Beverly didn't answer but simply nodded to him. They each took a deep breath and headed for the hallway that they both knew was the last place that Danielle Morgan had been alive in.

As they passed the living room on their right, Beverly paused to take several photos of the walls, furniture, television set, video tape collection, the coffee table, plus any items or magazines that were on or around it. She didn't know if they would matter much but was certain that they were the last tame snapshots that she'd be taking for the next several minutes.

They stopped at the narrow, dark hallway and ran into their first surprise obstruction. Burgess flipped on the lights but they could already see that a disappointment or two was awaiting them. They would need to tread carefully from this point forward.

"What the fuck happened to the floor, Perry?"

"It's gone," he answered, stating the obvious. He waited for a response from her along the lines of *No shit, it's gone*, but it never came and he was encouraged to see that she wasn't in the mood to be flippant about what they were currently viewing. "That must be why forensics came and went so fast. It looks like they tore everything up and took it with them. And if that's how it is then I'll bet they've got the better part of all six murder scenes consolidated into one lab right now. It's an interesting approach. Watch your step there."

The carpet, padding, and even the flat floorboards had been removed from the hallway, leaving only a few tufts of pink insulation poking up from the two-by-fours that remained. Slowly, they teetered across the narrow pieces of wood and searched for something to photograph. There were no sharp gouges in the boards beneath them, but the spots, sprays, and splashes of blood across the walls and ceiling more than made up for it.

"Do it quick, Bev," Burgess said, looking down at his watch. "These are the money shots."

He squinted against the bright light that he was sure would soon blind him again but after several seconds there was no flash to be seen. When he opened his eyes again with the utmost caution—he wouldn't put it past her to wait a moment and purposely burn his retinas again—he found that she wasn't trying to line up a decent shot or anything close to it. She was holding out the camera to him with two hands that appeared to be shaking.

"You go ahead and do this, okay? I'm just going to stand over here for a minute."

While Beverly stepped back and leaned against a door frame, Burgess aimed the camera near where the carpet used to be and worked his way up the wall. With the first push of the button, he could see the bloodstains transform into their natural color as the bright white flash overpowered the low-wattage, warmer toned bulb that had been dimly illuminating the hallway. The rusty shades turned into a deep maroon while the darker reds exploded into a dazzling crimson that hadn't been present only moments earlier. There was more than either of them had imagined.

"Oh, Christ," she said in an throaty tone, exposing the fact that much of what was happening with her vocal cords was way beyond her control. The same went for her respiration as she hitched in gulps of oxygen at very unnatural intervals. "Perry, I…just let me…" She choked on the words as her lungs tried to catch up. "I need to open a window."

When she disappeared through the doorway that was closest to her, Burgess sincerely hoped that there wouldn't be a screen on whatever window she ended up in front of. She said she needed air and it sure sounded like she could use some, but he suspected that the kind of breathing she was talking about would involve more exhalation than inhalation and would most likely be solid, too. He heard the blinds being opened up as a flood of natural daylight poured through the opened door and into the hallway.

"Perry?"

"What is it?"

"Jesus, Perry…I think you really need to…. This is…just so…it's. Fuck. Oh, fuck. Perry?"

Her voice hadn't reached a panic-stricken pitch quite yet, so he didn't move as fast as he could have. It wasn't fear he was hearing from her—as a psychiatrist, he knew it when her heard it. This was more like exhausted revulsion and it was way too early in the day to be as worn out as she sounded. When he heard the barely controlled gagging sounds, he started moving a little quicker.

"Are you okay?" he asked, taking swift, uneven steps across the beams that obviously used to be the floor in Danielle Morgan's bedroom. When he got his first good look around, he slowed it down again. "Holy shit. Now *this* is unbelievable."

Unlike the walls and ceiling a few feet away that were spotted and speckled with blood, the room they were in now was positively painted with it. Although the floor was missing, it was easy to see where all the action had taken place. The corner of the room that faced the window made it look like the house itself had an open wound that was still trying to heal.

"Bev, are you okay?"

"I'm fine…perfect," she replied sourly, swallowing a mouthful of saliva.

She'd given up trying to open the window a few seconds earlier, choosing instead to lean forward with her palms down, taking deep breaths as she kept her eyes pointed upwards to anything that might pass for a distraction. She stayed focused on the blueness of the sky, the whiteness of the clouds, and the occasional bird that flew by. Her eyes didn't wander anywhere inside the room. She didn't want to make that mistake again.

"I'm okay, really. Just get as many shots as you can."

Though she couldn't even see it, he nodded to her and did as he was told. While she stared out the window in a frazzled state that made Beverly furious with herself, Burgess shot each corner of the room then moved into each individual corner and took the same basic series of photos from different angles. It probably wasn't how a professional would have proceeded but it seemed like the thing to do.

"Okay, I'm finished here," he said, moving beside her but being careful not to touch her just yet. He could see that she'd started breathing normally again but she still looked like a cat that had been cornered. He waited for a minute before speaking. When he did, he spoke softly.

"Do you need any help or should I just throw you out the window?"

"No, I'll be fine," she answered with a sniffle, turning around on legs that seemed halfway sturdy again. She moved her eyes down to the floor and they took a step together. Then another. Her face wore an expression of both personal and professional humiliation as they made their way out of the room. "*Chapter Fifteen—Beverly McGrath Doesn't Puke Under Pressure.* How's that sound, Perry?"

"Technically accurate but a little misleading. You feel like getting out of here now?"

"I left five minutes ago."

He held her arm and she clutched his hand as they slowly teetered through the stripped hallway and back onto a solid floor with actual wood and carpeting. It was a relief. The ground stopped swaying and the feeling of claustrophobia dissipated once they'd exited what now seemed like a long black tunnel as they looked back at it. The nastiness was over and for a brief instant it felt like gravity had returned.

Neither was really truly surprised when it slipped right out from under them again.

"*Did you get whatever it was you came for, doctors?*"

The loud voice came from the kitchen off to their right, causing both of them to suck in air so fast that it probably altered the atmospheric pressure of the entire house. The man doing the speaking was casually leaning into the refrigerator, not even bothering to look in their direction as he addressed them.

"Yeah, I think they got it." The second voice came from the living room to their left. He was seated on the sofa with his legs crossed and a magazine across his lap. He turned his head from his partner and shifted his eyes to the startled pair. The brown suit he was wearing matched well with the cheap upholstery he was sitting on. "Some people are just too inquisitive for their own good. You shouldn't have pushed it."

The man in the kitchen pulled an apple from the crisper and closed the refrigerator door. He buffed it to a shine on the arm of his dark blue suit, just to the left of where the FBI ID hung from his pocket.

"Feel free to speak up anytime, doctor. You're trespassing."

"We're looking for Hildebrandt," Burgess spat out quickly, doing his best to appear startled and annoyed with their presence—which really wasn't difficult at all. "Where in the hell have you guys been hiding? Didn't you see us? We must have pulled up ten minutes ago."

"Special Agent Hildebrandt isn't here. And I think you already knew that. You've made a mistake in coming here."

"Hang on there, guys," Burgess argued. "The seal was already broken and the door was unlocked when we got here. We knew you were around here somewhere. We saw your *car* out front for Christ's sake."

"Is that right?" Agent Peck asked in reply, stepping to the living room window. He pulled the curtains open wide and seemed almost bored as he scanned the street in front of the house. "What car?"

Sure enough, the white sedan was gone, as was Perry Burgess's faith in his ability to bullshit any further. Since saying *whoops* with a foolish smile on his face wasn't going to cut it, he gave up trying instead.

~ 38 ~

Not like that. Not with those two. Not today.

The immediate impulse was to floor the gas pedal and clear the area as soon as possible but it would have made him look even more conspicuous than he already did. Instead, Floyd took it slow and casual, driving at the posted speed limit as opposed to lighting up his tires and screeching out of the neighborhood like he'd wanted to. He took regular glances in his rearview mirror and didn't start to relax until he was blocks from the house.

Of the few scenarios he'd been expecting, any one of them would have been more beneficial than what little headway that had been made in the last couple of weeks and he was willing to risk a certain amount of himself to take advantage of them. At the same time, there were risks that he couldn't take because of the principle involved as well as the kind of people he preferred not to be associated with.

Scenario-one would have put him head to head against a few feds, maybe some state investigators, or possibly just some geeks in thick glasses and lab coats, but they could each be valuable if the cards were played correctly. It would all be a bluff of course—getting them to show their hands even though Floyd was holding jack-shit—but that's what playing cards was all about. He guessed that the state boys wouldn't have been a problem since he could have steam-rolled over them or played on his former celebrity status to find out what he wanted to know easily enough. It was a California thing and probably wouldn't work in any other state.

The FBI certainly wouldn't be pleased with his presence but that was where the gamble came in. He knew he could be arrested quite legally for stomping through a closed crime scene, but he knew they wouldn't want to do something so stupid to themselves at this stage of the contest. Taking a look at the lack of progress the authorities had made since Hewitt's initial escape in Utah, it could only be detrimental in the public's eye if the one man they did arrest just happened to be the man who caught him the first time around. There would be serious questions as to the motives of such a move on the FBI's part; questions he hoped they would ask themselves before throwing cuffs on him and tucking him away in a cell while Hewitt's psychosis ran its course. It would be an unpopular move for them if the word got out, but there certainly wouldn't be any guarantees against incarceration.

These were the big risks—the red-card moments and personal fouls that got one ejected if they received too many. With luck, it wouldn't come to such extremes, but if it did, Floyd was ready to take the penalty.

Scenario-two didn't have anything to do with the FBI, the police, or any authorities at all for that matter and, instead, revolved around the two albatrosses he'd been wearing around his neck since Altamont. They were annoying and sickening creatures at times but, unlike the FBI, they held no particular spite or vindictiveness toward him; not yet, anyway. It all depended on how he chose to treat them when the time came, which also depended on how they were treated by the two feds who probably picking them apart at this very moment. It also depended on whether she'd seen him or not. He suspected she might have.

There was no recognition in Beverly McGrath's eyes—not much of anything, in fact—when he saw her appear in the late Danielle Morgan's bedroom window just a few minutes earlier. She was struggling to slide it open, leaving little doubt in his mind that she was onto him or at least onto *something*. They were moving awfully slow for a couple of unprotected, uninvited nobodies with two agents about to crawl up their asses, so he had to wonder about what their intentions were.

If it was an attempt to ditch through a window as Floyd himself had done, she'd stopped trying way too fast. She gave up too quickly and just sort of hung there, suspended silently in front of the window, staring outward from the most brutal room in the house. He was almost sure he'd been seen by her but she never gave any indication of it if that was the case. For all he knew, there could have been a glare on one of their windows or something.

They sure weren't a very stealthy pair, that much was certain. He suspected it long before they ended up at the Morgan residence but it was solidly confirmed when he heard them arguing on the front porch. Not just having a small, professional disagreement, but sniping at each other like children. They were so loud, in fact, that he got the feeling that they might have actually known what they were doing. It wasn't the greatest plan ever developed but Floyd could see how the stakeout team would want to chase them off the property as quickly as possible. If they were able to cause enough commotion, which they were doing adequately, then the agents would be forced to acknowledge their own presence and give away their position at the same time.

The doctors risked getting yelled at or even threatened a little, but no laws would have been broken and all boundaries would have remained uncrossed while a much sought after contact with the FBI would be initiated. After some additional thought, Floyd didn't really think the plan sounded all that bad. He had been listening and waiting for the fun to begin when he discovered that there was no such plan. No plan, no foresight—no thought involved at all. One second, they're calling each other names and the next Beverly McGrath is walking through the door like she owned the place. He could hear Doctor Burgess do everything but plead for her to cease her actions but she wasn't having it.

For the first time since Floyd had laid eyes on him, the man who wrote snuff books and didn't know how to drive a car started looking like a genius. Then he followed her inside and looked like an idiot all over again.

Floyd was down the hall and into the children's room before Beverly made it three feet into the house and he was out the window before Burgess had pulled the front door shut. Once he was outside of the residence, Floyd didn't poke his head around the corner or even bother to look for agents climbing out of the woodwork; he simply looked at his watch and began counting. At exactly two minutes—about thirty seconds longer than it would take the stakeout crew to identify them and enter quietly from the front—Floyd shoved his hands into his pockets and walked across the street to his car, making sure it took a normal amount of time to get there. It was hard to tell what normal was sometimes, which was why he relied on the timepiece so often.

He climbed into the car and held the door handle in an open position as he slowly pulled the door shut, being careful not to slam it. He only heard one click and the door was still ajar as he started the engine but he didn't worry about it, knowing that in a block or two he could slam it until the window shattered if he wanted to. He pulled away safely and didn't look back, though he was unable to stop picturing Beverly McGrath's horrified face in his head. He'd seen at least one face with that same look on it before, but never through a window.

From Floyd's experience, moments of emotional vacancy were private affairs and best handled far away from where others could watch your soul empty out.

Behind locked doors in front of a mirror worked for him most of the time. As he made his way to the freeway, he wondered if it would work for her.

She and the psychiatrist had botched his deal but would be forgiven this time if amends could be made. If they were taken into custody then there wasn't much anybody could do about it and he would be on his own again. On the other hand, if they were simply sent packing with nothing more than a warning then Floyd might be ready to deal with them personally—but only if he *had* to, of course. There were still principles to consider after all.

Cooperation with the feds? *I can do that.*

Arrested by the feds? *I can do that too if it gets me back in business.*

Arrested by the feds while associating with a couple of parasites? *Not like that. Not with those two. Not today.*

~ 39 ~

For over an hour Beverly and Burgess silently shared space on the small sofa, doing what they'd always done when it came to Special Agent Dwight Hildebrandt—they waited. They had waited in Utah, waited in Redding, and now they were waiting in Sacramento. It didn't seem to bother the agents that they hadn't uttered a word in sixty minutes. The two men had each other to talk to.

"What do you think the temperature's like outside?" Barnes asked.

"Eighty-four degrees with eighty-seven percent humidity," Agent Peck replied quickly, as though he was a walking weather station.

"That explains the smell then."

"Yeah, it's coming back." He turned his attention to the doctors on the sofa, speaking in a matter of fact manner. "That's Miss Morgan's blood you're smelling. It's reacting with the moisture and the heat and it's putrefying right there in all the cracks and crevices. It'll burn itself out and dry up for good in a while but we're lucky they pulled the carpet up or it would be about a hundred times worse in here."

"And we're lucky it's not the middle of summer."

"Very lucky," Peck agreed, nodding his head. "We're all-around lucky, wouldn't you say?"

"Definitely," Barnes replied, taking his seventh or eighth stroll to the kitchen, where he would soon turn around and walk back to the living room. He almost appeared to be practicing his entrances and exits. "How many years do you think they're looking at for this?"

"It depends on how many felonies they're charged with, what court they land in, if their sentences run concurrently or not—there's a lot to consider. It also depends on Hewitt's next move."

"How so?" Barnes inquired, keeping his eyes leveled between Beverly and Burgess. They both lowered their eyes, neither wanting to be the one to tell him that the phrase *How so?* didn't sound right coming from him and should be immediately dropped from his repertoire.

"Well, you see, Agent Barnes, this is what we call a crime scene. Maybe there was some little piece of evidence that would have pointed us straight to Hewitt's location—you never know. Perhaps he was even here looking for mementos and keepsakes but got scared away by something. Maybe we'd have him in custody right now if not for our two friends here."

"And when he kills again…"

"That's right—we'll know exactly who to thank for it."

There was a little emotion now and it came in the form of two flinty glares. It was the sixth time they'd resorted to dirty looks in the last hour but it wouldn't last very long. In a couple of minutes, both Beverly and Burgess knew that they would smooth out their faces and start from the beginning again, which was fortunate because at least one of the doctors was finding it harder and harder not to laugh. When the agents got back around to glaring again Beverly couldn't guarantee that she wouldn't start giggling. Compared to the bleeding bedroom she'd been in, the two men were a comic relief of sorts.

After a couple minutes of silence that was supposed to be edgy and uncomfortable, Agent Peck looked at his watch and returned to his seat across from the sofa. Barnes, as was his pattern, turned his shoulder to them and strolled back into the kitchen for a moment. If the waiting went on much longer he would be cutting a path through the carpet pretty soon.

"You didn't really think nobody would be watching, did you? Just tell me this one thing. Are you *trying* to screw this investigation up? I'm curious. Because you seem to be putting a lot of effort in that direction."

"Maybe they are," Barnes offered in reply, looking to his partner. "A couple of sharp, has-beens like these two—they've got to be loving this. If they didn't, I don't think we'd be seeing them every time we turned around. They must think it's entertaining or something. Do you think it's entertaining?"

"Who *me?*" Peck asked with a look of mock insult that disappeared quickly. "Do I look like a sick fuck to you? Why would anyone think that?"

"I don't know. Maybe we should ask."

"Ask who? Do you see any sick fucks in this room?"

"I might see a couple," Barnes answered with another scowl, apparently forgetting that he wasn't supposed to show irritation for another eight minutes or so. "I might see a couple of opportunizing, morbid, sick fucks with—"

"Agent Barnes?"

The voice was as soft as his entrance had been, though it grabbed an incredible amount of attention from the performers. Barnes quieted down quickly, losing a good deal of color from his face and Agent Peck stood up so fast that his feet left the ground for a moment. He spun around to find his superior giving them both a look usually reserved for the criminal element.

"Sir?" both agents muttered simultaneously.

"I thought I told you to isolate them and sit on them," said the only man in the room who appeared secure in his role, throwing his soft voice away like it was garbage. While agents Peck and Barnes had been mildly intimidating during their better moments, Dwight Hildebrandt made them look strictly second-rate. "I don't remember telling you to talk to them."

"We weren't, sir," Barnes noted with a defensive tone. "We were just speaking to each other."

"I didn't authorize that either. Hit the road—both of you. We'll talk in a few hours. Really...get the hell out of here. Go on."

"Sir?"

"I said hit it, Barnes. You ought to be running by now." Hildebrandt tilted his head slightly and reiterated the previous statement without having to repeat himself verbally. Both started moving. They didn't look back even as he continued to speak to them and he didn't watch them leave since he was too busy eyeballing the two people he hadn't been face to face with since Utah. "Check in with Agent Hargrove when you get there and wait for me. Don't improvise—just wait."

The two men nodded sourly and attempted a rapid exit.

"Agent Barnes?" Beverly called out suddenly, causing the man to stop as he pulled the door open. It was the first time she'd spoken in over an hour. "I think the word you were looking for back there was *opportunistic*. *Opportunizing* isn't proper English."

"And that's not really blood we're smelling, Agent Peck," Burgess added, only willing to smirk a tiny bit. "It's ninhydrin. It's a chemical that forensics uses to bring out latent fingerprints and it doesn't smell like blood at all—just so you don't look stupid in front of anyone important."

~ 40 ~

There was no reply except for the front door slamming shut. The jarring sound seemed to please Hildebrandt to some degree. He took the seat across from them, looking much more at ease than Agent Peck had looked in it and stared at them for almost a minute.

"I'm sorry if my men were a little intense with you there," he finally said. "If I'd have known it was you two who were going to pollute my crime scene I would have sent someone else."

"Listen, agent, we didn't mean to—"

"Just be quiet for a minute," Hildebrandt said, holding a finger up to his lips. "Let's try to remember who you're talking to, doctor. And you can relax about that whole crime scene issue—it's really just a gimmick at this point. I think you already knew that. There's nothing new here today and there won't be anything new in Pleasanton or Salinas or Santa Maria or Santa Barbara if it gets that far. But we'll use it if we need to, I hope you understand that."

Beverly was already nodding. "We understand, agent."

"Because all we really need is an excuse. Just one."

"Some of us understood that before we got here," Burgess said, shooting a nasty look in Beverly's direction.

"That's good to hear. You should listen to those instincts sometimes." Hildebrandt began to clean one of his fingernails and seemed to focus all of his attention on it as he continued. "I know you have other instincts as well—impulses, actually—but you've got to learn to set those things aside and stick to whatever your main task is. If your task is to write yourselves a book, then go ahead and do it. If you want a bunch of red artwork from every murder room from Vancouver to Santa Barbara—just ask for it. We're not unreasonable people."

"That's what I tried to tell *her.*"

"Shhh," Hildebrandt hissed, holding up a finger again. He lowered it quickly and went right back to digging dirt from underneath the nail. "I can get you site access, sealed records, interviews—*real* interviews with *real* people; not that shit you've been doing—and maybe even some better accommodations so you'll be more comfortable while you're doing it. With proper motivation, I might even be able to manage some autopsy photos if you were interested."

"That's quite an offer, agent," Beverly replied. "And it makes me nervous. I'm sure an arrangement could be worked out, but if you honestly feel like sharing what you know with us, I need tell you something about the business—*our* business, I mean."

"And what's that, doctor?"

"Now, this is going to sound wrong in a lot of ways. But our audience—the readers of the genre and our main demographic—they don't read thirty chapters just to get to the conclusion of a story. These aren't novels that we're talking about and closure is not what they're looking for. We write about events that have already happened and they already *know* how it's going to end, which basically leaves only the little details for them to read about. Now, it's nothing against you personally…" She paused for a moment. "It sounds bad, I know this, but in *our* line of work…it really *is* kind of a villain's market. I guess what I'm saying is that when it comes down to it, people aren't buying these things to read about a valiant US Marshall or a Texas Ranger or a supercop with the LAPD…"

"…or an FBI agent," Hildebrandt concluded for her. He didn't look surprised. "I've read your books, you already know that. Your readers want the wet stuff. The screams, the pain, the suffering, and whatnot. They want to watch the car crash in slow motion and see the aftermath in living color. They want to see, smell, and taste the blood while looking at it from the killer's mind. I understand, doctor. I get it and I've got a pretty good idea what your fan base looks like."

"Then you also understand there are limits to what we can do for you while catering to what our publisher will expect from us," Beverly replied cautiously. "I had to pull teeth the first time just to get Agent Schultz that one chapter in *Understanding The Sickness.* I…*we* can't guarantee you any more than a few consecutive pages mixed in with all the other people who've put time and effort into the various manhunts."

"Not my concern at all, Dr. McGrath. If you think I'm requesting some personal ad space then it's obvious that we're not following each other too well. Like

I told you back at that dungeon in Utah; keep my name out of it. I meant it then and I mean it now. This is just another job for me and I'll be on to the next one as soon as I'm finished."

He crossed his legs and sat back deeper into the chair. Exercising some patience, he didn't throw out a counter proposal and instead waited for them to ask for it. Burgess and Beverly exchanged a wary look before they did.

"Are we going to need a notebook to write all this down?" She tried not to look as concerned as she suddenly felt. "Because I'd like to hear it all in one shot instead of having you show up in a couple of days asking us for another 'favor'. Our book is a work in progress and we've got continuity to consider. I'm sure you understand."

"And I'm sure you don't," he replied. "You're only right about one thing; I've got a request and it *does* involve your work. But don't try to con me by telling me that the two of you will write something that will make me famous. It's presumptuous and insulting coming from where you're sitting…and I mean that in all the bad ways you're thinking. You can take offense if you want to but I'm just telling you how it is."

"What is it then, agent?" Burgess asked in a more submissive tone. "We're listening to you. One way or another, I'm sure we can find a way to insert whatever it is you want to get across."

"It's not what I want put into your book, doctors," he replied, locking eyes with both of them before returning to the fingernail that was fascinating him so much. "It's something that I want left out. Dr. McGrath, I'm referring specifically to you in this case but since you're working together, I'll need to hear a commitment from both of you if you want to see this thing to the finish line. You see, I have an issue or two with that *Sickness* book of yours, doctor. Actually, I have a lot of problems with that piece of crap but we don't have nearly the time to go into all of them right now."

"Your point, agent?"

"My point is that I'm not going to be terribly concerned with who gets the credit for this bust when it happens. It'll happen, trust me on that, but the main thing—the *one* thing I want to be *absolutely* clear on—is who *doesn't* get the credit. Are we on the same page yet?"

"You can't be talking about—"

"You know exactly what I'm talking about." Hildebrandt finally started sounding as though his patience was waning. He leaned forward closer to them and locked his fingers together as he spoke, his squinty eyes settling on Beverly.

"Floyd Madison did *not* track down and catch Stanley Hewitt on his own. I think you already know that."

"I don't know any such thing."

"I think you do. You glossed over all aspects of Madison's role in the hunt aside from the capture itself and you made hardly any mention of the several hundred federal agents involved—aside from Agent Schultz's five page rant about the bureaucracy of the organization I work for, of course. Not a great career move on his part…or yours."

"I'm still not seeing your point," Beverly said with a shake of her head.

"Floyd Madison didn't identify Hewitt using DNA and two solid weeks of evidence collection—that was us. Madison didn't throw Hewitt's photograph onto every television screen in the country, offering cash incentives for information—that was us too. He was never involved in any investigation and didn't even break a sweat for nearly a month of murders before he stumbled across the guy in Santa Barbara. Have you even looked at the timeline, Dr. McGrath?"

"What timeline? And what do you mean he 'stumbled" across Hewitt?"

"I've done the math, doctor," Hildebrandt answered sternly. "Any idiot with a calendar and court records could verify that Madison was down in Los Angeles County until the day before he captured Hewitt. He was, you know. He was busy bringing in a felon named Kirk Faust for processing, which means he had *nothing* to do with *anything* until the day he found himself involved. How did he *get* involved, Dr. McGrath? Well, I have a theory."

They didn't ask for it, but the expressions on their faces asked anyway.

"I think Floyd Madison was in Santa Barbara for whatever reason. Maybe a really great hooker he knew lived there or it was ten-cent beer night at some dive on the beach. I really don't give a damn what brought that scumbag up north and it's not important anyway. But while he's there, some God-awful miracle happens and he spots Hewitt. Just *sees* him somewhere, maybe. He glimpses him crossing a through an alley, wading through the surf—I don't know, but it's got to be off the beaten track because his face is all over the TV by now. What does he do, Dr. McGrath? You wrote the book. Tell me."

She wasn't sure what he expected to hear but the picture in her head was just as clear as when she'd originally written the book and she would never forget it.

"Okay, I'll tell you, Agent Hildebrandt. He made the initial ID—he wasn't one-hundred percent sure yet, which he freely admitted—then followed him from a safe enough distance not to be spotted if he turned out to be correct about it. As we now know, he was right on the money."

"Then what?"

"Then he moved in closer and tailed him back to a residence a few hundred yards off of the campus. As it turned out, the house was rented to three students including a young woman named Gail Rainier. She was alone and on her way to becoming Stanley Hewitt's tenth victim. Thanks to Madison, that didn't happen. He entered the property, located Hewitt, subdued him, and placed him under citizen's arrest."

"Knocked the door right off the hinges, did he?"

"There's a picture of it in the book if you want to see for yourself," she answered, thinking it was indeed a powerful photo. The twisted metal and splintered wood of the woman's front door contrasted well with Hewitt's brand of violence and showed it being put to a good use for a change.

"So he busts through, beats Hewitt to the ground, and cuffs him," Hildebrandt mused, nodding to himself. "He finds Miss Rainier nailed to the floor in her bedroom and grabs hold of Hewitt's hammer. While she's bleeding all over him and screaming in pain, Madison pulls the nails out of her feet all by himself."

"No time, agent," Burgess interjected, heading him off before they were forced to dwell on the obvious medical questions. "With a heavy bleeder and no realistic estimate on a 911 response, you've got to act fast and I have to agree that he did the right thing. It may not have been a calculated move on his part or even the smartest, but it turned out to be the right move considering the timing issues involved."

"Oh...the *timing*. Now I see." Hildebrandt managed to look embarrassed for a moment but it didn't ring true. By now, both doctors knew that if he actually felt anything close to an emotion, they certainly wouldn't have known about it. "It must be this timing thing that's got me all screwed up. Yeah, that's probably it."

"Well, I don't know what it is, agent," Beverly said with a tired sigh. "But it's obvious you hate the man and I have my suspicions that it's little more than a jealous reaction on your part. It almost sounds like you would have rather had that young woman die than to have Floyd Madison be the one to save her. That's my opinion and I can write that down if I want to. You can go ahead and arrest us if you feel the need, but I can still write as long as people can still read. I'm done talking to you, Agent Hildebrandt. Do what you have to do."

"Does that go for you too?" Hildebrandt asked as his focus shifted to Burgess.

"Yeah," he answered nervously, looking anything but certain about it. "I guess I'm done talking too."

"Good, because I just want you to listen. Doctor McGrath, I don't hate Floyd Madison for catching Stanley Hewitt. Somebody had to do it and I'm glad it got done. I don't care that it wasn't a federal agent doing the arresting and I don't care that we got brushed aside when it came to getting patted on the back. I just care about timing and I think you should care too."

"What are you—?"

"*No*, you're *listening*, doctor. Listen to me and think about this while you're on your way to Pleasanton, which should be in just a couple of minutes if you don't do or say anything too stupid before then. I want you to consider everything you know about Hewitt, his MO, and how he does everything that he does. Think about Madison locating him, regardless of how it happened, and then tailing him to the Rainier girl's house. Now, you know as well as I do that once Hewitt gets started, he doesn't stop until the job is done. You told me that yourself back at Woodhall, remember?"

Beverly nodded to him. It was a thoughtful kind of nod.

"Well, that's the timing I was just talking about. I've asked the question but I can tell by the look on your face that you're only starting to ask it right now. Floyd Madison didn't tail a blood-covered man going back to the scene to finish what he'd started, did he?"

She didn't nod or shake her head. Burgess remained mute as well, keeping his eyes down while checking his own fingernails for dirt this time.

"No, he tailed a killer on his way to a murder that hadn't even *begun* yet. How long did he wait, Dr. McGrath? That's my question. That's the big one. How long did it take for him to crash through the door in that picture you were just talking about? I've seen the photo, and to the casual observer it would appear that whoever went through it was in one hell of a hurry. But really, doctor—how much of a hurry was he really in? Ask yourself that. Ask yourself how many cuts Gail Rainier had to endure before she was in bad enough shape to rescue. Before she was worthy enough. Before she was *news*worthy enough."

Special Agent Dwight Hildebrandt sat in silence, looking both pleased with himself and halfway sorrowful for his audience. It was pretty much what he'd expected.

"It's about a two hour drive to Pleasanton," he said, rising up from his seat. "I'd like you to give some serious thought into who you want on the other side of the door while nails are being hammered through *your* toes, Doctor McGrath. Just consider it. And while your thinking about that, you should also think twice about that superhero of yours and what he's really all about. Or you can go ahead and ask him yourself because he'll probably be driving right behind you. He's been there for a week now."

~ 41 ~

Pleasanton was warm, slightly muggy, and had less than six hours before it would lose another inhabitant if the pattern remained consistent. Unlike many of the previous cities, not much was done in the way of prevention or curfew this time and no one would have cooperated even if told to do so considering how much good it had done in the recent past. It seemed that the residents already knew the odds and believed it was more likely that they would slip and die in their showers than become a victim of Hewitt's aggression. A sort of gallows humor was even settling in as the big night approached and more than a few of the gambling types had wagers going on it.

Color of hair, age, weight, height, whether there would even be a victim or not—these were the general topics of discussion. Most thought there would definitely be a victim and some clever genius had already defaced the freeway signs entering Pleasanton, editing the last digit of *Population* down to the next lowest number. City officials weren't amused by the cavalier attitude, but most of the people in the area went home from their jobs that evening with confidence and optimism, more curious with the following morning's news than what would occur in their own neighborhoods when the sun went down.

It wasn't panic or irrational fear that hung over the city but the good kind of fear, most thought. It was a time to reevaluate one's safety. Time to check your windows and lock your doors; security issues that weren't always considered so much in a nice place like Pleasanton.

A few of the alpha-males would even keep all night vigils in their living rooms or organize with neighbors for a safety-in-numbers approach to the threat, feeling smarter and better about themselves for their preventative measures. These were the people who thought they were least likely to fall under the blade, but there was more at stake than just survival, of course. There was the embarrassment of death to worry about as well because, as everybody already knew, Stanley Lewis Hewitt wasn't the only one who would be on the prowl tonight. The spirit of Charles Darwin would be out there too, making sure that those who weren't smart enough to take a few simple precautions wouldn't have the opportunity to breed and pollute the collective gene pool.

To the more shallow of the species, dying horribly was already bad enough. Dying stupidly and so publicly would have been unimaginable.

It was day-three in Pleasanton, which meant the waiting was just about over. The requisite dark sedans were visible and the police cars were abundant as the sun began to make its dip toward the horizon. It hadn't gone down yet but more than the usual amount of sunset watchers took an interest in it. Not many of them thought it would actually be their last one but the just-in-case crowd was out in big numbers tonight.

~ 42 ~

The window was open and the Venetian blinds were angled to where nobody could see clearly into the hotel room from the outside, leaving bright, sunlit stripes across the walls. The same stripes covered the men looking out from the window and at the proper angle made them look like they were wearing old style prison uniforms. It seemed funny for a minute but they'd stopped laughing about such small things a couple of hours earlier. As the time had worn on and their conversations slipped into darker terrain, both found that they were laughing less and less frequently.

"What if they'd made it and were still out there somewhere? I mean, I know they didn't have a prayer—but what if they did? What would it mean?"

"Well, Stan, it would mean that they were made of asbestos and take bullets better than the average guy. Those troopers in Utah weren't fucking around."

"No, Spence. I mean…"

"Christ, I *know* what you mean, man. I'm just fooling around. If Marty and J.J. were still alive, they sure as shit wouldn't be around here. Not California, not the US…probably not even this hemisphere. I know what you're thinking and you don't have to worry. They wouldn't be stealing our thunder no matter what they decided to do with their freedom if they'd made it."

In regards to Jensen Carroll, Spencer's mild but daily hazings were more of a hobby than anything else. Cruel but friendly, like felonious neighbors often get. It was just something to do on top of his regular busy days of thinking, drawing, and eating, though passing time had never been an issue with him. In the end, a relationship of sorts had been forged and it was the main reason they'd made it as far as they had.

Martin Carroll and Stanley, however, were the real deal when it came to out-right hatred and could have very possibly killed each other if given the chance, which was serendipitous because it made the whole thing that much easier. He also didn't want those two speaking to each other during the planning phase any-way—a phase that Stanley hadn't been aware of right up until it happened. He was still in the dark about most of it.

"What if it didn't work out right, though?" Stanley asked, looking worried even though it had already worked out just fine. "What then?"

"Then we'd probably be squished up underneath a shitload of concrete."

"Wow, I didn't even think about *that*." It was obvious he hadn't. "But what I was really thinking about was what would've happened if *none* of it happened at all? Not just the wall coming down, but the whole thing. No escape…no noth-ing. What then?"

"Don't worry about that. I never had any doubts about those two guys. They wanted out quick and they hired the best men to get the job done. I knew they would."

"How'd you know, though? About them, I mean. And getting them to do it right when we needed it. It sounded a lot harder than you made it look."

"It wasn't," Spencer replied, not wanting to make a big deal out of it. "For some guys, all you need to do is tell them exactly what they want to hear to get what you want. It was lies mostly—like I'm fucking trustworthy or something—and you did half the work for me. You know that, don't you?"

"With Marty, you mean? Yeah, I said some pretty bad stuff to him."

"You worked him like a professional, Stan. A supermax effort if I've ever seen one. If he wasn't such an emotional turd we'd have played it differently but it still would have turned out the same way. There's no question about it."

And there really was none; not in Spencer's mind. As far as he was concerned, he could have picked any week, any day, any hour—maybe even the minute of that hour if he needed to be that precise. He guessed he might not have even needed the Carrolls to get the job done. They were simply the easiest route to go with the limited amount of time they were dealing with.

"Listen, Stan, if it wasn't those gangster boys it would've been someone else knocking the walls down for us…or something else instead. Hell, a guy like Mat-thew Chase could have walked us out through his own front gate if I asked him in the right way. He fucking loved us for Christ's sake. There's always gonna be a way to get something done if you want it bad enough. Always."

Stanley looked as though he had a follow-up question or something to add, but didn't quite dare. He decided to wait for an adequate amount of time to elapse before he pursued it any further or he knew he might risk a tongue lashing from the only man on earth that he respected. When the fifteen or twenty whole seconds was up, he took a shot at it.

"But why—?"

"How about killing that *'Why?'* and *'What if?'* shit for a few minutes. The clock's ticking and I'm starting to feel like a moron over here. We've only got a few hours. Are you gonna help or just sit there and ask stupid questions?"

Stanley continued to gawk at him for a minute then grudgingly took over Spencer's position in front of the window. He didn't respond, keeping his mouth shut instead as he kept an eye on what was happening a couple hundred feet below them. He was in no mood to talk now; not even enough to thank Spencer for grabbing them a room on the top floor. It felt like he could see forever.

"Try to ignore the silent treatment. He gets like this sometimes." Spencer was still looking at Stanley's back but was actually addressing the other two people in the room with them. It was the polite thing to do after all.

He moved in behind them, putting his face between their heads and placing an arm over each of their shoulders. If not for all the tape and bed sheets that kept the traumatized newlywed couple bound to their chairs, they could have been posing for a picture together. Using what looked like an overly friendly and double-sided headlock, he pulled them in close.

"George? George's lady-friend?" They were Jonathan and Marilyn Yost respectively; the latest in a long line of Georges. "My two newest and truest…latest and greatest pals on the whole fucking planet. I want you to look at that man over there. Go ahead, look at him."

They did. The two young adults in their early twenties had seen him practically everywhere they'd glanced in the last eighteen or nineteen days. TV, newspapers, magazines; they had certainly seen enough of him to feel badly about their current situation.

"Look at that face and those eyes and try to think of the last time you saw something like that. When was it? Unless you've been on safari lately, I'll bet it was at the zoo."

Like Stanley, their response was mute. It wasn't that they had no opinions on the subject; it was more a matter of fear and vanity. Since Spencer would force a reply from them every now and then, they would often have no choice but to hum their way through it. And since their mouths were taped so efficiently, their hums eventually turned into gurgling, bubbly rivers of yellow snot that ran down their faces, over the tape, under their chins, and all the way down into their shirts if Spencer was on a serious roll.

"Keep watching him. You're looking at a fucking animal right there. A rare and endangered species with some of the weirdest instincts you've ever heard of. You know what he's doing?"

Silence.

"*George*...do you know what he's *doing?*"

In reply, Spencer was treated to a choking, wet sound that sent a torrent of phlegm down his right forearm and onto the back of his hand. He decided to end the group hug right then but made no move to wipe the mess off. He wanted to—oh, how he wanted to—but was afraid it might ruin the whole beastly effect. If he wasn't currently working the horror angle, he would have been tempted to chase Stanley around the room with the mucous-covered limb and try to wipe it on him. Though it would have been the pinnacle of entertainment, he decided to remain on course and finish his business with the people who were footing the bill for the room.

"That's right, George. He's hunting."

He circled around them, appearing to be doing a little hunting of his own, though he'd stopped swinging the knife around a few hours earlier. With each circuit around them, he would pause for a moment and shift his eyes between them and Stanley.

"What do you think? Has he found what he's looking for yet? Has he found his prey?"

There was no reply and he didn't force one this time.

"And it's not you guys, if that's what you're thinking," he said with the least frightening face he'd worn all day. He thought he could see the air escape from them while he said it, as though a great pressure was suddenly released. "Because I've already *got* you two, baby." And he watched the pressure build right back up again. "I got you first and you're all mine. Now, what I'm gonna do with you...I'm not quite sure yet."

He looked back and forth between them, letting his eyes glide all over the young woman who hadn't changed out of the sweatpants she'd worn to bed on the previous evening. Her hair was matted and her makeup was long gone but Spencer managed a decent leer at her for the shape she was in. It didn't matter since the dirty looks were mainly for her husband's benefit anyway.

"She's some hot stuff, man. A sweet, sweet thing to behold. It's been a while since I've had something fresh like this, you know." While Jonathan Yost's face nearly crumbled, Spencer turned his own face away before the sick laughter could find a way out of his mouth. It would have been a wild, uncontrollable series of cackles that would have made him look more insane than he already did. "We're gonna give her a little workout, George. The both of us. What do you think of that? Me and my buddy Stan giving it to her from two ends at once. How's that sound?"

For the first time in a long while, Jonathan Yost began to struggle again.

"Yeah, I'll be down her throat and Stan'll be ten feet up her ass before she knows it. I'm thinking we safety-pin her eyes open, bend her up like a busted Barbie doll, then lift her up and twirl her around like a pig on a fucking stick. Like a luau but without all that nasty fire. We'll show her how it's done, Georgie-boy. You want to watch this?"

He struggled even harder now and Spencer readied himself in case the chair couldn't hold up under the thrashing. He knew that the man was imagining his young wife suspended in the air between two psychopaths, being skewered like a shish-kabob while spinning around like a rotisserie chicken even though there was no basis in reality for it. The visual was there, though, and that mental picture was more than enough for the young husband to temporarily lose his mind. He did it while Spencer watched and even drew a look from Stanley, who hadn't been paying attention to them at all. He didn't look too amazed by the reaction. He'd already seen it a few times by now.

With snot and tears running down his face, Jonathan Yost finally ceased struggling and didn't complain or even notice when his chair was tipped backwards. Spencer only tilted him halfway before dragging the chair into the bedroom of the second largest suite in the whole hotel. He then set it all the way down and rolled the man onto his side, still bound to the legs of the chair. It was all that was keeping him there now. Whether the man knew it or not, Spencer had sliced the tape that had held his arms in place. He was left alone in the room.

"And now the clock's ticking a little faster," Spencer said gleefully as he pulled the door shut behind him. A flinching and heavy-breathing Marilyn Yost was tipped back in the same fashion as her husband and dragged into the closet nearest the door. She was still tied up and left in total darkness. He closed the door on her as if it was a pantry and he'd just put away a can of corn. "Anything yet? We're gonna have to beat it out of here pretty damn fast. They need to know that we left before it got dark."

Stanley replied with more of the silent treatment. He was now standing and parting the blinds to get a better view down below.

"*Stan*…wake up, man. That guy's not gonna just lay there and drool on himself all night—well, probably not. Let's get our shit together and move along."

"Why'd you do that to me?" Stanley turned to look at him but hadn't started moving yet. "What did you shut me down for? I was doing okay."

"No you weren't. You went off track and started asking questions that weren't in the script. That's why I had to put the screws to that fucker. I had to keep his concentration in the right place."

"Did I mess it up?" Stanley asked with a worried look.

"Not at all, Supermax. We got the point across and they'll remember all the important stuff. We're still rock solid."

Looking back on all that was said and done, Spencer felt pretty good about how it went. When the Yost couple started talking—God only knew how long it would be before their brains would wobble back into proper orientation—they would be able to tell the authorities about every exchange that went on between the duo of Hewitt and Stoning.

They would be just like the Lang family back in Oakridge who told the feds that the pair was headed to Altamont. Much like the roommates in Redding who relayed the next bit of info they wanted known; like the math teacher in Chico; like the family of six in Yuba City. Even the ancient Mrs. Forbush in Sacramento had her own part to play. It was room and board plus quality time with a series of Georges, every move and every word having its own predetermined purpose.

They had conversations that meant nothing which led to clues that meant even less, but they would all add up shortly if put into the proper context. It was a game and this time it had been the Yost's turn to play.

When asked for details, they would be able to recall conversations about the Carroll brothers and how Martin and Jensen had been forced, pushed, prodded, and tricked into organizing an escape that was, in reality, made-to-order by someone else. As an afterthought, Spencer had tossed some of the credit Stanley's way by saying that he'd helped out a little, but he knew that the Yosts as well as the authorities would be able to see through to the truth. It wasn't any big secret who was in charge. In Spencer's mind it was clear as day.

While Hewitt was stupid, Stoning was intelligent. While Hewitt was dull and thoughtless, Stoning had wit and a sense of humor. While Hewitt had lived in a gray room, Stoning's former cell was adorned with a bright and colorful exit. And when they figured out and acknowledged who was the teacher and who was the student, Spencer guessed the news anchors might start using his middle name again.

James. He strongly suspected that those five little letters just might get him killed before this whole thing was finished.

"The sun's falling, Stan. Time to go to work."

"Just give me a minute."

Stanley was still staring down below in a trance like state. Stepping to the window, Spencer expertly twirled the knife in his hands, weaving it through his fingers as the blade spun around and around.

"What is it, man? You see something of interest?"

"Maybe."

"Really?" It was a pleasant surprise. Most of the time that he put Stanley on lookout it was just to give him something to do; like putting a toddler in front of a television set. "Well, is it good or bad, man? And I swear, Stan, if you tell me there's fifty guys in body armor rushing the building right now, I'm gonna be *so* pissed."

"It's nothing like that…but it might be something. Or maybe nothing. It's down there, though. Down there in the clouds. Hiding. Trying to blend in."

Spencer stopped spinning the knife and gave him a narrow and questioning look. It appeared that Stanley remembered all that cloud bullshit from back in Sacramento, which was a little freaky. "Are you just fucking with me? Because if you are, now isn't the time."

"Down there," he repeated. "They're getting ready to fan out like they always do."

"So?"

"Right across from the lobby. Check it out." Stanley tried to point but stopped when his finger banged into the glass that he forgot was there. "Other side of the street. See?"

"Yeah…yeah, I see. Have you been watching them long?"

"As long as you have, I guess," he answered, knowing that Spencer had seen the same thing but hadn't recognized it for some reason. Either it was too obvious or too well hidden—or maybe there wasn't much difference between the two. Like Spencer's clouds, though, it might have meant nothing. "They look like they're staying behind. What do we do?"

"We get closer." Spencer twisted the rod that put the blinds back into a fully closed position. "We're out of here anyway."

"We can't. We're already too close."

"Just get out there and do what I tell you, Stan," he replied impatiently, grabbing up one of the suitcases. "I'll get close enough to smell her perfume if I want to. And try not to forget, I'm doing this for you."

~ 43 ~

Standing across from the lobby of the Embassy Suites hotel, Beverly watched in amazement as the world she had been ignorantly wandering through began to change right before her eyes. She and Perry Burgess weren't anywhere close to being tight with Special Agent Hildebrandt but he was kind enough to let them know a few of the smaller details that they had been previously unaware of. Apparently, Floyd Madison wasn't the only thing they'd missed completely.

Darkness was approaching rapidly when the first man of many—this one dressed as a mail man—exited a cab in front of the hotel's main entrance and went in without any bags. Neither took much notice of him until he emerged a few minutes later looking much more like what he actually was. His tussled hair had been flattened out and swept back and his gait had changed considerably in the very short timeframe, but it was the fresh clothes and the weapon that flashed from under his jacket that really gave him away.

"Did you catch that?" Burgess asked. "I swear I remember that guy from way back in Redding. He was wearing flannels and a big…"

"…backpack," Beverly finished for him, feeling a little lightheaded. "It was a big green thing with black and red straps on it. If he's who I'm thinking of then I'm pretty sure I saw him in Sacramento too."

"The flowery shirt with the black socks."

"Yeah, that's him," Beverly agreed, taking a longer look as he climbed into the back of the taxi that he'd arrived in. "Oh, God…the cab. The fucking *cab*, Perry."

There it was like it had always been; even in the smaller towns where yellow cabs were seldom seen. If they weren't driving their own rental they might have tried to hail the vehicle a few times.

"They're going for total invisibility. How many do you think there are?"

"Jesus…a *few?* A *thousand?* Who knows?"

As they put the question to each other and considered it, they were forced to step aside for a man who was moving by them very slowly. He wore a sweater and slacks and his feet sort of shuffled as if he had all the time in the world and was simply enjoying a leisurely stroll. His eyes stayed focused out in front of him and it appeared he was preparing to cross the street to the hotel. Only once he had walked past them did he turn back and give them a brief glance.

He wore a knowing and somewhat familiar look that said two things to them: *More than a few. Less than a thousand.* He picked up the pace and crossed quickly without looking back again.

"This is unreal," Burgess muttered quietly as he watched the man disappear into another car that had pulled up out of nowhere. "And off he goes."

With both of their heads spinning, they moved a few yards to the bus stop on their right and dropped down onto the empty bench. Feelings of both encouragement and disillusioned fright bounced off of each other as they tried to make sense of it. Deciding whether they were completely safe or in mortal danger was a hard one to figure.

"How could they not have been caught by now?" Beverly asked. Even as she spoke, more vehicles were coming and going at odd intervals from all around them. "This isn't even the command center. There could be hundreds of them all over the city. They'll be caught tonight, right?"

"At least we're not in Sacramento anymore," Burgess offered optimistically, thinking in terms of population. "It'll help, but Pleasanton isn't nearly as small as it used to be. A lot has changed here since Hewitt blew through the first time. The whole area's been transformed."

They quieted down as another man walked by—a man in a baseball cap who moved with a swift and jaunty step. He bounded by them, only turning his head in their direction once. He continued on without slowing but Beverly kept her voice down anyway.

"I wish we could be with Hildebrandt tonight. Or at least we should be where they're running their communications from. He can't expect us to go back to our rooms ordering room service all night."

"Why shouldn't he?" Burgess countered. "These aren't cops giving out free ride-alongs to citizens. They work for the federal government and they've cut us a ton of slack already. All we have to do is stay off of their toes for a little while longer and we'll have the best book out there."

"I hear what you're saying, Perry, but it feels really wrong to be thinking so much about the book right now—well, tonight anyway. This is the real world here. How can you not be getting caught up in this at all?"

He got up from his seat on the bench and extended a hand to her as she stood up. "My patients live in the real world too. I don't get caught up in *their* lives."

"Neither do I," she stated firmly. "But none of these people are patients. They're innocent people with lives that have nothing to do with us or Stanley Hewitt or any of it. They're just here to be slaughtered so Stanley can…" She trailed off, looking for cars as they crossed back to the hotel.

"So Stanley can *what*, Bev? I've been waiting for you to answer that question since Utah. Why such a precise repeat of his old killings? What's he doing this for? Average psychosis isn't going to sell this all by itself. We've got all the tools to make this work, but at one point or another we're going to have to be really specific and put it in writing. Hewitt could be pretty damn important for that end of it. What if he's not taken alive?"

"He won't be." She hoped not. Since her long day at Danielle Morgan's house in Sacramento, Beverly's hopes for a post-capture interview were no longer a priority. "They're going to kill him the first chance they get."

"And that's fine with me too. As long as we can explain all of this with some degree of believability."

She hesitated for a moment and considered her words carefully. "I still don't believe all of it. He couldn't pull this off. Something's got to be driving him—pushing him. Maybe I should ask *you* what it's all about?"

"Why me?"

"Because Stanley isn't a glory-seeker and you know it. There's no thrill associated with what he does. That's Stoning's thing—not Stanley's."

Burgess understood the message and didn't seem to mind. He even brightened up a little, looking up to the sky and the stars that were slowly filling it. "So, I won't sound like the raging egotist if I agree with you on this one?"

"With you, that's always a risk," she replied. "But if you're willing to concede that Stanley doesn't have the drive or the mental capacity to mastermind this thing then you might actually have something to write about. Because other than scaring the shit out of everyone he comes into contact with, Spencer Stoning hasn't really…well, he hasn't…"

"He hasn't been very busy, I know." Unless they could prove otherwise, Spencer James Stoning was just like Perry Burgess; along for the ride. From all appearances, they were both actively participating but only in advisory roles. "That is, unless what's been happening over the last few weeks has been Stoning's doing, which would be a performance unto itself. And as far as glory-seeking goes, I can tell you a thing or two about Stoning and that pretty face of his. If you think *I'm* vain…"

"And I do."

"Then you should spend some time alone with Stoning for a few days. He redefines the word *vanity*. TV, magazines, newspapers—he couldn't get enough of it. So, if you wanted to formulate a theory that Stoning is the one who…*shit*, wait a second."

Burgess didn't say a word as he rose from the bench, motioning for Beverly to do the same. Both remained silent as they quickly crossed the street and made their way to the hotel lobby. Once they were a few feet inside—just enough so that the sensor wouldn't keep the door open—they stopped and peered back.

"Why does Hildebrandt still have a guy on us?" Burgess asked, waiting for the glass double doors to part again. He looked insulted. "Where's the trust? Since when can they afford to waste manpower on us?"

"They can't," Beverly replied, peering around as they stepped deeper into the lobby. She tugged on his hand, moving them further away from the entrance. "Who was it?"

"It was probably one of Hildebrandt's street guys but I didn't get a good look. I guess once you know about them, they aren't so invisible anymore."

Beverly continued to pull him along with her. It wasn't until they were a few steps from the restaurant's bar that she let go of his hand. She was already looking for a place to sit. "If we see him again, I say we buy him a drink. I'm sure having one."

She had an idea of what was coming and knew she would need it.

✳   ✳   ✳   ✳

"Okay, here's the pitch if what you're telling me about Hewitt is true," Burgess said, sipping his drink through a straw while Beverly downed her second shot. They had settled into a corner but made no effort to maintain a low profile. If Hildebrandt was still having them watched, they didn't want him to think that they'd broken any rules. "Spencer James Stoning; spree killer extraordinaire who loves the limelight, spends a quiet ten-year stretch in federal, rides off into the night with the scariest serial killer in lockdown, and then—wait for it—convinces that serial killer to have another go at it. A fifteen year-old repeat guaranteed to put a couple of names in lights."

"A repeat of crimes that Stanley didn't have any control over the first time around," Beverly reminded him. "He didn't even want to talk about them if you recall. The man that I interviewed didn't remember those nine victims and didn't want to. I swear, by the time I was finished with him, I think he was actually sickened by what he'd done; as much as a person like him *could* be anyway. We're talking about a compulsion—not a choice."

"So, if he's doing it again?"

"Then he feels compelled to do it," she answered quickly. "Choosing to do it or not to do it isn't an option."

"Or?"

"Or someone's compelling him to do it. Someone who craves the spotlight and wants some for himself. He'd have to be pretty damn convincing, Perry." It was sounding right to her but wrong at the same time. "It would take a lot more than a nudge from Stoning to get him started again."

"Or?" he asked again. This was the one that counted and Burgess had knowingly led her right to it. He had a strange, victorious smile on his face that she wanted to suddenly slap off.

"Or *Stanley's* not even the one *doing* it. *Fuck!"* Only twenty or so patrons turned to look at them. "I threw that out there three *weeks* ago, Perry. Spencer Stoning was *your* end of the deal." She pointed a finger at him and tried to keep her voice from shaking while he looked around the bar nervously. "You should have listened to me and at least considered the possibility. You wouldn't hear it, though, would you? You told me I was wrong. You told me to stop saying he didn't do it and to stop calling him fucking Stanley."

Now she had tears in her eyes but they weren't the crying kind. They were tears of rage and frustration. The alcohol helped a little too, as did the smile that was still on Burgess's face.

"Hey—I'm sorry, Beverly."

He couldn't keep the silly grin from his lips, knowing that they'd just come to a major turning point in the book. The star—the *real* star—was very possibly *his* star with everyone else being little more than sidekicks and bit-players. Spencer James Stoning was his monster and nobody else's, though sharing him a little wouldn't be out of the question. A deal was a deal, after all.

"It doesn't change a thing. It moves a few things around and switches priorities a little, but it's still a two-person, coordinated murder spree. It's also still a two-person job to document it. Every bit of information we've gathered is still relevant. All of it."

"That wasn't my concern."

"I'm sure it wasn't. I'm just letting you know that we're in this together no matter what. It's *our* book and I'm committed to that."

"Yeah, committed is what you should be," she fired back. "I think you're actually enjoying this."

"I'm not," he said, forcing a serious expression as he looked into her eyes. "Whether we're right or wrong—it doesn't even matter who's doing it. It could be both of them for all we know. They're equally dangerous and we'll figure it out when they're both in custody. It shouldn't be long."

"They'll catch them here, won't they? Tonight, Perry?"

"I'm sure they will, Bev." As Burgess's voice easily betrayed, his confidence was lacking in just about every respect. "Pleasanton's just a dot on a very big map and this is where they are. It's not like we're in San Francisco or anything."

~ 44 ~

Floyd Madison kept his ears on the radio and eyes on the road as he crossed the Bay Bridge, getting an eerie sense of deja-vu. He had been here very recently but coming from another direction, which was why he guessed it felt so strange. The reason was the same, though. It was a different job with a different purpose but there wouldn't be anything different about what he came for.

Only twenty minutes earlier he had placed a call to an old friend—the kind of friend who Floyd usually paid for their friendliness—and gave her a long identification number that he could hear being tapped out on a keyboard as he read it. He held on for less than a minute before two street names were read back to him. A moment later he received confirmation that the target wasn't in motion. He hoped it still wasn't, though he would find out very shortly if the situation had changed or not. The one incredibly short phone call to Floyd's GPS lady cost him two hundred fifty dollars.

As he left the bridge and moved inland, he realized that he felt bad for what was about to happen in the city that he'd skipped. Pleasanton was about to go down and he felt badly about not being there. He'd thought about it all night and most of the day in his hotel room in Oakland, where he'd run to after the debacle in Sacramento.

About forty miles to the east of him, he knew that a woman was going to die in a few short hours and he knew there was nothing he could do about it. It wasn't that he had any strong feeling's about laying his hands on Stanley Hewitt—the chances were as slim as they'd always been. The problem was that he wasn't even trying this time. There was no effort in that direction at all. It was futile two weeks earlier and was just as futile now. From this point forward, all his current moves would be based on the future and assumptions of what that future would be like.

As for tonight, a girl would be dead. That's all he knew.

Just south of Chinatown and the Nob Hill area, Floyd dropped below the speed limit and started eyeing each of the vehicles as he passed them. He went up and down three side streets before flipping a U-turn and nearly running into the vehicle he was looking for. He parked directly behind the white Cadillac that was as big as a house, then got out of his sedan and felt the hood for engine heat. It was slightly warm, meaning that the target was somewhere nearby.

On the four corners that surrounded him, Floyd noted a gas station, a twenty-four hour donut shop, an apartment building, and a bank. His gut feeling told him that the man was in the bank but it was late and the bank was already closed. After less than five minutes of looking, Floyd found him at the donut shop instead, thanking God that the he hadn't been keeping house in one of the apartments. When Floyd sat down across from the small man reading the out-of-town newspaper, Henry Torres didn't even lower the page from his face.

"Tell me you're not fucking broke already."

Floyd didn't tell him anything of the sort and didn't hold anything back. He simply laid out the full story as he understood it and hoped for a little help from an old friend—the kind of friend who usually paid Floyd for his friendliness.

*   *   *   *

"No, we don't have to go anywhere," Henry Torres said with a smile, motioning for Floyd to sit back down. His laptop computer lay on the table between them. "I can do it from here through the network. I'm hooked in with a wireless setup that's talking to another wireless terminal that was left on by some dipshit who doesn't know anything about security. I'm doing it right now. See—no cables."

"In a donut shop?"

"I'm not in a donut shop," he replied, clicking away with his mouse and banging on the keys occasionally. He took a sip of coffee from a paper cup. "I'm in that bank across the street. I'll probably be on the top ten most wanted list in less than a year. I'll be worth something then, won't I?" He laughed a crazy little laugh in his high and wheezy voice.

Floyd looked over his shoulder and was happy to see that his gut feeling had been right. One way or another, he knew Henry was in the bank.

"Don't ask what I'm doing, Floyd. I'm just kind of borrowing their network for a while. Hey, you want me to open a Swiss bank account for you? It'd take me, like, twenty-five seconds. You can time me."

"Maybe another day," Floyd replied, sadly realizing that the thirty thousand dollars in his glove compartment was the type of money that Henry Torres probably lit cigars and wiped his ass with. "It's just some straight info that I'm looking for right now. Should be pretty easy for a smart guy like you."

Henry's eyes didn't just narrow. They nearly went Chinese on his pudgy face. "No money? See, now that's the kind of shit that makes me paranoid. Floyd Madison showing up twice in one month and he doesn't want any money from me? It's odd, don't you think?"

He knew where Henry was coming from and started to wish that he'd asked for a little cash just to keep their relationship on a normal level. It wouldn't have felt right, though. He couldn't explain it. It just wasn't right.

"Yeah, it's strange, Henry. But it's not as strange as a genius like you not knowing when you're wired. I find that odd and it makes me wonder about *you*. Have you seen Devereaux lately?"

"I haven't seen that prick since he bagged me in Reno. Are you saying that motherfucker cheated and wired me up? Man, that's dirty. He's really got me wired, no bullshit?"

"Not anymore." The two words made Henry's face light up. "He probably knows you're in Frisco, though, so I'd think about relocating if I was you."

"I just might do that. What do you need, Floyd? Name it."

"I already did."

"That's it? No fooling? You must be pretty fucking desperate."

Floyd watch the man's chubby fingers fly across the tiny keyboard without making a single mistake as he plumbed through a seemingly endless pile of information. It was all Greek to him but he couldn't ignore the results once the query was finished. Henry hit another couple of keys before spinning the laptop computer around for Floyd's approval. The whole thing took less than ten minutes.

"How'd you do that?"

"It's a secret," Henry replied with a laugh. "In your line of work it surprises me that you don't have someone like me on the payroll. There are twelve year-old kids that know how to do this shit. They're not as good as me but it'd be damn useful for the future. You should keep that in mind when you score big again."

"But this is FBI information."

"No, it isn't," Henry corrected. "It's just a credit card trail from a private citizen named Beverly McGrath. You can see a definite hotel pattern starting in Oregon which goes clear down to Sacramento. It ends there…but it doesn't."

"But I can see it right there, Henry. Embassy Suites. Pleasanton. Now I even know what rooms they're in. How can you do that without her credit info?"

"I don't need it," Henry beamed. "Based on the pattern, I can tell that she's in-house but somebody else is picking up the tab for the room. Then working backwards and reexamining the pattern, I can tell you who's paying for everything now. And I'll tell you what, Floyd…it isn't your standard account. I haven't exactly hacked into the FBI's precious files—it's a lot easier in the spy novels than in real life—but you don't need to be a super-genius to read a credit card statement and cross-reference it with certain criteria. Hey, you want a wide-screen TV? We'll bill it to the feds. Where do you want it shipped?"

"Just the stuff I asked for, Henry. Where are they headed next? It'll be in a place called Salinas, so that should make it easier for you."

"It's already done," Henry stated with absolute certainty. "I already know where they're going. Reservations have been made and deposits are down. You asked for it, you got it."

"All of it? You've got everywhere they'll be for the next nine days?"

"And then some. No problem—just like I said."

"And then some *what?*" Floyd asked. "We're already looking at Salinas, Santa Maria and Santa Barbara."

"Yeah," Henry replied with a nod as he finished the last of his coffee. "And Camarillo, Diamond Bar, San Jacinto, Coachella, Palm Springs—the list goes on. Same three-day setup as all the others. Do those places mean anything to you?"

No they didn't. They were a strange mix of medium and small places that were probably pulled out of the ass of an FBI profiler based on Hewitt's own patterns. Perhaps they knew what they were doing. Perhaps not. Did the cities mean anything to Floyd?

"Not yet, Henry."

It was getting late but they passed another hour or so just shooting the breeze. It was something that neither Floyd nor Henry had done with anyone in quite some time. Covering everything from Henry's chronic thievery and polygamistic pursuits to Floyd's gross fortune and nearly equal misfortune, they chatted like old friends who hadn't seen each other in years. Before they were done, a certain amount of parity between them was achieved. Floyd also decided he was going to drive on to Pleasanton tonight.

It was late already and the reasons not to go were many, but something almost seemed to be pulling him there whether it was a conscious decision or not. While Henry jabbered on, Floyd tried repeatedly to convince himself that tonight just might be his lucky night, but he was having a little trouble listening to that self and it's bullshit right now. It could have been as simple as a sense of guilt for all of his failures or payback for his successes, but in the end he decided to shift the blame to his rotten instincts. They were as good a reason as any.

"I hope this helps in some way," Henry said with all sincerity as he copied down the list of cities, dates, and hotels that had come from his . "That ought to do it."

Floyd took the sheet of paper and folded it up, placing it in his front shirt pocket. He wanted to thank the felon for all his assistance—assistance given without threats or other pressure—but he simply nodded appreciatively and gave him some advice instead.

"Like I said, Henry, you should really get the hell out of here. Devereaux is still gonna be on your ass and a little thing like a lost GPS transmitter isn't going to slow him down too much. The longer it takes, the more you'll be worth."

"And the less negotiating I'll be able to do," Henry agreed. "I've got it. Anything else I should be aware of? You know—transmitters and the like?"

"You're clean as a whistle. Be safe and don't go through Pleasanton if you can help it. Every federal agent in the state is just an hour to the east of us. So, unless you've got business that you just can't pass up on, I'd steer clear of that place."

"Don't fret over me, Floyd." He was back to his newspaper before the door swung shut. "I don't even have a wife there."

*   *   *   *

The drive to Pleasanton took less time than he'd imagined and he found himself cruising the streets as usual with as much as two hours to spare. It wouldn't make Stanley Hewitt or Spencer Stoning any more visible or save any lives, but he felt his presence was necessary for reasons that he couldn't explain and he was glad he was there for it anyway. Regardless of what happened, no one would be able to say that he didn't try his hardest—except for himself, of course.

~ 45 ~

It was around eleven-thirty in the morning when the first loud scream was heard by every person in a one block radius. There were many screams to follow but the person who found their twenty year-old daughter nailed down to her own bedroom floor had shredded most of their voice box with the first one. The high-pitched shrieks came one after another and were still audible even after the ambulance door slammed shut on their source. They fought with the siren in terms of volume all the way to the hospital and continued to pierce ears until the subject was finally medicated. When they woke up two hours later, it started all over again with renewed zeal and vocal strength.

Richard Verner was a hard-nosed corrections officer with the Federal Detention Center in Pleasanton and was known for his stony and intimidating appearance as well as a toughness that was unmatched in his field. But when he found his little girl stuck to the floor looking like a battered and bloody voodoo doll, he screamed like a woman and didn't stop for three whole days.

*   *   *   *

A few hours after Richard Verner stopped screaming, Brandy Shepard of Salinas, California became statistic number eight. She was twenty-six years old and was discovered in a frightening state of disrepair. Whether it was because her feet were situated too far out in front of her or because she was a little on the heavy side, both knees had hyper-extended completely, bending them at a nauseating angle and leaving her a close second to Sacramento's Danielle Morgan on the unofficial scale of all things fucked up.

It was a tough few days for everyone involved. Not really tougher than any of the others, but only because a lot of folks were getting used to it by now. It also didn't help that there were still the cities of Santa Maria and Santa Barbara to worry about.

Not to mention whatever came next.

~ 46 ~

"Vancouver, Altamont, Redding, Chico, Yuba City, Sacramento, Pleasanton, and Salinas," Spencer noted, then whistled through his teeth. "You're quite the eclectic traveler, Stan. Did you pick these places because they were pretty, or what?"

He was sitting Indian style in the dark brown dirt in between two rows of what he believed to be grape vines. Whatever they were, thousands of similar rows surrounded them for miles, obscuring them from view of anyone who cared to look. They'd chosen the highest point in Santa Maria that they could find and had been resting under the sun and the moon for two days. Picking a new residence in town was too risky. Practically everything was now.

"Just places I went, Spence. I was scared and confused and I was turned all around most of the time. Running was all I was doing. Pretty is just how it worked out. I never really noticed."

Spencer thought he looked plenty scared, confused, and turned all around even as he was speaking. Stanley always seemed to have that look about him, though it was probably aggravated by the fact that they had only woken up twenty minutes earlier. His eyes were puffy and still crusted with sleep and his hair stood straight up in the back. He also looked at peace with himself, however, having grown accustomed to a long life of fear and disarray.

"But why Vancouver? I would have headed north and far away from Washington myself."

"That's what I tried to do," Stanley replied, not looking the least bit embarrassed by it. "I thought I was in Canada, man."

"Vancouver, *British Columbia?*"

"Yeah, and it ain't funny either. I told you I was confused."

*   *   *   *

"Confused can't be the right word," Burgess argued as he skimmed over a few of the later chapters in *Understanding The Sickness.* Their morning started earlier than most since sleep was something they'd both found harder to do lately. Even in their own large rooms at the nicest hotel in Santa Maria, the last two evenings had passed somewhat fitfully. "He obviously wasn't so confused that he couldn't keep track of the days and the time. In one breath he's a complete moron and in the next he's a Swiss watch. You bounce all over the damn place in this thing."

He set the book down next to his orange juice and took another bite of his waffle.

"How about *disoriented* then?" she asked, stealing the book away before something could spill on it. "I wrote this for true-crime section, not the New England Journal of Medicine. Most people don't know the difference and I wouldn't want anyone to get…"

"*Confused* by it?" he finished for her, feeling like the king of wit.

"Something like that. There's so much back-story going on that I decided to keep everything sequential and in it's proper order before diving into Stanley's head. I'll bet half the people who bought it didn't even care about the reasons involved. I know it's just a slasher book up until the final few chapters—you don't have to tell me that. The title was for marketing reasons…at the publisher's insistence."

"Don't you hate that?" he asked, still sore ten years later that his own book had to be titled *Man Of Rage.* He'd originally wanted to call it *Kill Switch;* a truly kick-ass title if he'd ever heard one.

"I'm not too worried about it this time. I think we should be able to write our own ticket. And you're right; we'll be able to cap off the manuscript with whatever angle turns out to be the truth. If Spencer Stoning's pushing the buttons and pulling the strings, it'll only make it that much more interesting."

"But what would that make Hewitt then?" he asked. They'd been dancing around the same questions for days. "It's like one of those Mad Libs and we're going to need a noun pretty soon. Would it make him just another murderer? A co-conspirator? An accomplice?"

"A *victim?*" Beverly offered, knowing that she could get away with such sentiments for the moment. If Special Agent Hildebrandt was around, she wouldn't have tried it.

"It would make for an interesting approach. Hewitt as the victim. We'd be hated for it."

"Not after we present his background in the final chapters. I've done it before and ended up selling fifty thousand more books than you did. If we do everything exactly right, nobody will hold it against us. I mean, it *is* a sad story, Perry."

✳   ✳   ✳   ✳

So what if it's a tragedy? That's no excuse for anything. There'll never be an excuse good enough, Dr. McGrath. Never.

Floyd firmly believed all those things, though he still thought her book was hard to read without feeling at least a little sympathetic. It was more sympathetic than anyone would ever feel for Spencer Stoning in Perry Burgess's book anyway. He was just an imbalanced freak as far as Floyd was concerned.

Aside from being in Santa Maria this time, nothing was too different from any other place on a bright and sunny day-three. They were eating food together, Beverly McGrath had driven them there, and she would soon be paying for the meal too. All in all, it was a standard Burgess and McGrath outing. The interviews with past participants were done and another chapter or two was probably on paper, leaving them with little more to do than wait for the next act to fulfill itself. Everyone knew it would be over in less than eighteen hours unless the world happened to end before then. After that, they'd all be bound for Santa Barbara. It was already in their mental calendars.

He'd read through *Man Of Rage* a couple more times since Sacramento but had shifted his attention over to *Understanding The Sickness* in the last few days. Floyd still didn't understand and didn't want to, but reading about Hewitt's childhood seemed to even things out a bit. It was like experiencing Hewitt's punishment for his crimes but from retroactive viewpoint, as if he was exacting a refund for payments made to him over thirty-five years earlier.

It was still no excuse, though.

From a parking lot across the street, Floyd watched them dine but paid much more attention to the book than their breakfast. He could see their car clearly anyway and would know if they tried to evade him. He suspected they just might since Special Agent Hildebrandt had probably spent a decent amount of time with the both of them in Sacramento and he wished he could know what the agent had said. He hoped it wasn't a reason for concern.

For two weeks, they had tried to avoid the FBI as much as Floyd himself, but they were obviously all in league together now. He wondered what had changed since he'd first seen Hildebrandt way back in Altamont.

✳   ✳   ✳   ✳

"So, what about Altamont then? I know you wanted to get the hell out of Washington but why head on down to Oregon? It couldn't have been as arbitrary a decision as it sounds."

"It wasn't," Stanley replied, not having any idea what the word *arbitrary* meant. Whatever it was, he was pretty sure he wasn't it. "I was just kind of driving around—I don't know where—and I saw a sign."

"What, like a sign from God?"

"No, like a sign on the freeway. It said *Altamont*. I decided to go there."

"What the hell for?" Spencer asked, wishing he could be taping the conversation they were having. If he ever found himself in a crappy mood at some point in the future, he suspected that listening to the tape would make him laugh a little and brighten his day up. It would also help him remember his friend Stanley who would probably be dead before long. He guessed there was a good chance they'd both be. "Why did you want to go to Altamont?"

"NASCAR. I liked watching those cars go round and round. They're so fast. All of 'em painted real cool and stuff. I'd seen it on TV but I never been to real races before."

"And I'll bet you still haven't," Spencer replied, pursing his lips together and making nervous little ticking noises with his tongue and teeth. "You never made it there, did you?"

"Yeah, I never did. How—?"

"You probably didn't even ask around, huh?"

"Well…no," Stanley admitted.

"And you never found it. You just looked all over for it until you found something totally different to do."

"*Exactly*. It's so *weird* when you do that." It was weird and Stanley loved it. "How'd you know?"

"Magic, Stan. Fucking magic."

Since Stanley already thought Spencer was god-like, it didn't make any sense to ruin the image and make him feel dumber at the same time. If he explained that the city of Altamont in Oregon was a completely different entity than the Altamont Raceway in northern California, Spencer could only guess how ignorant Stanley might feel. Then, if he told Stanley that Altamont Raceway had been less than thirty miles from where they'd stayed in Pleasanton a few days earlier, it would be even worse. He knew it would only hurt his feelings.

∗   ∗   ∗   ∗

"It goes a lot deeper than simple hurt feelings, Perry. Parents leave their kids all the time and they don't always go bad. They get divorced, they get remarried, they come, they go—these are all normal things and nearly half the children in the world are exposed to it. Stanley is light-years beyond the standard parental separation trauma, but it really is the root of everything that made him what he is. He wasn't just your average damaged kid. It was almost like he had every force of nature working against him from day-one."

"Is this the part where I'm supposed to start crying?"

"Not yet," she replied, brushing off the sarcasm. "With Stanley, we're only talking about one parent right from the start. An alcoholic mother…"

"Not to mention a heroin addict and a prostitute as well."

"A real winner," she agreed. "And her drug use was prevalent long before and long after Stanley's birth. I know I already covered that in the first book but times have changed and we can recycle it with newer and harder data to back it up. Hell, fifteen years ago I could have smoked a cigarette right here at this table. Prenatal narcotic intake is a no-brainer now and there's no way anyone can hold him responsible for what she did while he was in the womb. That would just be the beginning of making the reader feel sorry for him. A poor, innocent little boy with a drug addicted whore for a mother? Anyone with kids would feel something for him and his story hasn't even started to get original yet."

"Good. Because we'll need a hell of a lot more than that tired shit. Half of the serial killers that have been identified had alcoholic hookers for mothers. It's not a big discovery. It's a cliché. I could rattle off a list of them for you right now."

"I'm sure you could. But throw in the multitudes of deviant boyfriends, dealers, pimps, and clients walking in and out of the house all day long, not to mention a bunch of those 'special uncles' we love so much. Look hard at the old hospital records and you're starting to see a pattern of physical and sexual torture on a daily, if not *several* times daily basis. Views on sexual abuse have changed even more than drug, alcohol, and physical abuse since back when *Sickness* hit the shelves and Stanley had all kinds of it thrown at him starting as early as his infancy. We can use the exact same words and phrases from *Sickness* if we want to but it'll be even more powerful now."

"Not good enough, Bev." Burgess was shaking his head at her, wishing she would just stop. "As sick as it sounds, it's not uncommon. Terrible parent destroys the child; state takes away the child; mother cleans herself up enough to start collecting checks from the state again; child goes back into her loving, track-marked arms. Wash, rinse, repeat. How many times did she leave him with somebody for months at a time?"

"At least twelve. Probably more."

"And how many times did Hewitt revolve through the state's doors?"

"Five times that he went back to his mother and at least twice as many foster homes in between. And they weren't exactly a picnic either. He was a hard one to place anywhere."

"Why's that?" Burgess asked with a sarcastic laugh. "Is it because he was the only five year-old on the block with crabs?" He chuckled even louder. "Because I'd guess that having to wipe down your tricycle seat every time another kid wants to ride it would tend to make *any* child bitter."

He continued to laugh to himself but stopped abruptly when his eyes moved back across Beverly's face. He was expecting the usual scowl of disapproval, which he would have completely ignored, but was treated to a look of woeful disappointment instead.

"He was four years old, Perry—not five. And it wasn't crabs—it was syphilis. He was four." She glared up at him for a moment then returned to her notes. "Four years old. You're an asshole."

In an unexpected state of shock, Burgess had no witty reply to that one and didn't say a word as Beverly scribbled several more lines in her notebook. He usually found her pouty looks to be mildly arousing if not blindingly sexy, but now wasn't one of those times.

"It was just one of the little details that the publisher wanted edited out," she said coldly, still scratching away with her pen.

"*Jesus.* Do you mind if I ask why? I'm sorry, Bev. I've heard some shit before...but..."

"The book was called *Understanding The Sickness*, not *Pity The Sick Man*. Saying he was abused was all the understanding they needed to sell it."

*   *   *   *

Smooth as razor wire, Doctor Silvertongue. What the fuck did you go and say this time?

He couldn't hear them and was too far to read their lips—not that he'd ever been endowed with such a skill in the first place—but it was obvious that Dr. Burgess had screwed the pooch again. It seemed he couldn't go more than an hour without sticking his foot in his mouth in one way or another. And it looked like he enjoyed it most of the time, which was the strange part. Here the man was, traveling for weeks with a beautiful woman and all he could manage to do was antagonize her. It was strictly third-grade behavior and Floyd thought that Dr. McGrath was at least at the junior-high level. In fact whenever he thought of her he still pictured her in that old candy-striper uniform, which really was a very hot look.

Even in the interviews that followed Hewitt's capture and Floyd's rise to celebrity status, she had a sweet and youthful shine to her regardless of what she wore. She was impressed with him, perhaps even in awe of him, and he liked it. Where he fit in now was a total mystery and he didn't like that nearly as much. He hated not knowing for sure.

What did he say to you, doctor? What did Agent Hildebrandt say about me? He wasn't there and he couldn't know anything. What lies did he tell you? I've checked my phone and my answering machine back home—they're working just fine. I'm in the book—White Pages, Yellow Pages, and directory assistance—why haven't you called?

Do you know that I'm here? Did you know I've been watching? Do you even know why?

Talk to me, Dr. McGrath. What did Hildebrandt say to you? Be honest.

*   *   *   *

"But to be honest with you, Stan, Altamont Raceway is right here in California." He wanted to be kind and tried to hold back—really he did—but letting people know just how painfully dumb they were had always been one of the many things that Spencer found hard to control. "The city of Altamont is just a plain old town in Oregon. You are *so* fucking stupid sometimes."

"Are you sure about that? *California?* For reals?"

"Yeah, *for reals*, man," Spencer replied with a snort. "I take it you didn't go to Redding for any serious reason, though. You were just running like mad by then, right?"

"I guess so," Stanley answered with a bewildered and uncertain look. "I wasn't thinking right. I probably should've worn gloves or something. Like in the movies when they want to do something bad...they always wear gloves. I should have done that too."

"Yeah, you definitely should have, Stan. Gloves are the most important item any fine killer can own. You've got to have them. You know it and I know you know it, so I won't bother going there."

He didn't want to ask why Stanley didn't bother to cover up those tell-tale fingerprints of his, so he let it pass without another word. He suspected he already knew the reason even if Stanley didn't.

Besides having a smooth three-word name that sounded neat, the best serial killers in history had another thing in common; they got caught. They *had* to get caught. Without people knowing that three-worded name, there was no point in having one and fingerprints were only one of the ways a person could throw in the towel and step out of the ring. But he still wasn't completely sure if Stanley was capable of seeing it as such.

"The only gloves I ever wore were the ones I put on when it snowed. And you can't do anything with those things on. They're all big and stuff and you can't grab nothing and you can't hold your knife or your hammer or your..." Stanley turned both palms upwards then stopped looking at them, moving his eyes up to the sky instead. He leaned his head back and remained in the position long after his hands drop back down to his sides. "I should just shut up now."

"No way, man. Don't even think about it. This is what I paid admission for. You don't talk about that old shit nearly enough."

"But I don't remember that stuff. Like it didn't *really* happen, you know? I mean, it's like I *know* it didn't happen—but it turns out that it *did* if you know what I mean." He searched Spencer's face for understanding and thought he found some. "Do you *know* what I mean?"

"I might know something about it," Spencer replied. "I may not know it exactly the way you do since I don't have the same types of experiences you've had, but I know that odd feeling a person gets when certain things don't seem quite...real. Like they never even happened at all."

"Yeah, yeah—that's it," Stanley agreed, growing excited as he always did when he and Spencer were within a few chapters of being on the same page. "And it's like a dream you had once. An old one. A beautiful dream from a long time ago."

"Beautiful? What the fuck could be beautiful about it? I figured it'd be more like a nightmare."

"A nightmare?"

"Yeah, man. I'd think that whenever you remembered something from back then it would be one long dream of total fucking terror. I read the book, Stan. I read *her* book—the one she wrote about you. I know about your mother and a lot of the other stuff too."

"My *mother?*" Stanley's eyes lit up at the very mention of her. "What about her?"

"What do you mean *'What about her?'* You nailed her to the fucking floor, Stan."

His eyes only dimmed for a moment before lighting up again. "Oh, *that.* Yeah, I definitely remember that. What about it?"

~ 47 ~

"No, Perry, it wasn't about anger or frustration or any of the usual aggression triggers. It wasn't even an aggressive act as far as he was concerned. Just a simple solution to a reoccurring problem."

"And nailing her into the corner of her room achieved that?" Burgess asked, doing his best to keep any incredulous expressions in check. "Hewitt was twelve by then; a prime age to become a runaway. There were plenty of options other than what he decided to go with."

"*Decided* had nothing to do with it. He must have loved his mother to some extreme. No matter what happened to him, he'd never known anything different and after a while anything can become normal to anybody. Now, I don't know what made him pick up that hammer or what drew him to it in the first place, but he did what he did out of an instinct that had been getting more and more warped with each passing year and he didn't feel like he had a choice in the matter."

"He could have tied her up instead or locked her in the basement," Burgess argued feebly. "That would have kept her at home."

"Nails are more permanent. They hold houses together for years. How's that for poetic?" It was the first time she'd phrased it in such terms and thought it sounded great. The words went into her notebook as fast as they'd come from her mouth.

"Okay, it's a wonderful piece of prose you're working on there. So what? What about the blood, Beverly? Now, *there's* an instinct that's in all of us. We may react differently but we all definitely react to the sight of blood. How could he see it squirting out of her toes and not know the damage he was causing? There must have been quite a bit of pain involved."

"Maybe," Beverly agreed, but already had her answer lined up. She'd written the book after all. "But there were no signs of preparatory strangulation or head wounds like on his murder victims—not even a small bump, so she was probably in a drug induced stupor when he started hammering. She *had* to be unconscious when he did it."

"Why?"

"Because you couldn't just stand there and take it. Nobody could. But if she did happen to jerk away reflexively and even if she bled all over the place, it wouldn't have made any difference to Stanley. Blood and pain were normal daily occurrences by then. Nobody stopped when *he* screamed. Nobody stopped when *he* bled. And as far as pure agony goes, he wouldn't know it if he saw it. Normal is a relative term and Stanley's mother got a serious dose of the normality he'd been raised with."

"And you're one hundred percent sure that he didn't kill her?"

"Completely," she stated. "It was only a basis for the MO that we know of today and, unlike any of the others, he actually gave his case worker a detailed explanation of why he did it. He understood this one and could put it into words. At twelve, it made perfect sense in that messed up little head of his."

"And how much sense did it make to you?"

"Just enough to let me know that I wanted to write the book on him," she replied, wondering about the wisdom of her decision even now. "Stanley didn't want his mother to leave and he made absolutely sure that she didn't. Sticking her into a corner of her room that he could see from both the inside and outside of the house was the only goal he had. It's horrible yet it's as simple as it gets. And as bad as it might sound to anyone but Stanley himself, it was probably the most comforting three days of his whole miserable life."

"That's a lot of days to be nailed to a floor."

"Especially when you're withdrawing from every drug in the pharmacy at the same time," she said with a slow nod. "Under those circumstances cutting into her own arteries must have seemed like the best way to go. Maybe the only way."

"And then he walks in and finds her drained out onto the floor," Burgess said with a long sigh, trying to picture the scene but knowing he could never see it the way Stanley Hewitt had. "An imperfect end to an imperfect relationship."

"It was more perfect than you might imagine. Sure, she was nailed down and dead…but at least she was still there when he went looking for her."

Having said that, Beverly put her notebooks away and quickly finished off the last of her coffee before rising from her seat. She scribbled her signature on the credit card receipt and stepped away from the table, having nothing more to add.

*   *   *   *

Noting the exhausted and uneven pace as she walked away from what had obviously been an uncomfortable breakfast conversation, Floyd kept his eyes on Beverly until she disappeared back into the hotel lobby and out of sight. Guessing she was only headed back to her room, he felt confident that she wouldn't be vanishing on him too easily as long as their rental car was within his visual range. Perry Burgess was still sitting at the table where he'd been abandoned and it didn't look like he was going to get up to follow her, which was just as well since he didn't look invited anyway.

Balancing his attention between a few chapters of *Understanding The Sickness* and the rented Pontiac, Floyd didn't leave the parking lot or even his own car as he waited patiently for the next move.

The morning had already given way to noon and he would wait until darkness came if he had to. Though it felt like the standard day-three event was rapidly approaching, Floyd had a suspicion that he wouldn't be cruising the streets tonight.

~ 48 ~

Shade encroached on their last few warm spaces of earth and the sun was all but gone by the time they finished transferring their belongings the back of their latest vehicle. Spencer had only been gone for an hour or so but it was long enough for Stanley to slip back into his normal state of doubt and vulnerability.

"I was almost afraid you were gonna leave me here, man. Just a little bit, you know? Not like you'd do that, but I was just afraid a little."

"Don't be. I'm here until we're done mopping up." Spencer carefully unfolded what clothing they had and draped several different outfits over the open lid of the trunk. He took a few steps back and looked at each item, glancing back and forth between the clothes and Stanley. "Formal or janitorial? What do you think?"

The blue suit was nice for a cheap Giorgio knock-off but he could sense that Stanley's interest was drawn to the simple gray coveralls with the long zipper in front. "I used to have jammies like those."

"Well, we're not gonna be sleeping in them, Stan. What'll it be?"

"Does it even really matter?"

"Not unless they're going to bury you in it," Spencer replied with a dry smile, trying hard not to picture Stanley in little one-piece jammy-jams with bunnies and bears stitched into them. "If that was case I'd go with the suit, but it isn't so I'd dress for comfort if I were you. We'll be in close tonight; closer than is really safe for us, but it can't be helped. Either of them will be fine."

"Give me the gray ones then."

He yanked the coveralls from the trunk and kicked off his shoes before putting his legs into them. After pulling the zipper up to his neck, he put his shoes back on and bounced around for a few minutes as he tried to figure out why they felt so familiar to him. Spencer simply stood back and watched the spectacle, wishing he had picked up a pair sooner. It was pretty close to what their old prison uniforms back at Woodhall were like and he knew Stanley would feel comfortable in them.

By the time his partner calmed down, Spencer had picked out a matching cap for him to wear and he put it on immediately. The whole outfit looked very natural on him and Spencer thought that maybe it was how things were originally meant to be. Not the prison part; just the clothing aspect of it.

Maybe in another life or in another time it was supposed to be *Stan the maintenance man* instead of *Stanley Lewis Hewitt, serial murderer*. It would never be *Stan the professor* or *Stan the biochemist*, but *Stan the exterminator* or *Stan the groundskeeper* might have conceivably worked out. It was as unimportant as ever and time was shorter than ever, but Spencer couldn't help but wonder about the alternatives.

"It'll be showtime soon," he offered as he slipped into his own outfit. "I'm guessing I don't need to tell you that this is going to be a little more difficult than before."

"Yeah, it's a miracle we've made it this far. We ought to be dead, man."

"And we will be if we're not extra careful on this one. We'll only get the one shot at it tonight if we've plotted it all out right."

"What if we blow it?" Stanley asked.

"It sure as shit won't be from a lack of trying. And I'm not just trusting your instincts on this one, Stan. I saw the same thing you did and I think tonight just might be our night. The poor girl's been begging for it for weeks now. It's tragic, really."

It was almost six p.m. when they said a final goodbye to the plot of land they'd occupied for the last few days and wound their way through several back roads on the outskirts of Santa Maria. Finding a secluded location—much more secluded than the vineyard had been since nothing would ever be harvested in the dense vegetation—Spencer pulled the car off of the road and started driving haphazardly through fields and brush. They only had to drive for a few minutes before stopping.

"What do you think about this place?" Spencer asked, though it was merely a formality. He'd found the perfect spot and it didn't matter what Stanley thought.

"Looks private. How deep do we go?"

"Since we're in the middle of nowhere, I'm thinking we don't need to go down more than a couple feet," Spencer replied, dropping the shovel onto the soft earth at Stanley's feet. "I'd do it myself but I'm not really dressed for this."

~ 49 ~

It was close to seven p.m. and the sky was fading quickly from orange into a rusty shade of gray as the volume began to rise. There were fewer state and federal authorities involved than the pair of doctors had seen before and there was something depressingly electric in the air around them. It felt strangely like panic, which was unsettling since most of it was coming from bigger than average men carrying all sorts of automatic weaponry. The preparations were steadily picking up steam but the hopelessness of it all was more than evident.

Beverly and Burgess had been sitting quietly at the same table for over two hours, taking additional notes and making corrections to a manuscript that was all but complete. The beginning sections that started in Black Pine, Idaho and Woodhall Penitentiary were well documented as were the agreed upon background chapters on Stanley Hewitt and Spencer Stoning. In keeping with the general theme, the middle of the book followed Hewitt's current escapades compared to the original murders as well as whatever domestic nightmares Stoning had produced along the way. As far as Burgess was concerned, Stoning's disturbing interludes were some of the most entertaining portions he'd written in years.

The end was still up for grabs, though, and the latest suspicion between the pair was that Santa Maria wouldn't finish up anything other than another redundant chapter full of somebody else's pain. They hadn't shared such feelings with anyone else but the sentiment could practically be sniffed out of the air and was visible on nearly every face present.

Santa Barbara was where it would happen if it was going to happen at all. As for the citizens of Santa Maria; they'd be in a lot of folk's prayers tonight.

"Dr. McGrath?"

The voice came from behind her as she and Burgess watched the scene that was old hat by now. She hadn't spent too much time in his company but Beverly could tell who it was before she turned around. The look on Burgess's face as he peered over her shoulder helped too.

"Aren't you supposed to be doing something important, agent?" she asked, turning in time to see Dwight Hildebrandt pull a chair from an empty table and take a seat with them. He exhaled deeply and made himself right at home as he stared out through the tinted glass that enclosed much of the lounge, watching a few of his own team's cruisers go through the usual moves. "It looks like you're taking the evening off."

"I'm just getting started, doctor. The *evening* your referring to will probably last until tomorrow afternoon, so setting a decent pace for myself will be important. I was curious about how you two are holding up."

"Splendidly, agent," Beverly replied, painting a weak smile on her face while she studied his own discomfort. They'd had brief conversations with each other and Beverly had been handed four separate envelopes of carefully selected FBI information by the agent since their meeting in Sacramento, but this was the first time he'd acknowledged both doctors so publicly.

"Dr. Burgess?"

"Me—I'm fine," he answered, shifting his eyes around the room. Special Agent Hildebrandt had come alone.

"Good," he said with a thoughtful nod. "How about those pictures I gave you? The interviews—can you use them?"

"The autopsy shots will have to be cropped like mad and a few names will have to be cut out, but it's all useable."

"And how are those rooms working for you? A little nicer than Motel Six, I hope."

"Great rooms, Dwight," Beverly stated, her tone shifting to one of impatience. "Go ahead and ask for whatever it is you want. We've already been through the whole getting-to-know-you thing. Now, what can we do for you?"

"You can get out of here tonight—as soon as possible," he replied in a serious tone, speaking directly to Beverly. Burgess would have had to lean across the table and wave his arms to grab his attention. "You won't miss anything here, doctor. I think you know how it works by now."

"And just where do you expect us to go?"

"Santa Barbara," Hildebrandt answered as his pager began to beep. He ignored it in the same fashion that he was currently ignoring Perry Burgess.

"You'd be headed there tomorrow anyway and I'm sure you've got to be somewhat anxious to get back home even if it's only for a few days. Besides, I could really use you there."

"For what?"

"For help. It's a sixty mile drive. You can be there in an hour."

"Why?"

"A person of interest to us hasn't been too keen on cooperating and I suspect she might react a little better to you than the men I've had her surrounded with. I know it, in fact." Hildebrandt's pager beeped again but he simply muted it and kept his eyes on Beverly. "I could really use your assistance on this and if my sources are right then Santa Barbara is where it comes together."

"You mean you still have faith in your sources?" Burgess quipped.

"Oh, they could be wrong," Hildebrandt replied with a shrug as he turned back to Beverly. "I'm not entirely sold on it myself, but let me ask you—just how crazy would Stanley Hewitt have to be to go after his number ten again?"

"Gail Rainier?" Beverly nearly choked on her coffee. *"He couldn't..."*

But of course he could, Beverly reminded herself. He or somebody else. If Stanley and Spencer Stoning could walk out of maximum security, traveling freely and undetected to predesignated locations while producing a steady body count, then they could really be expected to do just about anything.

"Ah—it's probably nothing," Hildebrandt offered, seemingly dismissive of his own words as he waved the suggestion away and checked his pager. "But I thought I'd run it by you anyway. We've been sitting on her for almost a month now and she's about ready to snap. Some people need more than the normal kinds of protection, Dr. McGrath."

"And you just want me to drive down there talk to her?"

"Or whatever it is you do. Sit with her, talk with, stay with her for a few days—if I knew what to do I'd have done it by now. Calming her down would be a good place to start." Hildebrandt pulled his phone out and dialed a number. "Her husband's on the faculty at UCSB and her kids are in the fourth and sixth grades. None of them have been to work or school since Stoning and Hewitt ran off and...." He stopped speaking and held up a finger as though it was a pause-button to their conversation.

"What is it?" he asked of the person he had just called. He looked annoyed by the interruption but continued to listen. "I know that. We've had sixteen of them over the last two days alone." Mild annoyance gave way to irritation as he lowered his pause-button finger to the table and took a sip of coffee. "So?" He waited a few seconds then repeated himself a little more vigorously. "*So?* Send *them* over to check it out."

A second later Agent Hildebrandt lost all interest in the party he had joined. He quickly spun around in his chair and lowered his voice, leaving Beverly and Burgess with only each other to stare at. He listened quietly for over a minute before speaking again and going back into motion.

"Are you sure about that?" He was already rising from his seat. His mood appeared to fall somewhere between rejuvenated and terribly bothered—a combination he wore remarkably well. "Don't just tell me what *he* told you. I asked if you were sure or not. Are you?"

Hildebrandt pulled the phone away from his face and exhaled loudly as he shook his head with a bored expression. He took another gulp of his coffee before putting his mouth to the phone again. His disinterested face didn't match the words that began pouring out.

"Then you should already be there. No...*no*, Hargrove. Just give me the address and get there. Seal it off and I'll be along shortly." He listened again for a moment but the moment didn't last long. "That's right—me and everyone else. Ten minutes until I'm there and twenty's all you're getting after that. We'll be in full swing in half an hour anyway. Feed it to the locals when we're done but don't be an asshole about it. It'll sound like we got close and missed them."

Beverly and Burgess's ears perked up at the last sentence and they both got up to follow him as he attempted a quick departure from the lounge. He made no move to stop them and even gestured toward the main lobby as he finished his call.

"Then do it. I'm on my way and I want it clear when I get there." Hildebrandt folded the small phone up with a sharp snap and stuffed it back into his pocket. His attention was quickly returned to Beverly.

"So, this Santa Barbara thing with Gail Rainier—what do you think?"

"Sorry, agent, I'm not going to miss whatever's happening here," she said. "You made that sound awfully important."

"This is a management type of position I've got here, doctor, so everything has to sound important. It's nothing to get excited about—just another Hewitt sighting. We get fifty to sixty a day. I usually wouldn't be going myself but there's a stolen vehicle from Salinas involved, which requires me to be on scene."

"And that's not important?" Burgess asked with an awestruck expression. "A car stolen from Salinas? How can you not put the two together and—?"

"It probably *is* the car they've used for the last few days, Dr. Burgess. But they're done with it now and they won't be anywhere close to it. We'll find some clothes and some food wrappers and little else aside from a spare tire in the trunk. I've done this eight times in the last month and I'm pretty sure I know what to expect."

He looked down at his watch and actually started moving this time. They both followed him through the door. "Now, Dr. McGrath, I can't keep Gail Rainier in Santa Barbara if she doesn't want to stick around and play target for us…but I'd really like her to do just that. Some of my people are telling me that Hewitt might be ready to walk through bullets, hot coals, and broken glass to get to her to finish what he started. You know what they say his reasoning is for it?"

"What?" Beverly asked.

"Closure," Hildebrandt answered and nearly laughed out loud. "The Bureau's budget is about three and a half billion dollars annually and what do I get from my profilers? *Stanley Hewitt wants closure*. Don't quote me on this, Dr. McGrath, but I'm beginning to think that Special Agent Schultz wasn't entirely full of shit."

"What do you think his reasoning is then?" Beverly asked.

"Whose reason—Hewitt's or Stoning's? Or have you not figured it out that far yet?"

"We're at *least* that far," Beverly answered, shifting her eyes toward Burgess, who looked happy to see that they were finally all in agreement on something. "The jury's still out on all the particulars, of course."

"Of course," Hildebrandt echoed. "And in three or four days I'm guessing we'll know for sure—that's if Ms. Rainier can play the role and wait it out. I'm not really sure if she can."

They kept pace with him as Hildebrandt made his way to his car in the parking lot. By the time he got there, two more men approached from different directions and stood by as they waited for him to give the order. While Burgess took note of the seating in Hildebrandt's sedan, Beverly's eyes moved back and forth between the agent and the hotel she'd just walked out of.

"Is she at home or do you have her stashed somewhere safe?"

"Moving her to an unknown location wouldn't help us at all," he replied, pulling his keys out of his pocket. A small business card came out as well and he handed it to her. "She's listed in the phone book, meaning that anyone who really wanted to know where to find her wouldn't have much trouble. That's her current address—same place she's lived for the last ten years—and I've got seven men in and around the property on a rotating schedule. The number on the other side is for Special Agent Denker. He's expecting you around nine p.m. Call him if you'll be more than fifteen minutes early or late."

Beverly, bewildered by the unexpected request, didn't look ready to accept the mission quite yet. "And what am I supposed to do?"

"Whatever you have to do to keep her in place tonight," Hildebrandt replied as he opened his door and unlocked the others. The two agents got in, leaving room in the rear driver's side. "Get her to commit to at least one more night under our protection then you can go home and spend the night in your own bed. First thing tomorrow you go to work on her again and keep her from running. We'll play it one day at a time until they're caught or have moved along."

"What'll you be doing?"

"Cleaning up here until tomorrow evening most likely and then we'll meet you down there. Make sure you have your keys." Hildebrandt turned his attention to Burgess. "Climb in, doctor. I think we can keep you entertained for the next twenty hours or so."

He didn't have to be asked twice and pulled open the door before the agent could take the offer back. His excitement was only slightly dampened by the apprehension of his co-author.

"It's not even a full day, Bev. What do you think?"

She glanced nervously to Burgess with a questioning look, feeling strangely like she was asking his permission for something. When he nodded to her, implying that permission was granted, the idea of it only made her angry with him.

"I think I can be there by nine."

Hildebrandt was behind the steering wheel within seconds. As she started back to the lobby, Beverly could hear the engine start up and rev loudly for a few seconds before the tires started to squeal. By the time she turned to look back, they were a hundred yards away with several other vehicles joining in behind them.

~ 50 ~

Uh...don't anybody pay attention to me over here, Floyd thought as the cloud of blue smoke from the sedan's tires wafted past his car. He was now surrounded by dozens of other empty automobiles but still tried his hardest not to stand out for any reason.

From the moment he'd seen them crossing the parking lot, Floyd had frozen in place, leaving his beaten up copy of *Understanding The Sickness* propped up on the steering wheel as it had been for the last couple of hours. It only partially obscured his face but was preferable to laying down quickly across the seat, which was his first instinct to keep from being noticed. He felt fortunate that he was able to ignore it since nothing screamed out that you were spying on someone more than rapid motions designed to hide it. As it turned out, nobody even looked at him anyway. In fact, there was only one person out of the whole entourage who was still around to see him.

As he watched Beverly McGrath make her way back to the lobby he had to wonder what it was that made her stay behind. Whatever was going on—he had learned over the last month that there was *always* something going on with these guys—Floyd guessed it wasn't much to be concerned about. If it was truly important she would have been in the back seat instead of Perry Burgess and she certainly would have put up a fight to go along, even if it happened to be a fight with an FBI agent.

The amount of time they took getting to Hildebrandt's car was another thing that tipped him off as to the importance of their sudden departure. The other federal vehicles that he hadn't even noticed, not to mention two news vans and a few other cars, didn't begin their tear out of the parking lot until Hildebrandt took the lead and set the pace. If Floyd was correct, he guessed they were probably heading to the location of Stoning and Hewitt's latest getaway car from Salinas to search for clues that wouldn't be there or wouldn't be helpful if they were. Even Floyd was familiar with that pattern.

The good news was that the place was practically empty of FBI now. Most of the more obvious vehicles had disappeared within the last hour and the last of them were now on the latest wild goose chase. Aside from one or two of the low profile, plain clothes guys that he'd identified and seen repeatedly over the course of a few weeks, Floyd didn't see anything threatening enough to get in his way.

He put his book down and removed the key from the ignition. Locking the car door behind him, he crushed his cigarette out and took long but slow strides across the parking lot. He steered clear of the lobby and its automatic doors, choosing instead to slip around to a side entrance. The doors were locked from the outside but Floyd knew that all he had to do was wait.

Staring down at his watch and counting down, he guessed it wouldn't be more than seven or eight minutes before someone would exit the building and give him unfettered access to Dr. Beverly McGrath in the process. It only took four.

~ 51 ~

"I told you he wouldn't go with them. Do you see him, man? Do you see him?"

"Yeah, I see him."

Spencer was sitting on a patch of grass only twenty yards from the furthest edge of the hotel's parking lot, carving small figures and designs into the earth with the knife as he watched. They'd studied the area from afar in order to have the best viewing angle while retaining some coverage, but right now the coverage didn't seem so important. Most of what they had to fear had just driven away. Fortunately, all the important stuff had stayed behind.

"I wish we had some x-ray vision and could see into all the cars," Stanley said as he climbed to his feet. "Feels kind of like a trap, doesn't it?"

"As it should," Spencer agreed, rising to join him. "I think we're good for at least thirty minutes while they're posing for the networks in front of some asshole's Buick."

"You're sure they won't expect this?"

"Relax, we're coming unannounced. Unless you called ahead and got us a room or something stupid like that."

"Nope. Just the one to the cops about our car."

Stanley started fishing around in his pocket until he came up with the cellular phone that they'd acquired in Pleasanton and handed it over to Spencer. It's service wasn't deactivated yet since the newly married Yost couple hadn't taken the time to report it stolen—if they even realized that it was missing. They were currently trying to get over the honeymoon that never got started and would still be recovering from it mentally for many months to come. The marriage would fall apart a few months after that.

"You must have a great phone voice, Stan, because it looks like they really ate it up."

"They sure left in a hurry, didn't they?"

"See how popular we are?" Spencer pulled his arm back and hurled the small phone off into the brush. He dusted off any dirt or foliage from his suit and took his first step out into the open. "He's just about there so I'm going on ahead now. I'll signal when I know where we're headed and I'll let you in. You'll need to keep your eyes on that door for this, okay?"

"I'll be watching."

"And I'll need to take that from you." Almost as an afterthought, Spencer reached back and relieved Stanley of the sawed off shotgun, wrapping the awkward chunk of wood and steel in a newspaper and placing it under his arm. With only a little pause, he then handed Stanley the knife that hadn't left his side since he'd first grabbed hold of it at the Spitfire Steakhouse in Black Pine, Idaho. "Can I trust you with this, Supermax?"

"*Jeez*, Spence..."

"No, really, Stan. I need to know. It's important."

"I can handle it," Stanley replied, pulling it away before it might be grabbed back from him. "You should hurry up and go. I'll be watching."

Without another word on the subject, Spencer turned and started across the parking lot, weaving in and out of the empty cars that concealed him as he neared the building. Darkness was almost total when he found the door that would be their entry point. He hung back in the shadows and waited for it to open for him. When it finally did, he waited for the other man to go first.

~ 52 ~

Floyd checked the room number that Henry Torres had written down for him even though the three digits were already burned into his brain from days of staring at the page while he figured out the next move. He passed a few people in the halls as he worked his way to room 212, though he still didn't have a solid idea of what that move would actually be. He suspected he might not really know until he was there, staring her in the face. There were things they needed to discuss.

Clearing up any confusion about what Special Agent Hildebrandt might have said to her was first on the list. He hadn't even met the man but he remembered Agent Schultz's reaction to the way things had climaxed fifteen years ago and he knew a lot of the other agents felt the same kind of professional animosity toward him. He didn't care much back then since life had been a completely different game and things had gotten exciting faster than he could keep up with. Of course, he sure as hell cared about it now. There were things like reputation to consider.

Regardless of his current lack of work and the accolades that came with it, he was still hopeful that a noisy and celebrated comeback wasn't out of the question. He had name recognition after all and even though the name hadn't been used on-air in a good many years, he was sure they would remember him. With enough prompting and a good enough reason for all the attention he knew he deserved, Floyd was ready to go public once again.

In Beverly McGrath's *Understanding The Sickness*, Floyd Madison was a tracker with uncanny skills and a rabid dislike for those who harmed, used, and exploited those who couldn't defend themselves. He was a man who flew under the radar and moved stealthily, sniffing out the information he needed to complete any task without the assistance of vast, resource-rich, networked departments and agencies that were supposed to be keeping people safe when the world got scary. He was so good that he could enter a city of thousands and use nothing more than his own precognitive abilities and intuition to guide him to the target.

Floyd thought it looked fantastic on the printed page and dutifully tried to buy into his own myth as everyone else had done, though it hadn't been close to true then and was even further from it now. Either it was wishful thinking on a young journalism major's part or was simply a totally conscious and very big lie; he couldn't decide which.

Checking each of the numbers as he passed, Floyd finally completed his wandering at the end of a long hallway, leaving him face to face with what he was looking for. As he neared the door to room 212 he found himself questioning her motives again. More than that, he suddenly questioned his own. He pulled his balled up fist back only an instant before it could knock on the door.

What in the hell are you doing, Floyd? What are we trying to accomplish here?

Slowly, he backed away from the door and stared at it for a few seconds before stepping away. Since he didn't want to get caught hovering around her room and still had no answers for the questions he'd asked himself, he decided to think about his options a little more. An answer would come to him shortly. It always did.

~ 53 ~

More than the clothes and other unimportant items she'd been toting along with her, Beverly took a careful inventory of the notebooks that contained nearly every bit of information that she'd put together on their journey. The rest of it could be soaked in gasoline and torched for all she cared since she'd probably never wear any of the over-worn outfits again.

The only thing she was more tired of than her clothing was currently being driven around on his first cooperative effort with Special Agent Hildebrandt. She wasn't sorry she was missing it.

While juggling her suitcase, briefcase, and rental car keys in two hands, Beverly took one last look around to make sure nothing would be left behind. Most of her data was already duplicated in multiple forms and she had copies of everything, but she couldn't stand the thought of something as simple as a stray floppy disk undoing almost a month's worth of work by falling into the hands of a hotel maid who'd always wanted to write a book. It was unlikely but she double-checked anyway.

Only once she was finally secure in the fact that her writing wasn't going to be lifted by the help, Beverly dragged her luggage to the door. She reached for the handle but was stopped dead in her tracks when the door in front of her came to life with a series of heavy and unexpected rapping sounds. The sudden noise drove Beverly back several feet, sending her tumbling over her own suitcase and onto the floor with a loud thump.

Her first reaction was fright. Not the kind of fear one gets from something dangerous, but rather the startled variety that makes a person flinch involun-

tarily—like a bee landing on your arm or a car's tires squealing behind you…or a
door knocking in your face right when you go to open it.

Her second reaction was one of embarrassment and she prayed that whoever
was on the other side of the door hadn't heard her ass hitting the floor. In her
own head, it had sounded quite loud; much too loud for a petite woman like herself, she thought. Even as she got back to her feet, Beverly started working on a
story involving a heavy suitcase that had slipped off of the bed or something similarly believable. Whether it was Perry Burgess and Hildebrandt returning for her
or just one of those infamous book-stealing hotel maids, they would all get the
same face-saving bullshit.

She was still thinking of the story and the embellishments that would follow as
she put her hair back in order and approached the door again. Her only fear now
was that the person on the other side would knock again before she could get her
eye up to the peep hole. She was certain she wouldn't go sprawling again, but she
had a long evening planned and didn't feel like appearing twitchy to anyone she
might encounter. Placing her two hands flat against the door, she closed one eye
and put the other to the tiny hole.

Unlike some of the other places she'd stayed before the FBI started chipping
in, the peep hole was free of gum, wadded up toilet paper, and any other obstruc-
tions that she'd become familiar with. She had a clear view of the hallway as well
as the person who was paying her a very unexpected visit.

Instead of tripping and falling noises, it was now the sound of her own breath
being sucked in that she hoped didn't broadcast straight through the door. If he'd
heard it, he didn't give any indication at all and even kept a passive grin on his
face while he waited. He also wasn't staring directly into the peep hole, which was
something that always freaked Beverly out a bit whenever anyone showed up on
her doorstep at home. Usually they were strangers trying to sell her something
but the man at the door didn't qualify as such. It was only because Hildebrandt
had recently informed her of the various presences around them that she wasn't
completely surprised to see him.

Rattled but curious, she watched him as he knocked again, sliding her hand to
the door knob while she tried to figure out what had brought him to her room.
She only waited another second before turning the knob, still not sure if she'd
have to invite him in for a few minutes or if they would simply have their chat on
the way to the lobby where she would be checking out.

As the knob made it's first clicking noise, the face in the fish-eye lens quickly
changed. It wasn't the kind of face she would have invited in.

Beverly didn't get a word out before the door suddenly rushed inward at her, forcing her backward and creating more than enough space for the man to step easily into her room. She didn't see him kick the door shut but heard it slam quite clearly as a large hand was pressed against her face. Her heart began to hammer as doubtful shock gave way to the terrible reality of the situation.

For an instant—a very short instant—she entertained the notion that this might be one of those movie moments; the one where the hero sneaks up on the heroine then covers her mouth and speaks in a hushed tone so she doesn't cry out.

Shhh, Beverly, don't scream…it's only me, was what she was hoping to hear.

"Scream, you fucking bitch—I dare you," was what she got instead.

Before she knew it she was being whisked across the room by her hair and the strong grip on her face as she struggled vainly to do exactly what he'd dared. All attempts at anything approaching vocal ferocity had been nullified by one hand. The other flailings with her arms or legs were just as ineffective and in one quick spin he was suddenly behind her.

The hand was removed from her mouth just long enough for his arm to wrap tightly around her neck, cutting off her only form of oxygen. She knew what came next and could feel the constrictive blackness approaching, but it wasn't what she feared the most. Even as the furiously rushing blood from her heart made every pulse point on her body vibrate, Beverly was certain that the true terror wouldn't begin until she regained consciousness.

She knew how it worked. She'd written the book on it.

~ 54 ~

Deep down, somewhere in his heart or in his head or maybe both, he felt he might be doing the wrong thing. Such displays were often just a cry for attention and he didn't like the idea of being one of those guys. It was a tough world out there, though, and using the lovely Dr. McGrath had always been the plan, although using her in this fashion was the last of all last resorts. Floyd was almost ashamed of himself.

He couldn't help it that things weren't shaping up the way he'd intended but he certainly wasn't about to stop what he was doing out of some ethical obligation. He had way too much invested and he knew he might not get another chance for some alone time with her. Hesitation at crucial times had almost always been his own worst enemy.

He'd hesitated in Santa Barbara fifteen years ago and nearly cost a girl her life by his lack of action, which was something he wasn't sure if he could live with back then. At the same time, it helped his future a great deal since he got credit for saving that very same life, but if he'd been more confident of what he thought he'd had in the first place the whole ordeal would have been unnecessary. Maybe it was because of the odds involved or a simple lack of faith in himself, but Floyd couldn't believe that out of every experienced law man in the region, Stanley Lewis Hewitt had ended up crossing his path instead. In every literal meaning, he knew that it was exactly what had happened.

If Tom Devereaux hadn't called him back at the LA office and informed him that he was moving from Santa Maria on to some other places ahead of the feds, Floyd would have never thought to go looking. He was already busy enough with whatever menial chores Tom had left in his absence while he traipsed across the west coast in search of a killer. It could have been a twinge of spite that made Floyd lock up the office that day and head north, but he knew it was more of a celebration than anything else. He had just hauled in his first multi-thousand dollar bounty in the form of a man named Kirk Faust and didn't feel much like being the hired help for at least a few days. He'd felt above it somehow.

Tracking his boss down in Santa Barbara was easy and required only a minimum of effort on his part. Locating Stanley Hewitt was much easier and had required no effort at all.

While Tom Devereaux slept in his cheap motel room, unaware of his underling's presence in the city he thought Hewitt most likely to strike next, twenty-six year-old Floyd Madison did what came naturally to him and drove to the university to get an idea of what girls who didn't go to USC or UCLA looked like. The campus was still somewhat lively regardless of the Spring break vacation and there looked to be plenty going on wherever he went. Since he didn't want to get a ticket from campus security, he parked a block away off-campus with the intention of walking his way in.

Instead, he had parked directly in front of a car containing a man who looked suspiciously like the man that his boss was after. He knew that it couldn't be the person that all the fuss was about, but the resemblance to the photos he'd seen on TV was uncanny to say the least.

More as a personal game of skill than anything else, Floyd found a decent vantage point and waited for him to exit the vehicle to get some physical specifications and to see where he would run off to. Two hours and a half a pack of cigarettes later, Floyd was surprised that he hadn't left the car yet. He was even more surprised to find himself still interested in the pursuit. He didn't believe with any certainty that he was onto anything huge, but for the man to sit for two hours in a dark car on a dark street was more than a little curious. Floyd began to wonder how long the guy had been there before he'd pulled up in front of him.

He could have walked up to the vehicle and taken a closer look at the driver…but he waited to see what would happen instead. When the man finally got out, Floyd could have accosted him there on the street and confirmed or erased the growing suspicions he had…but he hung back and paused for further developments. By the time he was led to the small apartment that housed a young woman named Gail Rainier, Floyd suspected strongly that he was tailing Stanley Lewis Hewitt…but still he hesitated.

In the end, it took her screams to get him moving and she'd almost died anyway. Everything that followed was a blurred recollection that Floyd didn't know whether to completely trust or not.

After smashing through a door that hadn't even been checked to see if it was locked, he followed the screams to their source, where he found a young woman in the corner of the room. In what had to be the epitome of discomfort, she was stuck in a horribly awkward position—not quite standing, not quite sitting—and all ten of her toes had been impaled by nails that kept her feet firmly in place. On the floor in the middle of the room sat Stanley Hewitt and two very common household items. Both of them—one hammer and one medium sized kitchen knife—were within easy reach of the form that was stationary aside from a slight back and forth rocking motion. When Floyd stepped into the room, the only attention he received was a slow glance up from the floor.

In a haze of horrified adrenaline, Floyd grabbed the intruder and violently yanked him backwards with two strong hands. Like a rowdy drunk being tossed from a bar, Stanley Hewitt was dragged from the room and into the hallway, where he took what Floyd could have easily referred to as the beating of a lifetime. Resistance to the vicious assault was futile, allowing Floyd to complete the task as if there had been no struggle at all.

It was easier than he'd expected, which didn't really surprise him after putting some thought into it. Noting that all of the victims had been women, he guessed that his perpetrator simply wasn't used to tangling with men very often; especially men of Floyd's size.

He suspected that their next meeting might go down in a similar fashion. Maybe even more brutally...and hopefully more permanent. But none of that would matter in the least if he couldn't be located.

He wasn't going to catch Hewitt this time; that much he knew. It really left only one final option in his mind and he was ready to proceed if he could bring himself to sink to such a level. It didn't take him long to decide that he could.

Floyd took a deep breath and steeled himself for the humiliation, then actually knocked on her door this time.

It still felt wrong—all of it—but he was so desperate to get back into the game that he was willing to do anything to remind people that he was still alive and still capable. He would do anything at all; even beg the lovely Dr. McGrath to work him into a chapter or two of the new book he knew she was working on. There had to be angle for him in there somewhere.

Nervously, he waited almost thirty seconds for the door to open. When it didn't, he got ready to knock again but his arm froze in place before his knuckles could make the short journey to the door. His skin suddenly broke out in goose bumps as a cold shiver ran across the base of his neck. The cold felt frighteningly solid. Instinctively, he knew what it was even though he'd never had a gun barrel pressed into his flesh before.

This ain't right. This ain't right at all.

~ 55 ~

"Fancy meeting you here," Spencer said from behind him, reaching around the much taller man and into his jacket. The giant's shoulder holster was emptied of his gun before the short sentence was finished. "Turn around, Madison. Let's get a good look at you."

Spencer could tell right off that Stanley's pursuer didn't have a clue about what was happening and he had to resort to a few nudges with the shotgun just to get him moving. As he did, the large figure spun slowly and cautiously, taking special note of the fact that the twin barrels never left contact with his skin—something Spencer appreciated since he knew it was about as close to a show of respect as he was going to get. It also meant that the man saw through the bleached blond hair and sparkling blue eyes and knew exactly who and what he had come face to face with.

"*Ah*...shit. This is fucking perf—"

"*Shhhh,*" Spencer said, putting a finger to his lips before Floyd Madison could say something inappropriate and ruin the moment. "Just give it a second. It won't be long."

Together they waited silently, both fully aware that they were currently in the middle of the hallway of a pricey hotel that was at more than half capacity. One man standing tall and dangerously defiant; the other wearing a scary grin as he toyed with a shotgun that had lost most of the newspaper that obscured it. If Spencer was wearing a watch and cared at all about the time, he would have seen almost two whole minutes flash by before whatever they were waiting for started to happen.

At the first hint of it, he watched as Floyd's expression shifted quickly from the uncertainty that he'd been hiding into a rage that he didn't bother to camouflage in the slightest. Spencer, who was still confident as long the two guns were in his possession, merely smiled back at him as he tilted his ear to the door. There it was again.

"Take a guess what that is, Madison."

It was just a sound; a thumping sound that could be felt as well as heard. They could both hear it and both feel it down by their feet as it lightly shook the floor beneath them in a tapping, repetitive rhythm. A moment later the first human sounds found their way through the door as well. They were muffled and nasally, but both men knew that there were terrified shrieks of pain underneath the duct tape that had been applied to keep the noise in. They knew it all too well.

"And that's our cue," Spencer said with his first sign of urgency. "Now back the fuck away from the door."

For a moment, Floyd didn't move anywhere and still seemed to be thinking about his options, as though he had all the time in the world to mull it over. Spencer didn't care for the lack of cooperation but issued a final warning anyway just to be a swell guy.

"Seriously, man, you'll want to back it up. Swear to God."

Grudgingly, Floyd complied.

The moment he stepped clear, the ears of both men were quickly filled with the sound of loud, clumsy footsteps approaching at a frantic pace. The enormous bounty hunter didn't have the time to make sense of what was going on before two-hundred thirty pounds of Stanley Hewitt flew past him and slammed into the door of room 212.

~ 56 ~

Floyd could only watch with a stunned expression as the most bizarre of scenes unfolded before him. Stanley Lewis Hewitt, the serial murderer that everyone had been searching high and low for, had just bounced painfully off of Beverly McGrath's hotel room door and was already backing up for another shot at it, regardless of the obvious futility of the effort. The man was just as huge as Floyd remembered but he could tell immediately that busting through the door simply wasn't going to happen. He felt almost embarrassed for him as he watched him try it again. Then again.

While Stanley was putting his full weight into it for the fourth, fifth, and sixth times—the end result being the same—Spencer took in the scene as well with a look of genuine amusement. He appeared to be cynically gauging the strength of the door compared to the size of his zealous partner, having the first visible signs of doubt about what was possible and what wasn't. After what looked like some serious thought, he stepped even further away and leveled the shotgun toward Floyd's face.

"You on a break or something?" he asked, motioning to the door with the barrel. "Put some shoulder into it. Let's see what you got."

"Wha—?" Floyd started, but wasn't given the time to ask. Spencer's smiling face had already shifted into a frustrated frown that would have looked more at home on an impatient eight year-old child throwing a tantrum.

"Can we *please* get through this fucking *door?!*"

Stanley, who was already winding up for a seventh try, paused long enough to allow Floyd to take position beside him. It was an awkward moment for the both of them.

They stood shoulder to shoulder; Stanley looking much more confident in his current role than the man who had subdued him fifteen years prior. The tapping sounds on the other side of the door—the human sounds too—started coming at a greater frequency and volume.

Shrugging off the strangeness as best they could, Floyd and Stanley only eyed each other uncomfortably for another second longer before throwing themselves into the thick, solid obstruction together. They both crashed into it, grunting simultaneously as the heavy fire-door gave no indication of movement. They drew back even further and created more distance to increase their momentum for the next attempt, though all it achieved was to increase their pain when they hit the unyielding door yet again.

Spencer, whose patience was reaching limits he never thought possible, was practically bouncing up and down in place and looked ready to go out of his mind completely. He was still smiling, though. And still enjoying himself.

"You guys are fucking *killing* me," he whined, pacing back and forth rapidly as the two men lined up another lunge at a door that seemed to want to hurt them right back. *"You..."* he spat, pointing his finger at Floyd's chest. The shotgun hung limply at his side as he blasted the words out. "...get ready to put your foot right fucking there." He pointed to a location on the door just to the right of the locking mechanism. *"Stan*...when his foot nails that spot, you need to be banging into this sucker with everything you got. It's gotta happen at exactly the same time or we're just jerking off here." As an extra precaution he added, "And hit it as far to the left as you can without crushing the guy that sent you to prison for life. This might not work the first time."

Both men were breathing heavily when they backed up again. Floyd moved to his left and tried to make some room as he prepared his foot for the kind of action that had always looked much easier when the cops did it on TV. He was nowhere near to understanding what was happening but he was glad he had help with this part of it regardless of where that help came from. They both inhaled deeply and steadied themselves for the next attempt.

"Christ...aren't you even gonna *count?"* Spencer moaned, bringing his hands up as though asking God what he ever did to deserve the incompetent forms of assistance he'd been saddled with. He also looked to be one twitch away from accidentally blowing his own head off with the shotgun. *"Jesus*, guys. Gimme a one-two-three and get that fucker *open* already. *Do it! Do it!"*

They only paused for an instant but weren't going to get the chance to debate the issue. Too keyed up to wait, Spencer aimed the shotgun at whatever would be on the other side of the door as soon as it opened and started counting.

"One..." he called out, glaring crazily at both of them—his own special form of motivational support. *"...two..."* But he couldn't hide his smile as he watched Stanley's fists ball up repeatedly in anticipation of what was coming. Likewise, Floyd Madison's right foot was dug into the carpet and had begun to hop a little. He looked like an Olympic sprinter who didn't know why he was in the race but was just dying to get off of the starting block anyway. As he called out the next number and waited for the fun to begin, Spencer wished he'd thought to bring a camera.

"...three."

~ 57 ~

"…three."

She could hear it on the other side of the door as sure as the man kneeling in front of her could, but the only significance that the number three had for her at the moment was the amount of nails that had been driven through her toes so far. The pain was exactly the variety she would have expected from a thin steel spike being pounded through toe nail, flesh, bone, then flesh again as it exited through the other side and buried itself deep in the floorboard beneath the carpet. *Unbearable* or *excruciating* would have been a couple of ways to describe the feeling, but those adjectives and many like them had been overused to the point that they couldn't relay her discomfort adequately. It was a special kind of pain that would probably require a whole new word in the dictionary.

Inside the room that she had been only minutes from vacating, Beverly was crammed into a corner in the most unflattering position she could imagine. With her ass planted on the floor and her bare feet placed together just a foot and a half from either wall, it left her legs spread apart in a fashion that fell somewhere between porn and yoga. The hammer had repeatedly swung down, striking the nails only a few inches from delicate parts of her that were currently anything but private. It seemed a ludicrous thing to be concerned about; especially since she was certain she wouldn't be found in such a crude pose.

At one point or another, Beverly knew she would be pulled upright and forced against the walls that joined behind her. Her feet, which would be part of the floor soon, were situated far enough out front so that her knees would lock into place quite nicely when the time came. She had no idea when that would be and found the whole concept of minutes and hours to be more confusing than it ever had in the past.

Time had ceased to function normally from the moment she had been rendered unconscious and it still hadn't quite caught up with her even though she was partially aware. Beverly couldn't think of her own last name right now, but somehow knew that the disorienting effect was most likely a result of shock combined with the lack of oxygen that had separated her from her wits the first time around. She also knew that the strange but not unpleasant dreamy feeling she experienced intermittently was due to a heavy release of endorphins designed to make one's death that much more acceptable. And she was almost ready to accept it a couple of times over the course of the last minute or so, which she found odd when she was coherent enough to think about it.

It wouldn't be that easy, of course, as every time she wished it could be over quickly and had submitted to the inevitable, another blow with the hammer would send a bolt of angry pain through her whole body. Fighting for survival would then take charge of her faculties and start the cycle over again. They were just short little bursts of instinctive reactions but came very closely on top of one another, creating the perfect mixture of mental torture and startling pain. And as she very well knew, the person at her feet could keep it going for hours and hours. He might not have been Stanley Lewis Hewitt but he was obviously a fan.

"...*three.*"

Beverly couldn't tell how long it had been since hearing the word and was beginning to wonder if she'd really heard it at all. In fact, she thought she had heard all kinds of noises coming from just outside of her room but doubt was piling up in her head along with everything else. Even as she struggled to think about it, the hammer came down again, ripping another ferocious howl from her lungs that could only travel as far as the tape on her mouth would allow. Mixed in with all the other sounds, it was hard to tell whether the next loud crash came from the hammer, her own muted screams, or the ruckus on the other side of the door—a door that suddenly looked like it was no longer there.

From her schooling, Beverly knew to possibly expect delusions under the trauma she was experiencing but hadn't prepared herself for what she was currently witness to. Her mind could have played any number of tricks on her but this one just wasn't even funny.

~ 58 ~

"You…dirty…thieving…motherfucking…piece of SHIT!"

He didn't stop to look for any additional threatening presences or even bother to check the status of the woman who'd written a whole book about him. Stanley simply stepped through the splintered door frame and began a slow, stomping journey to the other side of the room as he sized up the reason they were all here. His jaw was clenched tight and his lips were drawn back on a face that didn't take a genius to read. He was all teeth and all business as he covered the distance between them.

Floyd was prodded through the door a few steps behind him. He wasn't moving as fast and even slowed down a bit when he saw what was waiting for them but was forced ahead nonetheless. Aside from Stanley and the pale and bleeding woman who was shoved into the corner, there was only one other person in the room with them. He had a hammer in his hand and seven nails sticking out of his mouth. Floyd recognized him immediately. They all did.

"Stan doesn't lose today," Spencer barked quickly from behind him, giving Floyd another light shove in the proper direction. "Not this time. You understand me, Madison? He's not gonna lose."

Floyd turned his eyes back to Spencer with a look that he hoped would make things clear between them for at least the next minute and a half if it lasted that long. He didn't like him and he sure as hell didn't trust him, but he didn't need to be shoved anywhere right now. At the moment and *only* at the current moment it wasn't too hard to tell the good guys from the bad guys—or better guys from the worse guys, or something like that. The whole thing was confusing, but making a decision about who to back up and who to beat down wasn't at all the brain-teaser that Spencer Stoning was making it out to be.

"Whatever you say, chief."

It looked to him like it was going to be one of those dirty affairs with lots of knees and elbows, not to mention one average sized hammer, so getting into the middle of it would be avoided if possible. As it was, most of his attention was directed at Beverly McGrath, who was halfway nailed down and trying to cover herself while she gazed up at him as if not quite believing that he was really there. Judging from the company he suddenly found himself keeping, he could hardly believe it himself.

The fact that Spencer Stoning had opted not to slaughter everyone in the room didn't slip by him either and Floyd could tell that the trigger-happy spree killer had no intention of simply shooting the man to death. It would have been done by now if that was the case. He wasn't sure if it was just an attempt to keep the volume down, but whatever was about to happen, it was obviously an intensely personal matter between them.

"I *knew* it was you—I knew it a *week* ago, you dirty *thief!*" Stanley squealed as he waded into the corner just outside of the other man's striking range. He briefly turned back to Spencer, who still hadn't ventured more than three feet into the room. "It's *him*, Spence. This is the son of a bitch who's been stealing from me."

Stanley's eyes were tearing up with emotional anger as the man stared back at him with what looked like utter fascination. After all the time crammed into cars, ducking their heads head at every turn, and eating food from stranger's refrigerators in strange houses, they finally found what they'd been looking for. Stanley hadn't been certain about much of anything over the last few weeks but now knew for sure that he was laying eyes on the man that had ripping him off for more than half a year. It was about time they met.

Spencer pushed the ruined door shut and held it closed with his foot. He hung back away from the action, keeping his eyes on either Floyd Madison, the wall, or the floor directly in front of him. He hardly looked up at all. "Finish it up then. Tear his fucking head off."

~ 59 ~

The carpenter's nails were spit from his mouth onto the floor and the hammer was quickly flipped around so that the claw end was now out in front. A defensive posture was taken, though the man looked ready to go offensive without much provocation. All words remained unspoken but the dialog that went on between the two pairs of eyes was as loud as any heated argument. The man stood completely still as he waited for Stanley's invitation, but if he had taken a few steps in any direction, each person in the room would have known exactly how he would look doing it. At one point or another they had all seen it by now.

He would be walking with the same bouncy, jaunty, and strutting gait that he had never been able to shake no matter what city they were in. It wouldn't make a difference what clothes he wore or what style his hair was in or whether he had bothered to shave or not. He wouldn't have been able to walk ten feet without giving himself away if the subject was aware of him and if they weren't too keen on being stalked—a category that all four current occupants of room 212 fell into, though each thought he had been more of an annoyance than anything else.

Even with a hammer in his hand and blood on his fingers, Hang-around Guy still looked like one of the many low profile feds they'd spied over the weeks. Just like Black-Sox, Taxi-Fed, and Agent Sloth, he took his time, performed his job with maximum efficiency and stayed low to the ground.

This one didn't stake out addresses of victims that were fifteen years dead just in case Stanley Hewitt's repetitious nature strived for more accuracy. He didn't keep tabs on family members of victims like the others did and didn't track down, isolate, and protect women who happened to share a first and last name with a previous victim. He didn't take notes on what the journalists were talking about when they thought nobody was listening and had never spent all night with headphones strapped on, trying to keep track of multiple tip hotlines while going over sheet after sheet of stolen vehicle reports. He had also never shown up at a victim's funeral with a notepad, camera, and binoculars, recording each license plate number and every face in search of a man who stood out too much or too little or was a repeat mourner with no ties to the family and no press credentials. That was the FBI's job and they were good at it, but Hang-around Guy's job was even easier. All he did was search for opportunity wherever he could find it, and so far there had been plenty of it to go around. Even though it had put a slight kink in his plans, opportunity was the reason he was now standing face to face with the closest thing to God that he could imagine.

After deciding that he might not get such an easy chance again, Beverly McGrath had been pushed up to victim number fourteen in Santa Maria instead of number fifteen in her home town of Santa Barbara as he had originally wished. It would leave him with only one more victim to worry about in Santa Barbara if he wanted to keep up with the goals he'd set for himself; goals that even surpassed what Stanley Lewis Hewitt had achieved. He didn't have any particular target mapped out in Santa Barbara yet but he definitely knew who it wouldn't be. The heavily guarded woman named Gail Rainier meant absolutely nothing to him and as far as names went, Dr. McGrath's was really the only one that mattered.

Her ironic death would surely be counted as number nine in the official records, newspapers, and on TV, but it wouldn't be the truth and he didn't care what was fed to the masses. As long as Stanley Lewis Hewitt knew who she was and where she actually rated on the tally sheet, all of it could be justified to himself.

Stanley Lewis Hewitt—he never thought of him in any other way. Always three names and always with reverence. He'd read the woman's book hundreds of times and got a little more from it with each reading. It was beautiful and tragic while it explained the malady in terms that no therapist had ever been able communicate to him. He'd always thought that there was an abundance of wickedness in the world—much of it residing deep within himself—but valid reasons for horrifically absurd behavior had never been spelled out so clearly before and excused with such ease. And thanks to the bitch with all the big words and fancy writing, he had finally come to understand the sickness. He understood it and appreciated it. She'd made it so easy.

It helped him understand his hero a lot better and gave him some insight into his own demons as well, but mostly what it did was give him ideas. They were terribly unoriginal ideas and had already been done to death a decade and a half earlier but old or not, they had stood the test of time remarkably well. The good ones always did, which was the main reason he started off his homage with five old Seattle murders that were probably known only to Hewitt himself. They were sloppy and thoughtless with only a very slight resemblance to the MO that would make him famous one day, but everybody had to start somewhere.

Stanley Lewis Hewitt—serial killer, artistic genius, idol, and role model. Up close and personal for the first time, he wondered which one of them would still be living in a couple of minutes.

It was plain to see that the man was upset with him and he understood all the reasons perfectly well, though he'd hoped it would end on a better note than this. While he did expect a butting of heads over what amounted to thirteen cases of blatant copyright infringement all the way from Seattle to Salinas, the thing he hadn't considered was that Stanley might bring friends to help sort his business out. And if indeed he had thought about it at all, the very last name on the very short list would have certainly been Floyd Madison—yet there he was, big as life and only a few feet away.

For the last few weeks he'd felt that Spencer Stoning's brand of evil wasn't half bad, meaning he had rightly earned his place alongside the dark angel that was Stanley Lewis Hewitt—but where Madison had come from and why he was along for the ride was a complete mystery. It was also a major disappointment.

The knife usually wasn't unsheathed until all the nails were in place but this was rapidly becoming an emergency. As he was reaching around to his back to extract the long blade, he felt the first strong blow meet with his face and heard the distinct and unsettling sound of his jaw dislocating from the rest of his skull.

~ 60 ~

For several seconds he had hesitated again—maybe it was only one second; it was hard to tell—but the tension had finally gotten to be too much. While Stanley Hewitt looked to be waiting for the starter's pistol to go off, the other man was just gawking at him with a crazy stare that might have passed for admiration to some people. It was a sickening display on the part of the man with the hammer but Hewitt's naked animosity let him know in no uncertain terms that he wasn't about to be flattered by it.

The physical aspect of the argument still hadn't started, however, and Floyd began to wonder how long it would be. When the man reached behind his back for what could have been anything, Floyd started it for them. He didn't even bother to check his watch this time. He knew all those numbers by heart.

The hooking left hand was thrown out of instinct and landed directly in the spot on a person's face that bulges out when they clench their teeth or bite down on something very hard. Everything beneath the layer of flesh and muscle gave way easily and Floyd could actually feel the movement of the man's lower back teeth sliding away from the molars above them as his jaw unhinged. It felt grisly and wonderful in the same moment and Floyd quickly stepped back so there would be room for him to fall before his blindly swinging arms made contact with something.

When he didn't drop to the floor as he should have, Floyd could only watch as the claw of the hammer buried itself into Stanley Hewitt's shoulder. There was a brief sound of discomfort from him—nothing more than a muted, angry yelp—but, strangely enough, it didn't appear to be the focus of his concern.

Hewitt's own vicious assault then began, leaving Floyd with a thankful feeling for pulling away as he'd done. Stanley had apparently brought a weapon of his own and there were now three pieces of steel whisking through the air.

*   *   *   *

It got loud very quickly and Spencer lost track of much what was happening on the other side of the room the moment it had started. He wasn't even pretending to help out this time while his gun-filled hand jittered anxiously. Leaning back against the closet with one foot on the opposite wall and the other still pinned in front of the door, he spared very few looks at the fracas. It was just enough to be prepared if any of it started heading his way.

He was lucky that it didn't since the only places that his eyes wanted to go were to the floor, wall, or ceiling. Those were the only safe areas; places where spatters or streaks of blood wouldn't be able splash across his field of vision and send him into the same dreaded blackness that they always had. Aside from two knives and a hammer, he was the only one in the room who was armed in a truly serious way. Right now, he wasn't sure if that was a good thing or a bad thing.

He hummed softly to himself as he chanced another glimpse into what could have accurately been called the *crowded* corner of the hotel room. For all the information he got out of the glance, it may as well have been a cartoon fight on Saturday morning TV since it was nothing but a swirling, noisy blur from where he was standing. Plus, any opportunity to be bludgeoned was something he didn't care to get too deeply involved in. His eyes scrolled back over to the door and his humming grew louder as he waited for the grunts and moans to cease, at which point it would be time to see who was left standing and decide how they would be dealt with.

Until then, it would be murmuring a verse with no melody to no particular song while keeping his left ear pressed tightly against the door. There was no thunder of heavy footsteps from the hallway yet, but he didn't really expect there to be for another minute or so. He couldn't be sure if every federal agent in Santa Maria was still out on the streets being useless while snapping photos of their stolen Buick several miles away, but it still could have left plenty of local cops in the area or even a few hotel security guards to spoil all the fun.

Time was finally ripping right along like it did in the real world. It was pretty much the way he remembered it.

*   *   *   *

Her first reaction was to get out of the way as quickly as possible; a reaction Beverly regretted the moment she started working under her own steam again. While she was alone with her intruder and the three nails were being pounded through her toes, all normal thought patterns had turned to a cloudy static of disorientation and her paralysis was legitimate. But with her faculties returning like a shot of pure adrenaline, not to mention the sudden life and death struggle that was occurring inches away from her, she did what came naturally and tried to flee.

In one quick movement, Beverly was filled with a renewed respect for Danielle Morgan, a woman who'd felt she had so much riding on her life that she practically died in two rooms at once. Unlike the mother of two from Sacramento, Beverly had only given her foot a single light tug before the realization took hold that she was going to stay put and ride out the violent storm that was taking place almost on top of her. The pain that kept her situated was very different from the helpless and hopeless variety that had overwhelmed her a minute earlier, but it still wasn't going to allow her to simply get up and walk away; not if such a conscious, self-administered dose of complete agony was the price she would pay for it.

Giving up on the idea of any sort of exit from her tiny plot of carpet space, she pushed herself as far into the corner as she could and brought her knees back together, trying to cover herself with the skirt that had been hiked up around her waist for what seemed like two days. There was no vanity in the gesture since she cared as little about it as a person bloated with starvation cares about how bad the food tastes, but it was simply another layer of protection for her to hide behind, both mentally and physically.

It helped on some level, though she was still aware enough to know that the two thin arms she pulled over her head were tokens at best. They wouldn't do much to deter the clawed end of a hammer from entering her from any angle and would fare even worse against the sharpened blades that were now part of the show as well. And those were just the annoyances that might prove fatal.

The knee she took to the side of her head was preferable to any of the inanimate solid objects that were currently cutting through the air but it still hurt regardless and sent her brain flying into another dizzy tail spin. The shot in the ribs; the elbow that may or may not have cracked in a few places; the worst charley horse of her life—these were minor and were, to some extent, appreciated for their lack of permanence. She didn't keep track of the injuries as they occurred and wouldn't have been able to count them all if she tried.

It wasn't until a shoe that felt more like a bear-trap landed firmly on the one part of her that was guaranteed not to move anywhere that the world lit on fire and went cloudy on her again. Beverly's hands fell to her sides and her fingernails began tearing at the surrounding carpet, her face twisting involuntarily with a pain that her entire body absorbed and couldn't shake off. Consciousness was fading and she did nothing to fight the drowning feeling that accompanied it as her head tipped back into the wall behind her.

Through vacant eyes that bled dark mascara, she could barely make out the three tangled figures as they grappled for final position in the closing seconds of a game that seemed mainly for her benefit. The sights, sounds, and vibrations that had been overwhelming her senses reached their peak at the same time that Beverly's ability to worry about them was fading.

There was a sound, though. A sudden, odd sound that stood out from all the other distractions for reasons she couldn't begin to understand. A moment before her mental light dimmed out completely she could have sworn she heard someone die.

~ 61 ~

"Still with us, Stan?" Spencer asked quickly from his own protected corner, his tone not filled with it's usual overpowering confidence.

He wished he didn't have to ask the question, but the one look he'd spared to the other side of room once the silence finally came told him absolutely nothing. None of the players were still standing, which was expected considering the amount of energy that had spilled out of them in such a brief amount of time. They were now out of time, though, and he didn't want to have to guess why his partner wasn't busy doing a victory dance.

"Stan? Come on, Supermax. It's time to finish up."

There was still no response from him, though he could hear at least two pairs of lungs doing some heavy breathing. He could also hear those footsteps in the hallway that he'd been waiting for. They were right on cue and there were a lot of them.

"Stan? We've got to—"

"Your friend doesn't look so good," Floyd said in a deep, huffing voice as he hoisted himself up off of the carpet and leaned back against the window ledge. Peering hopefully down at his torso and each of his limbs, he appeared to be searching for any injuries that he might have been unaware of. Only once he was finished with himself did he look back down to Stanley. "He's still alive but I don't think he's—"

Floyd stopped speaking abruptly and scooted further away as the man he was talking about rose to his feet. A quick wave of nausea came over him but didn't last long. He'd seen worse; but those people were dead at the time. *"Sweet fucking Jesus."*

"Is he staying down, Stan?" Very carefully, he took a squinty, one-eyed look at his partner to verify his status. Stanley was alive and on his feet, which he had genuinely been concerned about, but it was only the first of many things they still had to deal with. "Just kick the guy a few times and make sure so we can—"

This time it was Spencer's turn to slam on the brakes.

"Fucking *shit*, Stan," he uttered sickly, looking at and speaking to the floor again. It was easier now because he had dropped to his knees. His labored breathing now matched that of the other men in the room, though he hadn't lifted a finger. "Cover that up. Use a towel or something. Do it *now*, man."

"I'm fine, Spence—really," Stanley finally said, his face only looking a little stunned.

The area to the left of his neck—closer to his shoulder than the very major bloodline a few inches away—didn't look the way it used to. The clothing he was wearing had been torn apart in much the same fashion as his skin, though they would be much easier to sew back together than the living parts that were strewn about. The hammer had been plunged terribly deep before being yanked around and wrenched out, taking quite a bit of Stanley with it as it exited. Solid white fragments were mixed in with fiery redness where shards of his clavicle poked out at odd angles.

To the only person who viewed the scene close up, he looked like an organ grinder in coveralls whose monkey had exploded. Floyd couldn't stop looking at it.

Stanley couldn't do anything to wrap the injury, having only one functioning arm, so a quickly emptied pillow case was simply thrown over it. It was still flowing freely but was adequately masked.

"I'm *sure* you're fine…" Spencer replied with an unseen grimace. He struggled back to his feet. "…but just do what I tell you, okay? We've got a bad situation brewing here and we're not done yet."

That was when Floyd stopped merely observing and decided to open his mouth again.

~ 62 ~

"What the hell's left to *do*, chief? You ain't nowhere even *close* to being in the clear, but you two actually have a chance of going back to your cells alive because of this. I was here…I saw what happened. I was *part* of it for God's sake. The doctor saw it too and she'll tell them the same thing that I will."

"How's she doing anyway?" Spencer's voice was slightly muffled since his mouth was up against the door underneath the peep-hole he was currently staring through.

Both men looked down at her but it was Stanley who leaned over to readjust her skirt. He then pulled the layered strips of duct tape from her mouth in a smooth but painful looking jerk. Blood dripped from his wound like tea would spill from a saucer but he still took the time to hold his hand in front of her face to make sure he could feel her breath.

"Looks like she's sleeping, Spence. Sleeping really hard."

"Well, she's had a rough day," he replied, still watching the crowd grow outside their room. It was mostly average people just wondering what all the noise was about, but he knew security would be along shortly. People like the kinds he was seeing didn't go to check out the noise themselves unless they'd called the front desk to whine about it a little first. "What about the other guy? How's he look?"

They both already knew how he was doing but didn't know exactly how to describe it. *Immobile* might have been one way to put it.

"Uh...he's...," Stanley started but couldn't figure out where to go with it. With eyes that were growing more dull by the second, he turned to Floyd who found himself almost chuckling out loud at the insanity he had just partaken in.

"Oh, yeah—he's fucked up all right. He's definitely not going anywhere."

"Sorry, *chief*, but he most definitely is. I need you to give me your keys."

"What—you mean *me?*" Floyd was already digging for them, though he knew that Stoning and Hewitt going anywhere was a pipedream now. "There's nowhere to go. Just let me make one goddamn phone call. Just one. You'll get out of here. You got my word on that."

"We're getting out anyway, so what's the difference?"

"You'll never make it."

"Keys, please," Spencer ordered, sighing one of those *I mean fucking business* kind of sighs. They were tossed over the bed and landed at Spencer's feet.

"Listen, Stan. You're gonna be the boss for a few minutes. I want you to take this." Without looking up or moving his foot from the door, he tossed the shotgun from his sweating hand onto the bed and removed Floyd's handgun from his waistband at the same time. "Go ahead—take it." He waited until he was sure that the weapon was in the proper hands before stashing the semiautomatic back into his pants and looking through the peep-hole again. He spoke softly to Stanley, though the words were for Floyd's ears as well. "I'm going for the car. If Mr. Madison here tries to give you any shit, I want you to shoot his ass. If the guy on the ground comes back to life and starts wiggling around, I want you to shoot his ass too. Okay?"

"Sure, I guess," he replied, staring at the twin barrels skeptically. "But there's only one shell."

Another loud sigh came from Spencer but it didn't sound like a particularly bad one. "Fucking, *Stanley*. Thank God we don't rob banks or something. I'm gonna get going now. Give it a minute or two and meet me down in the parking lot. Don't forget our friend. You got that?"

"Got it, Spence. Parking lot."

"You're not gonna pass out or die on me, are you?"

"What...*now?* I don't think so."

"I'll see you in a couple minutes then."

Spencer took his foot from the door and yanked it open. He didn't look back before stepping through it into the hallway, pulling the door shut behind him and leaving the two large men with nothing to do but look at each other. Stanley, scratching at the open wound on his shoulder, was the first to speak after a long silence. He was suddenly beaming. "Did you see me kick that guy's ass?"

*   *   *   *

"Out of the *way* people! Sick man coming through. Out of the way *now!*"

As instructed, the crowd of curious onlookers made way for the fast walking man who appeared to be in need of some kind of assistance. The few that he actually came close to stepped further away.

"We've got an emergency and need to clear this hallway! Get out of the *way* goddamnit!"

When he reached the end of the hallway, Spencer rolled past the elevator and headed for the stairs. Only after the stairwell door closed behind him did he begin to run.

The short journey from the second floor to the first was completed in five seconds and he was back out into a similar looking hallway in less time than that. The elevator doors in front of him had just closed as he walked by them. He guessed that security was finally getting their shit together.

He only saw two people on his way to the same door he had entered from and hadn't made eye contact with either of them. He simply stormed his way to the least visible exit in the place and hoped for the best. Just before stepping out into the chilly air of the parking lot, Spencer pulled the fire alarm.

About the same time that the shrill alarm started wailing, he could see multiple pairs of headlights pulling up to the lobby area and even more of them following close behind. Less than thirty seconds later he was behind the wheel of Floyd Madison's white sedan, feeling around for the seat release since his feet were at least eight inches from reaching the pedals.

~ 63 ~

"Yeah, you sure did a hell of a number on him," Floyd agreed, though he had his doubts about who exactly did what to whom.

After making sure that Beverly McGrath still had breath in her lungs, he stared down at the man that he'd been mistaking for an FBI agent for almost a month and tried to recall the last time he had seen a man as broken as he was. While Hewitt's injury looked not too different from a close up gunshot wound, the man on the floor appeared to have been twisted from top to bottom, over and over again. The worst part was the area from his chest to his neck since the upper spine bent off at an angle that was now perpendicular to an equally distorted jaw-bone. Stoning had told Stanley Hewitt to tear his head off but it was Floyd who had nearly accomplished it.

He distinctly remembered taking him from behind after Hewitt's hammer-in-the-shoulder bit of nastiness, but he didn't think the overdone headlock would be so brutal that it would drag much of the backbone right along with his skull. He guessed that Hewitt might have helped like he'd said but Floyd couldn't think of any moment that his hands were free enough to get a really good grip on anything. There was also the fact that his arm was hanging like a tire swing from a tree limb.

"Anytime you want to tell me who this guy is—feel free."

"Who...*him?*" Stanley asked in reply, nodding to the floor.

"Sure, I guess we can start with him," Floyd answered, trying to imagine what it would be like to travel with Stanley Hewitt for a few weeks. He'd suspected it fifteen years ago and was now almost totally convinced that the man who had made him a legend was retarded. Medically, technically, and certifiably retarded. "Where did he come from?"

"I don't know."

"Well, who is he then?"

"Just some guy. Some thief. The papers called him the Roadside Butcher for a while, but he never did get it right. Ask Spence, he'll tell you. He stole some old stuff from me and then started swiping the ones that everyone knows about and he couldn't do that right either."

"What did he do that was so wrong?"

Did I really just ask him that? *Wrong* was a word that seemed beyond definition lately.

"The hammer," Stanley said, nodding toward it. "It says *Craftsman*."

"And what's wrong about that?"

"The one I used said *Stanley* on it. I swear, it was written right on there in big letters. Weird, huh?" He dropped the subject quickly and looked back down to Hang-around Guy. "Spence called him a hack. Said he was stealing from me and ripping off my style…whatever that means. He told me it would only get worse and said my reputation was on the line. I didn't even know I had one. Man, that guy's smart."

"I've heard a little about that Roadside shit. What the hell does it have to do with you?"

Stanley looked at him with an expression that fell somewhere between shame and denial. "Well, they say I did some stuff a while ago. They always say that, you know? They're always saying I did stuff. Stuff like this…" he gestured to his biographer and the nails poking out from her toes. "…but not really like that, you know? I guess it was…a little different. I don't know. I never know. They tell me I…"

He was interrupted simultaneously by a loud alarm going off and voice that suddenly came from the floor. Stanley didn't flinch but Floyd nearly jumped out of his skin.

"You cut them, didn't you, Stanley? You cut them and got rid of all of them the same way." The words were weak and still filled with pain, but Beverly McGrath was back among the living. "You dumped them out onto the side of the road."

~ 64 ~

Beverly shifted herself around slowly and swallowed hard as her eyes clenched shut for a second. She gasped for breath when her foot tilted in the wrong direction but seemed to have regained enough composure to speak without moaning.

"They were a month and a half apart. There were five in all. It was before that first one in Vancouver fifteen years ago. Isn't that right, Stanley?"

Stanley stopped looking in her direction. "Yeah…five. I guess that's about right."

She glanced around the room and her eyes settled on the still figure that laid only a few feet from her. She could tell he was dead but pushed herself further into the corner anyway.

"Who's the Roadside Butcher, Stanley? How did he know about those five?"

"How does anybody know anything?" he replied, trying to shrug his shoulders but noticing with a keen interest that only one side was moving up and down. "Man, would you look at that?"

They both already had. For Beverly, it was simply another gruesome tidbit she would never forget. For Floyd, it was a sign that at least half of the nightmare was closer to being over. He didn't see a way for him remain conscious for too much longer and there was certainly no way they were actually going to walk out the door and meet Stoning in the parking lot—if indeed Stoning had made it himself. The loud alarm going off told him that he probably hadn't.

He started thinking about the spree-killing mass-murderer and what his next move was supposed to be. He also started thinking about the single shell in Hewitt's shotgun.

"Okay, how did *you* know then? Did Stoning tell you that too?"

"I can read a newspaper, you know. I don't need Spence for that."

"And they give you a paper every day at Woodhall?"

"Only sometimes."

"Paperboy brings it?"

"No, we don't have—" Stanley caught himself before continuing. "Paper-boy—I get it. That's funny."

"Where do you get them from then?"

"One of the guards, I guess."

"Which guard, Stanley?" Beverly then asked, lifting herself up slightly so she could see the look on his face better. "Was it Ryan? Did Ryan Williams give you those papers, Stanley?"

"Ry's a good guy…" His eyes narrowed into little slits, though the look was obviously directed internally at himself rather than anyone in the room. It almost hurt to watch him think. "…and I should just shut up now. How long has it been since Spence left?"

"A couple of minutes," Floyd estimated.

"Man, we've got to get going, then." Stanley moved quickly away from the door and stepped over the bed to where Beverly awaited. He picked up the hammer that was gummed up with bits of his own flesh and handed it to Floyd. "You need to take those nails out of her, but be careful. That last girl howled when you did it."

Without another word and without putting the shotgun down, Stanley bent down to a knee and jostled Hang-around Guy up into as close to a sitting position as he would ever be again. Then, in a motion that almost made Floyd and Beverly yell out with pain, Stanley leaned forward and hoisted the man up over his one good shoulder. He bounced him a couple of times to get the balance right.

"I already told, you won't even make it to the elevator," Floyd warned.

"He didn't say to meet him in the elevator," Stanley replied. He then took a short running start and sent Hang-around Guy crashing through the window. "He said to meet him in the parking lot. You better get those nails out or he'll be pissed."

~ 65 ~

Nice toss, Supermax.

Spencer didn't have time to put their latest stolen vehicle into park before he heard the loud crash of breaking glass—a sound he'd always loved—and saw the shape of a man fall from the sky onto the hood of a car six feet away from him. He hoped to God it wasn't Stanley taking the short dive from the second floor, but it was hard to tell with him sometimes. If his old psychologist was capable of speaking yet, it probably wouldn't take much for her to talk him right out the window; a feat Spencer suspected that he could do himself if he cared to, though from a much greater height.

He left the engine running and waited in the car.

✳   ✳   ✳   ✳

"Faster's better," Stanley offered as he awkwardly ripped another pillow from it's cotton case with one hand. "Like a band-aid, man. Take this."

The pillow case was tossed to Floyd, who had no idea why he was now holding it. Even Stanley recognized the confused look.

"Have her bite down on it. It makes things hurt less. I swear it does."

After quickly folding then twisting the brown pillow case into a near-solid object, Floyd could see that it made perfect sense and he wished he'd thought of it first. There was no conversation going on and there were no questions as he held the bound up fabric to Beverly's lips. She opened her mouth and bit down hard, her eyes only meeting his once before they were shut tight in anticipation of the worst.

But it wouldn't be, of course. This would be painful—maybe even more painful than when they were hammered in—but worse? It was doubtful. Regardless of what happened and how it felt, the next bout of torture was designed to free her from the floor and she was ready to accept it.

"Here we go," he cautioned, grimacing as he slid the V-shaped, meat-ridden claw into place.

He wanted to be gentle, so the handle of the hammer was pulled with the utmost care—too much care the first time. The nail came halfway out of the floor before slipping out of the claw and bending somewhere inside the toe it was supposed to be exiting. The muted shriek that followed hurt his ears and heart at the same time, leaving him with no choice but to speed the process along.

"No, like a band-aid," Stanley repeated. "Real fast."

Wiping the sweat from his forehead, Floyd decided he was right and was going to do what he could to ignore Beverly McGrath while he worked. It was difficult but not impossible.

Crack.

He didn't even think about it as he repositioned the claw and slapped the handle, as though pulling a nail from a piece of wood. It came from the floorboard quickly but slowed as it had to be wrested from the bone and skin that had swelled around it. He paid no attention to the doctor's wails and moved onto the next one.

Crack.

The pillow case was already soaking through with saliva and the fresh tears that rolled down her face. As he tore the second nail free, he thought deeply about the item she was grinding her teeth against and how easily Stanley Hewitt had come up with the idea. It was a *good* idea; one he'd come up with so quickly that Floyd deduced it was experience rather than brains or education that had planted the seed in his head.

Crack.

While the last nail was easing it's way out, Floyd wondered how many pillow cases Stanley had bit down on in his life. How many times he'd resorted to chewing halfway through his bed to quell whatever the pain of the hour was. How old he was when he took that first bite. He didn't like thinking about it.

"You did good," he said to her as he removed the tooth-bitten gag from her mouth. In turn, Stanley took it from him and started flapping the wet, wadded up mess back into it's original shape. Since he only had one arm to work with, he had put the shotgun down on the bed. Floyd didn't grab for it, though he guessed he might have been able to if he'd tried.

"Okay," Stanley said, sucking on his teeth as he tried to remember what to do next. After a few pensive moments, he tossed the pillow case back to Floyd. The shotgun was quickly back in his hand. "Put this over her head and wrap it really tight."

"Why in the fuck do you want—?"

"*Feet!*" Stanley blurted out with an embarrassed face. "*Jeez*, I meant *feet*. Put her feet in there and wrap it around a few times. She's bleeding and Spence has bad reactions to the stuff."

With a loud sigh—Floyd didn't even want to *think* of the reasons they'd want a pillow case over her head—he gently covered her rapidly swelling toes. He put an arm under her and lifted her up. Beverly stood on one foot looking ready to pass out again while he kept her steady. Stanley stepped to the broken window and could see Spencer in the car waiting for them.

"Down you go." Stanley was already kicking the rest of the glass from the pane. "Just hang and drop. Then her—you'll probably have to catch her." After a look down at his useless arm he added, "And you'll probably have to catch me too. Sorry, man."

It wasn't such a far drop.

~ 66 ~

"I hate to break it you," Floyd said from the passenger seat of a vehicle that was much smaller than he was used to. "But this ain't my car."

Once Hang-around Guy had been shoved into the trunk, the rest obligingly helped each other get into their predesignated seats. Taking a long arc around the nearly black parking lot, they drove off of the hotel property, bypassing the rush of dark sedans that had been fighting to get in a minute earlier.

"I know it isn't your car," Spencer replied curtly. "We haven't gotten to that part yet."

"It's true—you *are* crazy, Stoning. If we're going back later then where in the hell are we going now?"

"We're going to say goodbye to a friend. A serious-as-fuck bon voyage, if you know what I mean. You got a problem with that?"

"No—no problem here, chief," he replied, wondering how well Stoning could shoot while he was driving. Floyd never left a round chambered in his gun and hadn't seen the spree killer cycle the weapon yet; not in his presence, anyway, which didn't help much. Meanwhile, Hewitt was directly behind him and probably had the shotgun aimed straight into his back. If there was any hero left in him, he guessed it would have to wait to come out.

As Floyd would have done, Spencer drove slowly and surely, using turn signals and stopping at all the red lights. They drove in the same fashion until the street lights disappeared and, finally, much of the city itself. The road they eventually found themselves on was illuminated in no way except for their own headlights and that was when Spencer started stepping harder on the gas. A minute or so later they weren't even on the road anymore. Aside from the engine all they could hear was the sound of dense foliage scraping across the bottom and sides of the car. It wasn't too long before they dropped speed then slowed to a crawl.

When they stopped and Floyd got his first look at what lay ahead of them, the fear that had been slowly turning into concerned curiosity came racing back to him. He started thinking about shotguns and pillow cases over people's heads again.

Spencer killed the engine and removed the keys. He left the lights on and turned to Floyd. "We're getting out here. You and me."

Even though he was staring at what was obviously a freshly dug grave, Floyd felt himself slide out of the passenger seat anyway. His options were limited to the point where he really had no choice in the matter. Grabbing for one of the weapons would be suicide and dashing off across the dark field would have been a little too cowardly for his taste, not to mention how stupid he would feel when he was gunned down after four or five steps.

With Spencer walking a few feet behind him, they moved to the rear of the car. Spencer unlocked the trunk and took a few more steps back as it popped open. Next to the twisted shape that used to be Hang-around Guy, there was a shovel.

"What time do you have, Mr. Madison?"

For the first time in an eternity, he looked down at his watch. He was shocked by what he saw. "Says seven twenty-three."

Spencer had to raise his own eyebrows a bit. His estimate of a timeframe for the whole thing since they'd met Floyd in the hallway was in the twelve to fifteen minute range. Floyd's guess would have been about ten minutes since his first knock on Beverly's door and he would have been almost as wrong as Spencer. According to the watch on his wrist, the whole thing took a little more than seven minutes, including the time spent driving. The ordeal felt like it had taken forever. As he took another look at the pile of dirt and the empty space next to it, time started slowing down again.

Spencer seemed to read the look right off of his face.

"You don't need to be gentle with this one and we've only got a little time to spare. Just get him into the hole."

Though it was another nasty thing that served to remind him of his younger and darker vengeful days, Floyd had never been so happy to get his hands dirty from a dead guy.

~ 67 ~

With the job completed and their location readjusted yet again, the group of four prepared to navigate their way to the wooded area where Spencer and Stanley had been waiting about forty minutes earlier. Even from their current position, which obscured much of the hotel, they could see the red, blue, and bright white lights swirling through the sky as they reflected off the misty air from down below.

Besides Beverly, who was cradled comfortably in Floyd's arms, they were on foot for the time being. While they watched and Spencer supervised, Stanley awkwardly splashed the last of the gasoline into the opened trunk, one arm still flopping at his side. Most of the can had already been poured throughout the interior but the orders were to be very thorough. He was.

"Okay, leave the can right there in the trunk." Spencer put the gun back into his waistband and approached Floyd with his hands out. For a moment, it appeared that he was about to take Beverly from him, causing Floyd to take a nervous step backward before he could. "Don't be an asshole, Madison. Just lift her up a little bit and stand fucking still."

Spencer approached him again and he did as he was told. With a tired grin, Spencer calmly stared him in the eyes as he rifled through his pockets. His hand came out holding a pack of cigarettes and he removed a single one before putting them back. He held the cigarette up for a few seconds and scrutinized it before tearing off a quarter inch of the unfiltered side. After a second look, he tore off a little more.

"Give me some matches."

"Don't have any. I've got a lighter in my front pocket."

"Lighter...*shit*," Spencer whispered to himself, his eyes darting between the cigarette and the car that he desperately wanted to be on fire very shortly. He looked back to Floyd. "I can't do the cigarette-in-the-matchbook trick without a matchbook and it's the only fucking trick I know."

He'd learned it from Jensen and Martin Carroll. Those guys had rigged them up to paper airplanes to keep their written correspondence private back at Woodhall Penitentiary and it certainly wasn't beyond them to burn up a body or an automobile when they needed it. They had always been good with tricks involving corpses, vehicles, and fire.

"We need a few minutes before it goes. Any thoughts?"

"It'd have to be dry," Floyd offered, hoping he wasn't giving tips to a man that was about to burn him up. "Something that won't soak up the gas before the butt burns down. Dry but combustible."

"Something like gunpowder, maybe?" Spencer had seen him eyeing Stanley's shotgun and decided to throw it out there before Floyd had to embarrass himself with such a ridiculous idea in front of the lady. "Sure, I'm hearing you. Take our last shell and dump the lead out. Great fucking idea, Madison. Stuff a lit butt in the thing and put it right there on that gas can. Problem solved and me and Stan are down to half the guns we started with. Doesn't sound like the kind of thought I was asking for, does it?"

"Listen, Stoning. I'm just doing what—"

"It'd probably work, though," Spencer continued, looking at the cigarette again.

He tore off another tiny piece of it then reached into his jacket pocket and pulled out the small, red, twelve-gauge shotgun shell that had been there since he'd given up the weapon to Stanley back in the hotel room. Floyd's face distorted and he grunted with frustration as Spencer smiled widely and handed it to him.

"Put her down and set it up."

In very short order, Beverly found herself standing painfully on one foot again with Spencer Stoning's arm wrapped tightly around her waist. Whether it was for her balance or his own protection, she couldn't be sure.

She found it interesting to watch Floyd Madison uncrimp the end of the small, explosive cylinder and do his thing, but not quite as interesting as watching Stanley, who was still covering him with the unloaded shotgun. She heard a hushed laugh to her right and turned in time to see Spencer shaking his head sadly, yet endearingly. A moment later his head turned as well and Beverly found herself almost nose to nose with him. It was her first really good look at his face while not in the throes of terror.

Surprisingly, she found him strangely appealing in a way that she would never be able to justify to anyone, including herself. At the same time, she wanted to wiggle out of his grasp but didn't quite dare.

"Is it lit, or what?" he called out.

Floyd nodded to him as the first wisps of smoke wafted into the air. After a quick transfer, she was back in his arms and they were all moving away at a brisk pace. Stanley took the lead but it was Spencer who told him where to walk from his position behind them. The hazy light in the sky grew brighter and the noise increased in volume as they stepped back onto the blacktop of the outer edge of the parking lot. Only a few feet in—as far from the buildings as possible—they found Floyd's white sedan waiting for them.

"Help her into the back," Spencer ordered as he walked quickly to the other side. He pulled open the door for Stanley and helped him in before taking his own seat up front. "You're driving, Madison. Slow and safe. Everybody get your heads down just in case."

Floyd assented quietly as he leaned into the driver's side door, but then stopped short of getting behind the wheel of his own car. Without thinking too hard about it, he reached under the seat and readjusted it to it's original position. Only once he heard Spencer loudly clear his throat did he realize that the gun was back in his face again.

"Not using your head too well, are you?"

"Sorry," Floyd replied with a tired and angry glare. "It's just that it looks like a fucking midget's been driving this thing. Where are we headed?"

"Just get us out to the main street. Slow and easy...like I said."

"They're gonna see us," Floyd stated with absolute certainty as they neared the exit for the second time tonight. This time, however, he was driving directly toward scores of vehicles with flashing lights and sirens. He didn't know if the fire trucks that were now there would help or hurt their chances of squeezing through unchallenged. "They know my car. I think the feds have been on to me for a while."

"They have," Beverly confirmed from behind him.

"Just keep it moving." Spencer had slid all the way down in his seat and was getting all the information he needed to know from the various looks on Floyd's face. "We're not so interesting. They'll find better stuff to look at in a..."

That was when he heard the loud pop off in the distance and stopped worrying so much about any eyes that might fall on the car. He thought the timing could have been a little better, but Spencer could picture the lit cigarette in his head as it burned down to the base of the shotgun shell and ignited the gunpowder. In turn, the nearly harmless detonation would ignite the gasoline and remove what he hoped were the last remnants of Hang-around Guy that existed above ground. It wasn't a huge blast, but sounded more like the thump of a fourth of July firework being launched from it's tube and into the air. The sudden roaring blaze was what really grabbed everyone's attention.

"I take it the coast is clear for the moment?" Spencer asked knowingly. "Who's the bad guy, Stan? Who's the fucking bad guy?"

Stanley looked first to Beverly, then over to Spencer. His own smile was evident but his eyes were somewhat blank. "It's getting harder to tell."

~ 68 ~

"South," Spencer repeated to Floyd, answering the question in the simplest of terms and happy to see the world finally flying by him at a decent rate of speed. They had cleared the city of Santa Maria and were cruising swiftly down Highway 101. "That's all you need to know. It's a nice night. You should try to enjoy it."

"She needs a doctor." Floyd turned and looked at Beverly, who was pressed as far against her own door as she could get while her naked, bleeding feet stretched across Stanley's lap. Her head faced forward and was resting on the window, which was fogging up with each heavy breath she took. It was pretty dark but he could see what kind of shape Stanley was in. "And, *damn*, so do you, chief. It's time to call it a day, guys. There's nowhere to go, I'm telling you."

"Stan's fine," Spencer countered. "The guy's made of tougher stuff than you and me. And quit sounding so negative. There's *always* somewhere to go, George."

Floyd gave him a quick, questioning glance. Spencer caught the look, then sighed and reversed himself. He wasn't in the mood and didn't have the strength for it if he was.

"I didn't mean that...*Floyd*. That's a great name, by the way. Low class but presidential at the same time. *Floyd Madison*. You've just got to love them hero types."

"I ain't no hero. Sometimes things just happen."

"I didn't call you a hero. I called you a hero *type*. Your size, your voice, your attitude—it's a good act, man. That's a serious look you wear on that face of yours. I bet you practice that shit in a mirror." Spencer didn't get any reaction to the comment. "But there aren't any heroes, really—just types. I think you already know that. Circumstance determines who gets credit for what. There's no way around it. You just got lucky."

"Lucky how?"

"Well, for starters, you got lucky that Stan didn't kill your ass the first time around. My buddy back there has a hole in his shoulder that a family of fucking squirrels could live in and he hasn't moaned about it once. He's in his mid forties—that's an old man to some folks. Do you really think you could have taken him down when he was a whole fifteen years younger if he didn't want to be taken down? If he didn't *want* it to stop?"

Floyd stared out at the road ahead and considered it. If he went back to his first encounter with Hewitt, which had ended with relative ease, and compared it to what he had witnessed during the last half hour, he suspected that there might be some truth in Stoning's statement.

"You saying he took a dive?"

"Do I really have to? You could ask him yourself..."

"Yeah, you could ask me yourself," Stanley agreed cheerfully from behind them.

"...but it wouldn't help."

"Wouldn't help at all," he agreed again.

"It may as well have been a hundred years ago. He's not a mean guy, Mr. Madison; not in the same way that some people are mean. The way some people are cruel. People like me, for instance. I think the doctor might even agree with me on this one. She gets it. She understands."

Beverly finally peeled her face from the window and shifted her feet around. They'd been elevated since driving away from Santa Maria but it only helped ease the pain a little bit. "I understand nothing. *Nothing.*"

"Well, I think you do. I think you understand it better than anybody and you'll be able to put it into words when people start asking questions. You're one of only two people out there with first hand experience."

"Experience?" she asked. "Experience with what?"

Spencer's reply was swift and incredulous. "Experience with Stanley Lewis Hewitt the multiple fucking murderer, you silly girl. He busted into your hotel room and nailed you to the floor. A hammer? Three nails? I find it hard to believe that you're having trouble remembering something like that."

While Beverly merely caused herself more pain by trying to sit up too quickly, Floyd came close to driving them off the highway. He reined in the steering wheel fast enough to straighten them out but his mind was on anything but the road. He could hear Stanley chuckling from behind.

"What the hell are you trying to pull, Stoning?"

"She sure is lucky you showed up when you did," Spencer went on, ignoring the question. "Stan wasn't so lucky—that hammer in the shoulder was some cold-blooded shit, Madison."

"Cold-blooded, man," Stanley echoed with a chastising tone to his voice.

"But I got the drop on you. Don't think that I didn't. Thank God I'm a quick thinker and moved the party along before the feds showed up. Me, Stan, and my two hostages. Right out the window and into the car I had waiting. I swear, I'm a fucking criminal genius sometimes."

Pulling his eyes from the road again, Floyd took a look at Spencer's face. "What happened to that hammer, anyway?"

"Room 212. Stan's prints are all over it. Yours too. Too bad it's a fucking *Craftsman* instead of a *Stanley*…but what can you do? I guess Hang-around Guy didn't get the joke."

Even as he said it, Spencer wondered if the others in the car had gotten it either or if this was something completely new to them. All he knew for certain was that Stanley had never seen any connection between the brand of hammer he used to drive nails through women's toes and his own name. Like many of the things that slipped right by his shattered brain on any given day, it simply did not compute.

"What about the knife?"

"Ask Stan."

"I've got both of them," Stanley called out before anyone bothered. He was chuckling louder now. "The one from the restaurant and the one that the guy used in all the…"

"What guy?" Spencer asked harshly, cutting him off. *"What fucking guy?"*

Stanley's face went blank. His head shook back and forth. "No guy. There's no guy."

"You see? There *is* no guy. Never has been." Spencer paused for a moment as he checked the road behind them. "What time do you have?"

"Coming up on eight p.m."

"Good. Drive a little faster, will you?"

Floyd accelerated to sixty-five miles and hour and took his own look in the rear view mirror. There were no headlights staring back at him; just Beverly. He gave her what was supposed to be a comforting nod while trying to figure out if they had even spoken to each other yet. After more than a little thought, he came to the conclusion that they hadn't uttered but a frantic word or two.

"I don't know what you're trying to achieve," she said, balancing on her bad elbow even though it was killing her. "But there are so many tiny details involved that whatever you're thinking is just not going to work. I'm talking about DNA, hair and skin samples—they've got a whole lab full of evidence like that."

Spencer didn't blink at her lack of confidence. "The feds might find a consistent DNA pattern in a few places—sure. But what are they going to compare it to? *Nothing.* What will they say? *Anything that works for them.* How will they explain it? *Any fucking way they want too.* Or maybe you're thinking that after this string of nasty murders has stopped, the feds are going to go on the air and announce to a national audience that Stanley Lewis Hewitt didn't kill a bunch of women *this* time."

"I—"

"No, this is Stan's deal and it won't be stolen from him. I won't let it. This Roadside Butcher thing was nothing but a total fucking rip-off from the start. And the sad thing is, there wasn't really anything about those first five killings that was worthy of stealing. No offense to my man Stan, but they were crude warm-ups at best. He hadn't even evolved into his true sick self yet and some motherfucker comes along fifteen years later and swipes them. I mean, the guy got a *name* out of it."

"A real bad-ass Jack the Ripper kind of name too," Stanley added indignantly.

"That's right. And *we* knew what came next. He wasn't going to stop with those five. Shit, he probably only did them so he could segue into the others more easily; so he could emulate the master with more accuracy." Spencer rolled his eyes, growing more and more irritated as he spoke about it. "Man, he had that shit coming *so* bad. I only wish we could kill him again."

"And one more time after that," Stanley agreed.

"It might seem like a crazy thing to be remembered for—and it is, I already know this—but it's all he's got. It's all he's gonna have in his whole damn life. I don't expect you to grasp it completely but that's not my problem. Inconsistencies in the book that I'm sure you and my old shrink are working on—that's not my problem either. Figure it out yourself. Make up a bunch of shit and fill in the blanks with it. It's what you writers do."

"But the Carroll's escape?" Beverly persisted. "There's no way that just happened. It couldn't have been a coincidence. The timing was too close. How—?"

"Let's not discuss the Carrolls right now, doctor. The less you know, the better. Trust me on that one."

"But the walls in your cell." The pain must have been climbing. She was nearly in tears again. "The *windows* you painted. The *door*. The—"

"There's nothing to see." It was Stanley replying this time. "They're just clouds. Don't you know that?"

She had no response to that one. She was glad she didn't.

~ 69 ~

They had been driving in absolute silence for almost fifty minutes when Floyd heard the words he'd been waiting for. He wasn't waiting in anticipation; quite the opposite, in fact. These were bad words to be hearing and made him glad he'd decided not to mention that they were almost out of gas and would need to fill up the tank in less than half an hour.

"Pull it over, Madison. Right up ahead about a hundred feet." He was pointing as they began to slow down. "Get us off the road a bit. No lights."

Floyd looked off to his right and saw nothing but more of the same dense brush they'd been driving by since leaving Santa Maria. The only visible light came in the form of the moon, which was very bright and hung directly overhead. They came to a stop and Floyd killed the lights.

"Where in the heck are we, Spence?" Stanley asked in a shaky, dry voice. He sounded as if he had just woken up, though Spencer had his doubts. With the kind of shape he was in, Spencer guessed the next time he slept it would be for a good long time.

"It's time to lighten the load, Stan. Relax and just stay put, okay?"

Stanley nodded and let his head drop back against the seat. He squinted against the dim illumination that the dome light gave off and was starting to wonder why he felt so damned tired. His rapidly glazing eyes settled on Beverly and she stared back at him. Whatever fear she had was now floating somewhere beneath the surface, sharing company with the special kind of exhaustion that comes from horrible pain.

"I'm guessing you'll want me to get out of the car now." Floyd's voice remained steady.

"You guessed right. Leave the keys in the ignition."

Ah…fuck, Floyd growled in his head. *Out in the middle of nowhere.*

Even as he eyed the gun that Spencer was gripping tightly, he wondered if there was a hole dug somewhere out there for him. He supposed not, but only because a clean disappearance wasn't necessary for him. It would be birds and rodents picking away at him instead of the underground dwellers that would reduce him to soil. Sadly, Floyd guessed he would be missed even less than the secret that he had been forced to bury back in Santa Maria.

"Come on," Spencer beckoned, motioning with the gun. "Let's take a walk."

Floyd didn't argue. He strode alongside Spencer at a steady pace—as steady as he possibly could, anyway. He'd made the same walk a few times before, though never on the receiving end. Two of the three men that he had personally dealt with back in the day had walked as easily as Floyd was walking now, knowing what was coming and knowing exactly how it would turn out for them. They were usually all out of fight by that point and he knew that the truly guilty didn't cling to hope like normal people did. There was no reason they should.

Floyd didn't feel guilty, though. He wasn't particularly hopeful either but it wouldn't stop him from trying. Every three or four steps, he moved a foot closer to Spencer, estimating that they would only need to walk another thirty feet or so before he could try for a final attempt at greatness. Unfortunately, they only walked ten before Spencer stopped. There was a full six feet between them but Spencer backed up a little more anyway, keeping the weapon out of range as if he'd read his mind.

Floyd moaned quietly as he heard a sliding, metallic sound from his own gun. Only then was he certain that Spencer hadn't cycled a round into the chamber all night long.

"You're lucky I didn't know about that," he said. "You'd be wearing it up your ass right now if I did."

Spencer's grin widened into a full blown smile as he raised the weapon. "You see, that's the attitude I was talking about. You're a fucking sport, Floyd Madison. The real thing, I swear. I'm glad it gets to be you instead of someone else."

With no reply, Floyd pulled his shoulders back while steeling himself for a bullet from his own gun. All he could do was stand tall and wait for it. It felt like he waited a while before Spencer startled him by speaking again.

"What time do you have now?"

Floyd cursed silently. The short sentence had caused him to flinch and he hated himself for the lapse. He only looked down at his watch because he was curious about it himself. "It's just about nine."

"Okay, that's prime-time here and midnight on the east coast. What do you suppose they're watching on TV in New York right now?"

Floyd didn't have to guess at it. He used to make appearances on the shows that Spencer was referring to. "Late night guys—the regular stuff. Why?"

"Because in twenty minutes they won't be." He sounded eerily sure of himself. Even more so than usual. "You can listen to me now and do what I say or you can die a really, really bad death whenever I choose. What'll it be?"

Floyd decided that he could listen, which was good because Spencer was already speaking again.

"At one point or another—pretty soon, probably—there are gonna be some people wanting to ask you some questions. Lots of them. Understand?" Spencer waited for Floyd's response, which was a simple nod. "Good, because I'm gonna give you all the answers. I recommend you get them right."

*   *   *   *

Spencer knocked on the window and Beverly rolled it down. He stared past her and got his last look at Stanley before the driver's side door closed and extinguished the dome light. His breathing was shallow and his eyes were closed. Consciousness had finally faded. He thought it was just as well.

"See you later, Supermax," Spencer said softly, pulling his head away from the window and giving Beverly one last glance. He kicked at the rear tire as he backed away from the car. "Now, move it along before I start getting fucking emotional."

The car was started and Floyd gunned the engine a few times then put it into drive. They rolled forward very slowly but didn't make it two feet before the brake lights came on, bathing everything behind them in a red glow. He knew he should have been racing away as quickly as the car could take them but it just wasn't possible yet. Out of all the unanswered questions, there was really only one that he couldn't let go of.

Spencer leaned back into the window. "Problem?"

"Just one thing, Stoning. Seriously. I need to know something."

"You're killing me, man. What's so important?"

"I've read *Man Of Rage* a couple times."

"I read that piece of shit too. What about it?"

"Those things you made on your lathe back at Kerslake Machinery—the metal rods you worked on all day long." He'd read the book too many times not to know. "What were they for?"

Spencer didn't speak right away and for a second it looked like he wasn't going to answer at all. The tiniest of smiles played around his lips as he turned away and looked up into the sky.

"Man, I have no *idea* what they were for." He laughed out loud, noting the supremely tortured look on Floyd's face and continued to smile as he watched the white sedan drive away. Only once their tail lights were gone did he finish answering the question for him.

"But seeing as how I was a drill-press operator, I guess I can't really be expected to know, can I?"

~ 70 ~

On that fateful day...

He still laughed out loud when he thought about that stupid line.

To Spencer, *Man Of Rage* wasn't just another piece of shit book. It was an absolutely *horrible* piece of shit book. It was almost as bad as the investigative team who happily allowed him to take credit for two mass killings in two states with little more than a confession, some fingerprints, and a gunpowder residue test. They were pathetic and lazy but he couldn't blame them too hard for wanting to slam dunk the case before the bodies even got cold. It was an honest-to-God national tragedy for a whole week. They had to blame somebody.

Spencer could still picture his best friend spacing out like he did every day in front of a machine that he just knew was going to gobble the kid up one day. When they got hired on at Kerslake Machinery he couldn't believe that they put Kenny Keyes in front of the lathe instead of himself. As machinists, they were both checked out on all kinds of heavy equipment, but those spinning gears with so many places to get fingers, hair, and clothing stuck always made Spencer nervous. He wasn't jealous by any means since the drill-press was simpler to operate and let him do his own spacing out that much easier, but he was always waiting for the accident to happen.

You're on fire, Kenny.

When it finally did happen, it wasn't such a big deal. Not at first.

With the exception of Stanley Hewitt, Kenny Keyes was easily the dumbest person that he had ever known. It didn't make him any less of a friend and, for reasons that were always known to him, Spencer had made a habit out of finding himself buddies that were sub par in the brains department. It guaranteed a chain of command and he needed to be at the top of it even if the lower links were about as smart as tadpoles. As long as he could remember, he'd always been that way.

Kenny, if you had a brain you'd be fucking dangerous.

It was hard to believe, but he knew that it was the line that got everyone killed. He knew Kenny was a sensitive little shit and he knew that it would piss him off. The problem was that watching him slap at his lathe with a shop rag was just too much to let go without a little commentary.

Forgot about the kill-switch, didn't you?

A direct misquote. One of many. As far as Spencer knew, nobody in the whole shop had ever referred to a power button on any machine as a kill-switch. Not once. Never. He chalked it up to creative license on the part of an author who thought it sounded cool and knew that there was no one left alive to contradict him.

Way to go, moron. That one was accurate, though.

Jack Holley, the shop's foreman, was the one who put the finishing touches on Kenny's anger and if he'd known what the end result would be he probably wouldn't have sent him packing. It was an hour and a half before they saw him again.

On top of being stupid, Spencer had always known that Kenny was a little nuts. It wasn't just the guns that he adored or the violent movies that he liked; there were also the scary faces he would make from time to time—deep, deep furious kind of looks—as well as his freaky, disjointed way of talking when he was upset about something. When Kenny wasn't around, Spencer would do imitations of him for the rest of the crew at Kerslake. It was a spot-on match of the real thing. It used to kill them.

Spencer didn't see Kenny at first when he got back to the Rockford site but, like everybody else in the shop, heard him loud and clear. When he burst though the door and onto the shop floor, Spencer got his first look at Kenny carrying the weapon that they had both fired at cans and other targets on numerous occasions. He wasn't shooting at cans this time and a sickening panic of screams quickly filled the room.

Like many of the others, Spencer took refuge behind the nearest heavy piece of machinery he could find. It seemed to go on forever and the hideous sound of masculine squeals was slowly cut down to a few gurgling gasps before it faded to deadly silence. The only sound after that was one set of footsteps as his good friend Kenny slowly found his way to him.

"I tried to remedy the situation," Kenny had said, dripping with more melodrama than blood even though he had just put an end to twenty-nine lives.

There was more to the quote on the back cover of *Man Of Rage*, but Spencer had made up the rest of it for Dr. Perry Burgess. Perhaps he really would have finished the sentence *"...but I ended up killing everybody instead,"* but Spencer never got the chance to find out. That was when Kenneth Keyes dropped his AR-15 rifle and pulled out a handgun. He put it to his temple and, looking Spencer dead in the eyes, shot himself in the head.

In response, Spencer did what he always did when he saw the red, viscous fluid in all it's glory. Whether it was jutting out in a great stream or trickling slowly from a paper-cut, his reaction to it was the same as it had been since his childhood—he blacked out.

To put it more accurately, he fainted.

*   *   *   *

And when I woke up, I knew I had a decision to make. I know it was an impulsive one but I'll tell you, I wouldn't change a thing; not even for the ten years I spent at Woodhall. Did I want Kenny to go bugshit and kill all those folks? No way, friends, but it happened and I couldn't do a goddamn thing to stop him. It was done and there was no undoing it.

I couldn't let it go to waste, though, could I? Think about it. Think about how often this situation presents itself. I sure did. I thought about it really hard in those few minutes I had before the cops would start arriving in droves. It was a tough one.

Sole survivor...perpetrator. Sole survivor...perpetrator. Okay, it wasn't really that tough. I was guilty as hell anyway. I've always had a soft spot for my gimpy-minded underlings, even since grade school. I always controlled them and dictated their actions, either by example or request, so I guess a certain amount of responsibility has to go with it. I'm willing to accept that—not to mention the perks that come with it.

I mean, what's a hemophobic drill-press operator from Rockford to do? Go on TV for a week, recounting a tale of horror that was pretty much my fault? Nah, let's bite the bullet for Kenny Keyes, take our medicine, and be on TV for a lifetime instead. I didn't have to think about it too long.

In fact, the more I thought about it, the more I started thinking that they'd hang the whole damn thing on me anyway. Shit, why wouldn't they? I'm looking at all these spent shells laying around thinking to myself, "I wonder how many of those rounds have my fingerprints on them?" I probably loaded some of those clips myself. Me and the sick-boy used to do a lot of shooting together, you know.

Every one of Kenny's guns was unregistered and untraceable. I should have seen it coming. Maybe I did. Maybe it really was my fault. Hell, I'm sure it was, which meant that all I could do at that point was to reconcile it in one way or another.

I guess that's when I took the gun from his dead hand and emptied it into him. It wasn't like he was gonna get any deader. They say I got him in the chest with most of them. Not impressed? Well, you should be since I had my eyes closed almost the whole time. I barely even opened them when I groped around for a phone, called 911, and told them that Spencer Stoning was shooting the place up. I didn't even change my voice for them. Not a very thorough investigation if you ask me. Thank God for that.

You know what my middle name is? It's James. I am Spencer James Stoning: spree-killing, mass-murdering, ringmaster of the psychotic circus.

Spencer James Stoning. That's three names. Beats the shit out of Spencer Stoning, the fainting drill-press operator, doesn't it? I think so. And so do you. I know you do.

I killed twenty-nine people by being cruel to an idiot. Maybe I saved that many by being kind to one.

As if I care.

The end.

✳   ✳   ✳   ✳

Right there. That's how I would've written it if the truth was what I was interested in. Simple and straight to the point. It's me and it's honest. Much better than Dr. Burgess's twisted translation of the words that I told him, isn't it? Maybe it's not as exciting since I'm not quite the evil fuck I've made myself out to be, but who's gonna know? Poor Kenny's dead and he's not gonna tell a soul. And he won't tell anyone that I'm a thieving liar just like Hang-around Guy was either.

Don't tell Stan, okay?

~ 71 ~

Up until nine-fifteen it had been a slow and quiet evening. The emergency room doors had opened and closed a total of twelve times since the shift change and most of those admitted had all been involved in the same low velocity traffic accident. When the doors opened for the thirteenth time, however, they wouldn't close again until they had a chance to be repaired. In the same instant, the hospital itself would lose every bit of the serenity that had been enjoyed by the staff thus far.

When Floyd Madison exploded through the double sliding panes of glass—actually shattering one side this time—his heart was thumping in his chest hard enough to make him feel fortunate that he was already in a hospital. It wasn't just the fact that he was exhausted and supporting the weight of two people. It was that for the last hour and a half he had been absolutely positive on more than a few occasions that he was going to die. He wasn't quite feeling like a million bucks yet but he was pretty sure it felt better than dying would. He also knew that the people with him felt significantly worse.

"We need a doctor over here," he stated in a voice that grabbed more attention than the noise they made coming in. It was as deep as ever but, more than that, it was calm. Not just unrattled and unfazed by what was occurring, but *calm*.

"Make that two doctors."

Floyd guided the bleeding woman on his left to the nearest available chair. Only once she was seated did he kneel down and gently lower the handcuffed man from his shoulder onto the ground.

"And security," he added. Stanley's eyes were open again, though his face wore no expression whatsoever. "A shitload of it."

The first group of people that came running over were dressed in various shades of blue and green and they moved with purpose, acting in a manner befitting their given professions. Drawn to the more seriously injured first, the man on the floor was carefully rolled into a position where they could view his wounds and gauge the level of severity. They only got him halfway over before noticing the handcuffs. A man in green clothing looked up to Floyd.

"Why are these—?"

"Like I said," he interrupted, letting his arms slip behind his back in a gesture that could only be described as casual. He nodded once toward Stanley. "Security."

The ER doctor looked down then jumped back as if he'd been bitten by a snake

"*Whoa!* You've gotta be fucking *kidding* me."

That was when everybody else moved in and it was safe to say that all professionalism took a side-step. The man in green wasn't the only one to scoot backward and think twice about how badly he wanted to continue his medical career, but the sentiment shared between all of them only lasted a short time. Once the initial shock wore off, work ethic and Hippocratic oaths were remembered and Stanley Hewitt was quickly covered by several pairs of shaky hands in latex gloves.

"*Security!* Get security down here *now!*" someone yelled. It was hard to tell exactly who because the tiled entryway to the emergency room was quickly becoming crowded.

There were murmurs that flowed from one person to next, moving further down the various hallways like a flash flood. The name heard repeated more than anything else was *Stanley Lewis Hewitt*. Even though Beverly McGrath was a hometown girl, well known, and highly regarded in the community, the other name that fell mostly from their lips was *Floyd Madison*.

Floyd stepped out of their way and gave them room to work, moving over to Beverly, who was being tended to by a single RN. He sat down next to her and watched as the awestruck nurse got a firsthand look at the kind of thing she'd only read about in a newspaper. Beverly watched as well, thinking briefly about her treatment of Gail Rainier and not feeling too happy about being a curiosity herself. With a loud sigh, she turned to Floyd, who was having trouble pulling his eyes from her brutally swollen toes.

"Hi, I'm Beverly McGrath." She extended a weak hand to him. "Nice to meet you…again."

"Floyd," he replied, grasping her fingers lightly. "Floyd Madison. Good to see you."

"Good…yeah," she agreed, swallowing hard. She was on the verge of tears again but held it in before any serious crying could begin since there was no telling when it might stop. She leaned in close to him and lowered her voice. "What in the hell are we supposed to say now? To Hildebrandt and the FBI, I mean. What?"

The nurse had given her toes a quick antiseptic wipe down but had stepped away and was now hailing a gurney. It was being wheeled over as they spoke.

"I don't know. I guess that depends," he answered as they watched Stanley being maneuvered onto a gurney of his own. Once he was situated, the rolling bed was raised to their eye level and locked into place. The handcuffs were still on and Stanley's blank eyes were directed at both of them. "You know what his story's going to be, don't you?"

Beverly considered it as he was wheeled away from them and down a long corridor. "I think we already heard it in the car. He might even believe it himself by now."

"But do *you* believe it?" Floyd asked. The two men with the gurney were approaching quickly. "Because my mind's pretty goddamn open right now and I can believe anything if I need to. It's up to you."

Beverly shut her eyes and ran through it all in her head. She thought about everything she *thought* she'd known over the last few weeks and everything she'd taken as fact—things that *everyone* had taken as fact. Believability of what the real truth actually was would become a factor. It might make her choice that much easier.

"Well…"

"We've got to agree on something here," Floyd said more urgently. "They're about to roll you out of here and I'm a few minutes from getting tackled by…" He trailed off for a moment, trying to figure that one out. "…*Jesus*, everybody."

Everybody. Everybody and then some. Though he hid it expertly, his knees had begun to shake.

"So, just tell them then," she replied, her words coming faster. "Tell them what they're sure they already know. A couple of hours ago I was positive of it myself."

"Is that smart?"

"Well, there's only one other person who knows what we know," she answered with a fearful stare. Images of a maniacal and strangely motivated Spencer Stoning were still vivid in both of their minds. "And I don't know if I want to argue with his version of the truth. He's still out there."

"That he is," Floyd agreed. "I'd sure hate to disappoint the motherfucker."

The gurney arrived and Beverly was carefully hoisted onto it. Floyd took her hand and walked along beside her to a set of swinging double doors, where three more people in scrubs joined them. Behind him, Floyd could hear the sounds of the authorities arriving on the scene, which told him he was about to become very busy. The grip on his hand squeezed tighter then released as she was rolled through the doors.

"You're going to be fine, Dr. McGrath," a gloved man said as they wheeled her down the hallway. He spoke calmly, though his hands were trembling mildly. "We're taking you to examining room six to have a better look at you. Is there anything—?"

"I don't care what room you're putting me in. Just make sure it has a television."

*   *   *   *

It was the exact same setup as before. They were on the same steps of the same police station with the same low-budget, quickly thrown together news conference set to roll. It was like deja-vu except for the fact that all of it had definitely happened before. Only a half hour had passed since she had been admitted and stashed away in a private room to hide her from the press, but the network gods were already hard at work.

Spencer Stoning's prediction to Floyd Madison had been fulfilled twenty minutes earlier. Nobody was watching Leno or Letterman tonight. They, along with any show that didn't have *news* in the title, had been preempted.

Beverly leaned her head back against the pillow and watched the scene on her television as self-administered doses of Demerol made their way from a plastic bag to the IV tube then straight into her bloodstream. Her toes were already numb from multiple injections of local anesthetic, which, understandably, were semi-difficult to receive. She hadn't needed to be held down, though. She had that much to be proud of. The only thing bothering her now was a certain grating and unpleasant voice that wouldn't go away.

"Can you *please* tell me what happened?" Perry Burgess asked for at least the sixth time in five minutes. "Beverly? Jesus, Bev. How? *How?*"

He, Special Agent Hildebrandt, and about a hundred other men in uniform had only been in Santa Barbara for five minutes. While the FBI's tardiness was duly noted, Perry Burgess was hardly noticed at all and wouldn't have been let into Beverly's room unless she'd specifically requested his presence. With every word he said, she considered revoking the privilege.

"How did he get in, Bev? *Jesus Christ*, Beverly, talk to me. Beverly. *Beverly?*"

"Perry?" she asked in a groggy voice, slowly dragging her heavy eyes from the screen. "Sorry, I forgot you were here."

"Bev, I'm just—"

"*Shhhh.*" The finger that was supposed to touch her lips poked into her left cheek instead. Her hand dropped back to the sheets with a thud and her eyes rolled back to the TV. "It's about to start."

The lights came up, flashbulbs started popping, and several men took position in various locations on the police department steps. There was only one person from the whole group that truly stood out from everybody else, but he stood out an awful lot. He wasn't front and center but was getting most of the attention anyway.

Burgess squinted his eyes and moved closer to the screen. "Tell me that's not—"

"*Mmmm-mmmm,*" Beverly answered in the positive with a drug-laced smile, her voice a dreamy, half-stoned imitation of what it usually was. "He's going to be big, big news, Perry."

"But how—?"

"And so…are…we," she finished, letting her eyes slide shut.

She wasn't awake when Floyd Madison was reintroduced to an admiring and very national TV audience, though just about everybody else on the planet was. Before he even got the chance to answer a single question, Burgess could see that Beverly was indeed correct. He was going to be very, very big news.

Like a door slamming shut, the Stanley Lewis Hewitt chapter was over. Dr. Perry Burgess would never know the exact how's and why's of the abrupt ending, but that was only because nobody would ever tell him. And due to circumstances that had been way beyond his control, he would get left out of the climactic final pages of their soon-to-be published best seller, too.

~ 72 ~

The bidding had started before the first rough draft was even completed and it would sell in record time at a record price. Dr. Beverly McGrath, Ph.D. and Dr. Perry Burgess, M.D. split authorship down the middle and would never have a single argument about who pulled more weight. The one who suffered the most over it was already obvious enough for Burgess to refrain from ever questioning the fact and Beverly was satisfied with the agreement as well, having much more than the one book to be concerned with anyway.

On top of her half of an advance so large that the publisher probably lost a few ounces of blood just writing the check, she was booked coast to coast for a series of lectures that were set to launch at about the same time her book signing tour with Burgess would be ending. There were interviews on all the big networks and talks were already under way for an hour on the Biography Channel. Her co-author hadn't heard from that group of people yet, but it didn't upset him too much.

While the manhunt for Stanley Lewis Hewitt was fading like a bad dream, Perry Burgess's widely acknowledged specialty was still a very live nightmare and was still at large. For the once-again noted psychiatrist, Spencer James Stoning was a well that showed no signs of running dry. And when he wasn't busy discussing the intricacies of Stoning, he spent his time playing psychiatrist to a multitude of celebrities or pandering to a jury when his expertise—a very expensive commodity lately—was required in a trial.

He was back in business and had accomplished the feat without breaking a sweat or losing a single drop of his own blood—unless facial cuts from a deviously blunted razor counted, of course. Beverly never did confess to her childish actions in Sacramento, but he'd always had his suspicions about it.

They were both big names again and it smoothed over many of the rough patches they'd encountered during the month on the road together; rough patches that would not have been forgiven so easily under different circumstances. There was still a fairly large emotional gap between them but nothing that would ever keep them from posing together with wide smiles while holding copies of their number-one best seller—an unoriginal number-one best seller that contained almost nothing but old, used, recycled crimes and characters.

Stanley Lewis Hewitt: the dim-witted and semi-retarded serial killer who was coaxed into repeating his past crimes by a superior mind. Spencer James Stoning: the cruel handler and enabler of Hewitt who masterminded an inconceivable escape while personally escorting the formerly infamous gangsters Martin and Jensen Carroll to their own fiery deaths. Dr. Perry Burgess: a man who made or broke cases by his testimony regardless of whether he was working for the prosecution or defense. And Dr. Beverly McGrath: a wildly popular writer, therapist, and Hewitt-survivor who didn't pose for *Playboy* until the offer reached a cool million, though she would have done it for much less. They had all been recycled, reused, returned to service, and put back into circulation.

Then there was Floyd.

For Floyd Madison it was as though he'd never been gone at all. Madison Investigations had a brand new message on a brand new answering machine before Beverly had been released from the hospital. His on-air time following his second capture of Stanley Hewitt eclipsed anything that the doctors, the serial killer, the spree killer, or even the Carroll brothers could have possibly imagined for themselves in an entire lifetime.

After a brief time of enjoying the spotlight, Floyd launched himself back into the kind of cases that he had come to learn to hate. There was nobility and hope in them again and they didn't seem so hard now that he had the funds to staff Madison Investigations properly. He wasn't alone anymore and didn't scrimp on hiring the best.

His first widely publicized case would be the return of a Congressman's daughter who had been recovered several states away from her last seen location. It was never mentioned that she was just another runaway—*even the smart ones are fucking retarded at that age,* he would remember with a laugh—and nobody knew that she had to be dragged back to her family handcuffed in the back seat of a car. That was Tom Devereaux's style, though, and Floyd wasn't about to criticize his lead investigator's methods. The man had taught him a lot about exploiting other's talents and Floyd had never forgotten it. In the following years, they would spend a fair amount of time on the covers of various newspapers together.

Two days after Hewitt's second arrest, Special Agent Dwight Hildebrandt appeared on the front page of many newspapers himself. It was practically every newspaper in the country, actually, and prominent placement of the photo had come at the request of the Federal Bureau of Investigation's own head office. The picture that had been taken by a photographer from the Chicago Sun-Times was shot at the same press conference in Santa Barbara that had announced Hewitt's recapture. It was a black and white image of Special Agent Hildebrandt fielding questions from at least a dozen reporters and it would receive a full page of it's own in the photo section of the book as well.

The focus of the picture was on the special agent. But the part that was highlighted and blown up for use on wanted posters that were quickly distributed across the country wasn't Hildebrandt at all. It was a blonde man with light eyes wearing a fake Giorgio suit and holding out a microphone. He had asked the agent a question and, according to several witnesses from the legitimate press, stood by patiently while getting a rather longwinded answer. Though Dwight Hildebrandt never got to appear on any of the popular late night TV programs, he would make it into a whole lot of monologs.

In many papers, the photo ran with a headline that read: *Wanted.* Most of them, however, just ran the man's name beneath the picture. It was a three-word name that rolled off the tongue easily and frightened people at the same time.

~ 73 ~

"Prisoner G32344-56 coming out!"

About the same time the last of Ryan Williams' echoing voice had faded away, another loud noise clicked directly in front of him and went on it's own sonic journey through the empty hallway. It was the lock that was controlled electronically by another man in another room, which rendered the key in his hand totally useless all by itself. It wasn't a big deal, but he knew that if Stanley ever felt the need to cram somebody's toothbrush up his ass again, it was going to be a lot more difficult.

"Hands out, Hewitt," he said, smiling as he always did when it came to his favorite inmate. "You know the drill."

Stanley definitely knew the drill. He loved the drill. In fact, the phrase *"You know the drill"* was an integral part of the drill and he enjoyed the repetitiveness of the statement.

The next part had Stanley approaching the heavy door and turning around. He bent forward slightly and placed his hands behind his back before shoving them through a rectangular slot. There was another slot down by his feet and every time Williams wrapped the heavy cuffs around his wrists and ankles Stanley felt so completely supermax he thought his heart might burst.

Stanley then took a few steps forward while Williams used his key to open the second lock. It was shower time in the newly completed D Block and it was Stanley's turn. He, like every other inmate on the D, showered alone. It was the only time outside of his cell that he wouldn't be chained.

The new cell block had been put up in record time since there was no demolition to wait for. It didn't replace any structure on the whole site and, was instead, it's very own building, totally separate from the other wings. On paper, it was still D Block, although anyone familiar with Woodhall Penitentiary knew that nobody ever called it that. They all knew that D Block was empty and dead, still in pieces as a monument to criminal ingenuity.

To those in the know, the new supermax structure was called the H Block. The Hewitt Block. Immeasurable tons of concrete and steel built to hold hundreds but dedicated to one man. Even Matthew Chase acknowledged it privately, though he had been thinking of two men when he signed the paperwork for construction to begin. Stoning would be back, though—he was sure of it. He just *had* to be. If not, why would ACT, Inc. have just spent millions of dollars building an escape-proof condominium for him?

"A little soap won't kill you, Stanley." This too was part of the drill; part of the routine. The words, the phrases, and the jokes—old but comfortable.

The cuffs were off and so were his clothes. Williams leaned against the wall like he always did and watched, always wincing when Stanley would cleanse that mangled shoulder of his. He didn't just wash the thing; he absolutely scrubbed the shit out of it and Williams suspected he knew why. The deep scars wouldn't come out and the arm would never work like it used to, but he sure did like to keep it clean.

It was his trophy, though few knew it the way Ryan Williams did. It was a battle-wound and he wore it the same way he wore his supermax status. After all the work, he guessed he'd earned it.

"Dry off, convict." Stanley loved being called *convict* and Williams usually saved it for special occasions. "Back to your cell." It was hardly an order since he was completely manacled and had nowhere else to go anyway. Stanley sometimes got the feeling that his favorite guard was there just to make sure he didn't fall down and hurt himself. "It's mail day."

"Mail day?" Stanley asked, stepping into his cell. Williams locked the door behind him. There was another loud click and the door was locked again. He backed up to the rectangular slots and let Williams unlock him. While it was being done, Stanley noticed the fresh newspaper laying on his cot.

"Oh...*mail* day." He turned as the cuffs were pulled through. "How'd you do that?"

"Magic, Stan," Ryan Williams replied before moving on to the next cell.

Stanley only waited until the echo of his footsteps disappeared before picking up the newspaper. It was local and had the current day's date on it. He went straight to the funny pages and that was where the single glossy photograph was. There weren't any words to read but the picture made him happy regardless.

It was a simple snapshot of three men standing next to each other with rolling, emerald hills as a backdrop. Spencer Stoning was in the middle and wore a large smile for the unseen photographer. His hair was back to its natural dark color and his eyes had returned to their original state of terminal blackness. On each side of him were men who smiled for the camera as well. If Stanley's best guess was accurate then all three of them—Spencer and Jensen and Martin—were probably somewhere in South America right now. Or maybe it was South Africa. He always had trouble telling the difference between the two.

With all the time Spencer had spent with him trying to locate one pesky, plagiarizing serial killer, Stanley was relieved to see that he'd made it across a few borders and was finally in safe hands. If there was one thing he remembered about the Carroll brothers it was that they *really* knew how to cover their asses. They also knew how to repay a favor. Sleep would come easier tonight than it usually did.

He took a long look at the picture then closed his eyes for a minute before looking at it once more. Convinced that he'd committed the photo to memory, he placed the four by six picture into his mouth and chewed the hard and shiny paper until it was in soft, wet pieces small enough for him to swallow. As he choked the sharp edges down, he thought about his old traveling partner and stared at his blank, empty walls.

When it would be time for Ryan Williams to come around again, Stanley decided he would ask for a Magic Marker and draw himself some trees and a big, bright, pretty sun. Or maybe a black one.

978-0-595-38156-2
0-595-38156-1

Printed in the United States
41889LVS00005B/97-123